For Hans, gone but not forgotten

…they see the light when they feel the heat…

~ ERIC HOFFER
1898 - 1983

The First Warrior looked out on the land and his Home.
He saw the hills
And the stars
And he was happy.
For giving him his home, the first warrior told the Great
Spirit
That he would fight and win many battles in His honor.
But the Great Spirit said, "No, do not fight for me.
Fight for your tribe,
Fight for the family born to you,
Fight for the brothers you find.
"Fight for them," the Great Spirit said, "for they are your
Home."

~ HENRY STANDING BEAR
Longmire TV Series

Part Two

Garret

Prologue

Skeeter Bronson loved the ocean. All he'd ever wanted to do in his life was become a shrimper like his daddy. As a child, during the summers and on weekends from the time he'd turned eight, he'd worked on his father's boat.

So when he somehow managed to scrape enough money together to buy his own shrimp boat, it was the happiest day of his life. Of course, he would never admit that to his wife, Adele.

Skeeter named his pride and joy the *Southern Star*, painted the name on her himself. The first time Skeeter had laid eyes on her, she was a beat-up old beauty, a double-rigged trawler with a two hundred horsepower engine. It took him almost two months of hard work to get her in seaworthy condition.

In thirty years of shrimping, she'd always been good to him, always brought him back to port in one piece, no matter how bad the weather.

The years had come and gone, some good, some not so good, but his home away from home would always be the sea. And God help him he loved the *Southern Star* almost as much as he did Adele.

During the good years he would upgrade the trawler with new engines, rigging, and every piece of equipment he could afford, including the latest and greatest fish-finding echo sounders. It had taken him forever to learn to read the damn thing and all the instrumentation that came with it.

In those early months with the modern technology, he'd felt like a blind man with his first guide dog. He'd been the first to install state of the art gear and immediately became the butt of jokes from the other shrimpers. For about two months he endured the ribbing. That is, until he was able to bring in twice the catch other shrimpers brought in.

These days, he could tell if the shrimp were large or small or where they schooled in massive quantities at the precise location on the bottom of the sea floor. With his knowledge of the ocean, he rarely bothered with tide charts because he knew the area around the Keys like an old familiar lover. No one was better at it than Skeeter Bronson. He'd shrimped in the west in the cooler Atlantic, but preferred the warmer waters to the east in the Gulf of Mexico.

Tonight, he was after pink shrimp, and maybe if things went well, he'd take a run around the Tortugas for some Royal Red. That would bring in some extra cash he could use to remodel the second bedroom his wife wanted to turn into her hobby room. The money would go a long way to getting her off his back.

He was two hours into his run, eyes glued to the fish finder, looking out for the telltale signs of the larger schools when an unusual echo popped up. For now, he ignored the strange blob on his screen and focused on the massive school of shrimp swimming along the sandy bottom.

Skeeter directed his crew to drop the tickler chain to get the shrimp moving and to avoid a large bycatch.

But the echo kept repeating. He realized his nets were about to get tangled up in whatever it was so he maneuvered the boat into position, avoiding the echo as much as he could but still aiming for the schooling shrimp. He ordered the outrigger lowered, the nets, and the bag line.

Everything was running smoothly until he felt the long line jerk, caught on something. God, he hoped he hadn't ripped another net. He should've heeded the echo and avoided the area altogether. Reluctantly he powered down the engine and ran to the winch, hoping like hell he hadn't torn a hole in the net too badly. In all his years of shrimping, he'd dragged up just about everything you could think of, tires, fishing gear, half a lifeboat, a buoy, a car hood, and even an old World War II mine that gave him gray hairs until the Coast Guard took it off his hands.

The winch began to strain with the load as it brought up some type of large cylinder-shaped object. Skeeter elbowed his crew chief, Bobby Joe Wylie, in the ribs and bet him five bucks that they'd snagged their first washing machine.

"Maybe it's one of those old bells. You know, like from the Titanic," Bobby Joe said hopefully. "Wouldn't that be something?"

"I don't think it's a bell. Too small," Skeeter declared with some maritime knowledge of such things.

So when a fifty-five-gallon drum surfaced in the net—a dull black barrel with silver markings, the kind used in chemical storage facilities—the two men traded annoyed looks.

"Damn illegal dumpers," Skeeter muttered. Every time someone dumped waste into the Gulf it screwed with his livelihood. If the markings on the drum could be traced back to an owner, he wanted to know who and what they'd dumped. But as he took a closer look he noticed all the key numbers had been sanded off, leaving nothing to identify the vendor.

"What the hell have we got here?" Skeeter asked as he angled the winch holding the drum and carefully lowered it onto the deck so Bobby Joe could work it out of the net.

"Check the net for damage," Skeeter called out as he grabbed his crowbar and tapped the drum a few times to determine if it might be empty or full. He decided the only thing to do was to pop off the lid to see what was inside.

He used the crowbar to chisel around the rim and pry off the sealed top. As soon as he was able to inch up the cover, the odor hit him and knocked him back a step. He recognized the smell of death from his two tours of duty in 'Nam. Fearing what was inside, he knew he had to finish getting the lid off.

He raised the heavy top high enough to get a peek in. The first thing he spotted was the long hair signaling an adult female body, and the plastic bag over her head. He took a few steps back to gain his composure and got a deep breath of fresh air before returning to the drum to open it the rest of the way. By this time the crew had gathered around the barrel to watch.

Skeeter had to find the mettle to take a good long look at what was in there. When he peered in, he saw immediately an additional smaller body, the petite head, a child's head with dark hair that obviously belonged to a little girl. Large chunks of concrete had been dumped in the bottom of the barrel and used to weigh it down and make it sink. If not for getting tangled in the nets, it might never have surfaced at all.

Skeeter stepped back in horror as the realization hit him. He knew then exactly what he had on his boat. He choked back tears, but tried to hold it together enough to get his mind right. "Bobby Joe, get on the radio and call the Coast Guard, give them our location, and tell them we may have found that missing lady and her daughter."

While the night spun out around him, Skeeter heard Bobby Joe's rattled voice in the distance. "This is the *Southern Star* calling the Coast Guard, this is the *Southern Star* calling the Coast Guard; Mayday, Mayday."

Chapter One

As far as waves went, Indigo Key was no North Shore, Oahu. But for Garret Davis Indigo, the island where he'd grown up held a special place in his heart.

Part of his childhood memories included tourists swelling the island's population. The natural beauty attracted sightseers like a casino lured gamblers. They flocked here year-round for the exceptional weather—temps rarely dropped below the sixty mark. They came to conquer its waves and fish its world-class waters, to angle for marlin and hook bonefish, or reel in barracuda. They'd make the trip from the frozen winter tundra to dip their toes in the warm blue waters, to swim, to snorkel, and to scuba dive, or watch sunrises and sunsets that rivaled exotic places in the tropics with names like Belize or Aruba or Barbados.

The youngest of four, Garret had mastered these waters early. Most times, the four-foot swells were barely enough of a crest to experiment with stunts or aerials. But somewhere along the way he'd discovered the secret to becoming a five-time world champion surfer. He could angle higher, carve and cut through a wave, barrel deep, and attack a lip with a combat mindset. On any given day, anywhere in the world, he'd try any wave. Whether it was beating out the competition at the Banzai Pipeline, coming in first at the Big Wave Africa, or winning at Bells Beach, Australia, Garret rode a surfboard like he'd been born to it.

In a way, he had.

His older sister, Olivia Shay—known as Livvy to her family and friends—was the one who'd first dragged him into the shallow part of Sugar Bay and put him up on her surfboard. She'd seen to it that he sailed through the waves without drowning. He'd been two at the time, to her eight. But his first solid memory of the event was probably around the age of four.

From that moment on, he'd lived in the water like he was two parts dolphin. At times, he'd skipped school to do it. Most of the time, he faced getting busted. Dealing with his parents' wrath meant taking the punishment Lenore and Tanner dished out by grounding him. To their credit, they tried everything to keep him from going to the beach during school hours. They took away television privileges, his access to music, his computer, his games, and even tried embarrassing him by walking him into class and standing guard at the door.

For all their efforts, most times their tough tactics failed miserably. There were other times, of course, when he buckled down to study. But when the notion hit or the water was just too beautiful to stay inside, Garret pushed the boundaries time and again. It wasn't until he was in his sophomore year that Livvy had taken him aside and straightened him out about cutting class.

Their six-year age difference hadn't mattered then. When his big sister said to straighten up and cut the crap, he stopped skipping school. Mostly.

Livvy had been missing now for more than two weeks, along with her husband, Walker, and their two kids, Blake and Ally. After the disappearance, his family had spent the first forty-eight hours hopeful. His brothers, Jackson and Mitch, had even formed search teams to scour the island for any signs of them. But that became difficult when certain upstanding members of the community went out of their way to stymie the efforts. Who knew Indigo Key fostered a dark underbelly, one that would roadblock finding a missing family of four?

He'd always considered his hometown a laidback, quirky community of like-minded people. That is, until his sister and her family had gone missing. He was beginning to rethink everything he knew about the place.

As each day passed, he came to realize Livvy wouldn't have disappeared without letting family know her plans, especially if it meant taking the kids out of school. If she'd gone willingly…anywhere…she would've called home at the first chance. That meant she hadn't left town on her own. She hadn't taken the kids out of school.

These days, he looked at everyone with suspicion.

Sometime during that first week, Garret had moved from hope and rescue into the sad land of recovery. He and his brothers had expanded their search from land to sea. They'd gone out every day as a team on Mitch's salvage vessel, *The Black Rum*, using sonar scans to hunt whatever looked promising on the ocean floor.

So far, they'd come up with nothing.

Maybe that's why he'd sought out a private detective from Miami. Anniston Marcelli had turned out to be a gorgeous Italian beauty with dark, shoulder-length hair. She had a quick wit and carried a sidearm she knew how to use. He wasn't sure which attracted him more, the easy way she laughed or the fact she could nail the center of a target dead on.

He had to admit Anniston wasn't his usual type. He often ended up drawn to a different kind of female, one who preferred no-strings sex, and whose idea of a serious discussion ran toward what to buy at the mall, or which kind of salad to order. In his mind, it was the reason a man had to explore all the different varieties before finding the one that stuck.

This morning he thought of all that as he paddled out into the swell.

In the rush of whitewater, he ripped through the wall, crouched low on his board and launched off the top of a six-foot wave, becoming airborne. He came down in the water with a splash, and tried the stunt again. This time he rocketed skyward, higher, whipped in a circle, rotated again until his board dropped into the foam.

He didn't realize he had an audience until he took his first steps out of the surf onto the feathery sand, clutching his board.

There she stood, pretty Anniston, with that mass of dark tresses fluttering in the sea breeze. Her chocolate eyes locked on his.

It took Anniston one look at Garret's sun-kissed bare chest to fully give thanks for his Seminole ancestors. His dark eyes reminded her of wood smoke with a little fire around the fringes. His hair had a shaggy look to it that came down past his ears. The color leaned toward a sultry coffee, a shade lighter than the jet-black of his brothers. Even now, the mass dripped wet, the bigger drops trickling down his fit, toned shoulders and his athletic body to his very large feet. With those long toes, it was little wonder he could cling to his surfboard like a bald eagle clinging to its dinner.

He ambled up to where she stood, and she immediately felt the hyper beat pick up in her heart.

"You're out early," she managed.

"If I plan to keep in shape and stay on the competitive circuit, I have to go through the paces. The Pipeline's a mere two months away."

What she had to say wasn't something she'd planned on telling him alone. But since the media would soon be on top of the story, she couldn't stall for time forever. "That's the one in Hawaii, right?"

"Oahu's North Shore, practically my backyard." He cocked his head, narrowed his eyes to study the anxious look on her face. "What time did you crawl out of bed? The sun's barely up. What brings you out here?"

It was tougher than she thought to form the words. Dack Hawkins, the lead investigator on his sister's case, had called her at five-thirty as a courtesy. The disturbing news had slammed into her brain enough to get her out of bed. She'd gone to the window of her hotel room and glanced out, only to catch a glimpse of Garret in flight, sailing through the water on his surfboard.

On instinct she'd known then that it might be best if she shared the news with him and he could pass it on to his parents. But back in her room she hadn't considered how difficult it would be to get the powerful words out. The impact they'd have would be devastating. "How about I buy you a cup of coffee?"

The offer held a lot more than the desire for caffeine. "How about you cut the crap and tell me what brings you out here? Let's have it."

Anniston swallowed hard and licked her suddenly dry lips. She moved closer. "A TV station out of Key West is reporting that last night a shrimp boat came across a barrel in its fishing nets. The skipper popped the lid on the drum and found two bodies stuffed inside—an adult female and a little girl. Dack said that even with the state of decomposition the bodies tentatively match Livvy and Ally."

Garret felt like he'd taken a blade straight to the heart. He actually staggered back and had to lean on his board to keep from dropping right where he stood. "Let me get this straight...Livvy and Ally were crammed inside a barrel and dropped in the ocean?"

He decided it was a good thing he hadn't eaten breakfast yet. "That's…I'm unable to think of a word for how horrific that is. Where? Where did they find this drum?"

"The Gulf waters."

"That's the other side of the Key. All this time, we were looking on the wrong side of the damn island. Is Hawkins absolutely certain this is a valid lead?"

"I called the Coast Guard myself for confirmation. It's true. The county coroner's office accepted the barrel and the bodies about an hour ago. Because there are no other missing persons cases within a hundred miles of here, the authorities are pretty sure it's them. A positive ID will take at least twenty-four hours. They'll compare dental records to be sure."

"What about Walker and Blake?"

She shook her head. "So far, there's no sign of father and son. But the Coast Guard plans to keep looking in the general vicinity. I'm sorry, Garret, so very sorry about Livvy and Ally." Even though he was dripping wet, she put her arms around his waist in a hug anyway.

He let himself soak up the comfort and lean into the embrace, kissed her gently on the top of her head. "Does Mitch know yet?"

"You're the first person I've told. Since Jackson's back in Nags Head with Tessa for Ryan's funeral and since your parents went with them, I haven't yet made the call. I thought you or Mitch might prefer to do it."

He rubbed his forehead. "Don't call. God, I'll have to be the one to tell them all. They barely get Tessa's brother in the ground and have to come back home to this. No matter how much I thought I was prepared for the news, I'm…I'm not. They won't be either."

"That's for certain. No one should have to prepare for this. No one."

His mind was a jumble of things that kept hurtling through his brain, but he couldn't quite settle on what to do next. Desperate, he stood his board upright in the sand long enough to wander over and pick up his T-shirt where he'd left it on the rocks. After stretching it over his head, he sent Anniston a look that could only be described as a plea. "I'm not sure what to do now."

Her heart went out to him. "Want me to go with you back to the house to tell Mitch?"

"Definitely," he muttered, retrieving his board.

"No problem." She ran her fingers down his muscled arm, took his hand in hers. "Garret, I think right this second, you might be suffering from shock."

With his free hand he gripped her fingers but ignored the comment. Instead, he stormed off toward the street forcing her to follow. "What kind of evil monster stuffs little girls and women down in barrels and throws them overboard?"

He suddenly stopped his progress and whirled around to meet her eyes. "That's exactly what someone did to Ryan four weeks ago. They killed Tessa's brother on board Walker's yacht, tossed him overboard and he washed up at Rumrunner Cove. Maybe it wasn't Walker who murdered Ryan after all. Maybe it was someone else, someone Walker got involved with in one of his sleazy schemes and they eventually came after Livvy and the kids."

He scrubbed lean fingers along the stubble on his chin. "Which brings up the question, where the hell are Walker and Blake? We have to bring them home, too."

She could tell his mind kept going in and out, testing logic and reason. "My guess is they're somewhere out there in the same area, disposed of in the same manner as Livvy and Ally. The Coast Guard's concentrating their efforts right there looking for another barrel."

Anniston watched Garret's smoky eyes flicker to black, hardening into a seething fury. The muscles in his jaw twitched. She'd seen rage before but this was a steely, determined wrath with a life of its own.

He bent his head to where he was a breath away from hers. "After we locate Walker and Blake, I want you to help me find the bastards who did this, help me find the why of it. An ordinary family doesn't end up like this unless someone wanted something from them so badly that murder became the prime choice. We've already determined this wasn't about the money they had in the bank. They didn't take Ryan's five grand he was holding. They didn't bother with Livvy and Walker's cash. So what the hell were they after?"

"At least nothing that went the normal way out the door," Anniston reasoned.

"Something else then," he mumbled before pivoting back toward the street, carting his surfboard, accompanied by enough anger to flash red across the blue sky.

"Do you want to take my SUV? It'd be a lot faster than walking," Anniston called out after him. "My Explorer is parked at the Mainsail Lodge. We walk right past the hotel to get back to your house."

His brow creased into a frown. "I'm not thinking straight yet. I could walk off the mad but I need to get to Mitch before he hears it on the news. You said the TV station already ran with the story."

Her eyes glistened with sympathy. "It was their *lead* story. That's just one station. By now I'm sure others have picked it up and it's all over the Internet as well."

"Damn. Let's move."

When they reached the paved lot, Anniston unlocked the car so he could toss his surfboard in the rear cargo area. She drove them past the saltshaker-style lighthouse at the end of the block and took the jag in the road onto Quay Avenue.

Garret spotted the crowd of reporters standing in front of a shotgun-style bungalow about the same time Anniston did. It was hard to say who let out a louder string of curses. "How the hell do the vultures get word so fast?"

"Police scanners, or in this case, their source in the police department—they all have them. There is a third possibility. Chief Sinclair leaked the info to the media."

She grabbed Garret's arm before he could open the passenger door and leap out into the swarm of news crews.

"Pull yourself together. Don't confront them in the state you're in, at least not until you bank that rage. I know you're pissed off, but think of it this way. If the world is watching, then so is the killer. You want the son of a bitch who did this to know you're motivated to find him but that you're in total control of your emotions and the situation. From this point going forward, act like you know something they don't. If you can't do that, then let me do the talking."

For the first time Garret truly looked into the depth of her sharp, nut-brown eyes. What he found there was a confidence he didn't feel at the moment. Obviously she'd already crafted a predetermined strategy to deal with all this. He squeezed her hand. "I'll follow your advice. It's good. But they've likely already talked to Mitch. There's no telling what he's said on-camera."

"If that's true, then we'll deal with it."

As soon as the car door swung open, newshounds surrounded them. Reporters clutched microphones and shoved them in Garret's face for comment. They all talked at once, bombarding him with rapid-fire questions.

He'd been used to interviews with sports reporters before, but this was a different thing entirely, a different tone. These people were asking about how he felt learning that his sister and niece had ended up stuffed in a fifty-five-gallon drum and discarded in the Gulf waters like trash.

He did his best not to take the bait. Tamping down his fury, he straightened his spine. "We don't know for certain it's them. But if it is, that means Walker and Blake are still out there. Our priority is to find them and bring them home to be with Livvy and Ally."

He cut his eyes to Anniston before staring straight into the camera lens. "I just want to say one more thing to whoever did this. Killing women and children makes you the lowest of the low. You're not even human. You're nothing but a sick coward. Our second priority will be to find you. And there's no place where you'll be able to hide."

Anniston spoke up so the journalists could hear her over the din. "That's it for now, guys. As you might imagine, Mr. Indigo needs to be with his family. I hope you'll respect their privacy while trying to deal with their grief. For now, I hope you allow them the time they'll need to mourn."

With her five-eight height, she shouldered Garret through the crowd, pushing them both toward the foursquare bungalow and up to the front porch.

Garret flung open the door and stepped into the tidy living room, Anniston following on his heels. He took one look at his big brother, two years his senior, and stopped in his tracks. He'd never seen Mitch's face so knotted with emotion. Mitch sat on the couch watching the interview Garret had just given replayed on one of the morning TV shows. Like an echo, Garret heard his own voice rerun the same words.

Mitch looked up at his baby brother. "Way to go, you said exactly what I couldn't. The reporters have been pounding on the door since they woke me up at six fifteen. I looked out through the curtains and saw the news vans lining up at the curb. And I *knew*. I just knew something had happened overnight. So I turned on the TV and heard about the skipper on the *Southern Star* netting the drum. I've been sitting here ever since, not wanting to go outside and face the reporters."

Garret went over, bear-hugged him, and dropped down on the other end of the sofa. "I'm sorry I wasn't here to tell you myself."

"It wouldn't have made a difference. I called Jackson, woke him up—helluva thing having to hear news like that over the phone. He's the one who'll break it to Mom and Dad. I don't envy that chore. He's making arrangements to catch the next flight out of the Norfolk International

Airport. If they can manage it, all four should be back here sometime this afternoon."

"So Tessa decided not to stay in Nags Head?"

Mitch shook his head. "I think she wants to be here for Jackson. And for Mom and Dad."

They heard someone pound on the front door. "Go away!" Mitch shouted, his head in his hands. "You got your interview, now go the hell away."

The female voice from outside hollered back, "Mitch, it's me, Raine."

Anniston got up to let her in.

Raine burst through the doorway, breathless and sobbing. "My mom heard it on the news and called me. I got here as soon as I could." She darted over to the men she'd known since elementary school, squeezed her way in between them and took a seat on the couch.

Mitch laid his head on her shoulder. Garret did the same on the other side.

"Thanks for coming," Mitch whispered.

"Why wouldn't I? This is beyond heartbreaking. Livvy's been my best friend ever since..." She started to bring up old baggage, but thought better of it. What would be the point on a day like today? Instead, she placed a tender kiss on Mitch's cheek, rubbed his back, and threw an arm around Garret. "Are they absolutely certain it was Livvy and Ally?"

Garret deferred to Anniston, who went over the same ground she'd already covered. "Several days ago Tanner provided the medical examiner with the name of the family dentist. Give it twenty-four hours and the dental records will tell us for certain."

"I'm surprised Dad did that," Garret noted, as the wall phone in the kitchen started ringing. "I don't feel like talking to anyone right now. In fact, I need a shower. Then I need to get dressed into other clothes."

So Anniston played buffer. She fielded calls from the close-knit neighbors, as well as curious strangers who kept asking about all the macabre details. Managing the phones was part of the job, she decided. But it struck her that this was a bizarre turn of events. Not surprising since this had been a weird case from the beginning. She did her best to remain calm, but the tether on her cool demeanor was tested when she realized the killer might be one the callers, making contact just to get a reaction.

She took care of several of the more persistent reporters before Garret snagged her hand and tugged her down the hallway to where he'd slept the night before in Livvy's old room.

"I want you to play decoy with the press. Go back out to your SUV and maybe they'll follow you."

"While you do what?"

"I need to get inside Livvy's house again."

"Why? I've spent hours in that house, Garret. There's nothing there."

"I don't care. The answers have to be there…somewhere," he shouted. "The cops missed something. You missed something. We all did. I want to take another look around before Mom and Dad get back. I'd like to be able to give them some answers, tell them why their daughter and granddaughter ended up tossed into the Gulf like waste."

"Garret," Mitch began from the doorway. "It's a good idea. We'll go back in and comb through everything, room to room."

Anniston threw up her hands. "I opened every drawer, looked through every closet. I'm telling you there's nothing there."

"Then *you* missed something," Mitch charged. "Something that tells us why Livvy and Ally were killed."

Garret turned to Anniston, gauged if there were hurt feelings at the comment. He decided she'd weathered the Indigo temper just fine. "Look, we're not accusing you of slacking off or anything like that."

Mitch moved his head from side to side. "I'm definitely not. It's a large house, easy for anyone to miss a piece of the puzzle, especially when we have no idea what piece we're looking for exactly. One person couldn't possibly cover every angle."

"I'll help look," Raine offered, coming up behind Mitch. "I'd intended to make everyone breakfast, but I don't think anyone's in the mood for food."

"Thanks for that," Garret drawled. "But we'll grab something later before we head to the airport." To Anniston, he asked, "So will you help us dodge the press?"

"No problem. I'll make sure they don't follow me to Livvy's. I'll even go back in the house and help you look as many times as you want."

She pushed past Mitch, stopped. "And you have a point. Of all the cases I've ever worked, it never occurred to me Livvy and Ally would end up dumped in the water in a rusty barrel. I want to find the person responsible for doing that to a mom and a little kid."

Chapter Two

Thirty minutes later, Garret and Mitch ducked out the back door and took off around the carport. They cut across the neighbor's backyard to get to the next block.

The corner house at the intersection of Blue Fin and Windward was a far cry from the Indigos' house on Quay Avenue. Doubled in size, its West Indies style suggested money and prestige. Not a surprise since Walker was the son of the wealthiest man in the county.

Walker had let Livvy paint the house a soft mint green while keeping the columns on each side of the front door and the second-floor railing a creamy white. The louvered windows sported shutters in the same eggshell tone that made the house look as if it belonged in upscale Nassau.

The brothers headed around back to the breezeway connecting the main house to the detached garage. Sandwiched in between was a small guesthouse built as a cabana-style getaway and designated as Walker's office.

They'd already gone through his man cave once without finding anything of value, which meant they'd likely save a second hunt there for last.

"Did you bring the house key?" Mitch asked.

"Crap. Last time I checked Anniston had it. I forgot to get it back." He dug out his cell phone to text her, asking for an ETA. A few seconds later a ding indicated she'd sent a reply. "She'll be here in five minutes without the press."

Mitch studied the house and the long narrow windows running the length of the utility room. "I don't like standing around. You could pick the lock."

"I forgot my keys. My gadgets for that are all on my key ring. But I could bust it down."

"Nah, no need for that. We could just crawl through one of the laundry room windows. There's a gap."

Garret stared at his brother. "What are you talking about?"

"When we were here last time looking around I noticed one of the windows above the washer and dryer had been left open about four inches." He held up his thumb and index finger for a measurement.

A disquieting thought occurred to Garret. "You don't suppose that's how they got in, do you? That Walker and Livvy never opened the front door at all."

Mitch's eyes grew wide with interest. He walked around the house until he stood beneath the same bank of windows he remembered. "That's a possibility. At the time, I assumed the window was located too high off the ground for anyone to crawl through. Plus, the screens on each one are still in place. See?"

"But the window is open wide enough so that someone could've used it to get inside and then shoved the screen back in place later. We didn't get to go through the house until a week after the cops got done with it."

"Garret, those windows are a good seven feet high. I'm a tall guy but I'd need someone to boost me up or use a stepladder to take off that screen."

"So the killer had help," Garret shot back. But as he took in the height, his face showed the disappointment. "Okay, so this isn't an entry point. Each time I think I've figured something out I take two steps back."

"I didn't say we should rule it out. When we get inside we should see if it looks like anyone messed with it."

Garret heard a car engine and recognized the motor in Anniston's SUV. He walked around the corner of the house in time to catch her and Raine pulling into the driveway.

"How about if I open the garage and you pull the Explorer in there out of sight?" Garret suggested.

"Why all the secrecy?" Anniston asked as she handed off the key to the house.

"Because I don't want any of the neighbors knowing what we're up to and tapping into Sinclair."

She slapped his set of keys into his palm. "I noticed you left these on the counter. It has several of those little wrenches you so often use."

"Thanks. I generally never leave home without them. But I was upset. And since we don't have the remote to open the garage..." He sent her a half-smile, dangled the key ring in the air. "I'll use one of these on the side door."

A few seconds later, he stood inside the garage. He hit the button to raise one of the three doors so Anniston could park her vehicle next to Walker's sporty Jaguar.

"This is the cleanest garage I've ever seen," Garret noted, looking around the tidy space. It was organized to the point that everything was in its proper place in a ridiculous, obsessive way. Four bicycles—two adult, two kids—hung from the ceiling so they'd take up less room. Plastic storage boxes were neatly arranged on the shelves and stacked on the sidewall. "Did you get a chance to search in here?" he asked Anniston.

She got out, angled her chin in Garret's direction. "I didn't have the garage opener and didn't want to face a B & E charge that might give the neighbors an excuse to call Jessup for doing what you just did."

Garret sent her a smug look as he hit the button to close the garage door behind them. "I keep telling you I'd've made a decent cat burglar."

He turned back to Raine and Mitch. "Instead of splitting up, I think we should stick together, go through one room at a time and finish it up before moving on to another part of the house. I say we might as well start in here."

"That'll work. This garage is as orderly as the house," Raine commented as she crossed over to get an up-close look at Walker's convertible coupe. "He spent some major bucks on this. You know he bought it on one of his trips to Miami, probably to impress the Ellerbee mistress. Livvy was furious that he didn't talk to her about the purchase beforehand."

Mitch made a derisive sound in his throat as he began to take down clear plastic storage boxes so they could rummage through the contents. "Yeah, to the tune of sixty grand. That's why it's so hard to believe the guy was having money troubles and couldn't pay his web designer."

"Any excuse for being a tightass," Garret muttered as he mentally counted the containers. "There's only twenty to go through. That shouldn't take long. I'll start at the back wall near the water heater, work my way to the front, while you guys flip the lids on those."

Garret opened the door to a storage closet on the back wall. It held nothing more than a lawnmower, an assortment of garden tools, a gas can, a bag of peat moss and potting soil, and the usual water hoses and sprinklers.

As he searched he remarked, "You know, I checked out Ryan's website, and it's a masterpiece of marketing. It should've taken the Vitamin Hut to the next competitive level. Which is another reason why it was weird Walker refused to pay Ryan his money."

Raine shook her head. "When you think about it, Ryan had no choice but to hound Walker to pay his bill. And yet, we're looking at a luxury car in his garage and he couldn't pony up a lousy five grand for the fancy website he ordered. Something's wrong with that picture."

A comprehensive search meant Garret had to stick his hand behind the water heater. "Not so clean over here," he grumbled, meeting sticky cobwebs along the way to the back. "I hate spiders."

"Don't be a wuss," Mitch ragged. "What's a little bite from a brown recluse in the quest for the truth?"

"Yeah. Well. There's something back here behind the tank."

That caused Anniston and Raine to abandon the cartons they'd been digging in for a closer look. The women went over to where Garret ran his hand between the wall and the appliance, watched as he brought out a simple binder, a day planner in soft brown leather.

"That's a Filofax, nice. I have one of those myself," Anniston remarked.

"It belongs to Livvy," Garret stated as he thumbed through the pages. "From three years back."

"You're kidding?" Mitch scratched the side of his face. "Do you suppose it's been out here all this time? Why would she hide it…out here of all places?"

Raine bumped him on the arm. "Why do you think? She obviously didn't want anyone finding it, namely Walker."

"But from three years ago?" Anniston's brow furrowed. "I'm not sure what good that will do us. Although it's an interesting find—and one we should fully check out from cover to cover—we should do it later when we can sit down and pick it apart. Anything like this, we box up." She glanced around for something to hold the day planner and settled on a box full of out-of-date fishing magazines. She promptly dumped the contents onto the concrete floor to make room. "Here. Use this."

Raine went back to delving through a bunch of infant clothing Livvy had preserved in plastic bags and kept as souvenirs from Blake's and Ally's baby days. Tears filled her eyes even as she tried to hold them back. She held up a white lace dress Ally had worn at two months old. "Ally wore this at her christening. I can't believe that baby's gone. It was just August when I went with Livvy to help pick out school clothes for both kids."

Mitch was in the middle of foraging through old high school yearbooks when he crossed to Raine, put his arms around her shoulders. "I know. I'm having a hard time believing it's real."

"It's real, all right," Garret chimed in while rummaging through a carton filled with holiday decorations. He was up to his knees in silver and red Christmas ornaments, wreaths, garlands, ceramic Halloween pumpkins, and bags full of plastic Easter eggs. "I don't care what Walker got involved in, they didn't deserve to die like that."

"Will you take *The Black Rum* and go out and try to find Walker and Blake?" Raine asked, wiping back the tears.

"If the Coast Guard doesn't find them, you bet we will. We won't have a choice. We won't let them stay out there like that."

After Anniston reached the bottom of the last box—a slew of bestselling hardcovers that went back ten years or more—she made a decision. "It's time to move on to the house. This is just typical stuff any family might keep in their garage. There's nothing here of value."

"Yeah," Garret said in agreement. "Nothing's surfaced that suggests a sinister plot."

On the way to the house, Mitch explained about the open window theory in the laundry room. As soon as he got everyone inside, they all four crowded into the twelve by twelve utility room, staring up at the windows.

Garret leaned over the stainless steel washer and dryer that sat directly underneath, ran his hand along the wall. "Are those scuff marks?" He pointed to a few obvious black lines that stood out on the white paint.

Anniston put her hands on her hips and studied the smudges. "I saw those the first time I was here. But if this is the entry point, then someone would've had to put the screen back on before the state police got here."

"Jessup Sinclair did a walk-through after Mom filed a missing persons report. That's at least a day before the state cops rolled into town," Garret pointed out. "If we think he's involved in this, he could've messed with the evidence."

Anniston wasn't so sure. "No question the guy has a dark past with the highway patrol. But I'm reluctant to hang every single thing that doesn't add up on the chief of police."

Mitch looked at his watch, intervened. "We're on the clock here. We don't have time to debate the issue. Whether Sinclair covered things up, we may never know. Right now our mission is to comb through as much of the house as time allows."

On the opposite wall, Raine had been going through the bank of cabinets and drawers. But all she'd found so far were the usual paraphernalia on hand to launder clothes. When she spotted Livvy's craft corner she took the time to go through the boxes and containers. It was an organized space, albeit small. But Livvy had found a way to cram her supplies into a limited, out-of-the-way nook.

When Raine opened the dryer she discovered where Livvy had done a load of laundry for the kids. Their little shorts and tops were still there, bunched together among the fragrant smell of lavender dryer sheets.

"I don't think I can do this," Raine announced. "Everything I touch reminds me that I'll never see them again."

"Want me to take you home?" Mitch offered.

Raine puffed out a sigh, scrubbed her hands over her face. "No. No. It's okay. I'll buck up. I just have to keep telling myself I'm doing something to help find out who did this to them."

With that, Anniston ushered them into the kitchen. They divided the room into quarters, each taking a section. They looked behind bowls and dishes, sifted through silverware drawers. They even removed each drawer from its rollers, one by one, turning it upside down to make sure nothing had been taped to the bottom. They scoured the pantry, found a brand new bag of Oreos they passed around to share for breakfast.

Mitch and Garret practically took apart the little corner desk. They found reminders of dental appointments for the kids, a hair appointment for Livvy for a trim, and a notice to Walker that his subscription to *Florida Sportsman* was about to expire.

With four snooping people, it didn't take long for them to pronounce the kitchen clear. Following the slate tile floors into the dining room, they repeated the process, combing through the hutch and buffet. But so far the search had yielded nothing.

They rifled through the cabinets under the huge aquarium that separated the middle wall from the living area and focused on making sure the fish tank wasn't holding back a surplus of secrets.

Leaving nothing to chance, Raine and Anniston even decided to check all the potted plants. Going from banana tree to Norfolk pine and everything in between, they picked up each pretty container to look underneath and came up with nothing.

They checked every cubbyhole in the living room, went through bookcases, even dug into the sofa cushions. They turned the spacious entryway upside down. Even the umbrella stand didn't escape scrutiny.

But they found nothing that sent up a red flag.

Upstairs, they went through Ally's and Blake's rooms, including their closets, before making it to the master bedroom. They dug into the chest and dresser drawers, repeating the standard search for anything hidden on the bottom. They practically disassembled the king-sized bed, lifting the mattress to see what was underneath. But there was no smoking gun diary, or journal, or some slip of paper that shed light on why this had happened.

Garret poked through the nightstand on Walker's side of the bed and lifted out the only interesting thing he found there. "What the hell? *The Successful Guide to Treasure Hunting.*" He looked at his brother, then tossed the book to him. "Do you really think Walker had the chops to go after something like this?"

"Huh. There was another hard copy downstairs in the bookcase about the same thing. *The Top 20 Lost Treasures of The World.* I didn't think anything about it."

"Did he ever talk to you about hunting for, you know, treasure?" Garret asked.

"He emailed me a couple of times about the 1715 Spanish treasure fleet. And cornered me once last Christmas, trying to pick my brain about its whereabouts. But he was never specific about anything so I passed it off as nothing more than trying to make small talk at a family function." Mitch slumped against the wall, looked at the others. "I'm getting a bad feeling about the choices Walker made. What if Walker really did take an interest in the hunt for lost gold? What if the *Patagonia Pike* is here because of Walker?"

Garret traded looks with Anniston and Raine. "So Walker contacted this Dietrich guy down in South America and got him up here looking for Nazi gold?"

Anniston began to pace in front of the French doors. "Tessa did mention that as a kid Ryan talked about going in search of treasure one day. And he ended up dead. I think we might be onto something. The search for treasure has to be the connection."

Raine couldn't imagine it. "But you're talking about them getting killed over such an innocent pursuit. Would Walker and Ryan actually believe they could find such a thing without having any experience at all?"

Mitch needed to set her straight. "It's not such an innocent pursuit, especially for someone like Dietrich." Or for him, he decided, if he was honest with himself. "Most guys have a fantasy, whether it's quarterbacking in the

NFL or pitching in the major leagues, some people dream big."

"And some people dream about finding gold," Anniston added. "There's all kinds of different treasure rumored to be within the Florida Keys. Not just Spanish gold, or Nazi gold. There's one tale about Confederate gold going missing at the end of the Civil War and historians have long thought that it ended up in the Gulf waters near the Florida coastline."

"And pirate gold," Raine tossed out, beginning to think back to another time. "There are plenty of stories floating around here about that." She turned to look at Mitch. "Remember the big find by an Australian crew back in high school? That's what got you all jazzed about doing this kind of thing down the road. What were you, fifteen at the time? Those Aussie divers found a Spanish galleon right off the coastline. For months that's all you could talk about. You must've known then that's what you wanted to do for a living."

Mitch nodded wistfully at the memory. And realized that's when everything had changed for him. "From that point on, it's what I knew I'd be good at, going after sunken treasure."

"You certainly have given it your all," Raine declared, as a chunk of resentment fell away.

Garret dragged a hand through his hair. "But the *Patagonia Pike* specializes in hunting down *Nazi* gold, they wouldn't make the trip here for Confederate."

Alarm tightened Mitch's face. "That's right. And Dietrich is not a man you want to mess with. He's rumored to be the wrong guy to form a partnership with in excavation endeavors because he doesn't like to share. With anyone. Not a country or a state. This is beginning to make more sense to me. Maybe Walker got a crazy burr up his ass that he could throw in with Dietrich."

"If only we had something concrete to tie Dietrich to Walker and Livvy," Anniston stated. "We'd have to get our hands on his email account to see if Walker ever contacted Dietrich."

"How good is your relationship with Dack Hawkins?" Garret asked. "I know it's a lot more than your daddy knowing his." He held up his hands when she started to protest. "Your past is your business. I just want to know if you can get your hands on Walker's emails."

Anniston eased back with the attitude. "Maybe. Hawkins might've released the house, but he kept the family's laptops, computers, and their phones. Although he did share the two calls I mentioned the other day. Now that he's working this as a homicide, though, we're back to square one. I'll be lucky to get him to share anything at all. It's standard policy for cops to dig in and not want to discuss an ongoing investigation. Plus, it's a great way to stonewall people like me in the business I'm in. It forces me to think outside the box."

"I've no doubt you'll come up with a way." Garret moved to the French doors to stare out at the neighborhood and the street below. "I know you said you went door to door to canvass the neighbors. I know they said they didn't see anything. But what about the house across the street— the one that's catty-corner from here? It has a security camera installed by the front porch."

Anniston's brow tightened. "Where?"

Mitch followed Anniston to the window and watched as Garret pointed toward the intersection at the end of the block—the other side of Blue Fin and Windward. "That house. That camera."

Anniston thought back. "I knocked on the door once, but no one was home. I'd have to check my notes, but I'm almost positive I learned that it's a vacation rental, empty now, has been since the end of summer."

Mitch slapped his brother on the back. "Good catch, but the angle's all wrong. It doesn't cover Livvy's front porch at all, certainly not the side or the back."

Garret chewed the inside of his jaw. "Doesn't matter. The angle would capture all the people who drove their car back toward town. They'd have to go directly past that camera to do it. It's the most direct route back toward the business district. If the same car traveled back and forth on the night they went missing and we eliminate the neighbors—"

"We might have something," Anniston finished.

"Do you know what a long shot that is?" Mitch argued.

The private eye wheeled on Mitch. "You have a better idea?"

Mitch stuffed his hands in the pockets of his jeans. "Not at the moment. Fine. I'll go ask if they'll let me look at the feed that covers, say, two weeks ago."

"I'll take care of it," Anniston promised. "You guys take care of picking up your parents and Jackson and Tessa from the airstrip. I've got this."

"Are you sure?" Garret asked.

But the go-getter detective was already on the phone looking up tax records to see who owned the rental.

Chapter Three

Garret borrowed Mitch's rented Titan pickup to haul the family from the little airfield that served the Florida Keys back home to Indigo. Luckily his brother Jackson had been able to get them nonstop tickets from Norfolk to Miami where they'd boarded a commuter jet for the last leg home.

As soon as Garret spotted his parents coming down the steps, he noted how exhausted they looked. Jackson and Tessa had the same worn-out appearance. Ryan's funeral had obviously taken its toll on Tessa, but the others were suffering from the grief of knowing Livvy and Ally wouldn't be coming home.

Garret rushed toward his mother. Without a word, he caught her up in a big hug. "I'm sorry, Mom." He draped an arm around his dad. "You okay? How was the flight?"

"Longest six hours of my life," Tanner groused. "Remind me again why anyone bothers to go anywhere."

Garret went over to help Jackson with the luggage. "How are you holding up?" He thumbed a hand over toward their parents. "The media will likely be waiting for them back at home."

"I know. I'll try to run interference as much as I can. Dad's beyond upset. Who knows who he'll accuse if they stick a microphone in his face. The last thing we need is for Dad to go off on the press."

Garret related the morning's events, sticking to the reason they'd gone to Livvy's. "We went through that house top to bottom for almost six hours, found a few interesting items that I need to talk to you about."

"Yeah. Well, I need to tell you a few things, too. But it's not a good idea for Mom or Dad to hear, at least not yet. They'll likely explode when they do. Now's not the right time."

"Is it about Livvy and Nathan having an affair?"

Jackson fumbled the hold he had on his and Tessa's suitcases. "How do you know about that? I just found out before I left. It was more of a hunch really. How do you know?"

Garret leaned closer, lowered his voice to a whisper. "I found Livvy's Day-Timer from three years back and thumbed through it. Saw where she'd scribbled in Nathan's name over and over again with the purpose of meeting up with him, mostly on Tuesdays and Thursdays. Jackson, the thing was hidden behind the water heater in the garage."

"I had no idea it had been going on for that long. I thought maybe within the last year or so they'd gotten hot and heavy."

Garret stopped his progress so his parents wouldn't hear. "From what I could tell flipping through it, their affair goes back to Livvy's thirtieth birthday. We should probably confront Nathan about it."

"Yeah. Well, good luck with that. Nathan went out of town on a supposed business trip to Denver, a banking convention. That's what he told his wife five days ago. When I had some time on my hands back in Nags Head, I called the Chamber of Commerce in Denver. No bank convention in town and hasn't been since last summer."

"Nathan lied?"

"Looks that way, since he's dodging my phone calls and won't return an email. Funny thing is that was right before the shrimp boat found Livvy and Ally."

"Do you suppose Nathan is mixed up in this in some way?"

"Why else would he take off like this without a word? What is it they say about coincidences?" Jackson narrowed his eyes as he shot a glance over at his mother. "So we'll find a quiet spot and talk about this later. Does Mitch know?"

"Are you kidding? I'm not gonna be the one to drop this bombshell. He'll leap to her defense. There'll be a scene and he'll accuse us of disparaging Livvy's good name. He'd likely punch me in the face if I even tried to bring it up."

"Okay. We'll pick the right time to tell him before moving on to Mom and Dad…at some point. But it won't be today. What were the other items you found?"

"Two books about treasure hunting written by so-called experts in the field. Mitch opens one, I thumb through the other, and you can see where Walker highlighted certain key passages in both books that pertain to going after and acquiring a financial backer."

"Who would that be? Royce or Dietrich?"

"Mitch and I are leaning toward Werner Dietrich. Why else would he come to the Florida Keys? Another coincidence? I don't think so."

"Wow. Okay. I guess we have a lot to talk about. I'll have to find a way to take Tessa aside and let her know."

"How'd the funeral go? I didn't want to ask Tessa outright. But how'd it go with her weird family dynamics?"

"Her stepmother is a piece of work, I'll tell you that much. Suzanne Connelly tried to run the whole show. It didn't sit well with Tessa. She butted heads with that woman over numerous attempts to turn Ryan's service into a damn circus."

"What did her dad do during all the head-butting?"

"Mostly stood back and let Tessa take the lead to try and muzzle Suzanne. At least Tessa tried to. We took her father out to dinner last night. Nice guy, by the way, and tried to tell him he ought to do something about the insane amount of life insurance Suzanne has on him. Turns out, it's something like four million."

"Holy shit. And?"

"He said he'd think about it."

"Sheesh. Sounds like he's not ready to stand up for himself."

"That's part of it."

The conversation came to an abrupt end when their dad grew impatient and laid down on the horn. "What's taking y'all so long? Let's get a move on. I'd like to get home sometime today."

The brothers exchanged amused looks and finished dealing with the luggage. As they stuffed it into the bed of the truck, they agreed to table any more theories about Livvy until later. Jackson made room in the cramped backseat for his mother and Tessa while Tanner crawled into the front to ride shotgun.

The ride home was somber. No one said much. That's why Garret was surprised when his mother cleared her throat and stated in a clear voice, "Your father and I have decided we're going to skip having the funerals at Life Stone Church."

"We plan to pick an alternate location. That is once we find Blake," Tanner added. "We've thought about this long and hard since I confronted Boone that day at the church. If it ended up this way, your mother and I agreed to make other arrangements. We've decided not to set foot inside Life Stone ever again as long as Boone is standing in the pulpit."

Lenore sat with her hands folded in her lap. "We have to consider that maybe he already knew where Livvy and Ally were and that's why he thought the search was a waste of time. Why else would he derail it like he did? We came to this decision because we don't want that man anywhere near our daughter and grandchildren."

Jackson reached over and took his mom's hand. "That's probably a good idea. We have some time yet before…" His voice trailed off, knowing there would have to be autopsies done. "Plus, there's no guarantee Royce will agree with you. He may choose something else entirely different for Walker."

"That's fine," Tanner tossed back. "We've thought of that already, too. We don't care what Royce does with Walker once the Coast Guard finds him. But Royce will have a fight on his hands if he tries to block me from burying Blake with his mother."

After spending the past week in Nags Head dealing with her family, Tessa could better understand the feelings in play now. "What about having a service in the park? Use that one closest to the beach, the one with all the palm trees. From there, you can even see the statue of Koda Indigo and the marina. You could call it a memorial service instead of a funeral, no caskets, just music and eulogies, and anyone who wanted to speak, could."

Jackson kissed the top of her head. "That sounds like the answer. Mom? Dad?"

Lenore reached over toward the middle seat, patted Tessa's hand. "That sounds like it might work. Tanner, what do you think?"

"That's fine. That's the way we'll go then."

While Garret was busy with family, Anniston spent her time running down the owners of the vacation rental. It wasn't all that difficult. Using tax records she found in a public online database, she discovered none other than Royce Buchanan owned the property.

She headed out of town to what the locals called Buchanan Hall, a nineteenth century antebellum plantation that looked like one day it would make an ideal location for a historical museum. Anniston could see it now, tours of people fanning out over the grounds and gardens. Wandering around might take half a day.

Turning down a long driveway with towering magnolias on either side, she had time to admire the house, the massive Greek columns, the long wraparound porch on the first and second floors, and the four chimneys poking out of the roof.

When she got out of the Ford Explorer it was like taking a step back in time. "Scarlett O'Hara here I come," she muttered to herself as she walked up to the porch and rang the bell.

A woman answered the door wearing the traditional housekeeper's uniform—black dress with a white apron, even a little hat on top of her head. It reminded Anniston that she could've easily sailed through the time machine beginning in the late 1800s right through to the 1950s in a matter of a few minutes.

"Hi there," Anniston began. "I'm here to see Royce Buchanan. I called first. He's expecting me."

"Yes, yes. Right this way. Mr. Buchanan is in his study."

She was led down a spotless corridor with rich wood flooring and into a massive office, complete with leather furniture, dark wood all around, and books everywhere. Walker's father sat behind a huge mahogany desk that seemed to swallow the old man up. He looked a little like Batman's faithful Alfred Pennyworth, tall and gangly in his prime, but now reduced to a frail scarecrow that seemed to have forgotten to eat.

"Mr. Buchanan, I'm Anniston Marcelli. We've spoken a few times over the phone."

"Please, come in. Won't you have a seat? Would you like something cold to drink?"

She dropped down in a tufted wingback chair with leather as soft as a baby's behind. "Sure. Whatever you have on hand is fine."

Royce waved to the housekeeper, who still stood in the doorway. "Muriel, will you bring us some of your fresh lemonade?"

"Yes, sir."

"Your father has an excellent reputation in Miami. I checked."

Anniston grinned. It always warmed her to hear praise for her dad. "Yes, he does. My brother and I try our hardest to continue that excellence."

"Quality is never something that goes out of style. Has there been any word on my son yet? Do you know if they've located another barrel? I spoke with the Coast Guard myself about an hour ago and they had nothing to report."

"I'm sorry, Mr. Buchanan, but I don't know any more than you do. I'll check when I leave here, if you like."

"Call me Royce. I keep making a pest of myself with them. It might be nice if someone else took a turn at getting answers out of them."

She'd always believed in that old adage that you caught more flies with honey than with vinegar. "I'll see what I can do."

Royce gave her a smile, showing off his pearly whites. "Thank you for that. When you called earlier you wanted to know about the vacation property down the street from Walker's. May I ask why the interest?"

"Someone noticed this morning the house has a security camera installed on the roof line and it's angled toward the street. If I could look at the feed, I might get a sense of who came and went at that intersection."

"Which might lead to who took Walker and Olivia out

of the house." It wasn't a question. Royce shifted in his chair and steepled his fingers. "Unfortunately that camera hasn't worked since last year. One of the winter tenants down here from Maryland did something to it. At least that's when my right-hand man reported it broken."

"Your right-hand man? Would that be your mechanic Roger Baskin?"

"Indeed it would." He paused to let Muriel bring in the tray with the lemonade and serve it up in highball tumblers rimmed in gold. As soon as the housekeeper left, Royce picked up his train of thought. "Roger also acts as my chauffeur when I require it, my property manager when needed, and in that capacity maintains the rental properties I own."

"You mean like a handyman?"

"When it's necessary, yes. As I recall, the Maryland couple stayed for three months, I believe, beginning December first, and left around the end of February. Snowbirds, I believe the locals call them. Naturally when they left, we had to charge them extra for the damage to the camera."

"Naturally." Anniston picked up her glass, politely sipped on the best lemonade she'd ever tasted. Even Lenore's or her own mother's didn't measure up. To put him more at ease, she asked, "What's the secret to Muriel's lemonade? It's delicious."

Royce smiled again. "I believe she boils the rinds to get out the full flavor of the lemons. But you'd have to ask her for the specifics."

"I will, thanks."

He lifted his glass in a gesture of friendliness. "I could give you a key to the rental. You're welcome to inspect the camera and see for yourself that it's been in a state of disrepair for quite some time."

"If you don't mind, I'll take you up on that. Is there any reason you chose not to fix it?"

"Not really, other than it seemed an unnecessary expense at the time. Either that, or Roger just never got around to it."

"Working on other things, was he?"

"Probably. I keep him fairly busy. And of course, Roger has his own lucrative car repair business."

"I see. It's a shame, though. That he never got around to fixing the thing. Looking back, I'd say it might have held the clue we needed to find out who's responsible for abducting your son and his family."

Royce leaned forward in his chair. "Is that what you think happened? Because from the very beginning I waited for a ransom demand that never came. I'd convinced myself that it was only a matter of hours before a demand for money would come in. But then days went by and then a week…"

Anniston noted how sad he looked. "I'm very sorry, Mr., uh, Royce. I promise to put in a call to the Coast Guard for you as soon as I get back to my hotel."

"You'll let me know if you hear anything, won't you? Anything at all?"

"I will. And thanks again for seeing me."

"No problem. I'll get you that key before you leave."

The rental wasn't as upscale as Livvy's house down the street but it still had that British West Indies feel to it. Out of curiosity, Anniston wandered through each room decorated in bamboo, rattan, and wicker.

She could appreciate the airy digs—high ceilings with tongue and groove planks and wooden beams. It made her think of warm tropical nights and sea breezes coming through the gabled windows.

She made her way out to the columned front porch where the video camera had been mounted to the roof. It didn't take a mechanical genius to figure out Royce had been right. It didn't work because the video card had been removed, disabling the ability to record. It was impossible to tell if the card had been taken out by the snowbirds back in February, or by Mr. Baskin himself a mere two weeks back.

Which meant another dead end.

Anniston got back in her SUV. Instead of heading to the Indigo house, she decided to leave the family to their grief. She drove back to the Mainsail Lodge with a headache from hell brewing at the temples.

She kept her promise to Royce Buchanan and called the Coast Guard. The official word from the petty officer on duty was they'd found no signs of Walker and little Blake.

Using a messenger service that the hotel provided, she sent the house key back to Royce with a note thanking him for his cooperation. After all, she might need his help again in the near future. She also included the update from the Coast Guard, which wasn't really any different than what he already knew. But she wanted him to know she'd kept her word.

What she needed at the moment was time to think. Maybe a hot bath would do it, or a run on the beach to get rid of her excess frustration. Maybe the run first and then a long soak with bubbles up to her chin.

She changed into a pair of running shorts and an old top and was just about to head out the door when her cell phone rang. Her brother's picture flashed up on the digital display.

"Hey, Sebastian. I hope your case is going a lot better than mine."

"I'm about to wrap it up by the end of the week, float some evidence I collected to the Daytona PD. Need some help with yours, baby sister? Yours is a big ol' nasty one, if you ask me. My missing persons case—underage girl from Syracuse meets older boy online and comes down to Florida to be with him—was a piece of cake compared to yours."

"I wish mine had been that simple. The coroner still doesn't have a cause of death for Ryan Connelly. It's making me crazy."

"You need to increase Chuck's kickback to make sure

he keeps you in the loop."

Chuck worked as a forensic pathologist in the county medical examiner's office. She and Sebastian often compensated him to provide details about autopsy results. Chuck acted as their eyes and ears—a window into the county morgue. He was also a close family friend and the older brother to Dack Hawkins.

"Believe me, I'm keeping Chuck supplied with plenty of expensive lattes and French wine."

"What's Dad's take?"

"That I have so many suspects it's insane. And now my missing family has turned into two homicide cases while I'm standing around waiting for it to turn into four."

"Want some advice?"

"I could use a ton of it."

"Go back to the beginning. Take your suspect list and run background checks on all of them. Don't leave anyone out because you think they're noble or virtuous or untouchable respectable citizens. And for God's sakes, remember to reroute the Wi-Fi signal and use the private IP address out of Miami so that no one's able to track your searches. You are, after all, in a hotel, using their public Internet."

"Good point. But just so you know, I don't think any of these people are all that virtuous or respectable. You don't go out of your way to sidetrack a search without having a major agenda."

"Amateurs make mistakes all the time and send up red flags. That was a big one. So it should be easy enough to dig up some dirt."

They chatted another twenty minutes about family issues before Anniston ended the call and headed for the beach and that run she wanted.

While she jogged, she thought about the six who made up her suspect list. At the top was Royce, the slick developer millionaire. But he didn't seem that slick this afternoon. If gut reaction counted for anything, Royce appeared to be genuinely grieving. She also didn't think he had it in him to hurt his own son. Not that he acted like he cared so much about Olivia, as he'd called her, or his grandchildren. Odd. She'd definitely slide that attitude to the weird column.

That left the five Tessa had seen at Royce's house. She'd already done her homework on Jessup Sinclair, the chief of police—a definite dirty cop in his former life at the highway patrol. He'd been forced into taking early retirement for unethical conduct. His jacket had been jam-packed with phrases like "once a bully always a bully" and "Wyatt Earp syndrome." All negative connotations for an officer of the law. But what possible motive did Sinclair have for murdering a web designer and a family of four?

Werner Dietrich. She'd already dug up the dirt on him. And according to Mitch, a very bad man. She'd give the rich guy five stars and move him to the top.

What she hadn't done were the backgrounds on Royce's so-called right-hand man, Roger Baskin. She'd take care of that chore tonight. She also planned to look into the mayor, Dave Oakerson.

That left the last man—Boone Dandridge, pastor and upstanding citizen who had in fact misdirected the search for the Buchanan family on purpose. Chalk another one up for the odd column.

By the time she'd sorted all this out in her head, her Fitbit said she'd logged two miles. Not bad if she rounded the corner and did a return jog back to the hotel.

An hour later, after indulging in a luxurious bubble bath, she sat on her bed with her laptop, running names through the system.

She started with the auto mechanic and sometime chauffeur to Mr. Buchanan, Roger Baskin. Her jaw dropped at what she saw on the screen. The hits just kept coming. Roger had quite the rap sheet. He'd started out life in the French Quarter as Roger Thornton. By his teen years, he'd become such a well-known all-around thug, the Dixie mafia out of Biloxi came calling. The organization recruited the young Thornton and later groomed him into a first-rate mob enforcer. Thornton would likely still be on the job there if not for law enforcement taking down his immediate boss, Faron Edwards—thanks to a cold case unit reopening two homicides the cops believed were connected. Edwards caught a life sentence for an execution-style double slaying he'd committed eight years earlier. The boss ended up in the East Mississippi Correctional Facility and Thornton packed up and moved east to Florida, where he'd changed his name to Baskin. Somewhere along the way Baskin had caught the eye of Royce Buchanan. Anniston thought it would be an interesting challenge to find out how and why a Dixie mob enforcer was now working for one of the wealthiest men in the county. She knew firsthand that a name change didn't equate to Thornton/Baskin altering his ways. Once an enforcer…

After saving Roger's information to another file and backing it up on a flash drive, Anniston keyed in the name Boone Dandridge. At first, she got zero hits on the preacher. Not a bad thing there. But she'd learned from the best that one should never stop digging. The red flag was Boone's brief financial history. For a man in his early fifties to have such a limited credit history had her leaning back to the odd category. Boone seemed to appear from out of nowhere twenty-four years ago. She took what Lenore had told her about the guy and keyed in several markers that came up empty. Which meant his church bio was a complete fabrication. That caused her to probe deeper into the bones of Dandridge's past, beginning with his age.

She leaned back on the pillows and realized she was in for yet another ride. The pastor at Life Stone Church had been born Roland Wainwright in Vancouver, British Columbia. After emigrating to Seattle when he was twenty, Wainwright became a street hustler. It didn't take long for the scam artist to get picked up on various cons he'd tried, but failed, to execute. After serving eight months in county lockup—and thanks to an early release—Wainwright claimed he'd found the Lord.

To prove it, he settled down in a small town in Oregon and created a ministry geared toward the elderly. But he couldn't quite leave his two-bit hustling days behind him. After getting caught defrauding several little old ladies out of their life savings, Wainwright faced fraud and theft charges, along with a subpoena over a stock scam. He chucked the ministry and went on the run, leaving the state and the little old ladies begging for their money back.

Shortly thereafter, Roland Wainwright became Boone Dandridge. The statute of limitations had long since expired on the fraud and theft charges. Boone had spent the last twenty years off the radar inside the Life Stone parsonage.

Now it all made sense about the golf course project south of town. According to Tanner, as pastor, Boone had started singing the praises about the resort land deal with gusto after offering his flock a piece of the action. If they backed and invested their money in Royce's vision, they could trust the millionaire to deliver a tidy return.

While Anniston could find no outstanding warrants now, Boone's priors certainly didn't equate to murder. His twenty years of what seemed like clean living went in the odd category, though, which just kept getting more crowded.

Again, Anniston saved off Boone's data to another folder and backed up the files before moving on to Carson Frawley, the doughnut shop owner. Carson had no priors and no aliases. At one time he'd been an outstanding South Carolina baseball prospect touted for his three-hundred-plus batting average and his glove in the field. His college coach had proclaimed Carson had a decent shot at the major leagues. But that all ended when a back injury in an off-season bar fight kept him from reaching anything higher than Double-A ball, a stint that lasted just under six months. Carson had been a washed-up never-was by the age of twenty-two. From his credit history, Anniston learned he was deeply in debt. He liked to gamble and according to the church roster was right in line with the rest of the congregation hoping for one big score off Royce's land deal, a deal that promised a casino in the area within a year of closing down the nature preserve. Anniston also discovered that not long after arriving in town, Carson had borrowed fifty grand from Royce to start his business.

An interesting bunch, Anniston mused as she moved on to Mayor Dave Oakerson. She found another guy deeply in debt, a public figure who had for the past four election cycles taken sizeable political donations from Royce Buchanan. That wouldn't be so bad if part of the cash hadn't started showing up in his personal checking account in increments of nine grand a pop. In turn, Oakerson had invested a sizeable portion of the money into the land deal in hopes the golf course would become an actuality. An interesting side note for the mayor, who needed cash fast, and had the town's funds within his daily grasp.

Not such an idyllic little island after all, she decided. She got up to grab a bottle of water out of the mini-fridge she'd stocked with various staples and took the time to stare out the window onto the beach. One question kept nagging at her. How had so many felons landed on Indigo Key and selected it to make a fresh start? Or had someone brought them to the island years earlier with one purpose in mind?

Chapter Four

An hour later, she was still going over the data when she heard a knock at the door. She glanced at the clock. In her mind it was way too late for visitors to come calling. Dressed in a pair of pale blue pajamas, she grabbed her Smith & Wesson off the nightstand and moved to check the peephole.

And saw a downhearted and forlorn Garret standing outside her door.

"Oh, for God's sake." She flipped the deadbolt, slid the chain aside, and opened the door. "What are you doing here?"

"Nice weapon. Even nicer PJs." He ran a slim finger from her throat down to her neck. "The soft blue brings out your olive skin. I'm sorry to show up like this without calling but I was afraid you'd tell me to go away."

"Insightful. Go away, Garret." No sooner had the words escaped her lips than she regretted her coldness. "What's wrong? Has something else happened?"

"I had to get out of the house. The atmosphere was brutal—neighbors stopping by, bickering over theories and the like. I thought you might want to go out with me and get something to eat."

"Garret, it's after ten o'clock. I ate supper hours ago."

"Okay. You have a minibar, though, right? Unless they changed it up from the last time I stayed here. I'll settle for a bag of macadamia nuts and a beer. Besides, I brought something you should see."

She raised an eyebrow, realized he was serious. He clutched Livvy's Day-Timer he'd found that morning to his chest like a prized possession. "Oh really. Well, come on in then. I can rustle up room service. They're open until midnight."

She reached for the menu on top of the TV. "What would you like? They fix a decent burger and fries."

He gave her a sheepish grin. "Come to think of it, I'm not all that hungry." He handed her the day planner. "You should read this. No one else but Jackson knows what's in there. Not Mom, not Dad. Not Mitch. That's why all their theories about what happened to the family started getting to me. It seems Livvy and Nathan Hollister were having a down and dirty affair."

"The bank guy? But you said this was from three years ago."

"It is." He let the implication land and hit its mark.

Her mouth fell open as she flipped through several pages, read a few calendar entries and noted the meeting places. "No wonder it was hidden behind the water heater. This stuff is…hot."

He crossed to the minibar, picked out a bottle of Rolling Rock, twisted off the cap. "There are dates, places, intimate details in the calendar portion. I'd say this might be in the running to top whatever Walker was doing down in Miami. Just don't mention this to anyone else until we're ready to pop the news out of a cannon."

Guzzling his beer, he roamed the suite. "There's more."

"Why am I not surprised? There's always more."

"Jackson says Nathan left on a business trip right before he and Tessa took off for Ryan's funeral. Nathan told his wife there was a banker's convention in Denver." He went on, "No such animal. Nathan's now been MIA for almost five days, won't return Jackson's phone calls or emails."

Anniston plopped down on the bed, reached for her laptop. "If he left the island by commercial airliner I'll be able to track his whereabouts. That is, if he used his credit card. Has his wife filed a missing persons report yet?"

"Not that I'm aware of. Which is weird. Don't you think?"

"This case is jam-packed with weird."

"Yeah. Well, I think this whole thing is starting to make me a little crazy. I'm used to my orderly life, my schedule, my routine. Now I come back home and hit this chaotic wall. I don't think I'm handling it very well."

She huffed out a breath. "I hear ya. My brother may come down from Daytona to help me out when he's done there. I don't like the idea of it, but this case is...I might've bitten off more than I can chew."

"I guess we're all struggling with the enormity of it." He took out his smartphone. "When I was waiting at the airfield, I tried to write it all down in my notes. My fingers started to cramp up because it took so long."

Her lips bowed up. "I have twenty pages of notes and created another ten spreadsheets on this case. And we're talking about less than three weeks in." She went to the mini-fridge she'd stocked with her own brand of beer and popped the top, then drank down a generous amount.

Garret frowned. "What is that? You have your own beer?"

"I don't like the crap in the minibar. I mean Rolling Rock, really? I brought my own."

He took the can out of her hand, read the label. "Big Rod Coconut Ale." He slammed back a slug and made a face. "Not bad, but a little too sweet for me. What else do you have in there?"

"Red ale, another Miami favorite."

"I'll try that."

She reached back inside, grabbed a bottle of the brew, and took out the bottle opener from the nightstand drawer.

He sampled the taste before taking a second, bigger gulp. "Very good. You're a mystery to me, Ms. Marcelli."

"How so?"

"Just when I think I have you pegged, you always find a way to surprise me. You brought your own beer."

"The fridge came with the room. And I like my brand of beer. I could say the same about you. You aren't exactly an open book. I went to see Royce today."

"Now see, that's exactly what I mean. And what side of the old man did you get today? Darth Vader, or the faux Jedi? Because that's about the only two sides the man has."

"An interesting way of putting it. You wanted me to check out the house with the potential surveillance value. Turns out, Buchanan owns the rental with the camera, the nonworking variety. It gave me the perfect opportunity to meet him up close and have a chat."

She recounted the details of her visit. "He was nothing like I'd envisioned over the phone. I have to tell you, Garret, I think the man's telling the truth. He comes across as genuinely distraught. Whatever happened to Walker and Livvy, I don't think he was part of it."

"He's a good con artist, Anniston. One of the best. You shouldn't believe everything that comes out of his mouth."

"I know that," she stated with some irritation. "You aren't listening. The face to face gave me an inroad into forming my own opinion. That was before I discovered his right-hand man—that's his description of Roger Baskin, by the way—has a questionable past."

She turned the screen around on her laptop so she could show him the data. "I haven't had a chance to print this info out yet and probably shouldn't here at the hotel using the printer in the lobby. But I've saved it off into its own file for now. These are the background checks I did on all the players. You aren't going to like it. This is what I found out about Royce's chauffeur, mechanic, property manager, and maintenance guy."

Garret took a seat on the bed and studied the laptop screen. As he read each line, his eyes narrowed into slits. "Roger Baskin was an enforcer for the Dixie mafia?"

Anniston tapped the keys to go to the next page. "He followed in his father's footsteps. Angus Thornton has been locked up in Angola for most of Roger's life. By the time Roger turned eighteen, he'd been working in the organization for almost a year. He's been around crime all his life. The question is why would a wealthy guy like Royce need a low-level mob enforcer on his payroll?"

Ah, Garret thought, so she wasn't as charmed by the old man as he'd first thought. "Royce obviously set him up in business with his own garage. My guess is he cherry-picked Baskin for his value as a minion, a man who'd do whatever was asked of him, no questions. Somewhere along the way he knew Baskin wouldn't hesitate to do his dirty work when the situation warranted it."

"That's not all." She showed him the other bios, sat back, waited for his reaction.

"My God, Dandridge is nothing more than a con artist. His larceny goes back years. And Oakerson? He's about as dirty as Jessup Sinclair. In fact, they all have something in their past that might be good blackmail material."

"You know, there's a lot more to you than a pretty face."

"That's the second time you've said that to me. Why is it women never take the time to get to know a man before sticking a label on how dumb he is based on his profession? Or making a judgment call about how much money he has or doesn't have just by looking at his clothes. Or how—"

Anniston didn't let him finish. "Oh, please. Men do the same thing all the time. If they see boobs out to here." She used both hands to emphasize her chest. "And a good body, they obviously assume the IQ is in the low seventies."

He cracked a grin. "So you think I'm basically the hunky athletic type who is woefully intellectually deficient? Is that it?"

"I think your pretty face hides a very smart guy. Jackson keeps saying how you're a computer whiz. And you were able to access and download the tracklog coordinates from Walker's yacht. Not an easy task."

He lifted a shoulder, got up from the bed and went over to the fridge for another brew. "That? A piece of cake. A beginner could've done it. All I needed was his password and enough time to—"

"And know-how," she butted in. "Which you obviously have in spades."

"Want another coconut thing?"

"Sure. Why not? I'm not driving." She shifted on the bed. "How did you find out about Sinclair's past?"

He brought her another can of the stuff she liked and took a seat back on the bed. "I've known that since before my senior year. It went down something like this. I was often bored in class and would rather be in the water. But second to that, I loved gaming, computers, spending time on social networks, the usual exploits of a teenage boy. Who didn't, right? I got to be pretty good on my PC. Anyway, I used to ditch quite a bit back then, I'd always take my laptop with me wherever I went. Since I knew the first place my parents would look was the beach, I'd find a secluded spot, open up my laptop, and cruise online instead. Sometimes I'd look up people that I knew. Sinclair busted me one afternoon, was a real ass about it. That night I went home, in trouble as usual, grounded absolutely, and knocked back in my room. I was pissed off about the bust and ran the old man's life story, found out how dirty he was as a traffic cop."

"But you didn't tell anyone."

"Are you kidding? Why would I? Back then, my father believed I'd likely end up a beach bum at best. My teachers all thought I was just plain stupid. You said it yourself, people in this town looked at me like I was intellectually challenged, a surfer dude with no future to speak of. So who exactly would've believed me, of all people, about their beloved police chief?"

"Okay. You have a point."

"The best thing I learned about high school is that it's a phase. You get pigeonholed as dumb, but afterward you get to break out of that and head toward the horizon, soar to any height you want." He shifted gears. "I'll tell you what I think. It's almost like Royce sent out a blast email asking for felons of all shapes and sizes. 'Want to make a new start? Try Indigo Key. Our little town is open to all phases of new beginnings.' It's like he held his own job fair."

"Maybe that's exactly what he did. Maybe at some point he looked around and said, 'I'm outnumbered here. I need more of my own kind to tilt the scales in my favor.' So he gets his own people to move here."

Garret picked up the thread. "Years go by, and before you know it, Buchanan's people become respectable members of the community: a beloved pastor, a mayor, the top cop, and various business owners. Before long you've compiled a list of people who'll back you up in every way possible. Want a resort or a golf course on protected land? No problem. Line up behind the man who brought you here and do what he says."

"We could follow that line of thought. Your mother is set on getting in Boone's face anyway."

"Tell me about it. That's one of the reasons I got out of there tonight. They were planning their attack. And that was before you showed me his rap sheet. What do you think she'll do when she finds out he bilked old ladies out of their cash in another state? I'll tell you what. She's likely to tear him into pieces before my dad gets hold of him."

"When do you plan to tell her about Livvy's affair?"

"Oh God. I'll make Jackson do that. He found out about it first."

She found that funny. "That is so like siblings."

"What do we do about Nathan's vanishing act?"

"Are we leaning that he left on purpose or because of foul play?"

"On purpose. Didn't you say you could find out if he used his credit card?"

"I said I could check the airline manifest. Fine. You want me to do that now?"

He cocked his head. "Why not? It's early yet. I get the sense you learned how to hack."

"Hack? Me? Not really. But I have a few other tricks up my sleeve that I learned in law enforcement."

"I'm having another beer."

She narrowed her eyes. "Garret Indigo, are you trying to get sloshed in my hotel room?"

"The night Tessa found out about her brother, she got plastered. It seems like two days have gone by since you walked out on the beach this morning and told me about Livvy and Ally. I don't want to go back to that house tonight and sleep in Livvy's old room. I can't." He used the bottle opener to lift off the cap, took a long satisfying drink.

Sympathy moved through her. She patted the side of the bed next to her. "Okay. That was the one card you could've played to get you a spot for the night. Platonically speaking, of course. I never get involved with my clients."

He sent her one of his charming smiles. "Fine. Then I'll just fire you. You can work for Jackson and Mitch. How's that?"

"Very clever. Not."

He sat down on the bed. This time, getting comfortable by scooting back to lean on the headboard and stretching out his legs.

"You might as well take off your sandals," Anniston suggested. "Strong-looking toes, by the way."

After removing the flip-flops, he began to feel the buzz of the alcohol kick in as he slid in next to her. Mulling over her skill with a keyboard, all the while her fingers clicked away, he started playing with strands of her hair. "You're very serious when you work."

"Murder *is* serious."

"It is. But there has to be a limit to what a person zeroes in on and for how long. I think we've reached our quota for the night. Tell me all about Anniston Marcelli— whose grandmother grew up in Anniston, Georgia. Where did the great-grandparents call home?"

Resigned to his talkative state, she indulged him in what she remembered from her grandmother. "Città di Domodossola, Provincia del Verbano-Cusio-Ossola, a little region surrounded by pretty mountains with a lake nearby, and beautiful countryside."

"If I remember my geography correctly, that's Northern Italy, right? Near the border of Switzerland? Is that the same town that once broke away from Fascist Italy?"

Her jaw dropped. "Yes, it is. What are you, some kind of prodigy? How do you know this stuff? The only reason I know is because my mother used to tell me about *her* grandmother, who spoke very little English. So how would you know the town's history?"

"When I travel, I like to go to out of the way places. Tell me about your folks."

"Well, my great-grandfather owned some land there, way before the war. But it was taken away from him in a property dispute. After that, the landlord demanded that he pay rent but still work the farmland. He was young and impetuous, not the type to let anyone tell him what to do."

"So it's an inherited trait?"

She gave him a half-laugh. "I guess so. Anyway, he'd just met my great-grandmother a few weeks earlier, and apparently it was…"

"Amore a prima vista?"

"You're just full of surprises, aren't you? Yes, apparently it was love at first sight. But I don't believe in love at first sight. How is it you speak Italian?"

"I dabble, a little French, a little Russian, a little Spanish."

"Hmm, well, the language thing would make sense because you've seen the world."

He didn't want to talk about himself. "So go on with your story."

"That's it, really. They decided to run off one day with the intent to come to America. They ended up passing through Ellis Island sometime in late 1924. My grandmother was born the next year. We often wonder why they decided to settle in Georgia of all places."

"That's easy. Your great-grandfather was used to farming, growing things. He probably looked around for the best land where he could continue to do what he loved. Georgia probably had the most fertile land he could afford."

"See, you're an enigma to me. I've told that story about my relatives a hundred times and not one single person has ever come up with a reason like that. You amaze me."

"I'm like that," he said with a grin. "What were you like as a little girl?"

"Worshipped my dad, wanted to be a cop just like him. And before you ask, I get along fine with my mom. She teaches English and computer skills to immigrants, mainly because, I guess, her grandparents came here and struggled to fit in, so Mom helps others to adjust to life in the US." She looked up from her screen. "But I don't have the patience for teaching like she does."

"You're a bundle of energy, an adorable bundle, but nonetheless driven to solve a puzzle. That's why you're a good cop. You're only twenty-five. I doubt many of your clients know that since you try to act a lot older."

"Act older? How do I do that? You're assuming quite a bit about me. And aren't you just as driven to be the best surfer in the world?"

"Every year I get a little less driven."

She studied his face, noted he was serious. "Really? Why? That surprises me."

"How do I put this? It gets more difficult to sustain the ambition to stay on top." He really did want to know more about her. "By the way, I've been meaning to ask, when exactly did you and Dack Hawkins hook up? And for how long were you a hot item?"

She cut her eyes, landed a heated stare. "That's none of your business. It isn't even relevant to the subject at hand, certainly not the case as a whole."

"It might be if it affects your work."

"It doesn't. At. All. That's over. Has been for...five years."

"No carrying a big-ass torch for him then?"

"God no. Look, we were together about two weeks during the time I was at the police academy. Getting through those early days of training is tough for a woman. I was twenty at the time and suffering little panic attacks along the way, maybe even a ding or two in my self-confidence. One day I walked into class and spotted an old family friend. I latched on to his familiar face, had a few easy dates where we spent our time reminiscing about growing up in the same Miami neighborhood and before I knew it we were sleeping together. It was a mistake from the get-go. We broke it off, mutually, when we both realized we got together for all the wrong reasons."

"Yeah, I didn't pick up on any residual chemistry between you two."

"Then why ask me about him?"

"To see if you'd tell me the truth."

Absorbed in the hunt for information on Nathan, she ignored the comment. But it was harder to do with the man getting sloppy drunk beside her. "Look at this. There's no indication Nathan flew anywhere. If he left the island at all he did so by car."

Garret shifted toward her, his body close to hers, and snapped the lid down on the laptop. "You're working way too hard tonight, Anniston."

He began to nip her neck and spoke to her in what she thought sounded like French. "Garret, how many beers did you have before you got here?"

"Mmm."

She tilted her neck to give him better access. "There are so many reasons we shouldn't do this."

"But there's only one reason for amore."

"Garret, you're drunk."

"I know. If not for that, I'd be all over you."

She laughed. "If you were any more all over me we'd be sharing the same bones."

"We're sharing the same bed. That's gotta be good enough for tonight."

With that, his head fell back to the pillow. She shook her head. "Son of a gun. You just passed out on me."

Chapter Five

Garret woke to a grating sound like a cement mixer grinding away at a construction site. Or it might be someone shouting in his ear. He tried to respond, but found his mouth was as dry as the Gobi Desert. He tried to form spit but the foul taste had his tongue glued to the roof of his mouth.

He focused on every other word because the whole of it made his skull hurt. Through heavy-lidded eyes, he watched Anniston's mouth move, full and sexy.

"Garret, wake up. Your mother's worried about you. She left a message on my phone."

Anniston saw him mumble something, but didn't catch any part of it, so she poked him in the ribs again. "What did you say? I didn't catch that."

He tried to lift his head despite his noggin feeling like it was about to tumble off his shoulders. The burn at the top of his head felt like someone had doused him with fuel oil. He spoke slowly because…well, because it's the only way his brain could engage. "I said I left Mom a note on the fridge. Now go away."

She'd watched him sleep for almost five whole minutes, wondering why she'd never noticed the slight cleft in his chin, barely a dimple, but enough that it set him apart from his brothers. "Aww, that is so sweet. You actually left a note for your mom? Well, I already told Lenore you were here with me. So…"

"Then why are you still yelling at me?"

She ran a hand gently over his hair until it was out of his eyes. "Aww, that's cute, 'cause I'm using my normal tone of voice. Does your head hurt and have a temperature?"

"Go away."

"Are you sure you want me to do that?" She leaned in and whispered in his ear. "Because I ordered strong coffee and a full breakfast. It'll be here in ten minutes or so. I didn't think you were up to heading to the buffet."

"Coffee?" He snatched her hand when she tried to crawl out of bed. "I need a shower and a toothbrush, but I want to do this first." He angled where he could cover her body with his.

While his lean torso hovered above her, she felt the jolt of his touch. His rangy body skimmed hers. There was no doubt all of him was awake and aware and hard.

Her heart took an extra lap in her chest while his mouth got busy. His skillful lips did things that made her warm all over. From somewhere inside she melted, yielded. The assault turned into a feast, a tightrope between want and need.

It was the situation they found themselves in—part danger, part attraction. She worked her hands between their bodies and up to his chest, then gave him a little push. "We shouldn't do this."

"I don't like the sound of that." Mischief winked in his eyes as his mouth grazed her lips again, tugging out a low, throaty moan. He felt her skin heat, her pulse pick up.

The knock on the door signaled room service and brought them full circle from the night before. They'd slept in their clothes, side by side, and still the heat between them created a fully engaged inferno.

She managed to get her breath back. "I'll get it. I don't think you're in any condition to make it five feet."

He huffed out a laugh and watched her dash across the room. "Make sure it's room service," he cautioned.

In one smooth motion, she picked up the Smith & Wesson from the nightstand on the way to the door. "This isn't my first rodeo. But thanks for the concern."

The server came in and set up breakfast. All the while, their eyes remained on each other, even as she signed the tab.

When they were alone, she brought the tray over to the bed, took a seat and poured the coffee. "Cream and sugar?"

"Black. Thanks."

She looked down, stared at his jeans. "I see you've recovered."

"Disappointed?" His eyes cleared and he patted his chest. "Right here, baby. Just climb on top, and I'll do the rest." He reached for her hand.

Anniston smiled and latched onto his fingers. "Don't push it. Now drink your coffee. If your stomach is up to it, eat your eggs. On second thought, maybe toast would be better."

She leaned over and kissed his forehead. "If you weren't so cute suffering from your hangover, I'd send you packing."

He lifted her hand, pressed his lips to her fingers. "Good to know you aren't heartless."

"I think you'll find I'm a very warmhearted person."

"I'm looking forward to finding that out. But right now, what I could really use is four aspirin if you have any on hand."

She placed a kiss on his forehead, turned his palm over, dumped several little pills into it. "You'll also find that I think ahead. When I ordered breakfast I thought you might need something for the hangover."

"I think I love you," he declared before he threw back the meds with his coffee.

She choked out a laugh, slid a hand down his cheek. "We'll see about that."

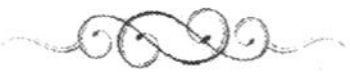

An hour later, Garret trekked through town toward the house on Quay Avenue to the sound of noisy seagulls. It occurred to him that it was already well into October. The days had flown by until it seemed he'd lost track. The month meant carved pumpkins on doorsteps and Halloween decorations popping up on windows all over town. In fact, he noted the blasts of orange and black plastered everywhere—the elementary school, the library, bars and restaurants, even city hall. Jack-o'-lanterns and ghoulish faces of all shapes and sizes adorned neighborhood porches and peered out, ready to greet unsuspecting trick-or-treaters at the end of the month. Scary witches took up guard over graveyard scenes spread out on the lawns. Any other time the displays depicting ghosts and goblins, even the ghoulish bloody exhibits wouldn't have bothered him. But today—the day after he'd learned his sister and niece had suffered a gruesome death—it all seemed too much.

Obviously that's why he'd sought out Anniston's company. It didn't hurt to pursue a distraction. God knows, he needed one.

He rounded the corner at the lighthouse and appreciated the bloom and look of autumn, although the temperature in the Florida Keys rarely dropped below a balmy eighty during the day. It was that time of year when people would start thinking about family holidays, like Thanksgiving, and getting their Christmas shopping done.

He realized Christmas without Livvy and the kids would never be the same again.

When he reached his parents' house, Garret quietly opened the side door and snuck into the little mudroom. Before making his move, he wedged himself between the door and the washer waiting to see if anyone was milling around in the kitchen. His teenage years came rushing back to him in vivid color, all the times he'd done the same thing to keep from getting caught.

Tanner sat at the kitchen table peeling an apple. As if his fatherly instincts went on radar, without even glancing in the direction of the utility room where his youngest son stood, Tanner said simply, quietly, "I told you to leave that woman alone."

"Technically…" Garret started to argue that the caveat had been that he would leave the private eye alone until she found Livvy. But since that no longer applied it was stupid, pointless, and just plain immature to bring it up to his dad now.

Instead, he went over to help himself to a cup of coffee and kept his mouth shut. He folded into a kitchen chair with honesty at the forefront. "I needed someone to talk to."

His mother came in, ruffled his hair as if he were twelve again. "Did you get any sleep at all? Want some eggs?"

"Nothing happened, okay?" Except for having her body up against his and a whirl of tongues mating that he'd like to repeat at the first opportunity, nothing at all had occurred between them.

"Anniston ordered breakfast for us." It wasn't judgment he saw in their eyes but rather compassion. "Look, I went over to her hotel last night just to socialize for a bit, to get out of the house. I couldn't sleep in Livvy's old room. I couldn't. We ended up talking for more than six hours about all kinds of stuff. By that time, I'd cleaned out most of the beer in her mini-fridge. I think she felt sorry for me."

Tanner put a hand on his son's shoulder. "Anniston has that look in her eye every time she's around you. Think about it. She strikes me as the levelheaded sort. If she hadn't wanted you there, she would've kicked you to the parking lot in a heartbeat."

"She didn't do that."

Mitch came in, trying to wake up. He poured his own coffee and helped himself to eggs still warming on the stove. "Morning, stud muffin. Have a productive evening?"

Garret sent his brother a broad smile and picked up his coffee. "As a matter of fact, I did. Want me to see if she has a friend for the lonely, solitary man you've become?"

Mitch started to raise his middle finger but thought better of it under his dad's watchful gaze. Instead, he dropped into the chair next to his brother.

"Where's Jackson?" Garret asked. "Did he make it official and move in to Nana's bungalow?"

The kitchen got even more crowded when Jackson and Tessa appeared in the doorway. "Sorry we're late but we slept in. Yesterday was an emotionally draining day for all of us."

"Want some breakfast?" Lenore repeated.

"Thanks, but Jackson fixed pancakes this morning," Tessa answered.

Lenore went to the cupboard, took out the Colombian java beans her sons seemed to prefer and dumped them in the grinder.

Garret had intended to wait and let Anniston relay what she'd learned from her research into Dandridge and the like. But since the gang was all here, before he knew what was happening, the details came pouring out of him beginning with the pastor's background.

As she brewed another pot of coffee, Lenore's hand went to her mouth in a gasp. "Boone stole money from the elderly? That's pitiful. I guess we aren't the only ones who trusted him. We've been a members of that congregation for more than twenty years. Since we've been back, he hasn't stopped by the house or telephoned us once to pass along condolences. Not a word from him. That's telling."

"Good God. For two decades he's been our pastor. Maybe he's the one who did something to Livvy. Did Boone serve jail time for this scam back then?" Tanner wanted to know. "Because that would explain his attitude when I mentioned visiting him at Raiford."

"You did what?" Garret asked.

"I told Boone that if he was into anything illegal, I'd relish the idea of visiting him every week in prison."

Garret rolled his eyes. "Sheesh. I can see how that would get a reaction. The scam he ran was back in Oregon when he was Roland Wainwright. I guess facing a subpoena, Roland took off and headed to Florida, somewhere along the way he morphed into Boone. It might be that Buchanan recruited all these people to come here. They all have questionable pasts."

Mitch sat back in his chair and thought that over. "Scamming little old ladies is one thing, a Dixie mafia enforcer among us is a lot more serious. And does Sinclair know Baskin's true past? I'm thinking he has to know about it."

"Yeah. Plus, if the mayor and Frawley are deeply in debt they could be blackmailed to do just about anything," Jackson estimated.

"Same goes for Sinclair," Tessa reminded them.

"You bet. But here's the kicker. Anniston doesn't think Royce is part of whatever hurt Livvy and the kids." Before Tanner could raise an objection, Garret added, "I'm not saying I agree with her, but you do have to wonder. Royce has always been protective of Walker, overly so. Why would he risk dragging Walker into something dark and dangerous at this stage of his life? He's already lost his wife and daughter. Wouldn't it be more likely that Walker wanted to impress his old man so much, he did something completely off the radar?"

Tanner nodded. "And incredibly stupid."

"Like going for the gold," Mitch tossed out in agreement. "And hooking up with the wrong set of partners, getting in way over his head."

Lenore pressed a hand to her chest. "Should we still plan to do those interviews? I'm not so sure I can. If I get in Boone's face now I can't promise I won't slap him silly."

Garret had been against the interviews from the beginning, fearing they'd yield nothing new. "I hear ya. Anniston's background checks change the game."

Mitch grunted into his coffee. "Something to consider. If we get any of these four to talk to us at all, we have to be in total control of our emotions. Anything else and we're liable to have confrontations with them instead of a simple Q & A session."

"But it has to be done," Tanner concluded, glancing at his wife. "We can't wait for law enforcement to get around to it. Your mother and I have known these people for two decades. We have to be able to gauge for ourselves whether or not Baskin, Dandridge, Oakerson, Sinclair, and Frawley were part of murdering innocent people."

Garret huffed out a sigh, knowing it was true. "Well, I doubt we'll get Dietrich to speak to us. But Royce seems to like Anniston well enough. He might open up to her. During these 'interviews' for lack of a better description, we need to find the weakest link in the bunch, do our best to cut him off from the others, and either exploit or break him."

Jackson nodded, getting on board with the idea. "That's okay by me. Any objections to that?"

"So it's a go," Mitch declared. "Now all we have to do is decide who gets to talk to whom. Raine already mentioned she wants in on this."

"I certainly do," Raine said from the back doorway, where she'd been listening.

"How long have you been standing there?" Mitch asked.

"Long enough. If no one else wants him, I'll take Carson Frawley. Carson and I went out a couple of times about two years ago. He likes me. He'll talk, especially about himself. I'll be able to wade through his BS well enough." She looked directly at Mitch and crossed her arms over her chest as if daring him to object.

Mitch returned her cold stare and stood up. "You actually went out on a date with that guy? Why? Carson's what, at least ten years older than you are? That's so…pathetic."

"Well, thank you very much, Mitch Indigo. You're such an expert on pathetic. At the time, I felt kind of like that. But you don't get to tell me who I date. Got it? Back then, I considered Carson a viable candidate for an affair. And why not? He's stable, owns his own business, and goes to the dentist regularly. You should see his teeth. But the best thing, and this is the icing on the cake, *Carson* doesn't take off to the ends of the world every time the wind changes direction."

Mitch threw up his hands. "Are you *ever* going to get tired of beating that same dull drum? I'm sick of hearing about it! I have a salvage business to run, a legitimate business that takes me around the world. It's what I do. I go where the treasure is. And it doesn't include scamming people or stealing because I'm in debt up to my eyeballs."

"Kids," Lenore pleaded. "This isn't the time or the place for bickering about something that happened a dozen years ago between you two. Let it go."

Raine bobbed her head. "You're absolutely correct, Lenore. That's why I'm happy to approach Carson. I think I'll be able to dig Walker's scheme out of him, if there is one."

"Well, I'm an outsider," Tessa said in an attempt to break the tension. "It doesn't matter to me who I get. All I ask is that Jackson go with me or I go with him. You know what I mean."

Mitch lifted a shoulder. "Fair enough. We want to draw straws for someone other than the doughnut man, or what?"

Jackson, who'd been leaning up against the counter, set his jaw. "I talked to Royce already. I'll take Dietrich."

"No," Mitch said quietly. "Dietrich's mine. Our professional connection should give me something to jam open the door. If Walker was trying to hook up with him to look for gold, then I'm the best person to talk to the treasure hunter, professional courtesy."

"Fine. Then I'll take Baskin."

"*We* will take Baskin," Tessa corrected.

"Right."

"Your mother and I want Dandridge," Tanner said.

"No offense, but do you think you'll be able to keep your cool enough to ask him about any kind of conspiracy?" Mitch asked.

Tanner glared at his son.

It was Lenore who spoke up. "I'll see to it that he does, because I'm going with him."

Garret chewed his jaw. "Anniston's already talked to Sinclair once, and it didn't go all that well. So I think we'll skip him for now. I'll go see Dave Oakerson. See if I can determine how deep the mayor's dirt goes."

"There's something else we need to discuss," Jackson said, cutting his eyes toward Garret.

"You're wading into dangerous water there, bro," Garret cautioned. "I'm not sure now is the best time."

"No, if we're splitting up to face the enemy, everyone needs to have all the facts." Jackson chose his words carefully before going on, "There's some indication that Livvy was seeing Nathan Hollister."

Lenore's brow wrinkled. "Of course, she saw him, every day. They were old friends. Livvy and Nathan were always doing something together." Her words bounced back as the implication hit her and everyone else in the room at the same time.

"Wait. You're saying Nathan and Livvy were having an affair?" Mitch put his hands on his hips. "You want to tell me what the hell you're implying?"

Garret waded in. "That Day-Timer I found behind the water heater is very…detailed."

Mitch whirled on his brother. "That's bullshit. That's the stupidest thing I've ever heard. Livvy wouldn't do that."

But Jackson was determined to stay on course. "Try to remember how unhappy she was, Mitch. I think Livvy had finally reached her limit with Walker and was ready for something else in her life. On the days he took off to Miami, I think she and Nathan spent that time together. I don't think Livvy cared Walker was seeing the Ellerbee woman."

"Based on what? Some stupid day planner?"

Jackson told them about all the emails Livvy had sent him, and that she always seemed to mention the banker. "Now no one can find Nathan. I've called. I've left messages. It's obvious he's avoiding me."

Acceptance came hard for Mitch. He slumped back against the wall as if he'd been punched. "You think Nathan might have killed the entire family and left town when he thought we were getting close?"

"I don't know. But if we're planning on sending the army out in attack mode, we need to keep an open mind about Nathan's part in all this. I don't think he could do such a thing, but then…you never know."

Mitch scrubbed his hands over his face. "I don't care if she and Nathan were having an affair. Let's say for argument's sake you're right. Maybe Livvy got fed up, gave the cheating thing a try. Walker was unfaithful, too. The marriage must've been over. Did you know, Mom? Dad?"

It was a long time before Tanner opened his mouth. "No. But if I had known, I might've done something stupid like encouraged my daughter to leave Walker and take the kids. I wanted her to be happy. Do you think Nathan made her happy?"

Lenore bit her lip. "I think he did. I don't think Nathan would've hurt her or the kids. But Livvy did spend a good deal of her free time with him. They'd go shopping or pack a lunch, even take the kids on picnics. They weren't exactly secretive about it. Livvy said they were friends, and I believed that's all it was."

"I asked Livvy about it, too," Raine admitted. "She and Nathan took a lot of trips to the antique mall. When I pointed out to her that she didn't own a single piece of furniture in her house that would be considered antique, she laughed and told me that she was helping him pick out stuff for his office at home. Livvy said they were just friends. I believed her explanation."

Mitch threw off the shock. "So how long do we give the Coast Guard before we go looking for Blake and Walker ourselves? You know they're out there somewhere in the same general vicinity."

Lenore shook her head. "I never thought for one moment it would come to this. But I don't want to bury Livvy and Ally without Blake. We'll need to talk to Royce about whether or not he'll want Walker to be buried with Carla and Winnie."

Mitch gave his mother a sympathetic look. "Okay, then I'd say we wait twenty-four hours. If they haven't located them by then, I'll get the precise coordinates where the *Southern Star* pulled in the barrel and start charting the waters. I need to give my crew a heads up on a time frame anyway. Walsh will stand by until I give the word."

"And how long do we wait before we start looking for Nathan?" Jackson prodded.

"I have Anniston on that already."

"So you knew yesterday when you found that thing?" Mitch accused, sending Jackson, and then Garret, a disgusted look.

"Yeah. I did. But then Jackson knew I wouldn't blow a gasket at the news. Instead of asking Dad if he's able to keep his cool, do you think you can do the same when you get in front of Dietrich? Because if you freak out with him like you just did, you'll demonstrate a weakness we can't afford to show."

Mitch's chest tightened. "I won't freak out."

Raine snorted. "That'll be the day."

"Don't start," Mitch warned.

Garret had heard enough. "Both of you need to lose the anger. We're all tired of listening to you bicker, or playing referee. Get over the past or walk away. It's just that simple. There's too much at stake for all this infighting every time we get together. It's a costly distraction. What do you say?"

Raine kissed Garret's cheek. "I'll do better. But I can't promise your brother will do likewise."

Chapter Six

Walsh Kingston had a past that very few people knew anything about. He'd learned at an early age that it was best to keep certain things about himself private. He'd gotten good at it over the years. But not before making some major mistakes.

His yearlong incarceration at seventeen occurred after a fight with a bully over a woman. Defending the lady's honor had come at a price. His rashness taught him a valuable lesson. Bullies were fine if they were left in control. When that control was taken away, they had a tendency to run scared into the nearest corner, crying all the way to law enforcement. Because he'd acted out of immaturity, a brash act over nothing, he did his best not to repeat the mistake. He'd learned to keep his temper in check.

Walsh knew the value of intimidation. It had kept him alive while surrounded by older, tougher, meaner inmates. He'd survived by serving each of those three hundred and sixty-five days growing wiser, getting smarter, learning to control certain urges.

He'd made a vow to himself never to take his freedom for granted ever again. So far, he'd been successful.

His military background in Special Forces was another matter entirely. He'd joined the Navy right out of Fort Madison lockup, spent ten years doing his government's dirty work in places like Somalia, Bosnia, and Libya before getting fed up with the lifestyle and chucking the entire thing. He'd long since obliterated his tattoos, turning them into tropical things like parrots or other frivolous wildlife so there was nothing left to tie him to his former life.

His training came in handy sometimes though, whenever he needed to handle a weapon or take up for a fellow crew member. He hadn't taken a life since his Navy SEAL days. But this thing in Indigo Key had all the earmarks of ramping up to a turf war.

He was getting a very bad vibe.

It was barely dawn when Walsh waited on the deck of *The Black Rum* sipping his first cup of Colombian roast. His light brown hair fluttered in the breeze, his olive skin glowed in the sheen of the morning light. His sharp, pale blue eyes watched as Mitch made his way up the ramp to the boat.

"Everything here normal?"

"We haven't had our ass blown out of the water yet, if that's what you mean," Walsh fired back.

"How's Prentiss doing?"

"He does his job, doesn't make trouble. What's the latest in this saga?"

Mitch let it all come streaming out. Because he trusted the man like a brother, he told Walsh about the interviews and what Anniston had discovered hiding in each man's background.

"I can't exactly throw stones at someone's past, now can I?" Walsh said as a reminder.

Mitch stared into his friend's face. "You ever steal from someone, Walsh?"

"Nope. Don't like thieves. But I've done far worse things."

"As a soldier," Mitch pointed out. "I'm talking cold-blooded murder here."

"Did you have any idea your hometown was such a hotbed for criminal types before now?"

"I don't think it was. Something changed. I'm just not sure when. I have a favor to ask. I want you to keep an eye on Roger Baskin for me."

"Sure, in my spare time, I'll see if I can out-slicker the mob enforcer. If I'd known I'd be asked to babysit like this, I'd've asked for a big fat raise. But since I don't care for cold-blooded killers who go after little kids, I'll do it without you doubling my pay."

Mitch slapped his friend on the back. "I knew I could count on you."

"That, too."

The banter went back and forth between friends until Mitch got serious. "I want you to keep your guard up out here. Pass the word along to the men to do the same. And tell them not to go blabbing around town about the case when they spend any time in town."

"They don't really know that much about the case, certainly not specific details. But it sounds to me like you have a major trust problem."

"I guess I do."

Chapter Seven

"It took me an hour to convince Wendy Hollister that it was weird her husband never made it to Denver. What a cold bitch," Anniston revealed as she breezed into the house on Quay Avenue.

In the heat, she'd changed into a peach sundress that set off her bronze skin. But with the humidity outside soaring, she was still fanning herself when she walked in. "Whew, it's hot out there. Sorry I'm late, but Wendy likes to go on and on, unfortunately it's all about Wendy. I don't think she mentioned her husband until I asked about him."

"So you got inside? Good for you. She wouldn't even let me in the door the night I stopped by to see Nathan," Jackson detailed. "Were you able to talk her into filing a report, making it official?"

"Eventually. But it was like dragging her there kicking and screaming. Something's off with the woman,"

Anniston declared. "I sat there while Chief Sinclair took the report, otherwise I thought she might get bored and get up and leave."

Garret came out of the dining room where he'd been helping Mitch pinpoint the exact coordinates of the shrimp boat. "Wendy works for the mayor. So maybe when we get Dave to talk to us we'll find out how and why she's off."

"The whole town's off, if you ask me," Anniston stated without holding back. "No offense."

"None taken," Tanner muttered. "Although it used to be a nice place to raise kids." He stared at Anniston still gripping her laptop. "You need a place to put that and work? Take the kitchen table. Mitch has charts spread out all over the dining room."

Later, they were all clicking in their respective zones when the doorbell rang.

Tanner opened it, only to see Royce Buchanan standing on his porch. He looked beyond the old man and noticed Roger Baskin leaning up against a Maybach sedan parked at the curb.

"What the hell are you doing here, Royce? What do you want? You lost or something?"

"Your oldest boy invited me," Royce explained in a gravelly voice. "'Course that was when we still thought our children would be found alive."

Tanner turned an accusing eye on Jackson before he snapped out, "What could you possibly want here with us?"

"Let me come inside. You don't expect me to tell you standing outside on the porch, do you?"

In a reluctant posture, Tanner opened the door wider so the old man could make his way inside. He watched while Royce used a cane to hobble over to the sofa and sit down next to Jackson.

Tanner let him get comfortable before he cleared his throat. "Okay, let's have it. What do you want?"

Royce lifted his cane in the direction of Mitch. "I need his help to find my boy. Walker's still out there in the water somewhere. I want you to help bring him home where he belongs."

Mitch clenched his jaw. "Why me? Why not ask your buddy, Werner Dietrich, for help? He's the one with the major bucks."

The name threw Royce off balance. They could tell it by the way his eyes grew wider. "What do you know about Werner Dietrich?"

"I know his boat, the *Patagonia Pike*, is outfitted a lot better than *The Black Rum*. And I know you Buchanans always go first class." Mitch had the satisfaction of seeing Royce go white as a sheet, so he went on. "I know the guy has a penchant for collecting artwork, circa World War II, and spends his time looking for Nazi gold."

Mitch thought Royce looked like he might pass out. "Which makes me wonder why you'd come to us for help when you could rely on a seasoned crew like Dietrich's bunch. Unless your buddy is busy with other more pressing matters, like trying to pinpoint the whereabouts of something very, very…lucrative."

It took a full minute before Royce recovered enough to speak. "I'm not in the habit of asking Werner Dietrich for favors. He isn't the type of man who hands them out, not without wanting something in return."

As much as Tanner loved watching his sworn enemy squirm, he lobbed another hard volley. "We already know you met with him during the height of our search for Livvy. In fact, the discussion got rather heated. What have you gotten mixed up with, Royce? What did you do that cost Livvy and my grandkids their lives?"

Royce's eyes watered with emotion. "You don't know what you're talking about. Werner is a businessman. He simply put in some money to fund the development of the golf course. So did a lot of other wealthy backers. My association with him is strictly a business arrangement, no different than other members of the community who want to see this deal go through. There are business owners who want a resort built here to watch the town grow and prosper. Not everyone is like you, Tanner, stuck in the bygone days. Some people actually want to see us grow."

"I'm not getting in a political discussion with you the day after I find out my daughter and granddaughter were discovered stuffed in a barrel."

"But they haven't found Walker," Royce tossed back.

"And little Blake," Tanner supplied. "Why do you never mention the kids? What are you up to, Buchanan? You've dragged Boone and your other cronies, even Jessup Sinclair, into your web of deceit. What are you hiding?"

"You're talking conspiracy-theory foolish. I'm the one who had Sinclair taken off the case right from the beginning. Do you understand that? I didn't trust a two-bit, rinky-dink, easy-to-bribe cop like Sinclair to find my boy. So I called Tallahassee direct, talked to a friend of mine up there, someone in charge. It isn't my fault the state sent me down some inexperienced dimwit like Dack Hawkins."

Tanner dropped into his recliner as if he'd been shot. "I don't know what to believe anymore."

Garret wasn't so ready to trust the claims. "But you are involved in something with Dandridge, Sinclair, Mayor Oakerson, and this Dietrich guy from South America, right?"

Royce looked tired and worn out. "Other than the development deal, I swear to you I don't know what you're talking about. All of you have gone crazy." His eyes darted around the room at all the disbelieving stares. A full thirty seconds went by before he decided to speak again. "All right. Fine. I'll tell you what I know. Last summer Walker came to me claiming he was putting together a business deal, a big one, one that would blow me away. When I asked for details, he wouldn't tell me a thing."

"Didn't you think that was odd?"

"Not really. It isn't the first time Walker attempted to stand on his own two feet. Of course that usually led to his failing but I always encouraged him to keep trying. I never gave up on my boy. Every son tries to impress his father at one time or another. Walker was no exception."

"That's pretty hard to believe," Garret pointed out. "That he wouldn't brag to you about the players he'd lined up. Any idea what type of deal he was working on?"

"I questioned him about it more than once. He was very vague. But he was also very excited, couldn't wait to get it off the ground."

"And you have no idea what this big score was?" Tanner went on. "Look me in the eye and tell me you're being upfront with us."

"I'm telling you the truth. Why would I get my boy mixed up in something that would cost him his life? Why?" Royce stabbed a bony finger at Tanner, tears streaming down his face. "Now I want help finding my boy. If money is the issue, I'm happy to hire your son and his crew to locate him."

"Them," Tanner amended. "There's an eight-year-old boy out there still missing, Royce. So kiss my ass. Mitch and his brothers already planned to go out tomorrow to do just that, and the day after if they have to, but not because of you. We're doing this for Blake. And when we find him…" Tanner's voice cracked. He swallowed hard. "When we find Blake, he'll be buried along with his mother and sister."

"I lost my wife to cancer, lost my daughter Winnie last year. Been eleven months since the car accident. Don't you think Walker should be buried with his mother and his sister?"

Relief moved through Tanner. "Yes. Yes, I do. So you don't plan to fight me on the grandkids?"

Royce leaned forward on his cane. "No. They may have died together, but I don't think they were all that close as a family unit, especially lately."

Mitch wanted to pounce on that, but Garret held him back. "Why do you say that?"

"The love had died a long time ago. Affairs on both sides. They stayed together because of the kids. I wanted Walker happy. I don't think he was, at least not with Livvy."

"Since we're being so honest here—"

From the kitchen doorway, Anniston cleared her throat. "Garret, could I see you in here for a minute?" She latched onto his arm in a death grip and practically pushed him into the other room.

"What are you doing? I was just about to grill Royce about Baskin."

"I know what you were about to do. And it's not the time. Do you honestly think that man's going to tell you he enlisted several felons to join him down here in paradise?"

"It's worth a shot. It seemed like the timing was perfect."

"No. Think about it. Your father's nemesis has just come to the enemy camp, hat in hand, so to speak, asking for help. Is that something Buchanan's ever done before?"

"Well, no, not that I know of."

"Then what does that tell you?"

When he gave her a blank stare, she fumed and lowered her voice. "Why would Royce ask Tanner for anything unless he's clueless as to what happened to his remaining child? I don't even think he knew what Walker was involved in."

"You actually think he's telling the truth? Come on."

"That's what I said last night. Besides, there's something you need to take care of now. Hawkins gave Skeeter Bronson my cell phone number. The shrimp boat captain wants to meet with a member of your family. He's not picky. I thought you and I could do that and get out of here for a little while."

"Good idea. I think we should meet the guy who found them. He probably wants his reward. I'm prepared to take care of that."

"What about Mitch and Jackson?"

"Jackson's plotting how best to corner Baskin. Mitch has his hands full contemplating a similar chess match when he gets to Dietrich. We're all sort of nervous about this whole thing."

"I've thought about this, long and hard. All the more reason I should put together a set of questions and persuade you guys to try to keep to a script."

Garret let out a half-laugh. "Yeah? Lots of luck on that with this bunch."

Before she could pack up her computer bag, Anniston's cell phone went off. She looked at the readout and realized it was Chuck Hawkins. The only time Chuck ever called was when it was time to collect on the hundred bucks promised for the latest news out of the county morgue.

"It's the medical examiner's office," she explained as she stepped outside to take the call. When she was clear of the house, she asked, "What do you have for me, Chuck?"

"A confirmation. The dental records prove the remains belong to Olivia and Ally Buchanan."

"No question?"

"Nope. It's them. Dack will make the announcement this afternoon. And Anniston?"

"What?"

"Olivia Buchanan was basically beaten to death before someone placed a plastic bag over her head. She suffocated. And, here's the big-ticket item. Mrs. Buchanan had recent sexual activity before her death. We found spermatozoa."

"Are you absolutely certain of that?"

"No mistake. The sample had deteriorated quite a bit, but it's there and useable for a profile. Dack will likely hold that tidbit back from the press."

"You're saying you have DNA?"

"Yep."

"Thanks, Chuck. I owe you. And there's a bonus in it for you when you get a hit in CODIS on the DNA."

"Better make it something nice. You'll be the second one I call after my brother. Oh, and tell Dack that Mom expects him there for Sunday dinner."

Anniston grinned to herself. "Tell him yourself."

"I just did when I gave him the update about the mother and daughter. You'll probably need to remind him before Sunday. This case has him jumping all over the place."

"Your brother's dealing with the biggest thing that's hit this area since the Kettering murders at Caruso Cove. Remember that one? And you want me to give Dack a message from his mama?"

"You know Kate Hawkins. Mom wants her baby boy there for pot roast."

"I'll see what I can do. I gotta go."

"Take care of yourself."

"I'll do my best." Anniston took a deep breath and headed back inside where Garret met her at the door.

"It's them, isn't it? The coroner confirmed it."

She patted his cheek. "I'm sorry, Garret. I need to tell everyone else inside." She took his hand, led him into the living room, and came up short when she saw Royce still sitting on the couch.

She took a deep breath. "I have very sad news. I have a contact I use in the medical examiner's office. He's a forensic pathologist, very reliable, very accurate."

There was no easy way to say what had to be said. "I'm afraid it's official. Livvy and Ally were identified through dental records. I'm so very sorry."

Chaos broke out when everyone started talking at once. Then came the sobbing, along with a lot of anger.

After several tense moments went by, Garret used Skeeter Bronson as an excuse to get out of there. But no one paid much attention. His family was too mired in grief to take notice.

The *Southern Star* had dropped anchor near a jetty on the opposite side of the island known as Oro Cay. That's where Skeeter Bronson had chosen to wait on the docks with a view of the Gulf waters.

Anniston had done the driving and once she parked the SUV in the little lot adjacent to the wharf, Garret shifted in his seat. "What else did your informant in the coroner's office tell you about Livvy and Ally?"

"I wouldn't call him an informant."

"Whatever. What happened to leveling with me? Or was that promise just a bunch of BS after you got us to sign on the dotted line?"

She tried for patience, knowing she'd just delivered appalling news no one should have to hear. "Garret, there are certain things best left to law enforcement that you don't want to know. Gritty details have a tendency to upset loved ones. It's a step I take to spare the family more pain."

His eyes narrowed at that. "To tell you the truth I never thought much about murder one way or the other, never considered what the family of victims should know or not know, until now. You told me once you'd be honest. That's the point of the question. You said candid and truthful were included in the deal, in the way you worked. Are you going back on that now?"

She turned to stare into his coffee-colored eyes. "Okay. I get it. They found semen inside Livvy. She had sex with someone before she died. It's not a smoking gun. It was probably Walker before they went to sleep that night."

"Probably. But even Royce admitted to us this morning that the marriage was basically over."

Anniston frowned. "Walker and Livvy were still sharing a bedroom. Does that sound to you like they were calling it quits? Not to me, it doesn't. Besides, Royce obviously doesn't know the play by play of what happens between two people cohabiting and sleeping next to each other. If things were so awful, there were other rooms Walker could've used. He didn't. There were no signs in any of the bedrooms that Walker was sleeping anywhere else other than the master. Sure, he might've bunked in his man cave once in a while, maybe on nights they had a tiff. But on the night of September twenty-third, he was in the bed next to Livvy."

"How do you know that for certain?"

"The first time I went in there, the bed was unmade, like two people had just crawled out from between the sheets, and the pillows on both sides of the bed showed where two people had slept. Plus, we found the how-to treasure hunt guide on his side of the bed. To me, that says he spent quite a bit of time there."

"Okay. Fair point." He rubbed his forehead. "This is so confusing. Were they nearing a divorce? Or was it nothing more than the seven-year itch on both sides?"

"It's one of those things we may never know with absolute certainty. Raine was Livvy's best friend and vice versa. Livvy didn't seem inclined to share her personal life with Raine on any level other than to occasionally bitch about Walker. I have married female friends who do that all the time. Their marriages aren't on the brink of divorce."

"That you know of," Garret supplied.

"True enough. That's why keeping an open mind is essential. Could Livvy have stayed with Walker because of the lifestyle, the trappings of being married to a Buchanan? It's something to consider."

"Nathan was no slouch in the money department."

"Yes, but he also would have to deal with Wendy, who would be the ex if Nathan and Livvy went so far as to try to be together. Greedy ex-wives have an inclination to demand alimony. The one thing I learned about spending thirty minutes with Wendy is that the woman *adores* money. It's all she talked about. She'd be motivated to fight for a sizeable chunk of her share of anything."

"So you're saying that Walker and Livvy stayed together in an open marriage concept? That's what they call it, right? You've tied the knot, but still play around on the side." He couldn't fathom Livvy doing that. "I'm blown away."

"Because Livvy's your sister?"

"Partly. Having an open mind is grand unless stuff comes to light that doesn't jibe with what you know about someone you grew up with."

"I see. This has to be difficult." She grabbed his arm. "I just thought of something. If Walker kept the how-to guide in his bedside table, Livvy must've had some inkling what he was doing, what he was reading about, what he planned to do with the information. Think about it. You're lying in bed together, your spouse takes out a book, your natural curiosity would be to look over and see the title. There's convo about the topic."

"Hmm. Maybe they were both waiting for the big score before they went their separate ways. Maybe that means Nathan was in on it, too. Or at least had some knowledge because she passed that info on to him." Garret looked around at the little strip of sand narrowed down to a sliver of land. The beach was dotted with Key thatch palm and patches of young almond saplings, along with a canopy of wild coffee trees.

"I say we get this over with. Is that the shrimper?"

Skeeter Bronson was waiting on the dock, tall and skinny as a beanpole.

Garret got out of the Explorer and approached the man, extending his hand out first. "My family's very grateful you went out that night. The sad thing is we were going out almost every day ourselves, searching, but we were looking on the wrong side of the island, the east side, in the Atlantic."

"Trust me, you didn't want to be the one who opened that drum."

Garret nodded. "That's why I'm prepared to give you the reward that was posted."

Skeeter shook his head. "No, sir, I don't want it. Opening that barrel, finding your sister and her little girl like that was the worst thing I ever laid eyes on in my life.

And I've seen war, arms blown off, dead bodies, even a drowning or two in the rice paddies in 'Nam. But I'll never forget your sister's eyes. They were open, big and brown, like yours. The little baby girl's were closed. No, sir. I don't want nothin' to do with no reward for finding something like that."

Dumbfounded, Garret shifted his feet. "At least take half. Seriously. You deserve something. Without you…" His eyes glazed over as tears formed. "We might never have known what happened to our sister."

"I'll tell you what I want. I want you to find the sumbitch that did this to that little baby girl. Monster like that, he don't deserve to live."

Garret reached his hand out, gripped the shrimper's again, and gave him a pat on the back with the other. "There should be more people like you in the world. I want you to remember one thing, though. Wherever you are, wherever you go, if you ever need anything, anything at all, you get in touch with me, hear?"

"That's a very generous offer," Skeeter said, scratching the stubble on his chin as if thinking about what all he could use. "You sayin' I could tell you my truck broke down or somethin' and you'd get me another one just like that?"

Garret grinned. "Sure. All you have to do is ask."

"Why?"

"Because I'll never forget what you did for my family."

"Well, I don't need no truck and my business has been damn good to me lately." Skeeter reached out his hand again. "But if there's another downturn in the economy, one of those recessions again, and if the shrimp business ever dries up, I might just take you up on that one day."

"Up to you. Thank you again."

Garret watched as Skeeter turned on his heels and walked down the wharf and back to the *Southern Star*.

"You do realize he's liable to ask you for a house one of these days, right?" Anniston advised.

Garret lifted a shoulder. "If he does, he does. But I think he would've taken the money if that were the case."

She looped her arm in his. "How'd you get so smart?"

"Smart? Not me. Jackson is the one with all the degrees. I'm just a beach bum who likes to hang out around the water."

"You're so much more than that. But somewhere along the way you've decided that image is the one you prefer to show the world." As they walked back to the parking lot, she said, "I'll drop you off at the house because I need a quiet place to get some work done."

He put a hand on her back and kissed her shoulder before dragging her closer. His mouth clamped down on hers as the energy between them surged. If the kiss at the hotel had been a delicious sample, this was a full course that prompted visions of a ravenous feast.

When he gave her time to come up for air, he whispered, "Did I mention you look beautiful in that dress?"

"No. But I'm beginning to get the idea."

On a path to possess, he devoured her mouth again, but then decided to change the angle. He drew out more little moans with light butterfly kisses that ramped up the juices.

A thrill shot through her, leaving her dizzy. She didn't get dizzy or lose control often.

A greedy seed took root, causing him to pull back. He murmured in her ear, "More than anything I want to go back with you to the hotel, but right now I need to be with my family."

"Of course you do."

"Why don't we plan to have dinner later?"

"Sure. Where?"

Running a slim finger down her throat, he said quietly, "I picture a candlelit dinner in a romantic dark corner of a restaurant with a view of the water. And then, a room with a bed."

Chapter Eight

After dropping Garret off, she stopped at the bank where Nathan Hollister worked. But she couldn't get anyone there to talk. From VP to teller they simply stonewalled her. One surly employee went so far as to have the security guard escort her to the door. She'd never been booted out of a bank before. But there was always a first time for anything in Indigo Key.

On the sidewalk, she weighed her options and texted Dack, hoping she could interest him in getting a subpoena for the bank's surveillance tapes. She needed to find out what Nathan's last day at work looked like via its security cameras. There had to be some telltale sign that he'd been prepared to bolt.

The day was already warm with temps edging toward eighty when she left the SUV parked in the business district and headed down to the marina. There was another stop she intended to make.

Ryan Connelly's remains had been found at Rumrunner Cove, a small channel that existed off the larger body of water known as Sugar Bay. She headed in the direction of Fast Willie's, a bait shop slash convenience store that had served the fishermen and boaters in this part of the Key for decades.

As she strolled along, she made note of every security camera within range. It was a short list. It seemed the downtown area had only installed a few, primarily near ATMs and liquor stores. Basically the town seemed to have opted out of a digital world. That included Fast Willie's.

It was the same stark reality once she reached the little inlet. The location of Rumrunner Cove was interesting. The area couldn't be seen even from the convenience store. Since it was hidden from view of the busy port, it provided a measure of privacy. Anniston surmised the locals had to be well aware of its out of the way location.

The waters here were calm, barely slapping up against the maiden cane and marsh grass.

Anniston took out her phone and zeroed in on the area where Ryan's body had been discovered. She tried to focus on an imaginary line that angled out toward the Bay. Her lens followed the sight line to an area less than a mile south of the port.

Garret had already proved that during Labor Day weekend while Ryan was in town, Walker's yacht never left Sugar Bay. The tracklog had indicated as much. But from where she stood now there was no doubt about one thing. She realized that if Ryan had died on the *Misty Dawn*, the boat had to have left its slip in order for the body to wash ashore at this point.

But what did that mean exactly?

She chewed her lip as she pondered a theory. Maybe once Ryan realized the situation on the yacht was becoming too dangerous and more than he could handle, he tried to get away by jumping into the water, hoping to escape the situation. What if he'd tried to swim his way to shore and…someone prevented him from doing that?

But the coroner had determined Ryan hadn't drowned. That meant he'd been dead before hitting the water. It didn't explain why the *Misty Dawn* had gone such a short distance from the marina to the mouth of Rumrunner Cove to get rid of the body here. Why not take it farther out to sea and dump it there? Time had been the deciding factor. The killer had needed to get rid of the body fast and couldn't do it at the busy marina. Throwing it overboard here was less likely to be seen by the fishermen who frequented the area. Even in daylight it'd be difficult to spot the boat because of the narrow gap in the tree line. And if Ryan had been killed during darkness, no one would've noticed.

He'd last been seen at the hamburger joint at four-thirty with Walker. She took out her phone and looked up the exact time sunset had occurred on that day. It was possible the killer had waited until nightfall to get rid of Ryan's body right outside the mouth of the cove.

With an idea brewing, she removed her sandals and eyeing the available coastal scrub—beach elder and golden creeper—she determined those were too brittle for what she had in mind. She weighed her options and snatched up a branch of bay cedar. She found it heavier, sturdier, perfect.

Before dipping a toe into the blue-green water, she used the long piece of stick to check for snakes. Stabbing the water with one end, she gingerly waded into the shallow channel, hoping like hell there were only fish and turtles to contend with.

Her feet hit the sandy bottom and with each step she questioned her judgment. But since the hem of her sundress was already damp it was too late to turn back. Instead of heading toward the mouth of the cove, she stuck closer to the grassy flats and wetlands. She had to fight off the wood storks that used the habitat to catch lunch.

While watching the stubborn birds use their beaks to break the surface of the water, she spotted a school of young redfish feeding off the crustaceans and seaweed. Her eyes tracked to a large batch of the stuff and looked closer. Something much lighter in color caught her eye. It was the contrasting bone white embedded in the brown stems and tangled in the vines that made her study it longer. With her stick she poked at the object lodged in the kelp. Closer inspection revealed eye sockets, teeth, and what appeared to be ugly, floating skin.

No amount of training at the police academy could ever prepare her for finding a head that had been exposed to the elements for four weeks. Fish, birds, and other wildlife had taken turns destroying the flesh. Still standing in calf-deep water, she took a deep breath and punched in Dack's cell phone number. When he answered on the third ring, she swallowed hard to get her mouth to work.

"Dack, this is Anniston. I need you to get to Indigo Key. Now! I think I just stumbled across Ryan Connelly's head near Rumrunner Cove, or at least what's left of it. There's not much flesh on the skull so it looks like it's down to mostly bone. And if I'm not mistaken there's a visible bullet wound in the center of the forehead."

"I'm on my way. Give me thirty minutes. Don't touch anything!"

"Hey, I'm not stupid," she shouted. But Anniston didn't have to be told twice to get out of the general area. She backtracked through the water, bunching up her skirt so she could hightail it onto land faster. She scooted out of there so fast she almost fell.

As she stood twenty yards from the skull, her first instinct was to call Garret. But since she'd already delivered devastating news to his family earlier, she held off. A few minutes later, however, she realized Tessa would have to be told about the discovery. She chewed her bottom lip and thumbed through her contacts for Raine's number. She'd ask Raine to go over to the Indigo house and break the news.

When no one answered at The Blue Taco, she tried calling Raine's cell phone.

As soon as Raine picked up, Anniston began her pitch. "Hey, I know you're probably swamped right about this time of day, but I need your help."

"I closed the restaurant. Put a sign on the door that read: 'In honor of Livvy and Ally Indigo we're closed for business.'"

"So you're at home? Good for you." Anniston went into the entire horrific find. "I'm standing here waiting for Hawkins to show up and I can't leave."

"And you want *me* to tell Tessa? What if she wants to go running over there?"

"That's a bad idea. It's up to you and Jackson to convince her not to do that."

"Okay. Sure. Do you need anything before I take off?"

"I could use a gallon of coffee and a new stomach. I'll never be able to erase what I saw from my brain."

"How did you make this discovery when the police searched that area? Twice."

"I don't know. That's a good question, and one I intend to point out to Hawkins. Look, I have to go. There are a couple of fishermen heading this way. They're getting ready to wade into the water and cast their lines. I can't let them do that."

After shooing away the anglers, a few minutes later she looked up to see Raine shoving through the curious throng beginning to congregate, carrying a to-go coffee mug.

Despite the circumstances, Anniston grinned widely. "I could hug you." To prove it, Anniston moved toward her and draped an arm around Raine's shoulders.

"No problem. I brewed it myself. Thought you could use this or a life-size poster of Channing Tatum. The java seemed more practical. Don't worry. I'm heading to see Tessa after this. Just not sure how to dump this kind of news on her."

"Yeah, I know, and so soon after Ryan's funeral." Anniston glanced around at the growing number of onlookers and shot a dirty look toward the fishermen, realizing they must've sent out text messages to everyone they knew. "The crowd seems to want a macabre show and I have to stay put. You and I both know word is bound to get out and when it does…"

"Don't worry, do your thing, I'll do mine. I decided to close the doors today at the restaurant because my mom and grandma thought it was the right thing to do. They both loved Livvy as much as I did." Tears formed in Raine's eyes and she knuckled a few away. "Please tell me you'll be able to find out who did this."

"You know I'm doing everything I can."

"But what are the chances?"

Anniston blew out a breath. "About fifty-fifty."

"Even with going through your suspect list? Even with the interview idea? I thought that was a great idea, by the way, especially after they made a point to say all those things about Livvy wanting to leave town."

"I have some ideas on that. We'll need to pull together to get those face-to-face sessions to pay off."

Raine's shoulders slumped. "I've lived in this town my whole life. It never occurred to me anything like this could ever happen here. I'm afraid there's a dark underside to the Key I didn't know existed. You let me know when you're ready for me to have that face to face with Carson. I can't believe he'd need money so badly he'd be a part of something like this. But I need to find out. Because since this happened, I don't look at my neighbors the same way I did before a whole family got wiped out. I guess I shouldn't assume Walker and Blake are…dead."

"I'm sorry." Anniston squeezed Raine's shoulders tighter. "Let me know after you've seen the Indigos. Try to make Tessa stay put."

"I'll do my best, but I'm feeling really down, Anniston. After you called, my mom and I decided to take some food over to show our support. Are you stopping by later…after this…chaos?"

She thought of Garret and his promise to take her to

dinner. "I'm supposed to have plans with Garret tonight. All the more reason I need to take care of this and head back to the hotel to get my work done."

"You and Garret have that look in your eyes."

"What look is that? Stumped? Baffled? Frustrated?"

Raine bumped her shoulder. "More like sexual frustration leading to the buildup."

"You mean the same way you and Mitch look at each other?"

"That's over."

"You keep telling yourself that, Raine. Maybe one day you'll even believe it. That anger you have for him has undercurrents about as…" She held her arms out wide for measurement. "Deep as the waters in the Gulf. Garret's right, you know. You two need to settle this once and for all or avoid each other entirely."

"But I want to help find Livvy's killer."

"That's why I don't think avoidance will work for you two. So you should really do yourself a favor. Figure out how to put the past behind you, and don't look back." She wiggled her eyebrows up and down. "Who knows? Getting along with Mitch might have its benefits."

Hawkins pulled up in a state-issued Crown Victoria, still wearing his fancy captoe Oxfords. Anniston shook her head at the sight. Didn't the man realize it might help if he lost the charcoal gray three-piece suit in the island heat? As she watched him cross gingerly over the little bayou, obviously afraid to get mud on his clothes, she wondered why she'd ever taken that step of sleeping with a family friend. Didn't matter that they were from the same neighborhood. Didn't matter that they'd known each other since…forever. Dack had a personable enough nature, she supposed. It just seemed as though these days he'd morphed into a stuffed shirt. On the other hand, his brother Chuck had a sense of humor.

"Took you long enough to get here," she grumbled when he got within earshot. "How could your team have missed something like this?"

Dack ignored the attitude and insult and stuck to the obvious. "Medical examiner is on his way, but it could be a while. Show me what you found."

She led him back to the edge of the tide pool. But when she waded in, she noticed he remained on the little spit of sand. She put her hands on her hips. "If you'd opt for casual clothes once in a while rather than the formal attire you seem so fond of wearing, you wouldn't be afraid of ruining your Sunday best."

"You said I should hurry, so I hurried," Dack snapped. "Just point it out to me. I'll get the gist from here."

Anniston sent him an annoyed eye roll. "The gist? Well, it's gonna be a little hard to see detail from where you're standing. You actually might have to get wet. You didn't answer my question. How could your team have missed the head?"

"It could've come in recently with the tides."

"Nope. It looks to me like it's been hung up in the kelp for quite a while." To prove her point, she took a picture with her camera phone, walked back ten feet, and held it up so he could see for himself.

Dack made a face. "It doesn't take long in this Florida heat for human remains to decompose that badly. How did you come across this?"

"I went looking. Besides, anyone could have stumbled on it. They just had to veer off twenty yards straight through the glade. As you can see, the seaweed snagged it, held it there for the fish and wildlife to destroy. It's about a foot down, but see how it dips in the current?" She tapped the photo she'd taken. "Isn't that a bullet wound in the middle of the forehead?"

"Yeah. Three murders now in a town this small."

"And two pending with Walker and Blake still unaccounted for," she reminded him. "This guy's got a hell of an aim."

"Not to mention he doesn't mind killing little kids. Do you realize this is the first case we've worked on together?"

She scowled in his direction. "We're working separately and you know it. Although feel free to share the contents of Ryan's laptop you found in his Civic, or better still, Walker's computer. I'm working under a handicap here. You aren't."

"You know I can't do that. Captain Briggs would have my head if I went against protocol and shared anything else with you. I won't risk my job, Anniston. So I'd appreciate it if you stopped trying to call in favors every now and again. You've about used them all up."

"Good thing Chuck doesn't feel the same way."

"Hey, that arrangement is between you and Chuck. But if he gets caught, it's his ass on the line."

"Chuck does that for Sebastian and me out of a sense of friendship. Your brother did mention I should pass along an invite. Your mother requires your presence back in Miami for Sunday dinner."

His lips curved up. "I know. She sent me seven text messages about it. Are you going back to Miami any time soon?"

"Nope. Not until I crack this case open."

"Any ideas what we're dealing with here, Anniston?"

"Let's be clear. You don't share with me. I don't share with you. I guess that explains why you ignored my text about trying to obtain the surveillance video at the bank for Nathan Hollister's last day of work?"

"It was a good suggestion. But it'll take time to get a warrant. Are you that certain his taking off is part of the whole picture?"

"I don't know anything that's one hundred percent. The security video from the bank should give some insight into Nathan's hour-by-hour schedule, though. Like what he did exactly from nine to five the day he lied to his wife about going to a bank convention. Did Nathan withdraw money?

Did someone come into his office and threaten him? What was happening in his head to make him split?"

Dack ran a hand through his blondish brown hair. "Okay, I'll get started on the warrant. And Anniston?"

"What?"

"I don't mind giving you a heads up if I think the situation warrants it. I always did think you'd make a first-rate cop. I'm glad you don't hold our little fling against me."

As the sun bore down on them, she patted his face, getting redder by the minute. "How could I hold it against you? I made up my own mind. 'A little fling' sums it up nicely. Back then, we were just a ripple on a pond. Just so you know, Sebastian is thinking about coming here at the end of the week."

"Really? You're actually calling in reinforcements? That doesn't sound like you. I'm a little green with envy that you have a Marcelli to rely on."

"Hey, I'm not afraid to admit I need all the help I can get." She held back telling him her plans to interview a bunch of seemingly upstanding citizens. After all, Dack didn't need to know everything. "Let me ask you something. There's a lot happening here in town. Your investigation is cemented here. Why aren't you camped out at the hotel like me?"

Dack gave her a sheepish look. "Sinclair was forced to clear out an office for me down the hall from him. But if you're talking about off-duty hours, I met someone. She has her own place up in Key Largo. I spend my nights there."

"Ah. That sounds serious. What's her name?"

"Shonna. Shonna Miller. I think it's heading toward serious."

"Enough to sell your condo in Key West and move to Largo?"

Dack smiled. "I already put it on the market a month ago. We're even talking about having kids. I'm taking her to meet my mother on Sunday."

"Good for you. Tell Kate I said to be nice to her."

"Yeah, well, my mother wanted it to work out with us. Remember?"

This time it was Anniston's turn to grin. "Our mamas don't always get what they want."

Knowing it'd be tough to get the good citizens to talk, Anniston hunkered down in her hotel room to tackle the pile of work that would make it happen. Leaving nothing about the interviews to chance, she decided to phone her dad and pick his brain.

Back in Miami her father picked up the phone in a good mood. "There's my baby girl. How's it going?"

"I'm good, Daddy. How are you doing?"

"I'm wonderful. Your mother spoils me more every day. Although she has been out foraging in that thing she calls an herb garden, tries to stick a bunch of green crap in front of me every chance she gets. A rabbit wouldn't eat that stuff."

Anniston snickered at what she'd heard for the past two years. "The doctor said you needed to change your diet. Green stuff is good for you."

"Not this awful tasting stuff. She's trying to feed me clover, dandelions, and something called burdock. On second thought, you mother may be trying to kill me."

"Daddy, stop complaining. She's hoping to get you to live longer. Did you get my last email about the one on one meetings the Indigos want to do with the people we suspect?"

"I did. It's a good idea. But I suggest consistency in the questions. You need to ask each man the same things to judge their reactions and get a read. You're taking part in all of the interviews, correct?"

She hesitated. "The family really wants to participate and do the meetings themselves, mainly because they know all these guys personally."

"I don't recommend it. It's risky. Either conduct the interviews yourself or don't let them go it alone, if for no other reason than to keep emotion out of it. And avoid using an accusatory tone. Making suspects comfortable, making it a friendly encounter will get you more results than a confrontational in-your-face every time. I once interviewed a pedophile who'd killed four little boys. You think I didn't want to reach across the table and plant my fist in his face? I did. But a good detective leaves his emotions outside the interview room."

Words to live by. Now all she had to do was persuade the Indigos to let her run with it alone.

"What if they're stubborn?" Anniston prompted. "Because in the event I can't convince them to back off, I'll need to prepare them better so they don't go in looking like bumbling *Keystone Kops*."

"There is another option." The older ex-cop detailed an alternate route that sounded like a decent solution.

From there, father and daughter went over a strategy, including how best to approach the four in question. Since she'd decided to leave out Royce, Sinclair, and Dietrich for this first round, that meant Baskin, Dandridge, Frawley, and Oakerson had to be dealt with as a unit.

After hanging up the call, she went to work formulating a exhaustive list of questions using key phrases that would fit all four. Gauging the responses would be critical. She itched to do it herself, but had to admit even Lenore had expressed an interest in taking point. The woman had even called dibs on questioning Dandridge.

Anniston wanted to please her clients. But that was only part of making up her mind. The main reason was simpler. Who had a greater stake in the outcome than the family? All she had to do was work on getting them to contain their emotions.

Not a small task.

So with that in mind, she'd do everything she could to make sure they were successful, even if she had to hold rehearsals to get the participants to follow the same script.

When it came down to the three men she'd shoved to the side, Anniston had already formed an opinion about Sinclair and Royce. Royce was certainly cunning, but she didn't think he'd have any part in murdering his own son. Sinclair, on the other hand, had a history of violence. Plus, the police chief didn't much like the Indigos. According to Garret, Sinclair had started out in friendly mode, only to slide into a defensive bear within a matter of days. And to hear the family tell it, Sinclair himself had gone to great lengths to make sure the Indigos knew he'd switched sides.

Which left the wealthy industrialist Werner Dietrich as the major wild card.

After a solid five hours of work on the project, Anniston closed her laptop to get ready for dinner with Garret. She refused to call it a date. But it wasn't a client meeting, either.

When he texted her with an ETA, she jumped in the shower and afterward slathered on fragrant lotion before spending half an hour fussing with her hair.

All the while she primped, she realized she was a little too excited about going out just to eat dinner. The eagerness she felt tipped more toward a sexual heat bordering on full-blown anticipation. Her stomach fluttered like a teenager's getting ready for her first car date.

Annoyed with herself, she finished with her makeup and looked at the clock. She grabbed her purse and dashed out the door, unable to fully tamp down her enthusiasm.

Chapter Nine

It hadn't been a good day inside the Indigo house. First Royce had showed up. Then Anniston had delivered the devastating news about Livvy and Ally. And now, Tessa had to deal with more pain.

Garret was glad to be out of there, even for thirty minutes.

When he rolled up to the hotel in Mitch's pickup, there she was waiting for him outside in the courtyard. She'd put on a creamy sleeveless georgette dress with soft turquoise blossoms. Her hair was up. She'd somehow managed to tame all those tresses into a sophisticated twist that reminded him of the one time he'd attended an art gallery opening in Paris.

He'd spent the evening surrounded by celebrities with a few icons thrown into the mix. It was enough glitz and glamour to last a lifetime. Thank God he'd come to his senses enough to never get dragged into that scene again.

Indigo Key was as far from that star-studded gala as he could get. And for the first time in a long time, Garret realized this was exactly where he wanted to be. The City of Love was nice and all, but nothing compared to that laidback world he'd come from.

Honking the horn when he came to a stop, he finished his perusal. Deep in appreciation, he saw Anniston had worn stacked-heel sandals on her feet. Big silver hoop earrings dangled from her ears. The bracelets on her wrists bunched with pops of blue-green. She looked ready for an elegant night out in one of the best restaurants in town.

"Wow, you look really hot," Garret proclaimed when she joined him in the front seat. She wafted into the car on a burst of Chanel. Knowing he'd have to disappoint her, he breathed in her perfume and added, "You have a great pair of legs there, Anniston."

"Aren't you sweet? Thanks." She made a quick study of his demeanor and decided there was a degree of distress hanging between them. She thought she knew why. "How's Tessa?" •

"Not good. But then, why would she be? She gets yanked back and forth in all this." He twined his fingers around hers. "You've had a busy day. Everyone wants to know, but they're afraid to ask—will finding Ryan's…head… shed any light on how he died?"

"Yes."

"Just that simple, huh? Then I guess there was some type of trauma visible."

"Gunshot wounds are usually hard to hide."

"Ah. Really? Raine didn't mention that to Tessa."

"Raine didn't know. Maybe it's best if no one else does either."

"She did mention there was a crowd standing around. That nugget's likely been passed around a dozen times or so since this morning."

"Nope, no one got close enough to see specifics. Dack and I made sure of that. What about your parents? How are they doing?"

"Ah. Well. About that. You'll get to ask them yourself. Change of plans. Personally, I've never seen them this devastated. Not even last spring when they buried my grandmother. They're coming to terms with having to plan another funeral. It's painful to watch. That's why I'm afraid we'll have to put our evening out on hold, at least having dinner by ourselves. My mother insists I bring you back to the house. Neighbors have been dropping in all day and leaving enough Jell-O salad and macaroni casseroles to last us through the zombie apocalypse. Mom wouldn't hear of us going out to a restaurant with so much food on hand. She wants you to help us eat it."

Anniston stifled a laugh. "It's okay. I don't mind your family. Did Royce manage to change your dad's mind…about anything?"

"That's another thing. My parents aren't sure what to believe. Royce came across convincing enough. Does that mean he was telling the truth? Not in my book. You know who's been MIA from stopping in to pay his condolences, though? Dandridge."

"What could he say? Livvy and Ally damn sure didn't take off for Maui all this time. And, your father did insult the pants off Boone, which is not a great visual." She let out a half laugh. "If we aren't going out, we should probably circle back to the hotel so I can grab my laptop. It has the questionnaire I came up with, plus all my notes. It'll be harder to make my case without them."

He squeezed her fingers as he veered the pickup to the curb. "I have faith in your ability to wing it. Just know that the house may be full of people. You may not even get the chance to bring it up."

That turned out to be true for the next hour. Anniston noted Lenore and Tanner looked tired but still managed to work up the energy to mingle with longtime friends and keep up a stoic attitude.

Lenore's best friend, Jule Mae Harriman, took over the chores in the kitchen. With help from Raine and Tessa, all three women dished out food, then worked to wash and dry a stack of plates.

Anniston walked up to Tessa and wrapped her up. "I'm so sorry my discovery dredged all this up for you."

"It's okay. Maybe it'll lead to Ryan's killer. I just don't know how the crime scene techs could've missed seeing such a thing there."

"Dack's trying to figure that out, too." Anniston pitched in and made a pitcher of fresh lemonade. She made the rounds refilling glasses. She cut pans of brownies into individual pieces and handed them out to young and old alike. It was a reminder that small-town neighbor showed up for neighbor, at least in these parts they did.

Anniston settled back with a glass of iced tea to admire the youngest Indigo son. She could easily admit that Garret was more than a mystery to her. Even as she watched, he was deep in conversation with Cara, a girl he'd dated back in high school. She knew a little of the history because Cara had mentioned that time of her life with great fondness. Unlike the animosity Raine showed toward Mitch, Cara seemed happy to catch up, reminiscing about teachers and students.

Even Cara's husband Wayne, got into the discussion, grilling Garret on the best place to look for treasure.

"Whoa, you're asking the wrong brother. That's Mitch's department," Garret declared. "Now if you want to know the best places to surf, I can hook you up."

"Hmm, that's what I thought," Wayne responded. "Which is the reason I never could figure out why Walker didn't seek out advice from his own in-laws about something he considered so important."

That got Garret's full attention. He put aside the high school reunion banter and focused on Wayne's comment. "What do you mean?"

Wayne looked puzzled. "You know, last summer when

the buzz was all about looking for gold, there were a few days when I considered chucking my bartending job and throwing in with Walker."

Cara leaned in, patted Wayne's arm. "But I put a stop to that kind of silly talk. Wayne and I have been thinking about having a baby. I wasn't going to let him waste our savings on something so stupid, especially after Walker mentioned to Wayne how much it would take to go in as a partner, I put my foot down on that."

Wayne nodded. "I couldn't afford twenty grand, let alone fifty."

Mitch and Jackson overheard the exchange and moved to within Wayne's circle. "Fifty grand to partner up?" Mitch asked. "That's a steep entry fee. How long had this talk been going on?"

"Pretty much all summer long. It was the main topic of conversation around here for months. I even know who started it, that old sailor, Hugo Reiner. The last time I saw Walker, he was in the bar buying drinks for the guy. Those two always seemed to have their heads together at the back table talking about latitudes and longitudes. Reiner did quite the sales job."

Garret traded looks with his brothers. But it was Mitch who seemed to know the most about Hugo. "That guy must be pushing ninety, old as dirt. Speaks with an accent. I don't remember where he came from exactly, just that he's been hanging around town since I was a kid."

"How come I don't remember him?" Jackson asked.

"I'm surprised at that. I thought everybody along the southern Keys knew Hugo. He's hard to forget. He has this old ketch, a relic that hauls him up and down the coast and back and forth to the Caribbean. He has this collection of gold stories he sells for drinks, hoping to land someone gullible enough to believe his tall tales and fork over a grubstake. I thought the guy had probably died by now."

Wayne scowled into his lemonade. "No way. That old sailor's been coming to Mattito's ever since I started there, probably five years or more. He comes and goes like clockwork, mostly moors that old bucket he calls a boat during the summer months here, sometimes hangs around until the fall. Last time I saw the old guy was before Walker went missing. That was about three weeks ago."

Garret looked at Wayne with disgust. "Why didn't you mention this sooner?"

Wayne's sheepish look said it all. "Didn't think it was all that important. Like everyone else, I just thought Walker and Livvy had gone on vacation and they'd be back. Cara and I talked about it. She tried to convince me it was something more serious. It never occurred to me they wouldn't be coming back. All this time…they were…you know…out in the Gulf."

Garret broke away to huddle with his brothers in a corner of the dining room. "When do all these people plan to leave? I'd like to tell them to just go far away."

"That's the way I feel," Mitch admitted.

Jackson was the voice of reason. "They're here because they care about Mom and Dad and don't know what else to do. Mom and Dad need them during this time. Hell, we all need some reassurance that Livvy and Ally were loved by the people in town."

"Why do you always have to do that?" Mitch bristled, impatience floating to the surface.

"Do what?"

"Be the good guy," Mitch began. "I want all these people to go away so we can put our efforts toward finding the truth. For the past twenty-four hours all we've done is stand around. I'm tired of it, tired of doing nothing."

"This isn't doing nothing," Jackson insisted. "It's coming together as a community, showing Mom and Dad, *us*, how they felt about Livvy and Ally." He dipped his hands in his pockets and turned to face Mitch. "If Wayne's right, it sounds like Walker fell for Hugo's pitch. We need to find this Hugo. What's the name of his boat?"

Mitch scratched his forehead. "I don't remember the name. But we need to spend some serious time finding someone who does. And we can't do that farting around here."

Garret realized they were all getting antsy. He raked fingers through his hair, caught sight of Anniston watching him from across the room.

As their eyes locked, lust stormed through him. It stirred an appetite he didn't recognize. Maybe it was the somber mood or something darker that had him crossing to her. He reached out his hand, tugged her out of the chair where she'd gotten comfortable.

He was oblivious to anyone else around as he angled his head to taste her mouth. She'd obviously nibbled on the fudge. She tasted silky sweet. He took his time with the flavor, setting a trail down the side of her neck, before moving to her ear.

Caught off guard by the display of affection, Anniston whispered, "Garret, what are you doing? People will talk." She tried to push him back a step, but he was like an unmovable brick wall. "What about your parents' guests?"

"Let them get their own women."

She saw the wild look in his eyes and recognized the feral way he moved, like a tiger on the scent of its prey. She let him capture her hand and tug her past the kitchen and out into the backyard so they could at least be alone. If his plan was to make out, it was best to do it away from the prying eyes of those who tended to gossip about such things.

The easygoing man who'd picked her up at the hotel had disappeared. In his place was a guy who acted like he didn't give a damn about protocol or correctness. It occurred to her this was a side of him that scared her just a little bit. "Garret, say something. Where are we going?"

"You'll see. Somewhere quiet. Away from all these people."

Outside, the sun took its final bow over the water in a bath of crimson and violet, its showy froth drifting to the color of merlot. Only the slimmest crescent moon could've carved out a chunk of the deep purple to get noticed. So that when the stars began to glitter, they looked like eager bits of white ice winking back at earth from the deepest blue of space.

It would be an October evening made for honeysuckle and jasmine, wood smoke and fire, he decided.

He twirled her in a dance to the corner of the lawn where a hammock hung between two giant magnolias. It wasn't until he looked down at her face that he saw the concern in her eyes. He took hold of her chin. "What's wrong?"

"You're scaring me just a little."

"Me? Why on earth would you say that?"

"Because I've seen that look on your face before. You get very intense."

"I get intense when I think about you."

"Oh. I thought…"

His face broke into a grin. "You've obviously had a stressful day. You need to relax. That's why I think you should get off your feet." Without another word, he seized her waist and swung her into the nylon netting of the hammock in one fluid motion.

She squealed at the unexpected movement and toppled into the dip of the sling. There was no time to think about anything else but the fall as his arms locked around her. She felt her hair tumble out of its clip and lightly punched his bicep. "Do you know what a tough time I had getting my hair to look like this?"

He combed a few strands away from her face so he could see those sharp, dark eyes. "I've never seen you look more beautiful than you do right this minute."

She took his face in both hands, pressed her lips to his. He tasted like sweet divinity with a streak of devil's food cake. "I'd get out of this thing if I thought I could climb over you."

He dawdled over her mouth, kissing each corner. "Why would you want to? It's like a cocoon." With great care, he touched his lips to her forehead. "Put all the bad stuff out of your brain and go with the flow. Close your eyes. Don't think about what you saw today."

She put her head on his chest, listened to the beat of his heart while they swayed back and forth to the motion. She let him nuzzle her throat while the night sounds played around them. There was a lilting chorus of crickets that brought out the playful fireflies. A string of bullfrogs broke into song trying to serenade a potential mate. From somewhere in the distance, she heard noises coming from the harbor, a seagull fighting for its supper, a horn sounding from a tugboat.

Just when she thought she had him pegged, he surprised her by singing softly in her ear. She recognized the lyrics to *This Must Be the Place* and poked him in the ribs. "You're a closet romantic. You should let that guy out more often."

His fingers traced along the curve of her breast, taking pleasure in its warmth. He took her hand and inched it toward the front of his pants. "It's no secret I want you, Anniston."

She breathed out a sigh, letting the night capture the promise. "It has to be soon."

Their solitude was broken when both of them heard voices whirring nearby. Lenore and Tanner were bidding farewell to the neighbors and slowly the others came drifting out of the house to join them.

She glanced up at the million diamond stars twinkling and took delight in the moment they'd shared. "Thank you for this."

"My pleasure." Their privacy had been too brief. Garret lifted his head and saw his brothers pulling up chairs around a circular fire pit. Jackson used kindling to build up the flame while Mitch brought over more wood.

Anniston heard the crackle and pop of a fire and breathed in the smell of the wafting smoke.

Tanner's voice cut through the magic. "Do you guys plan to stay over there all night and cuddle or join the rest of us?"

"Ah, civilization intrudes, or in this case more like a loud bear," Garret said with regret. He unwrapped his legs from around Anniston, swung them to the ground and stood up. "It was nice while it lasted. You need help getting out?"

"Probably, unless I want to end up on my ass."

"Can't let that happen. It's such an exceptional ass." Helping her out of the swing, he ran a hand seductively over her rear end, then swatted it with a light rap. "Oops. I thought I saw a bee. I got it just in time, though, before it took a bite out of you."

With his parents a few feet away, she batted his hand off her bottom and tried to wrap her hair back up into its twist. There was a snort from him as they walked over, hand in hand.

Garret left her momentarily to haul over two more chairs from around the side of the house. "Nice to have the crowd finally leave."

Lenore let out a tired sigh. "Yes, but I'm glad they all came. Everyone said such nice things about Livvy and the kids. Although Dandridge didn't show his face here today. I guess he knew better."

It was the perfect opening for Anniston to say what had to be said. She looked out over the faces glowing in the firelight. "Tell me, are you still bent on meeting with Boone and the others? If so, there are a few things we need to go over."

Lenore and Tanner exchanged looks. It was Lenore who nodded. "It makes my stomach curl knowing there has to be a reason he didn't want anyone searching for them. I want to ask him why."

"That's just it. You can't be upset when you get in his face. Bringing emotions into it is a recipe for disaster. Furious only takes you so far," Anniston explained. "You could let me do it."

Jackson rolled his eyes. "We've been all through this before."

Lenore agreed. "I thought we'd settled this already. We can't let you be the judge on this, Anniston. We can't. No one knows Boone like Tanner and I do."

Raine nodded. "That's the way I feel, too. I know Carson better than anyone here. I'll be able to tell if he's lying."

"Same goes for Dandridge," Tanner said. "I want to watch that bastard squirm."

Anniston held up her hands. "Okay. Okay. I had to try. I told my dad you wouldn't give in on this one point. This may not be the time or the place, but I want you to hear me out. This afternoon I came up with a list of standard questions and a script to follow. But halfway done, I decided to trash what I had and start over, go another way. I don't think asking the same stuff will work. So I revised some of the points and tailored the questions to each man. It'll be up to each of you to gauge their reactions to the various points. Watch the body language, the eyes. Is he evasive or straightforward? Does he squirm in his seat or meet the question head on?"

"You could go with us," Tessa suggested.

"No, after thinking about it, that would put these guys on guard. This way they think they're just having a conversation with people they've known forever, casual-like. And besides, I have a better idea. I hope you're all good at acting."

Mitch grinned. "Now we're talking."

"Since you're all determined to do this, there are certain topics you need to bring up to each of the respondents. Since we have a timeline as to when Livvy was last seen with her kids, pose that to all of them. Ask if they knew anyone who wanted to do harm to the family. Plus, it's imperative you bring up the golf course deal. Make them think that's why you're there."

Tessa grinned. "So Jackson and I shouldn't let on to Baskin that we know he's in debt to Royce for gambling losses?"

"Everyone seems to be in debt to Royce for something. And I'd like it if everyone brought up Ryan in the conversation. I'll email each of you a copy of the script. If you have to, act as though you think I'm a total idiot and you've been disappointed with my job performance. Make them believe you're hoping to get better results yourself. Tell them you can't rely on my talents as an investigator. Use any excuse, as long as you get them to talk. Even if it means you dupe them into believing you're doing this investigation on your own so you need to start from scratch."

Jackson rubbed the back of his neck. "You might as well put Wendy Hollister on that list. Tessa and I have decided to talk to her, mainly because we aren't sure Nathan left town under his own power. Until we know for certain, we need to find out what Wendy knows."

Anniston blew out a breath. "Wendy's another wild card, though. Personally, I don't think you'll get her to open up. That's my take anyway."

Tessa considered that. "Maybe we should wait. Give her more time and see if she makes mistakes."

"All right," Jackson said in agreement. "We'll let her play out this scenario and see where it leads."

"Okay then. You should know I stopped in at the bank earlier. Nathan's coworkers practically tossed me to the curb. And speaking of Nathan, that's one of the names I want each of you to throw out. Plus, I'd like everyone to record the meetings."

"Wear a wire?" Even Mitch raised his eyebrows at that. "Isn't that illegal?"

"In Florida it's a two-party consent. *But* we won't be wiretapping a phone, or going into anyone's personal space. We're not having a private conversation by intruding into their offices or homes. If we pick a public place where the casual conversation might reasonably be overheard, you're okay recording them."

She speared a finger at Tanner. "Don't even think about talking to Dandridge on church premises, though. Engage him anyplace but there. Pick a nice, highly visible spot. Pretend as though you've accidentally bumped into him at the coffee shop he frequents, or one of the places he likes to eat."

Anniston turned to Raine. "Don't approach Carson at his own doughnut shop. Try to get him into The Blue Taco, on your turf, or somewhere he likes to hang out."

"That might be tricky. Carson doesn't like tacos." When Mitch let out a laugh, Raine turned to him and smiled. "It's one reason I stopped returning his calls."

Anniston went on, "You'll figure it out. As for Baskin, buy him a beer at his favorite watering hole."

"That would be Mattito's," Jackson said.

"I think I'm getting the hang of this," Mitch admitted. "I like it. But why record these people?"

"Because I want to send the tapes to a voice analysis expert I know. He'll use the recordings to measure stress points in their responses, maybe tell us which ones we should eliminate altogether or which ones require digging further into their backgrounds."

"You're saying this voice analysis indicates who's lying?" Garret clarified.

"Yep. Better than a polygraph. That's why it's an investigative tool Interpol uses. I figure if it's good enough for them, it ought to benefit us. And it might cut through a lengthy process of elimination."

Tanner crossed his arms over his chest. "Where was this tape recorder when Royce waltzed in here trying to peddle his BS? I'd like to have had that analyzed. Does anyone really believe Royce didn't know what Walker was into?"

Garret cut his eyes to his brothers. "I would've said no before talking to Wayne tonight." He repeated what he'd learned about Walker and Hugo Reiner to those who'd missed the conversation.

But Tanner was stubborn. "I refuse to believe Walker actually thought he'd find a bunch of gold. Surely he wouldn't be dumb enough to believe that old geezer knows anything about finding it."

Mitch's back went up. "I hate to break this to you, Dad. But I find gold and other stuff that's quite valuable by following leads; leads that often originate from people just like Hugo. I like to think I'm pretty good at weighing in on the ones bullshitting me versus those with viable information."

"That's just it, that's the difference. You check them out, verify the lead," Tanner said. "Would Walker have the sense to do that?"

Mitch lifted a shoulder. "A rank amateur could get carried away. If Walker was desperate enough, thought he was invincible enough, he could bypass the verification part and go straight to the land of fantasy."

Garret patted his brother on the back. "Yeah, you have enough skepticism inside you that I doubt you'd take anything for granted. Are we suggesting Walker might've reached out to Dietrich?"

"Hey, Royce might have brought Dietrich in as one of his golf course buddies for backing. But who else would be dumb enough to wave a hunt for gold in front of Dietrich, known treasure hunter? Because if it sounded plausible enough he'd simply bring the *Patagonia Pike* up from South American waters to look for it himself. And since the crew is definitely here...I think Walker approached Dietrich with some kind of deal. And it got his family wiped out," Mitch stated.

Garret rubbed his forehead, turned to his dad. "Okay, here's my take on Walker. He was probably all those things you mentioned. Let's start with dumb. Absolutely. He underestimated the wrong person, more than likely it was Dietrich. Desperate? Certainly. He was rumored to be in debt and wanted to please his old man. We all know what that's like. It's easy to see the gullible side of anyone. What is that old saying? If something sounds too good to be true, it usually is. Hugo might've led Walker into a trap, double-crossed him for some cash. And to tell you the truth, *that's* what I saw in Royce's eyes this morning. Royce is scared, Dad, scared his son got mixed up in something he couldn't control for the first time in his life. Whatever it was, it got his wife and daughter killed. And since Walker and Blake are still out there, I'd say they ended up like Livvy and Ally. Which brings us to one question. How long do we wait before going out and actively looking for them?"

Mitch stood up. "I'll call the crew and get them ready to go out tomorrow morning."

"What about locating Hugo?"

All eyes fell on Anniston.

"Sure. I'll add that to my list of other things to do."

On the way back to the hotel Anniston noticed Garret had fallen quiet, not exactly a common occurrence. When he stopped to let her out at the front, she angled in her seat toward him. "You want to tell me what's bothering you?"

"It might take hours to tell you. I should probably come up and spend the night again."

A laugh shot out of her. "Oh, that's good. You're good. Women don't usually play hard to get with you, do they?"

"Why bother playing hard to get? You know you'll eventually let me spend the night, a night, I might add, that comes with a slew of carnal benefits."

"Carnal benefits? Maybe you should list your specific talents in that area." After he ticked off two or three, she held up a hand and fanned herself. "Okay. Never mind. I get the picture. You know your way around the female body. No wonder you come highly recommended."

"Say what?"

"Cara. She personally vouched for you."

Behind the wheel, he doubled over in laughter. "I guarantee my skill set's improved quite a bit since high school."

"I would hope so. Is it starting to get hot in here?"

Recovering enough, he cracked a grin and took her hand. "Steaming up car windows isn't exactly what I had in mind. More like naked bodies, stretched out on satin sheets, while we go at each other and get to know each other…a lot better."

"In the carnal sense?"

"Now you're getting the picture."

"I'm definitely in your corner. I'm even rooting for you. All kidding aside, it sounds like it's just what we both need to alleviate the pressure of this case. But, let's be practical."

"Let's not." He turned her wrist, found her pulse beating in double time, and pressed his lips to the spot.

His head was bent, almost in her lap. She raked her fingers through his hair, then tipped up his chin to meet her eyes. "Garret, if we do this, promise me it won't get complicated."

"I'll park the car."

Her cell phone lit up, once, then twice, then three times in rapid succession. "Uh-oh, something's happened."

She read the first text message from Dack. *At eight o'clock this evening the Coast Guard found a second barrel. They hauled it up and found two bodies inside. Adult male, little boy. On the way to the county morgue now.*

Anniston held out the phone so he could read the messages for himself. At the look on his face, she framed both sides of his cheeks. "At least you don't have to go looking for Walker and Blake tomorrow morning."

Garret pressed his fingers as hard as he could into his temples. "Will this ever stop? I have to tell Mom and Dad."

"And I should go see Royce, tell him in person."

"How about we tell my parents first, and then I'll go with you to the Buchanan estate?"

"That'll work. I really didn't want to go there by myself."

"Then we'll circle back to the hotel."

"You have that gleam in your eye."

"Honestly, I'm about out of gleams since I have to deliver more bad news."

"I'll be there with you."

"Then let's set this plan in motion."

But plans have a way of not working out.

Once they reached the Buchanan estate, the housekeeper had a hard time waking Royce up. She had to go ask Roger Baskin for help. It turned out Baskin lived in the guesthouse behind the main residence.

As soon as he appeared in the doorway of the study where they were waiting, he went into an explanation. "Royce takes an Ambien every night to help him sleep. It'll take some time to get him cognizant enough to know what you're saying."

"Some time" stretched out over two hours. Royce didn't come downstairs. Instead, they went up to him. His bedroom was massive, decorated much like his study, in dark wood and antiques. He was still in his four-poster bed, dressed in a tan silk robe, propped up by a dozen or more pillows. His eyes were glassy and confused-looking.

"Are you sure it's okay to do this?" Garret asked Baskin, who had taken a seat on the loveseat in the outer room. "He still seems pretty out of it."

Baskin lifted a shoulder as if he didn't really care one way or the other. "You're here now, might as well break the news."

"Royce," Anniston began as she approached the bed. "Remember when I told you I'd let you know if I heard back from the Coast Guard?"

The old man barely moved his head up and down.

But Anniston went on, "I heard from them. They found a second barrel. Walker and Blake were inside."

Anniston and Garret watched as tears streamed down the old man's cheeks. She reached for the box of tissues on his nightstand. But he didn't make a move to take one.

She jerked one out of the box and dabbed at his cheeks. "Are you okay? Do you want us to call anyone?"

He closed his eyes and slowly moved his head from side to side. His shoulders began to tremble. She squeezed his hand and realized he was starting to shake all over. The sobs came then, a moaning wail. Taking a seat beside him on the edge of the bed, she watched him come undone and glanced at Garret for help. But neither one knew what to do or how to make it better.

Chapter Ten

The longest night of Garret's life turned into the morning after, without ever having been to bed. He ended up taking Anniston back to the hotel around five that morning so she could catch a few hours' sleep. He, on the other hand, played the dutiful son and went back home to be with his family.

Now, running on zero shuteye, Garret was on the verge of a mental shutdown.

But since no one else had been to bed either, it seemed like no big deal. Sitting around the kitchen table with his brothers, he loaded up on more caffeine. "This stuff is actually beginning to make me sick."

"Don't barf on the table," Mitch warned. "You do look kind of green. I take it you didn't have the kind of fantasy night you expected."

"Fantasy would've been Anniston naked and a can of whipped cream on hand. I refuse to consider sitting around watching Royce Buchanan bawl his eyes out part of my fantasy, more like something out of Freddy Krueger."

"Feel free to provide details about the Anniston fantasy," Mitch prodded.

"My dreams, my fantasy. Seriously, Anniston and I left Royce at three-thirty this morning still crying like a baby. It was tough to watch. Baskin sat ten feet away looking like a damn statue. I'm not sure who was experiencing the greater shock, him or Royce."

"Maybe Baskin was shocked because he didn't expect the second barrel would ever be found," Jackson speculated.

"More like the first barrel. I sat there in Royce's fancy bedroom studying Baskin, or Thornton, whatever the hell his name is, and decided he looked every bit the enforcer. He has a vibe about him that's like a blank screen. He doesn't give off any emotions, or let on he has a touchy-feely side."

"I always thought he had a rough edge. I remember the time I took that old Datsun we took turns driving to him to get it fixed. I was trying to hide the fact that it needed a new muffler from Dad."

Garret nodded. "You ripped off the muffler when you drove over a speed bump doing at least fifty. Almost threw me into the windshield. My life flashed before my eyes. I think I was fourteen."

Mitch eyed his brother. "Don't exaggerate. Yeah, well, that speed bump shouldn't have been there. I should've just taken it somewhere else and saved all the aggravation. But after it happened I panicked and took it to Baskin thinking I could get it fixed with my own money. I'd been saving up to buy Raine a necklace. But Baskin said if I didn't pay him by the end of business that day he'd find me at school and drag me out of class. Now we know that threatening persona might've come from spending time in jail."

"Anniston did find a huge gap in his past, especially that time period he quit being Thornton and became

Baskin. It's not a leap to figure he's done prison time." Garret turned to Jackson. "Which makes me wonder how you plan to get this ex-con to open up to you in a public place."

"Tessa and I plan to hang out at Mattito's until he comes in. We thought we'd get him talking about Royce's rental property under the guise that we were interested."

"But you bought Nana's cottage," Garret reminded him. "That's common knowledge."

"Baskin might not know that. And even if he brings it up, we plan to make him believe Tessa's family wants to come here for the holidays. Thanksgiving's coming up. It works as a ruse. All I have to do is get Baskin to believe we need a rental and keep him talking, somehow find out whether he has ties to Dietrich beyond the golf course project."

Mitch got eggs and sausage out of the fridge. "I think I've figured out what the *Patagonia Pike* is doing in the waters off the coast of Florida. It took several trips to the library, but I narrowed it down to one Nazi sub that was rumored to carry gold bullion—thousands of pounds of the stuff—on a course from Germany to Argentina to help SS officers hide out and start a new life down in South America."

Garret whistled through his teeth. "On today's market that would be upwards of five hundred million dollars."

Mitch cracked eggs into a bowl. "That amount is enough to tempt the stupid and the brilliant alike."

Garret got up to help. Tossing the patties into a cold skillet, he turned up the heat. "What happened to the sub?"

"This particular ship was a class of merchant U-boats built for long range destinations. It had a thicker hull than most, with a top speed of twenty knots, which was almost unheard of during the time it was built. It apparently went down in April 1945, on a course that kept it hugging the US coastline not far from here. The last known latitude and longitude puts it somewhere between the southern Keys and west of Bimini."

"That's a lot of ocean, Mitch," Garret noted.

"Yeah. But something tells me Dietrich's crew has an inside angle that narrows down the precise location quite a bit."

Garret flipped the sausages to brown on the other side. "Question. What was the sub doing so close to the US coast?"

Mitch waved the spatula he'd used to scramble the eggs at his brother. "That's the thing. If the U-boat crew wanted to avoid detection, then why would they veer from the middle of the Atlantic and travel closer to shore?"

Jackson considered that. "Unless they had other business in Florida, a stopover for refueling maybe?"

"I don't know. But something brought them here. I think Hugo might know the reason."

Jackson made another pot of coffee, then got out orange juice. "So if there's no need to go out on *The Black Rum*, then what do we do next? Go looking for this Hugo?"

"How about we split up?" Garret suggested. "Jackson and I start the interview process, while you and Walsh go looking for Hugo, maybe get as close to the *Patagonia Pike* as you can, see if Hugo's anywhere on board."

Mitch dumped the scrambled eggs into a serving bowl. "We could do that, see what the crew is up to, and maybe intercept their communications."

Garret loaded up the four slots in the toaster with bread. "We need a plan, guys, one that keeps the focus on Dietrich. If we really believe Walker was involved with this guy, then we need to get better prepared. I've been looking him up on the Internet. He's the kind of guy who travels with a security detail. That means his goons will be armed to the max. We talked once before about going to see Michael Tang, but it wouldn't hurt to follow through this time."

From a buffet-style spread, the trio piled their plates high and sat down to eat.

Tanner had been listening at the doorway. "I like the idea of going to Michael for weapons. He's a good guy."

"Do you think Mom is up to facing Dandridge?" Jackson asked. "I could go with you instead."

"Thanks for the offer. But your mother and I are stronger than you think. Our main focus is finding out who did this. Dandridge appears to know something. We want to find out what it is."

"But what about the funeral?"

Tanner went over to the coffee pot, topped off his mug. "What about it? A bunch of flowers and music won't bring them back. We have four members of our family down at the morgue. Finding their killer or killers is all that matters now. Your mother feels the same way. We plan to go with Tessa's idea and have the memorial service in the park. Raine and Tessa offered to put their heads together and help your mother with all the details."

"What do you want us to do?" Mitch probed.

"Find the bastards who did this."

Anniston woke to her cell phone buzzing on the nightstand. After just three hours' sleep, she rolled over and stared at the display.

"Hi, Sebastian."

"Rough night?"

"Rough three weeks."

"I heard it on the news. I wanted to let you know I'm coming in Friday afternoon as planned. Tell me what you want me to work on and point me in that direction. I'll hit the ground running."

"Thanks for that. I'll send you an email with several suggestions. Feel free to pick one. In the meantime, I'm trying to run down a man by the name of Hugo Reiner. You could help me with that." She caught him up to speed on all the other players and the idea of the Indigos doing their own interviews.

"Wait. You have a former mob enforcer who works for the richest guy in the county? He might be your triggerman, Anniston."

"Triggerman would only apply to Ryan Connelly, who ended up with the hole in his head. It doesn't account for beating a mother to death and suffocating her children."

"I wish the Indigos would understand the folly of conducting their own interviews."

"Already tried. Hence the follow-along script idea. In fact, they'll probably have the interviews done by the time you get here. Are you up for the legwork involved? Because I need someone to hunt down every piece of surveillance video in town. I'm looking for any clip where Ryan Connelly crossed paths with any of our suspects, add to that Walker and Hugo Reiner together." She described the old German sailor and how he'd entered the picture.

"Sure. However I can help."

"Then I'll see you Friday."

She should've been nervous about Sebastian's offer. They'd only collaborated once before, one of those cheating spouse cases, the kind Sinclair had complained bitterly about. The twist to that one had been the deceitful wife, who'd sweet-talked a former lover into becoming a reluctant hitman. The wife had persuaded the dumbass to buy a gun, lie in wait in the bushes for the naïve husband to get home and then attempt to bring him down with a little .22.

Luckily for the hubby, the boyfriend had really bad aim and a peashooter for a weapon.

While still recuperating, the poor husband wouldn't believe anything bad about his wife. But after his discharge, he decided proof of that might go a long way toward saving his peace of mind. So he sought out Marcelli Investigations.

Enter Anniston and Sebastian.

The siblings pooled their talents and started the first of what would become hours of video surveillance on the unfaithful wife. Countless stakeouts produced confirmation the woman and her not-so-bright lover had conspired to do away with the hubby to collect on his ample life insurance. After months of work, Anniston and Sebastian delivered a thick file to the spouse and blew him away with the facts. They took what they had to the Miami PD, which in turn gave the case to the DA. The evidence had been enough to convict the boyfriend *and* lock away the conniving bitch in the women's correctional facility at Lowell for fifteen long years, no early parole for her.

For Anniston, the case was a source of pride. She didn't doubt what Sebastian brought to the table. No, she could always rely on her brother's expertise. But she wanted to be the one to find out what happened to the Buchanan family. She wanted to know why Ryan Connelly had to take a bullet to the head. But maybe, just maybe this case was too big for one person.

When she glanced at the clock, she realized if she wanted the breakfast buffet she had about fifteen minutes to make it downstairs. While throwing on a pair of yoga pants and a top, she made a decision. The case would benefit if she banked her ego and accepted help. The most important thing was finding a killer. She'd arrived in town cocky and certain that Ryan's death had kicked this whole thing off.

She just had to prove the connection.

That's why after breakfast, Anniston locked herself in her room. She re-routed the signal again to that private site Sebastian had set up so her searches couldn't be traced.

But after hours of dead ends, no matter how hard she tried, she couldn't find a single, solid thing on Hugo Reiner. She even called Wayne and picked his brain. According to the bartender, Hugo lived mostly off the grid, which could pose a problem finding a digital trail.

Frustrated, she switched gears. She texted Dack three times, bugging him about the caliber weapon that made the hole in Ryan's head. When he didn't call her back, she called him, irate.

"Look, I'm not your enemy here. I'm trying to be another branch, another tool to help you out."

"Okay, okay. I was on the phone to Chuck. We agree the gun had to be a large caliber, and not because of the visible hole on the flesh, which the marine life pretty much decimated, but because of the size of the hole it left in the skull. The shot was clean, meaning it penetrated and went all the way through. Chuck is certain that Connelly was dead before he hit the floor of the *Misty Dawn*. We found blood splatter to back that up, by the way. There's no doubt he was shot there."

"That's all great information, Dack, but what about the weapon?" Anniston insisted.

"Another thing my brother is fairly good at is ballistics. Chuck is sure it's something along the lines of a SIG-made P210. But there's a major snag with that way of thinking. Those guns were manufactured from 1949 to 2005, which takes in a huge market. But they're the type of weapon gun owners rank repeatedly as the Cadillac of the 9mm. Known for using high quality materials, it's built for accuracy."

"And it's pricey, something a rich guy would have in his arsenal rather than the everyday, recreational shooter," she added.

"You know your weapons."

"Damn straight I do. At one time I would've given a month's paycheck for a P210. That firearm sells for upwards of three grand. The low recoil alone is worth it. The weapon is so precise, it's the gun of choice for Special Forces and for the German police force."

Her own words stopped her cold. "There's no doubt we have a German theme going on here." Since Dack had shared the info about the SIG-made pistol, she told him about Hugo Reiner.

On the other end, Dack was silent. "You're suggesting all this started when Walker got a harebrained tip about Nazi gold? Anniston, that's nuts."

"Stranger things have generated a murder spree," Anniston pointed out.

"It's hard to argue with that. I once saw a guy lose it in a fast food joint because they got his order wrong. He ended up killing three and wounding five."

"There you go. All I'm saying is try to keep an open mind. And I'd appreciate it if you didn't make the treasure hunt common knowledge."

"That's the one thing I'll guarantee. I bring that motive up and I'm liable to get laughed out of the room."

Garret was able to catch a mid-morning nap that lasted three hours because the house finally cleared out around ten. He still couldn't sleep in Livvy's old room—not since her body had been recovered anyway. If he couldn't talk Anniston into letting him sleep with her, he preferred bunking on the sofa.

As soon as he rolled over and sat up, his stomach rumbled. But more than food, he wanted a run on the beach. He still thought it important to stay in shape—just in case he ever made it back on the circuit. Realistically he'd already considered he might have to pass on the Pipeline competition held every December. If this thing couldn't be wrapped up in the next two months, he'd consider selling his house in Oahu and buying something back on the Key.

Before throwing on his running shorts, he checked his emails. He still had friends checking in every other day to ask about the progress of the case and when he was likely to get back to his regular routine. One was from a former love interest, a model named Dominka Karetnikov. He hadn't seen her since she'd accompanied him to the Billabong Pro in Teahupoo, Tahiti. That destination had yielded some steamy nights and plenty of hot surfing. Ah, the memories.

He laced up his Nikes and headed out the door for a jog through the neighborhood to think... maybe reminisce about sex. After all, it had been a while since he'd experienced a woman's body.

He let his legs take him on a trip around the marina, during which he conjured up Anniston's curves and used his imagination to picture her naked.

He had to get a grip. He had a lot more important stuff to deal with at the moment than his sex-deprived state. Just when he decided he had his lust under control, an image popped into his brain—Anniston's bare midriff, showing a hint of belly button.

He really did need to find a way to get her alone.

Truth be told, he'd taken this route on the lookout for Hugo Reiner's ketch, a forty-foot Cheoy Lee clipper class probably a half-century old. Jackson might not remember the old sailor, but he did remember the boat. What he recalled from childhood was the unusual wavy white marking on top with squiggly blue on the side, at the water line.

He stopped in at Fast Willie's for a bottle of water. At checkout, Garret casually brought up Hugo to the owner and cashier, Willie DeSoto, a man who'd been born and raised here and knew every single resident by name. "Does Reiner ever come in here?"

"Sure does. He buys his supplies here whenever he's moored at the dock, which amounts to four or five times a year."

"When's the last time you remember seeing him?"

"Hmm, probably a week ago."

Garret stared at Willie. "Are you sure it couldn't have been three weeks ago?"

"Nope. I'm fairly certain it was the day they found Livvy and Ally."

That didn't jibe with what he'd pictured in his mind. "Any idea the name of his boat? I've racked my brain trying to figure it out, but I just can't."

Willie scratched the side of his face, scrunched up his

nose, and shifted his feet. "That's because that old tub has a funny name. No one knows how to pronounce it half the time."

"If you think of it, will you give me a call?"

"Sure thing. You gonna make it back to the circuit anytime soon?"

"Eventually. But not until I find out what happened to my sister and her family."

Chapter Eleven

Lenore and Tanner had Boone Dandridge clearly in their sights. They practiced all morning on the script, changing their tone of voice depending on the questions. They went over each point, line by line, until they'd put the high points to memory.

Eager to get on with it, the couple stopped by Anniston's hotel to pick up the recorder. They got a pep talk and listened to the private eye's final word of advice.

"Remember, all the while you're standing in front of Boone, you're wondering if he's our weakest link. Only you two can determine if we cull him out of the herd and move in to work on his guilty conscience, if he has one. In this case, blackmailing him with what you know happened in Oregon in exchange for rolling on his cohorts."

"But that incident was twenty years ago."

"Doesn't matter. The knowledge makes him vulnerable, or so we hope. But don't overplay your hand. Hint at his past and then sit back and determine if he'd be susceptible to it going public. I know it's a fine line to walk. This is about bluffing him into thinking you know more than you do. If you're good to go then make your encounter work to the fullest, because this might be the only time he'll allow you to get anywhere near him. Plus, his guard should be down since you're approaching him in public."

"No pressure there," Lenore breathed out.

Before walking out the door, Anniston gave them both a hug. "You can do this. I've no doubt. The circumstances are definitely in your favor. And don't forget to turn on the recorder."

The thing about Boone was that Tanner and Lenore knew his schedule as well as anyone around. They knew he'd be in the church office writing his sermon or catching up on emails until noon. He'd then stop for lunch and spend an hour and a half eating at a sandwich shop in the business district, where he'd linger over his soup, reading a book.

Which is how they were able to corner Boone at his table just shy of one-thirty as he packed up to leave.

Lenore eyed the lanky pastor who wore a pair of horn-rimmed glasses. "Hey there, Boone."

Tanner could tell they'd caught him off guard by the way he adjusted his glasses and fidgeted with the bookmark stuck down between the pages of his novel.

"Well, I was wondering if you'd ever come by to apologize to me for your outlandish accusations."

Lenore did what she knew Tanner couldn't, she held up her hands in peace. "Look, you know our family's been under a great deal of strain. That day in your office Tanner was extremely emotional about you having a hand in calling off the search. Naturally, you taking the stance you did on that upset him. At the time, we wanted more than anything to be able to locate Livvy and the kids alive."

Boone bobbed his head in understanding. "It was a drastic step on my part. I can see where you might've gotten the wrong impression."

"Yes, well, what's done is done. Since that day, I've tried to settle Tanner down over your position on the golf course development. I explained to him that it's just a differing opinion over politics, nothing more."

"Now see, I knew Lenore would get it. I just want the community to grow. Having that golf course would be such a windfall for the local economy. It would bring jobs here, which would bring in more people and grow our congregation."

Lenore gritted her teeth and continued to placate Boone. "Tanner doesn't think you had anything to do with Livvy's death. A religious man like you couldn't possibly have had anything to do with such an atrocious act. It would take a monster to murder innocent children, or to even be part of it."

"That's what I tried to explain."

"Then as a pastor, you should be able to forgive and forget. That's why we're here. After all, that's the business you're in. I'm sure over the years, in your line of work, you've had many situations where you've disagreed with members of your flock, only to set aside your differences long enough to console those who've experienced the loss of their loved ones."

"Most certainly. Why don't we take this back over to the office?"

"No need to do that. We're here now. Why don't you sit back down and I'll go order us some coffee. Tanner just needs to go over a few things with you about the memorial service." Lenore took a deep breath and handed off the rest to her husband. She left him to pick up the slack and hoped he didn't drop the ball.

Tanner took a seat across from Boone. "Before we get started though there's something I have to know. Did Livvy or Walker ever confide in you about having marital problems?"

Boone raised a brow. "I heard rumors. But neither one ever approached me about that sort of thing. If they had, I would've offered to counsel them. I often wondered if there was any truth to the gossip."

"Do you think Walker was into anything he shouldn't have been?"

Tanner noticed Boone cut his eyes away toward the plate glass window and look beyond into the street. It took some time before the pastor met his eyes again. "Walker was Royce's golden child. I don't think he would've put up with any type of rogue scheme."

Tanner nodded as if fully buying it. "Then tell me this, when's the last time you saw Livvy?"

Boone fidgeted in his chair. "That would've been at church on Sunday morning. She and Walker were both there with the kids. They didn't show up that Wednesday night for services, though. It wasn't unusual. Sometimes they passed on the prayer supper. Now what about the memorial service? Anything special you'd like me to say?"

"I'll get to that in a minute."

Lenore came over carrying a tray with three coffees. "Did Tanner ask if anyone ever talked about hurting Livvy or Walker? Did you hear any gossip about anything like that?"

Boone flinched at the question. It was so subtle, Lenore wondered if she'd imagined his reaction. But then he looked up at her and finally shook his head. "I'm truly sorry for your loss. But why are you asking me all this?"

Tanner cleared his throat and leaned across the table. "Between you and me, my boys ponied up a pretty penny to get that investigator on board. You ask me, she's not worth a plug nickel."

"Ah. I see. Well, anything I can do to help. It's such a tragedy when children are involved in something like this."

"Something like what?" Lenore asked. "Do you think Livvy and Walker got themselves into something they couldn't control? Maybe a financial jam?"

Boone adjusted his glasses again. "I didn't want to say anything but they had gotten a little lax on their tithing lately. Actually, they were months behind in their contributions. Susan Rauner keeps track of all that so she let me know right away there was a problem. I did what I could to prod Walker to get caught up."

"I'm sure you did. And I've always thought Susan does such a fantastic job as church secretary. You know there were rumors floating around last winter that you and Susan were an item."

Boone went on the defensive. "What? Why, that's preposterous. I wasn't aware people were talking about such things. When was this?"

"About a year ago. We didn't believe them, of course. Every time anyone mentioned those stories about you and Susan, Tanner and I would always take up for you. Why? Because we have complete confidence in our pastor."

"I'm just blown away by that sort of slanderous talk. I had no idea."

Tanner nodded in understanding. "You'd be surprised at the fodder people find interesting—affairs, money woes, people even babble on about a person's past—all those dark things no one's supposed to find out about. You know, a friend of Jackson's mentioned he knew you from the Pacific Northwest."

Boone suddenly looked like a deer caught in the headlights, frozen in place in the middle of the lonely Everglades, surrounded by hungry gators. He squirmed in his chair. "Me? Not me. Never even been there."

"That's what I told my boy, that it was impossible. You'd have told us if you'd ever lived in Oregon."

Boone picked up a napkin and dotted the sweat bursting out over his upper lip. "Maybe we should discuss the details of the memorial service now."

"Oh, about that." Lenore patted his hand. "Raine and Tessa—you know Tessa, the woman who lost her brother down here over Labor Day weekend when he came down to go fishing with Walker. Anyway, Tessa had this great idea. We're holding the memorial service at Estrella Park."

Boone looked horrified. "You can't be serious. Who holds a memorial service in a park? I'm not sure Royce will agree to that."

Lenore patted Tanner's hand signaling she had this covered. "Agree? There isn't much influence or pressure Royce can lord over us if we want to hold a nice service outdoors for our daughter and grandchildren. Surely you understand that, Boone. Livvy grew up playing in that park. She took her kids there almost every weekend. She loved the outdoors. Didn't you yourself tell us how much she wanted to travel and see more of the world? When you think about it, the park is the perfect venue. And Tessa, bless her heart, already got the required permit, although the mayor did make her wait several days before signing off."

Because his glasses had slipped down his nose again, Boone had to push them back up. "Well, yes…but…that's just so tacky. I mean, what about the casket? Where would you put the casket at the park?"

"No casket," Tanner grunted. "There'll be a separate service for burial, family only."

Boone persisted. "But who'll say the prayer? You're both talking crazy. What you're suggesting is so nontraditional, so pagan."

"It is, isn't it? Which makes sense because the park won't be so confining, no four walls to feel as though we're all bunched up. Blake's and Ally's little friends are free to run around and play afterward."

"But it would be so much more dignified in the auditorium where Joss Kade could play a string of hymns. And you'll want a processional. You can't have a funeral without a proper processional played on the organ."

Lenore waved her hand in the air. "It's a memorial service, Boone. I already talked to Joss and she agreed to play her flute along with her brother Quentin. They're both such good flautists, they also play at civic center events throughout the year. When Livvy was alive she adored listening to the sounds of Native American woodwinds. She used to say how she wished those instruments were part of our church service. And with Livvy's roots here…why, it's perfect. And when Tessa got involved with that part, she discovered Joss and Quentin might even be Tanner's distant cousins, certainly Seminole ancestors, for sure. The Kades were thrilled to be a part of the music. And my boys are planning to play several of Livvy's favorite songs. Doesn't that work out beautifully? So much better than in that stuffy auditorium."

Lenore steamrolled over Boone as he tried to sputter out an objection. "By the way, what do you make of Nathan Hollister going missing?"

"Missing? I heard he went out of town on a business trip. Denver, I think. Wendy definitely mentioned Denver."

"Did you ever talk to a man by the name of Hugo Reiner? He's known to hang out at the marina."

Boone's face went white as a sheet. "I don't know that name."

"Really? Huh. I guess Tanner and I've been out of the loop. Did you ever meet Tessa's brother, Ryan Connelly? Nice man, her brother. You know we just got back from his funeral in Nags Head. Beautiful service. Did you ever meet up with Ryan when he was down here visiting from North Carolina? Did you ever talk to him? It's such a pity what happened to him and right in our own backyard."

"What? No. Well, maybe once or twice I might've bumped into him in this very sandwich shop having my lunch."

"Now see I didn't know that." She turned to Tanner. "Did you know that?"

"Nope. Did you ever tell Sinclair about it or that state investigator?"

"Jessup? Yes, I believe I did." Boone was starting to get visibly more nervous at each question. They could tell because his forehead looked like he'd just stepped out of a sauna without wiping down his face.

"So what role do I play in the memorial service? You'll be sure to send me the time when you want me there."

Lenore and Tanner stood up to go, leaving the best for last. "That's just it, Boone. Raine and Tessa have it all planned out. I'm afraid there's not a single speaking slot left for you."

As they walked out and got away from the sandwich shop, they left a flustered preacher shaking in his boots and sweating. Once they got around the corner, Lenore took out her cell phone and sent a text message to Raine. *Finished with Boone. Will stop by the The Blue Taco and drop off the recorder. You're up now, darlin'. Now go get Carson.*

Raine left Tessa behind the counter at the restaurant and went home to get ready. She put on a short skater skirt that showed plenty of leg and a peasant top that left her shoulders bare. It didn't hurt to amp up the visual. She already knew the baker at Glazed & Dazed Donuts liked to hang out on the weekends at a nightspot called Theo's. But Raine had no intention of waiting that long to go after Carson Frawley. She didn't have to. The doughnut shop only stayed open from six in the morning until two in the afternoon. After that, Carson could be found losing money at a sports dive—betting on anything from college basketball to professional sports—on the other side of the island. It would likely be a noisy venue to talk, but hey, the situation called for a challenge to her creativity.

When Raine walked past the bar, Carson was in the process of putting the moves on a cute redheaded waitress half his age. But she glided on by and spotted Mitch in the corner who was there to springboard her act.

"You're late," Mitch snapped. "I told you I had to get back to the boat by three."

Within earshot of the baker and whoever else wanted to listen in, Raine began, "Same old Indigo. What is it with the attitude? You're the one who wanted to meet way out here. You want my help, the least you can do is lose the temper."

"You were supposed to be helping my mother with the funeral preparations. She's under a lot of stress. Now she tells me you're backing out."

"It can't be helped. I'm busy at the restaurant. I work sometimes from ten to seven at night without a break."

"That's no excuse. My mother was counting on you to follow through. You're leaving everything up to her. It's not right."

"There's no need to take that snotty tone. Lose the attitude. I do the best I can."

Mitch stood up. "As usual your best is hardly good enough."

After he stormed out, Raine let out a huge sigh. "There's just no pleasing that man."

As she'd hoped, Carson turned on his barstool. "Why bother trying? I thought you hated that guy."

Raine shrugged. "Old friend and all. His family is going through a tough time right now. I thought I was doing him a favor by trying to help with the funeral arrangements. After all, I feel bad for Tanner and Lenore, don't you?"

"Sure. But there's no need to put up with Mitch. He's never around here anyway."

"So true." Raine patted the seat next to her. "Why don't you join me? After that little scene, I could use a beer."

She waited for Carson to slide in beside her before she signaled the redhead over to take her order. "I'll take a Caribbean Pilsner."

She glanced at Carson's almost-empty cocktail glass.

"And I'm guessing you're still drinking malt scotch."

Carson drained the liquid and held up his whiskey glass. "You bet. If it's Wednesday, I'm throwing back Glenlivet."

"That's what I like about you, Carson. You always stay the same. And when you get going, you really know how to party." She leaned into him, giving him an ample view of cleavage. "Talk about partying, Walker *loved* to, didn't he?"

"Oh, tell me about it. That man would drink the craziest concoctions. He thought nothing of buying rounds of Johnny Walker Blue for everybody over at Mattito's." Carson snorted with laughter. "Used to ruin the taste by adding a damn soft drink into the mix. Didn't matter if it was Coca-Cola or ginger ale, that's the way he'd order a drink. Walker was either the biggest dumbass around or always trying to impress you with his money."

"You have to admit that man was generous with his liquor, you have to give him that," Raine reminded him.

"Sure. Sure. Couldn't hold his drink, though. More you poured into him, the more he liked to run his mouth."

"What about?"

"Oh, anything that popped into his head."

"Like that big land deal of Royce's that promised a casino in the area?"

"Exactly. Walker and his daddy pulled most of the church into that. But then old man Indigo had to go and stick his nose in, takes the fight to one of those environmental lawyers."

Raine shook her head in sympathy. "There's just no getting those Indigos. You'd think they'd want to see the town succeed."

"His own daughter was against her father doing that. She wanted that deal to go through as much as Walker."

"Livvy told you that?"

"That's what Walker said."

"What about that other big deal, the one, you know, involving Ryan Connelly?"

The corners of Carson's eyes jittered with a sudden nervous twitch. He suddenly did his best to fight the alcohol buzz affecting his judgment. "I don't know what you mean."

"Sure you do. People talk, Carson. You can't hope to keep a secret like that in a town this small."

"Ah, you mean the gold thing? That was all Walker and Livvy."

"Did Walker get his info straight from Hugo?"

Carson's face paled. "I...I...how would I know? But if Royce had known what Walker planned to do, he would've kicked his ass all the way back to Miami and beyond, probably smack up against that Ellerbee woman."

"So you knew about Walker's affair?"

Carson let out a soulful laugh. "Like you said, hard to keep a thing like that a secret in a town this size."

"So Royce didn't approve of Walker's affair?"

"He told him, on more than one occasion that I know about, to stop fooling around. But you know Walker, he did what he wanted to do."

"I thought it was pretty funny that you said Livvy planned to take a trip to see New York in the fall." She bumped his shoulder. "I knew that was a lie. She had kids in school. No one in their right mind believed she took off."

"Hey, I was just doing my part to keep the family's hopes alive."

Raine patted his arm. "You're such a good person that way."

Carson closed the space, got right up to her ear. "Why didn't it work out between us? I thought we were hitting it off."

She realized she might've overplayed her hand. She dug deep for a zinger, lifted a brow. "It probably had something to do with the rumor you were sleeping with Lucy Navarro, the dental hygienist."

"Oh. Yeah. I guess that's what did it. Lucy had a great pair of hands, though. You know, she gave fantastic massages."

"If it's a great massage you want, you should really try Lucy's cousin, Desiree. She owns the place out on the highway, Magic Hands. Sinclair even goes there, says Desiree really knows how to loosen a man up. Tell me, do you think Nathan going missing has anything to do with Walker and Livvy?"

"Nathan's gone missing? When?"

She leaned into him again for effect. "He went on a business trip, supposedly, a week ago. But no one seems to be able to locate him. Odd, don't you think, how all of a sudden there's so many people going missing? Why do you think that is?"

The jovial mood, brought on by the booze, seemed to abruptly end. "I really need to get going."

"That's a shame. We were just beginning to catch up."

Carson threw a twenty on the table and stood up. "I could call you. We could catch up *later*."

Raine smiled. "Sure." When hell freezes over, she thought, as she watched him head to the men's room.

Once outside, Raine met back up with Mitch in the parking lot.

Arms crossed over his chest, he was leaning against her roadster. Admiration flashed in his eyes as he looked her up and down. Petite at five-three, she still packed a punch, especially in those spiked heels she'd put on. "Nice outfit. Still driving Danny's old car, I see."

"You helped him put in the engine," she said, unlocking the car door.

"Nice job in there. Get anything usable?"

"Oh yeah. I told you Carson wouldn't disappoint. He was lying through his teeth every time his lips moved."

She dug out her cell and sent Garret a text. *Done with Carson. Giving Mitch the recorder to pass on to you. Good luck with Oakerson.*

City hall shared a building with the police department. Even if Anniston hadn't put the place off limits for a face to face, it was a bad idea for Garret to go in there and run the risk of bumping into Chief Sinclair.

He opted to wait until the end of the day, hoping Mayor Oakerson would be more open to a friendly chat that looked like a chance encounter, with his guard way down.

When he spotted the local politician heading across the street to the bar called Lime in the Coconut, he gave Dave a fifteen-minute head start.

As a kid, Garret remembered an exuberant young man who'd come to the Key to open up a scuba gear shop. If he'd been ten at the time, that meant Oakerson was an eager businessman of twenty-five. Dave had been a carefree, fun-loving man, who went on to become an effective diving instructor. Garret's recollection was of a man who taught him the ins and outs of the sport in a way that made it fun and worth doing.

But even then, Garret recognized the ambitious man who itched to branch out and make money. Almost overnight, his other businesses sprang up. It didn't take long before Dave owned a boat business that took tourists out on charters for fishing expeditions, and others that offered sunset cruises around Sugar Bay.

Before Garret had completed high school, Dave had become a full-fledged member of Royce's inner circle. He wasn't sure exactly when it happened. But somewhere along the way, Dave had veered off the path from happy-go-lucky guy to a money-hungry politician.

Since Anniston said she'd been able to track the large amounts of cash flowing into Dave's campaign coffers, Garret had to accept that the mayor could be a dangerous man if provoked.

Garret intended to push that in order to test the waters.

Happy hour was in full swing when he entered the bar. He took a few minutes to get his bearings, to judge whether or not the crowd had heavy Oakerson leanings or were more in line with an opposing viewpoint.

He spotted Dave at a table near the back and was surprised to see Wendy Hollister practically wrapped around him. The two were laughing and whispering in each other's ear.

The body language, thought Garret, said everything.

In a casual stride, he crossed over to their booth and found the couple already deep into their first round of drinks.

"Hey, Wendy, Mayor, how's it going?"

Nathan's wife barely took her eyes off Oakerson long enough to glance up. "Well hello, Garret. Long time no see." Wendy grabbed Dave's arm. "We should have a drink with our local celebrity surfer."

Dave reached his hand out in a hand-pumping shake like a guy used to running for office. "Good to see you again. I remember teaching you how to dive along with your brothers and sister. Livvy used to see to it that your successes made every issue of the *Indigo Dispatch*. I was very sorry to hear about your loss."

The mention of Livvy knocked Garret off his game. He had to remember to focus on the public figure before him, who owed his political existence and loyalty to Royce Buchanan, along with a host of others.

"Thanks, but I just have to ask. Are you concerned at all about how these murders will put a dent in the way tourists view our town? We thrive on their business. What happens if they think the island is too violent to visit?"

Dave laughed off that kind of suggestion. "I didn't realize you were such a fussbudget. Thinking like that is a drastic overreaction if I ever heard one. I don't think the general public has anything to worry about a crime wave here, do you?"

"Why not? The killer or killers are still out there." Garret purposely looked around, took in the other patrons sitting nearby. He angled his body to lean in and whispered, "He could be within arm's reach of us right now. I've heard rumors that residents are freaking out, locking their doors, gearing up their arsenals, staying home at night. If it's true, that means they won't be spending their hard-earned dollars in the business district."

Frown lines creased Dave's forehead. His demeanor changed from outgoing to closed off. "But what's it to you? You don't even live here anymore."

"True enough. But my parents do. I want to make sure they're safe after my brothers and I leave. And five murders should give anyone a reason to become concerned about their safety. Four of those belong to my family."

"A tragedy for sure," Dave said, glancing around, obviously getting bored with the conversation. "But the general public is safe enough."

"But how can you be so sure? Ryan Connelly was a tourist, and look how that turned out." Garret could tell his presence was beginning to annoy the mayor, so he switched gears. "I guess you must feel pretty silly since that day you stood in my parents' living room trying to convince them that Livvy had simply left town for Santa Fe? It was Santa Fe, wasn't it?"

"That was just an innocent remark. Why don't you move along now? Go find someone else to pester. There ought to be a surfboard somewhere around here for you to use. Go catch yourself a wave."

Garret smiled at the brushoff, then he locked gazes with Wendy. "I'm sorry to hear about Nathan."

"What about Nathan? Oh, that. He probably went off to be alone for a few days. He does that sometimes."

Garret was troubled by Wendy's indifferent attitude. But then she seemed a lot more interested in her boss. "How's that golf course project and resort thing coming, Mr. Mayor?"

Dave's face flushed a bright red. "You know damn well how it's coming, since it's your father putting a dent in the whole thing. Look, boy, I'm doing my best here to unwind after a long stressful day. Some of us work for a living. I think I want you to leave now."

As if he'd been waiting for the perfect opportunity, Jessup appeared to Garret's right. "You really shouldn't bother the mayor during his downtime."

"Since when? He's sitting in a public place, a bar no less, and I'm not allowed to come over to start a conversation? I shouldn't have to remind you that Dave's an elected official," Garret pointed out.

"Yes, he is. But, as the mayor already pointed out to you, you're no longer a resident here. You're not one of us. You don't vote in Indigo Key. Not anymore. You cast your ballot someplace else. Oahu, isn't it? Fancy name for a fancy place and a fancy boy like you."

In a show of force, using the uniform to display his might, Jessup blocked Garret's way to the door. "Why don't you apologize to the mayor before you leave?"

"I don't think so. But what I will do is ask him if he knows Hugo Reiner."

Dave's face, less red now, broke out in a sweat. "That old sailor who hangs around the docks? Why would I know a transient like him? Why would I care?"

"I guess if he doesn't vote, what's the point, right?" Garret said sarcastically as Jessup pushed him closer to the exit.

While Garret's brief confrontation ended at one bar, Jackson and Tessa waited inside Mattito's for Baskin to walk in. They took a pub table near the window that was still considered to be in the busy bar area. They ordered beers and nursed them until the brews grew too warm to drink. They munched on fries and chicken wings covered in spicy pineapple sauce—a specialty of the house—to make it look as though they'd come in for happy hour like everyone else in the place. Tessa had worn one of the sexy dresses she'd brought back with her from Nags Head. It was a pale green number that sparkled and showed off her hair.

"I hope this isn't a waste of time," Tessa grumbled.

Jackson picked up her hand. "It's never a hardship to spend time with you." He pressed his lips to hers to prove it.

"I didn't mean it that way. Sometimes I wonder when our lives will even out and get back to normal and we won't be dealing with all this…sadness hanging over us."

"We just have to hang in there. Think of it as play-acting in order to catch a snake in the grass."

"I know. I know." Jittery, she used two fingers to rub her aching head.

He took the hand that was so busy and kissed the palm. "You look beat."

"I am tired. I hope I don't make a mistake and blow this whole thing. There's so much riding on it. We may never have a better opportunity to talk to Baskin than cornering him tonight."

He patted her hand. "You'll do fine. We rehearsed this little scene three times before we got here." Jackson cut his eyes toward the front door and watched Baskin stroll in and head straight to a seat at the bar. "Show time. We let him order, get settled, and then act like we're heading out the door when we bump into him."

They waited an unnerving fifteen minutes before getting up to leave. Jackson crossed over to the bartender to hand him the little tray with their tab and the money to cover it. He sandwiched himself in between Baskin and another guy, leaning as far to the right as he could, bumping into Roger.

"Hey there, how's it going?" Jackson asked, friendly-like.

"I'm okay. What are you doing here?"

Jackson sent him an odd look. "Eating, drinking, trying to forget our troubles."

"Oh, right. Sorry to hear about Livvy and Walker."

"And the kids," Jackson added. "It's been a horrible few weeks."

"I bet."

About that time, Tessa joined him, tugging on his arm. She acted harried, shoving her hair out of her face. "I forgot to call my dad about Thanksgiving weekend. With everything that's been happening I haven't had time to look for a place."

Jackson introduced Tessa to Baskin as the bartender brought over his change. "This is Tessa Connelly. Her folks live back in Nags Head. We just got back from her brother's funeral. Ryan Connelly, the tourist who died here, that was Tessa's brother."

Baskin shook his head. "Heard about that, too. Nasty business with them finding the head yesterday. Makes you wonder. What's this place turning into? Never thought the Key could be such a mean part of the world. Nothing happens in this town for years and then all hell breaks loose. You ask me, it's a downright shame."

"It is. Royce mentioned yesterday that you're just the man who might be able to help us out. We're interested in getting a rental here for Tessa's parents over the Thanksgiving weekend."

Tessa was delighted at the look on Baskin's face. He took the bait, thinking about his commission. His closed-off demeanor almost morphed into chummy. "Sure. You guys leaving already? It isn't even nine o'clock yet. Sit down. Have another drink and we can go over the specifics of what you're looking for."

Jackson turned to Tessa. "What do you say? I know it's been a long day…"

"It is getting late, but sure, why not? We're here now."

Jackson dragged up a barstool and Tessa squeezed in next to Baskin. He ordered another two beers and turned to the dependable right-hand man. "How about another one for you? Looks like you're drinking a margarita on the rocks with a tequila chaser."

Baskin leaned over and laughed. "I'm fond of tequila, not the rotgut crap either, but the smooth stuff made from blue agave."

Tessa forced out a giggle like a schoolgirl. "If I hadn't already had too many beers with my chicken wings, I'd try it."

"Beer, never touch the stuff. Now tell me, little lady, how big a house you need for your kinfolk and for how long? I have several to pick from, a beauty at three thousand square feet down to a little cottage."

"Hmm," Tessa said, her brow creasing. "Nothing quite so large as that. I'd say something in between. And they'll only be in town for ten days. Is it possible to get something for such a short amount of time?"

"Honey, we rent them by the week, the month, or long-term, usually charge the tourists through the nose. I've got a nice waterfront cottage that's two-story, three bedrooms, about two thousand square feet."

"That sounds perfect. Could I look at it?"

"Absolutely. You just let me know when."

Jackson sipped his beer, but noticed Baskin was indulging faster than anyone could possibly keep up. Biding his time, he played out the scenario—Tessa's folks coming down—until he thought Baskin was enjoying a happy buzz. "Garret said Royce was really upset this morning."

"Oh, he was. Took him a while to calm down, too. Old man is heartbroken."

"Will you miss Walker?"

Baskin grunted into his drink. "Man was a putz with too much money on his hands. We should all have had Walker's problems."

"Did Royce know how you felt about his darling son?"

"Royce was well aware of his boy's shortcomings. No doubt about it."

Jackson acted like he'd had too much to drink when he tilted over toward Baskin. "Tell me the truth, did Livvy really tell you she wanted to fly out to San Francisco to see the Golden Gate Bridge?"

Roger's eyes glistened with humor. "What do you think? I felt silly saying it that day. But Boone suggested we should make your parents understand that she and Walker just took off, it'd make them feel better."

"That day at the house, it was like you guys had formed a club or something—you, Oakerson, Boone, and Carson—the four musketeers singing the same song. All that, and the whole time, Livvy and the kids were in a drum dumped in the Gulf. We didn't see that coming."

"No way you could have. Hey, it's no secret. The guys that day—all have a hefty stake in the resort coming to town."

"You mean the casino?"

"That too. Make us a pile of money if your dad would stay out of it. Boone decided we should downplay the missing family, not make a big deal out of it." Baskin lifted a shoulder. "It sounded good to me because I thought they'd just gone off for the weekend."

"Ever heard of a guy named Hugo Reiner?"

"Sure. Ask anyone in this place. Buy Hugo a drink and he'll tell you some fantastical tale about where the Nazi war chest ended up."

"Walker thought it was possible."

"Yeah, well, Walker thought a lot of things that weren't true."

"Do you think Royce knew about Walker's plans to find the gold?"

"Hell no. And I wasn't going to be the one to tell him. Besides, Walker was never gonna find that gold."

"You mean because Werner Dietrich's outfit wanted it more?"

Baskin narrowed his eyes. "Damn straight. You don't mess with a man like Dietrich." He threw back his glass of tequila, and in one gulp, drained the glass. "I gotta go. Nice talking to y'all. Now you be sure to call me about that rental, hear? Ol' Baskin'll fix you up."

Chapter Twelve

It was late when the group got together to compare notes. They sat around the Indigo dining room table grazing on sweets dropped off by the neighbors and listening to the voices on the recorder. When the last comment from Baskin finished, Anniston hit the stop button, munched on a soft chocolate chip cookie, and came to one conclusion.

"I'm no expert in voice matters but even I can tell they all come off as very anxious. This isn't just a normal tone to a casual conversation you'd have bumping into someone at the coffee shop or bar."

Raine paced in front of the window. She wasn't pleased with the way her encounter had turned out. "It was difficult to tell with Carson, because he'd been drinking for more than an hour when I walked in. He's usually more gregarious than that, doesn't take himself so serious."

"Which is my point," Anniston said. "It should've been easier for Carson to talk to you, but the conversation sounded forced and strained. He came off as a little irritated at you."

"It might've gone better if I'd gotten him to talk when he was sober. Although I doubt he'd have been as free with some of his statements."

"Yours was a lot more successful than mine," Garret complained. "Confronting Oakerson was a total bust. He was more of a jerk than I remembered. He was arrogant, basically a prick, and then Sinclair showed up to run me out of there. I didn't even get a chance to hit all the high points."

Jackson couldn't believe his ears. "And I thought the tougher nut to crack would be Baskin. Yet he turned out to open up more, which probably meant he was lying. At the mention of Dietrich, he certainly clammed up and was ready to get out of there."

"I thought your mother and I did okay," Tanner said quietly.

Anniston patted him on the arm. "You were both great. You handled Dandridge like pros."

"Because Boone seemed off-balance to me. More so than my getting in his face that day at the church. Which is odd. Plus, he got on his cell phone two seconds after we left," Tanner revealed. "That has to mean something."

Garret's spine straightened in his chair. "There's something bothering me about Boone grabbing his phone like that. Dandridge doesn't hesitate to send out an SOS to somebody. Think about it. Boone didn't call Carson, because Carson would've said something to Raine, right?"

"I think so." Raine turned to Mitch. "What do you think? You were there."

"I got to the bar before Carson did. He didn't once get on his cell phone. Nor did he take any notice of me sitting in the back. When Raine walked in, he appeared genuinely surprised to see her. So much that it was a little awkward."

Garret went on, "And as far as I'm concerned, I took Oakerson completely by surprise, too. He was initially into his charming mayor role, maybe somewhat distracted, what with trying to impress Wendy. So Oakerson wasn't the one Boone called to warn. And it seemed Baskin bought into the rental scam like he didn't expect it."

Jackson nodded. "Baskin was a little uncomfortable at first, but then he became downright talkative. If Dandridge had cautioned him to be on the lookout for us, he didn't act like it. I doubt Roger would've been so buzzed and chatty."

"What's your point? You're thinking those four played us after all and this was a complete waste of time?" Mitch speculated.

Garret cut his eyes to meet Mitch's. "I didn't say that. But…if Boone called to alert someone that we were on the attack, he didn't call the four we talked to."

Jackson took a peach tart from the platter in the center of the table, and bit into one of the corners. "Baskin would never have said anything against Walker if he'd decided to play us. He called Walker a putz. These guys are smart, I'll give you that much. But they aren't genius enough to outthink us."

Tessa broke apart a fudge brownie. "Maybe Boone called Sinclair. Maybe that's how the chief knew to hang out in protective mode around the mayor."

Anniston looked around the room. "Well, I, for one, think this was very productive, more so than I thought it would be. Something else came out of this and it's significant. There's no doubt each of these men blame one man for putting the kibosh on the golf course project and thereby blocking money going into their personal pockets."

All eyes fell on Tanner.

"Is there any way we could be missing that as a major motive?"

Tanner held his arms out wide above the table. "I don't think so. I'm still here, alive and kicking. If they wanted me out of the way, all they had to do was blow up my truck or my house. There's been none of that."

Lenore let out a gasp. "That's a disturbing thought. I'm still having a hard time with what Carson told Raine, that Livvy really wanted that deal to go through. She never said a word to me about that, not one word. I always got the impression she was proud of what her dad had done to stand up to the Buchanans. Carson's comment opened the door to doubt."

Raine patted Lenore's arm. "Carson admitted that info came straight from Walker. I wouldn't put too much faith in that."

Garret decided it had to be said. "Do we really know if Livvy had fallen in love with money? Was she so desperate to get out of her marriage that she wanted the big score like everyone else?"

It was Mitch who stood up and went nose to nose in Garret's face. "Why do you insist on saying things like that? Livvy was a victim in all this. I'm sure Walker pulled her into his crap."

"I loved Livvy, too," Garret maintained, but he wasn't willing to back down. "There are things about this scam of Walker's that simply don't add up. There's the book on treasure hunting in the nightstand. Anniston pointed out that Livvy had to know what he was up to. She was sleeping in the same bed, two feet away."

Before the argument could escalate, Tessa got to her feet. "Stop it, both of you. Since this whole thing began, I've had to accept things about my brother. He wasn't perfect. He died because he came down here to fish and got dragged into something nasty. I'm not sure how it happened or what he was thinking. All I know is that your sister ended up dead, just like Ryan did. Arguing over what Livvy knew is the same wasted fight about what Ryan did to get involved. That part doesn't matter. To find out who did this we need to stay on the same page, stay focused. So just cut the combative crap."

Everyone watched as she bolted out the back door.

"I'll go talk to her," Jackson said. "She's exhausted and hasn't been herself, not since Anniston found Ryan's…"

"We get it," Mitch stated, scrubbing his hands over his tired face. "I'm sorry I'm so touchy. In a way, Tessa's right. I guess it doesn't matter how deep Livvy was involved in this. But if it's true and she was interested in the money, then so was Nathan."

Garret nodded, but he was distracted with something he couldn't shake. A part of him was still fuming about the bar scene with Oakerson. "I think what bothers me the most is that the mayor dismissed five murders as if they offered no direct threat to the public. How does Oakerson know that for certain unless he has firsthand knowledge about why they were killed? No one in this room has yet to figure out why Livvy and the kids had to die. And as Jackson said, we're not dummies. Even if Walker messed up big time on some deal that went sour, why did the kids have to suffer?"

"Because they recognized the killer," Mitch uttered, barely above a whisper.

Garret's heart tightened in his chest. "Exactly. They were killed by someone they knew." He turned to Anniston. "We have to find something definitive that links Dietrich to Walker and Livvy. How do we do that?"

"I have to get my hands on Walker's emails."

Knowing that the kids had recognized their killer made Garret more determined. "So after listening to each of these jerks, which one comes across as the one we can shake down?"

As they listened to the recordings one more time, Anniston suddenly hit the stop button. "Maybe the link we're after isn't any of these people. Maybe the link we want is Nathan Hollister."

It was almost midnight when Garret took that notion and followed Anniston out to her SUV. Dark clouds had covered up the silvery moon and blocked out the stars. The whip of wind hit his face and made him think that a storm would likely make landfall before daybreak.

He helped load up the stuff that she seemed to never go anywhere without—briefcase, laptop computer, and all the legal pads of notes and research. He'd never met anyone quite like Anniston Marcelli before. The woman was the consummate professional who exuded law enforcement lingo like a scene out of *Dragnet*. Her cop persona and swagger should've been a turn off for him. Why it wasn't, he couldn't fathom. He only knew he wanted her more every day he was around her.

Anniston started to climb behind the wheel and stopped. She took that extra second to study the sadness in his eyes, the anguish on his face. That had to be the driving force behind her decision.

There were times a woman had to take the initiative. She wanted to be a part of changing that look to something else. Tonight she wanted to be Garret's distraction, as much for herself as for him. The weight of everything around them had taken its toll. Today had been long and brutal. As far as she was concerned, they'd more than earned the right to be together.

"Garret, why not come back to the hotel with me?"

His mind, she could tell, was a million miles from the offer. "I really should stay and be with my family tonight."

She framed his face with her hands. "After. You can come back after," she said softly.

The invitation couldn't have been clearer if she'd put up a billboard.

It took a few extra seconds for Garret to understand. When the implication hit and landed, there was nothing slow about the way he moved. He dragged her up against him. His mouth dived in to ravage hers. He let his lips and tongue show her the raw pleasure of what he'd been feeling while his arms wrapped around her waist.

It seemed like steam rose out of the ground. The air became hot, humid.

When he let her go, he rested his head on hers. "Are you sure this is what you want?"

"Certain. After that kiss, I'm not even sure I'll be able to drive."

"That's okay. I'll get us there. Let's not waste another minute."

They didn't. They climbed into the Explorer and Garret drove through town. He barely stopped at a red light, rolled through a couple of stop signs. It was a wonder the Indigo Police didn't clock them on radar.

"You might want to pull up to the main entrance," Anniston suggested. "We have to unload all my equipment and gear. We can't leave it in the car. I'll go grab a luggage cart so we only have to make one trip."

Garret groaned, but knew she was right. "That's all we'd need is to get the voice recordings stolen that we just worked so hard to create."

"Exactly."

He helped her transfer everything out of the car onto the trolley. Together they pushed it into the elevator to head upstairs. On the third floor, Anniston let them into the room by sliding her cardkey through the reader, and walked into the dark, hitting the lights as she went.

Garret dumped the gear on the little settee inside the hallway. "I'll be right back. I'll take the cart back down and then pull the SUV into the lot next door." He took her by the shoulders and kissed her mouth. "Don't move from that spot until I get back."

"If I don't move then how will I put on sexy lingerie?"

"Good point. That image just makes me want to leave the car where it is."

She shook her head. "The front desk will just keep calling and bugging me about it later until they make me move it. Here, take my cardkey…for when you come back. Interruptions aren't something we want to deal with…later."

Because it was true, he practically ran to the elevator and punched the first floor button several times just to get it up to third floor again.

Once he reached the lobby, he left the cart for someone else to use and walked through the double doors, back to the SUV. It wasn't until he started the engine and put the car into drive that he noticed something was off. The vehicle wobbled on one side, bumping along like the tire was flat. Because the adjacent lot was a short twenty feet away, he gunned the gas and pulled into the first available space he found. He got out to investigate and saw the damage. In the short amount of time it had taken for them to unload everything and take it upstairs, someone had slashed the back tire. His eyes immediately darted around the area to check for anyone watching him. But all he saw were the huge palms draped in shadows lining the pathway to the front entrance.

He took out his phone and took several pictures of the deep gashes in the rubber. He wasn't sure what else he could do about it now. A police report would have to be filed, but that could wait until morning.

Right now, all he could think about was getting back upstairs. So he hurried through the lot and back into the vivid light inside the lobby.

He waved to the front desk clerk—a man he was sure he went to high school with—and rushed into the elevator. When he reached the third floor again, he slid the cardkey into the reader and walked in to find she'd shed her clothes and changed into a silky red teddy.

"I thought you'd never get back," she breathed out.

His mouth went dry. He couldn't take his eyes off the vision. She was stretched out on the bed in a sexy pose, her gypsy dark hair spread out like an exotic fan in contrast to the white sheets. Her sultry chocolate eyes lidded in invitation, her olive skin was slick and satiny, sheened to perfection.

He wanted to rip off the lacy chemise. There'd been a force building inside him all evening. The juices that had stirred between them earlier was nothing compared to the heat building up now.

He kicked off his shoes, but when he started to peel out of his clothes, she got to her knees on the bed and motioned for him to come closer. "Here, let me do that."

Primal arousal kicked in. The seduction he'd planned went out the window as he crossed to the bed.

Her smooth fingers slipped inside the waistband of his jeans and worked open the button. She slid down his zipper, and found tufts of black hair there that had to be touched, stroked.

"Mmm, no underwear." With her tongue she left a wet trail.

"Baby, you do that again and I'm liable to explode right here." He backed up to push the rest of the way out of the denim while she grabbed hold of his T-shirt and yanked.

He ran a finger down her throat, found her skin soft as rose petals. The familiar whiff of Chanel drifted though his brain as he came back to plunder that eager mouth of hers.

He angled, led with lean abs that had her flat on her back. His muscles bunched as he slid the straps of silk off her shoulders, felt her go soft as mush when he exposed a shapely breast. His lips sailed along the curves, fusing and feasting on the ridges. His hand glided lower, dipping into moist, wet heat.

A jolt of lust shot through her as she latched onto his hair. She dropped her head back, then lifted her hips, encouraging him to take more, a lot more.

As his fingers played through the lace, he clamped onto her mouth again, and dropped into the kiss, open and fierce. He had her urgent now, her breath ragged. She clawed upward, trying to reach higher, ever so higher, before her body quivered and she shattered into a million bright stars.

It was his undoing. He tore the silk away from her flesh, ripping the lace to reveal all of her. He trailed his tongue along her belly, past a landing strip of black hair, and his tongue dived lower into the wet heat.

Dizzy with sensations, her fists dug into the sheet. She held on while he coaxed out a sultry low moan that rippled out of her like a seismic vibration shifting the earth. Flaming waves rose up, crashing onto shore. A halo of pleasure erupted. The room lit up like a Roman candle spiraled into the night sky.

She raised her head high enough to find his dark eyes locked on hers. She urged him up, to take as she opened— giving him everything she had in surrender.

He moved over her, dipped his head to take her mouth. He lifted and cupped her hips. The whip of desire bit and sliced into him as he dived in. Joined now, his blood pumped, his heart raced as their bodies slicked and thudded as one.

In a wild drumbeat, the rhythm winged up like a soaring bird in flight—with one goal in mind— grinding toward that soulful trip to the highest point of pleasure. They slammed into the curl on a thousand bursts of light. They rushed over and through the shimmering waterfall, landing into the calm, warm mist of blue on the other side.

Sated, he didn't think he could move. So he looked down, pressed his lips to the pulse at her throat. He kissed her mouth, long and deep, before rolling to his back. Still trying to catch his breath, he asked, "You alive over there?"

"I think so. I'm trying to figure out how to tell Cara she was right. You *do* aim to please."

He let out a snort of laughter. "Don't let me stop you, but I'm not sure I want to be around to hear that conversation. My little voice says never get two women together that you've slept with."

She raised up on one elbow, patted his chest. "Don't worry. Like Cara, I'd give you exceptional marks. You know a thing or two about a woman's body."

Again, he let out a laugh. "Women. Why do you insist on comparing notes about a man's performance? It makes me feel so cheap."

"Hmm, let's see. For one, it's fun to do. Plus, getting to sing the praises of a lover doesn't come along that often."

"Oh, jeez, please, nothing my mother might hear about, okay? It's a small town."

"It's okay. Your mom admitted a few weeks ago at the girls' night out, she's well aware her children engage in sex."

"This is getting more embarrassing by the minute."

She leaned over him, kissed his mouth. "Hey, I'm just trying to tell you I appreciate your giving nature. In fact, I have a giving nature myself."

She reared up, threw her legs over his body and straddled him. And she spent the next hour proving it.

Chapter Thirteen

Their bodies were still tangled under the covers when they woke to a gray dawn and a gentle patter of rain dancing on the roof.

Garret rolled to one side to watch her stretch beside him like a Cheshire cat truly pleased with her surroundings. He traced her lips with a lean finger. This was a mouth to savor, to feast on, he decided. "Tell me again why we hurried last night?"

"I can only speak for myself, but I was done waiting. I wanted you inside me."

"Mmm. There was that."

"As clients go, you're pretty damn talented."

"And as investigators go, right back atcha." He weighed whether or not to break the mood. Since it seemed like it wasn't fair to keep a secret, he went on,

"You know why it took me so long to get back to the room last night?"

"Why?"

"Someone took a knife and slashed the rear tire on the SUV's driver's side. I didn't notice it until I'd already pulled into the parking lot. My mind was on other things."

"Someone must've followed us to the hotel."

"It's the only thing that makes sense." Garret swung his legs to the side of the bed, reached for his jeans to pull out his cell phone. He showed her the photos he'd taken. "Do you have AAA? Because you'll definitely have to have a new tire."

"I have a spare," Anniston said as she studied the pictures then eased out of bed to throw on a red kimono. Her cell phone dinged with a text message. "Dack's texting me. He wants to meet at Rumrunner Cove. That's really odd. I wonder why."

"Make sure it's him you're talking to," Garret suggested as he yanked on his jeans. "Ask him something only he would know."

She smiled. "Look at you. World surfer turned protective lover." But she took the warning to heart and let her fingers fly. *Make me believe it's you.*

Want me to write it in code? You have a birthmark on your left shoulder and a scar on your ankle from falling off your bike.

She added a smiley face to the text and wrote, *Okay. See you in an hour. Flat tire this morning. Thanks to the locals.*

"Who should I call to change the tire? Baskin's shop?"

He gave her a pathetic look. "It doesn't open for another hour. I'll do it."

"You look miffed. What's bothering you?"

"All this cloak and dagger stuff is getting to me. Someone wiped out a whole family and I'm beginning to think we'll never learn the truth. They killed kids. We're no closer to finding out who did it. Some days this entire thing is surreal. I feel like I'm living a very bad dream and can't wake up."

She went over to him and cuddled his head over her heart. "Ask yourself why they were all beaten and tortured before they were murdered. Obviously someone was trying to get information out of them."

"Even little kids? That's disgusting."

"Whoever did this probably threatened to harm the kids if Livvy and Walker didn't talk. The killer or killers used that threat to try to get information. About what, I don't know. But even if Livvy and Walker cooperated they'd still be dead. Those people were not going to leave witnesses behind."

Garret let out a huge sigh. "So what do we do now?"

"My brother will be here tomorrow afternoon. In the meantime, I intend to find out if Walker got in touch with Dietrich."

"How do we do that?"

She held up her phone. "Dack just gave me an opening. I get in his face and beg for him to share details."

"I'm coming with you."

"Fine. But you'd better move that adorable ass of yours because I'm leaving in ten."

He sent her a grin. "Not without my changing that tire you won't."

She ran a finger along his jaw before curling her hand around his bicep. "Then put those muscles to work ASAP."

By the time Garret put on a new tire, the rain had slowed to a drizzle. They reached Rumrunner Cove on time, but the weather was still wet and dreary when Anniston and Garret pulled up beside Dack's Crown Vic in the parking lot.

Dack seemed nervous, but he motioned for them to come sit with him in the Ford.

"Why meet out here?" Anniston wanted to know as soon as she crawled into the front seat while Garret got into the back.

"I have a better question. Why did you bring him with you?" Dack asked, thumbing a hand toward Garret.

"Because I'm the client," Garret said flatly. "The victims were my family."

Dack rubbed his temple, stared through the windshield at two fishermen who had thrown their lines in the water. "Fine. Let's try to make this look like we're having a normal conversation about where Ryan Connelly was found."

"That doesn't even make sense. Why so secretive? Why do you look so stressed out? Not sleeping well? What's going on?"

"I have some things I need to tell you. I'd planned to walk and talk and act as though we're studying more of the crime scene. But because of the rain we might as well sit here and stay dry. You wanted to know the autopsy results for Walker Buchanan and the boy, right?"

"What have you got?"

"Walker suffered from blunt force trauma. He was beaten to a pulp and then suffocated with the same type of plastic bag used on his wife and daughter. The boy had considerably less head trauma but died from asphyxiation all the same."

Garret was glad he hadn't eaten breakfast because he thought he might have to open the door to be sick. "So if they weren't attacked in their own home, where did all this trauma take place? They had to have screamed, made noise. How did a beating happen right under our noses?"

Dack twisted in his seat to better answer Garret. "Not sure yet. But there's something else. On the morning of September twenty-fourth, early on that Thursday at 2:55 a.m., a Florida state trooper on routine patrol near Port Charlotte stopped a minivan traveling north at a high rate of speed on Interstate 75. The vehicle was registered to Olivia Buchanan. The male driver was ticketed for speeding, fifteen miles over the limit. The man's driver's license was issued to an Alton Rennie."

"But he wasn't the owner of the vehicle. Shouldn't that have flown up a red—?" Anniston began, jumping in.

"Would you let me finish?" Dack snapped.

"Sorry."

"When the trooper asked why Rennie was driving someone else's van, he got a story from Rennie about housesitting for a vacationing couple out of Indigo Key. The registration had the Indigo Key address and it didn't show up on the hot sheet. Rennie was supposed to pick up the couple at the Tampa Bay Airport later that morning, in their own van. That was the guy's story."

"And the cop believed that?"

Dack rolled his eyes. "Obviously, the trooper made a judgment call. But the real Alton Rennie had reported his wallet stolen at Hialeah race track two days before the traffic stop."

"Didn't the cop notice the photo didn't match?"

"That's just it. The photo looked similar to the driver." Dack reached for a file folder on the dash and took out a picture of Alton Rennie as it appeared on his driver's license. "Who does that look like to you?"

Garret leaned over the console to peer at the picture. "Son of a bitch. It looks like Boone Dandridge or his brother."

"That's right. The men have very similar features, which is probably why Rennie was singled out at the race track."

"Does that mean you have enough to get a warrant?" Garret asked, hopeful.

Dack raked his hands through his blond hair. "Not yet. It's all supposition at this point. I have no proof whatsoever that Dandridge was anywhere near the Tampa Airport dropping off the minivan at that remote parking lot. Whoever left it, picked the perfect satellite place to park with zero surveillance."

"From my understanding the lot was so far from the airport, they relied on a shuttle to get back and forth to the terminals," Anniston added.

"Let's just say it wasn't the handiest place to park, but it was the cheapest per day around." Dack pivoted toward the backseat again. "Are you beginning to see the problems with taking this to the state prosecutor this early? That's why I'd appreciate a little silence. Don't go spreading this around until I know more. There's a reason I'm asking for discretion."

"I have to tell my family," Garret insisted.

"No, you don't," Dack retorted. "Tell them about the results of the autopsies. Anything beyond that is off the record. Give me your word you'll keep this conversation between the three of us. If you don't, I won't share another item of interest."

Garret understood the weight of such a promise. "Okay. You got it," he said reluctantly. "I'll keep my mouth shut about the traffic stop."

"There's more to it than that, something bigger that requires a lot more digging. If the driver's license was stolen two days prior to the murders—"

"That means it was well-planned," Anniston finished.

"That's the way I'm leaning. Also, on the night of the murders a burglar alarm went off at 9:09 p.m. at one of the businesses across from the marina."

Garret swallowed hard, believing they were finally getting some answers. "The Vitamin Hut?"

"Exactly. One of Sinclair's patrolmen responded. He wrote in his report that a witness spotted a dark blue sedan, a late model Q50 near the store at about the same time."

Garret huffed out a breath. "It's probably not a coincidence that Roger Baskin owns an Infiniti."

Dack turned the wipers on to clear the rain that had collected on the windshield. "That's right, which means there's a likelihood that we're looking at more than one person involved." He stabbed his finger at Anniston. "You're usually decent with research. You want to tell me why you were off the mark with Dandridge?"

"What do you mean? I gave you everything I found on him."

"When Roland Wainwright was picked up in Oregon for petty crimes two decades ago, his rap sheet listed him at five-nine, a hundred and forty-five pounds. Boone Dandridge has to be six feet. After twenty years you'd expect a weight gain, but the man didn't grow three inches in height."

Anniston looked as though she'd been punched in the stomach. "If that's true then they aren't one and the same at all."

Dack turned to Garret. "Are you beginning to see the complexity of all this? I'm not sure how many are involved. Right now, today, everyone's a suspect. That's why I'm telling you it's more complicated than I could ever imagine. I need time to sort this out. I need personnel I don't have. If Captain Briggs—"

"Yeah, yeah, yeah, we get it, Dack," Anniston snarled. "You're in trouble with the higher ups if you share deets with us, but you're shorthanded, so you're willing to make an exception."

"It isn't that, Anniston. I'm limited as to where I can go here. You aren't. Understand?"

She tilted her head, eyeing him with open interest. "Are you telling me the state investigators are tying your hands? Why? Why would they do something like that?"

"To a certain extent, yes. And the short answer is I don't know. Sinclair is of no help whatsoever. Ask yourself why I was sent down here. Of all the detectives in this jurisdiction, they pick me to handle this particular case. At first, I was flattered. But this has taken so many turns I'm wondering if someone pulled some strings to get me here."

Garret suddenly remembered a key detail. He leaned over the front seat. "Royce Buchanan admitted he called Tallahassee when he thought this was a kidnapping. He asked for a special investigator to handle it instead of Sinclair. He wasn't happy you showed up. He thought you were too inexperienced. In fact, I guess we all did. I apologize for that."

"Yeah, well, you aren't that far off the mark. I've asked repeatedly for them to send me other detectives. So far, I've gotten stonewalled. I know other murders are happening all over the state, but…this thing is way understaffed. It's been strange from the get-go. But I'm beginning to think it's clinging to life support on purpose."

"Like getting the letter dropped on our doorstep that night from the killer. That was weird," a well-meaning Garret offered.

Dack looked puzzled and then stared at Anniston. "What letter?"

Her eyes narrowed at Garret's gaffe. She tried to do damage control. "It's not what you think. We weren't even sure it was legit. But whoever wrote it, did mention the beatings and the plastic bag, which I guess the autopsies proved did happen."

"I want to see that note," Dack demanded. "What else are you holding back from me? See, that's what I mean. No one wants to cooperate. It's impossible to fully do my job if I can't even trust a person I've known practically my entire life. I understand the chief of police is not in my corner. I'm not sure what's happening back at the capitol with my own department. But you? I trusted you. And we had an agreement."

"Okay. I'm sorry. You're right. It won't happen again. I'll see that you get a copy. But I've already had it analyzed by a lab and there were no fingerprints left on it. I do know the type of machine used, an HP LaserJet 9500."

"Why didn't you tell me this before now?"

"Because I wasn't entirely sure you wouldn't go running to the wrong person back in Tallahassee. I had clients to protect. I think of you as someone who doesn't bend the rules very often. I'm kind of surprised you're willing to bring me in like this. You told me not to ask for favors."

"I did, didn't I? Right now, I don't feel like I have much of a choice. I'm running out of contacts in this town.

Some days I feel as though I'm making headway. Other times, not so much. Today is one of those days I wish I'd listened to my mother and become a lawyer."

"We'll get more help when Sebastian gets here. What exactly do I have to do right this minute to get my hands on Walker's email account? I need to know if Walker ever got in touch with Werner Dietrich."

Dack looked around the dunes to make sure the two fishermen showed no interest in their meeting. "So you're still pushing the treasure hunt theory? I suppose it's as good as any. I have Walker's email file back in the office here. There's no smoking gun there, Anniston. There's no Werner Dietrich emails among his contacts."

Her enthusiasm waned. "Maybe Walker used another email account that we don't know anything about."

"It's possible. But he didn't create an account on his home computer."

"What about Livvy? Were there emails between her and Nathan?"

Dack looked surprised. "Hollister? A few. Mostly talking about meeting up to go shopping."

"I don't think they were buying anything, Dack," Garret clarified.

Dack lifted a brow. "Well, that's interesting. And now, Hollister can't be found either. No wonder his wife doesn't seem all that concerned about finding him."

"I had to twist her arm to file an official report," Anniston explained. "Even though you don't think there's anything in Walker's emails, will you still share the file with me?"

"Sure. I'll drop it off at the hotel later."

She made a face. "I'd rather you give it directly to me rather than leave it at the front desk. How about if I stop by and pick it up?"

Dack scowled at the offer. "I don't want you parading by Sinclair's office door to pick it up. Better still, we should meet somewhere out of town, away from the watchful eyes of the locals. How about that rest stop north of town?"

"The one with the Polynesian-style huts for restrooms?"

"That's the one. Say around seven o'clock tonight. I'll be heading back to Largo by then." He thumbed a hand toward Garret. "And be sure to bring him with you. Don't go skulking around without backup."

"I don't skulk." But Anniston grabbed Dack's arm when she saw the worry on his face. "You're really that afraid? I've never seen you this cautious before. You're starting to scare me."

"You should be scared. Whoever killed Ryan Connelly and the Buchanan family are monsters. We need to get them off the street."

On that warning, Garret and Anniston got out of the Crown Vic and back into her SUV. They watched as Dack put his car into gear and disappeared around the bend.

After she started up the Ford, Garret picked up her hand. "Sorry about letting the letter slip out. I thought he knew. I got caught up."

"It's okay. If I get Walker's emails it'll be a good trade for the note."

"That's a screwy way for things to work. And besides, Dack says there's nothing in Walker's emails."

"I'll be the judge of that. You want me to go with you to tell your parents about Walker and Blake?"

"No. I'll handle it." By the look on her face she seemed relieved, as if she already had another place to go, another strategy in mind. "Where are you headed?"

"Me? I'm gonna do the job you're paying me to do. For starters, I'll walk around town going from business to business and make a list of all the ones that use the right kind of printer."

Garret sent her a strange look. "That could take all day."

"Maybe not. It depends on where I start. I just have to think back to how long it's been since I've gone to church."

Anniston began on Bayside Boulevard, where Dandridge, or whoever he was, had set up shop at the Life Stone Church. Thanks to Lenore she knew the pastor left his office at noon for lunch. If things went well, maybe she could sneak inside and grab something with his fingerprints on it.

She waited until Boone got into his Land Rover before going up to the double doors that led to the auditorium. She held her breath and pulled on the handle, relieved to find it unlocked. She gingerly stepped inside, scanning the sanctuary to make sure it was empty. Once she was sure no one else was around, she walked past the rows of pews, down the corridor, and slipped into Boone's paneled office with his name on the door.

She took out her phone and started snapping shots of the interior. Her eyes landed on the desktop printer. She almost danced a jig then and there when she determined it was the right model.

Outside in the hallway, she heard the floor creak. Getting caught wasn't part of the plan. She opened the first door she came to, a supply closet, and flattened her body against the shelving. She hid inside the tiny space until the footsteps in the hall faded.

Opening the closet door, she grabbed the first thing she could reach that wouldn't be missed—a bunch of wadded up Kleenex out of the trashcan. She stuffed the wad of tissues into a plastic baggie she'd brought with her. As souvenirs went, it was pretty disgusting. But the lab might be able to test them and determine who Dandridge really was.

Before she got caught, she opened the door to the office and made sure no one was in the vestibule. When the coast was clear, she slipped out a side door that led to the courtyard and made a mad dash to the alleyway. She took off running toward where she'd left her car the next street over.

One place down, now on to the next, Anniston thought, as she jerked the car out of park and took off.

Chapter Fourteen

After delivering the results of the autopsies to his parents, Garret collapsed in his dad's easy chair with a headache brewing at the base of his skull.

He could tell his father took the news hardest. "It seems I was way off base about Walker."

"Don't do that," Mitch snapped. "Just because he was beaten to a pulp doesn't make him less of an ass. Our goal now has to be finding out how he got himself and his family murdered."

"It's just that I was certain Walker had killed Livvy and was out there somewhere hiding. It even ran through my mind that Royce knew where he was."

"I can't even fathom why someone would suffocate children," Garret muttered. Guilt spun through him like a mighty current. But he'd given his word to Hawkins that he'd keep his mouth shut about the other stuff. But maybe it didn't count if he made a suggestion. "I think we should keep an eye on Dandridge and Baskin, make sure we keep tabs on those guys and know where they are at all times."

"Way ahead of you," Mitch stated. "Walsh agreed to follow Baskin. And I've been sitting outside Dandridge's house every night until dawn."

Garret found the energy to get to his feet. "Why didn't you say something? There are three of us. We should take turns so one person doesn't burn out."

"I've only been at it for the last four nights. The evening I decided to do it, Mom, Dad, and Jackson were in Nags Head with Tessa for Ryan's funeral and you'd gone out to the preserve to see if you could locate any shell casings left over from the shots fired there."

"That excuse won't cut it. I've been back for days," Jackson said, sending a cool look toward his brother. "You could've said something. I'm happy to take my turn at watching either one of those men make a mistake."

"Thanks but I have it covered. Besides, I've nothing else to do with my nights." Mitch bobbed his head toward Jackson. "You've got Tessa. Garret's in the process of pursuing Anniston. Me? I'm free and clear to play detective for as many hours as it takes."

Garret paced in front of the window. "We've offered to help. I'm begging for something to do. Otherwise I'll go crazy." He angled toward his dad. "Surely there's a project you've been wanting to start? I need to do something, anything at all. I can still handle a saw or a paintbrush."

"That's not a bad idea," Tanner said. "I could use something to do myself. A couple of months back your mother bugged the hell out of me to build her some shelves in the utility room. That was July and too damn hot to think about starting such a job in close quarters. But now…"

Lenore set aside her knitting. "You three could practice on the songs you intend to play at the memorial service. Putting it off won't do any good. We're just waiting for the medical examiner to…" She couldn't finish the last part. "I don't think we should wait much longer to hold the service. I vote to have it next Monday at ten o'clock."

Tanner took in the sad look on his wife's face. "You've given this some thought."

"I just want it done with. The service is separate from the burial. The painful truth is we won't get to take Blake and Ally trick-or-treating this year. Thanksgiving won't be the same. I'd already bought Christmas presents for the kids. And someone has to go into that house and start packing up everything. That's something I'm not sure I can handle doing right now or even down the road. And then there's the fact that Tanner and I will eventually have to head back to work soon."

Garret chewed on that. "Shouldn't we have found a will by now? We've turned the house upside down before, been through it twice. We didn't find one." He looked at his brothers. "Want to get everyone together and go back in there?"

"Might as well. It beats sitting around staring at each other and doing nothing on a rainy day."

The brothers were on their own without help from the women. Raine and Tessa were swamped with the lunch crowd at the restaurant.

And Anniston had just gotten started.

She took her Ford Explorer over to Prospect Street where Baskin owned his auto repair shop, Baskin's Auto Clinic. She pulled up to the entrance behind an older model Buick. The "clinic" had three bays, all of which were occupied with an assortment of vehicles raised off the ground so the mechanics could do their thing standing underneath.

She cut the engine and hopped out without waiting for the tech to approach with his clipboard. When a man did emerge from the garage area, he sized her up. "What can I help you with?"

"Need an oil change."

"You have an appointment?"

"No. Do I need one?"

"It cuts down considerably on the wait time."

All Anniston wanted was to get a look at Baskin's office on the inside. "How long?"

"We're backed up. Probably an hour at least."

"Would you mind if I gave it a shot? The car's really overdue. I should've taken care of it before I left Miami, but I had no idea the case I'm working on would drag out this long."

Beginning to warm up, the tech nodded his head. "You're that private eye the Indigos hired."

"That's me." She rocked back on her heels. "You guys do a brisk business."

"We do. There's a body shop around the corner if you ever need that. And Roger also sells used cars from a lot down the street."

"Good to know. But all I need right now is an oil change."

"Then give me the keys and go wait inside. There's a place to get coffee and watch TV that helps pass the time."

She handed over her keys and crossed the lot.

The waiting room was tiny with six uncomfortable plastic chairs crowded along one wall. A simple coffee bar shared space with the ancient model TV that sat on a metal stand. There was a table jammed in the corner covered in car magazines. The walls were decorated with posters, all having to do with luxury cars.

She looked into a glass window where a female cashier stayed busy with paperwork. The office was smaller than the waiting room. It was easy to spot the huge printer at the woman's back because the machine took up an entire desktop. Anniston decided it looked like the right size and shape of the HP.

She strolled over to the beverage station and took her time fixing a cup of strong, stale coffee. She'd taken cold medicine that tasted better. She lingered, trying to make out the type of printer the woman used to spit out the invoices.

The woman looked up and caught her staring. "Can I help you?" she said from behind the glass.

Anniston shook her head. "Sorry. I was just looking to see if they'd gotten to my Explorer yet."

"We'll call you when it's ready."

Patience, Anniston reminded herself. She had a long wait time. The woman had to go to the bathroom sometime.

About thirty-five minutes into her wait, she spotted the tech guy driving her Ford into the garage. She stood up, only to realize the cashier was nowhere in sight. She stepped up to the glass and took out her cell phone and pretended to punch in numbers.

In a matter of seconds, she'd captured the images she needed. She went back and sat down, picking up a magazine from the table to hide her phone. She brought up the camera roll, zoomed in on the printer image and could make out the 9500 series and the logo. It was older than the model at the church, but it was still the same type of laser jet.

She sat back, got comfortable. Now she was stuck waiting until they finished with her SUV.

Once inside Livvy's front door, the brothers stood in the entryway and considered the daunting task ahead of them.

"Where do you suggest we start?" Jackson grumbled. "Since we're three pairs of eyes short, I'm not sure this will yield much."

Garret picked up a ceramic Athena statue off the hall table. "Think about packing all this crap up. I'm not looking forward to that chore. Knickknacks everywhere, a dozen years' worth of collecting household junk."

"Yeah. This is one reason I don't get married and stay in one place for too long," Mitch admitted. "Who needs all this clutter on a daily basis? Livvy must've spent half her life keeping it dusted. I don't think she threw anything away."

"Maybe this is a waste of our time," Garret decided. "We've been through all this stuff before right down to the books on the shelves and the linen closet upstairs. The last time we were here we tore up Livvy's bedroom, dismantled the bed."

Jackson put his hands on his hips. "You guys even went through the garage. So where does that leave to search?"

"We could go tear up Walker's office again," Garret suggested. "Maybe we missed something the first time. I'm not really in the mood for a long-drawn-out scavenger hunt on another trip through the house."

"Sure. We have to start somewhere. Might as well make it Walker's man cave."

The trio sauntered outside to the breezeway in between the main house and the detached garage. It was Garret who unlocked the door of the guesthouse and flipped on the lights. The studio-sized apartment was like a fancy lounge where Walker could relax and watch anything on his built-in seventy-inch, flat-screen TV.

Jackson dropped into one of the soft brown leather sofas and stared at the black granite fireplace, then the Murphy bed encased around the bookshelves. "Something bothers me about this layout. It did from the first time I saw it."

But his brothers ignored the comment. Instead, Garret immediately drifted to Walker's desk and printer, decided it wasn't the same model used to print the note and moved on to opening each drawer. He rifled through the contents and it reminded him of something else. "Why haven't we searched the Vitamin Hut? That's where Anniston found his credit card statements."

Mitch was in the process of rummaging through Walker's wet bar when his hands went still. "That's a good question. We'll make it our next stop."

As Jackson continued to sit and stare at the wall unit and built-in bookcase, Mitch had had enough. "Do you intend to move your ass off the couch any time soon? We could use a little help and the emphasis is on *little*."

"In a minute. Does that bed look like it fits into the corner of that bookcase snugly enough to you? It seems like it bulges out too much. It seems warped or something."

"Instead of staring at it, pull the damn thing down and take a look."

Jackson finally got up, went over and tugged on the handle. He lowered the bed down to the floor. The design wasn't too complicated. There was nothing fancy about the way the space had been utilized. He ran a hand between the mattress and the frame, ran it clear around the length of one side until he hit a lump. "Hey guys, I think I found what made the mattress so bulky." He pulled out a brown paper sack, weighing what felt like five pounds or more.

"What's in there?"

Jackson drew out a bundle of cash and then another. "I've heard of stuffing cash under the mattress but this is a new one. Saving for a rainy day?"

Garret jerked one of the bags out of Jackson's hand. "There must be four hundred grand in here, stacks of twenties and hundred-dollar bills."

Jackson cocked his head, studied the painting on the wall where the Murphy bed had been. The print was nothing special, a landscape depicting a beach scene available from a dozen retail outlets in the Florida Keys geared toward tourists. He reached up to get rid of the artwork. Behind the frame was a wall safe.

"That's weird. Why wasn't the sack of cash tucked away in there?"

"Good question. The only way to answer that is to get inside. Can you do it?" Jackson asked.

For a few minutes Garret stood there staring up at the metal box shoved into two feet of wall space that looked similar in size to a microwave oven.

"Well…any problem getting into it?" Mitch wanted to know. "It needs a digital code. How much do you think Walker spent on this thing?"

"No idea. Probably four hundred bucks. It's not worth ten," Garret decided.

"Really?"

"Yep. It looks like he cheaped out and bought an electronic strongbox they sell at most major retail chains. I'll have this puppy opened in less than three minutes." Garret brought out the key ring that held the torque and other gadgets he carried wherever he went. "It'll be a piece of cake."

He climbed up on the bed and went to work. He unscrewed the nameplate first, removed the bolts that hid the lock mechanism. In less than two minutes, he had the first side popped and then the second. The word "opened" appeared on the digital display. "There you go."

Mitch slapped him on the back. "Should I worry you might be a cat burglar in your spare time?"

"Nah. I make a good enough living on the water."

Inside was a stack of insurance documents, the will, a trust, a stack of maps, and notes. Jackson held up an old leather-bound book that looked like a Bible. They spread out the other stuff and began picking through the paperwork.

"The will's pretty standard," Jackson said as he reviewed the document line by line. "In the event one of them dies, the other inherits everything. If they both die, Mom and Dad get the kids. Walker set up a trust for the kids, again standard. None of it applies now. There are no surprises with the insurance policies. It's pretty routine stuff. Since Royce helped them get the house, the deed reverts back to him upon the deaths of both. According to some of these bank statements, most of the estate is mired in debts."

A ball of sarcasm knotted Garret's gut. "Was that before or after the bundle of cash showed up? Because I'd say that kind of money would go a long way in taking care of final expenses."

Mitch had his head buried in maps. His head whipped up when he realized what he was looking at. "Guys, some of these drawings include Walker's handwritten notes. He must've jotted down Hugo's directions all over the blue, indicating ocean."

Jackson studied the scrawled words and what seemed like the handwriting of a desperate man. "Please try to convince me this stupid ranting isn't what got them killed."

"I have no idea why people would be after these maps. They aren't even regulation, but hand-drawn. They look useless to me," Mitch asserted. "I can let Walsh take a look at them and see what he thinks. He's a whiz at that sort of stuff. But these are so badly disproportioned, I'm not sure how they'd help locate a navigational point, let alone a sunken sub."

Garret looked at his watch. It was getting time to go. "Can you guys box all this up and we'll go through it later? I have somewhere I need to be."

"Sure. What about searching the Vitamin Hut?"

"You guys go without me, or wait until tomorrow. Your choice."

"We'll wait until you can go with us. Who knows? We might need you to crack open another safe."

Chapter Fifteen

By six o'clock the rain had stopped. But a thick, milky fog had rolled in and settled over the coastline.

Before Dack headed north out of town he texted his girlfriend, Shonna, to let her know he was on the road. It'd be another forty-five minutes past the rest stop to Key Largo.

He'd met Shonna—a home health care nurse—back in Tallahassee at a Super Bowl party one of his coworkers had given last February. They'd hit it off immediately. For eight months now they'd been moving toward cohabiting, mostly talking it to death. This assignment had been an opportunity to make that happen. Since Shonna owned a little bungalow so close to Indigo Key, it seemed the right time for them to take that next big step together.

And now, come the weekend, he was excited about taking her home to Miami to meet his mother. And tonight after dinner they were supposed to kick back and watch the new *Mad Max* action movie on cable. In a thousand years he would never have believed he was considering making the move to settle down.

The beam of his headlights hit the mile marker nearest the rest stop. He took the exit and pulled off into the parking lot. There were no other cars around, but he did see the lights of another vehicle slide into the spot at the very end of the pavement next to the roadway.

He checked his watch before verifying the time with the clock on the Ford's dash. Both read 6:59 p.m. He was so tired his neck hurt. He leaned his head back and decided this case kept tying him in knots. He scrubbed his hands over his face and wished for coffee.

"Come on, Anniston. Don't make me wait. I want to go home," he uttered to himself.

Through the haze he caught a glimpse of a figure in the shadows. He assumed it was Garret since it looked like a male. Annoyed that Anniston hadn't come with him, he got out of his vehicle, stood with hands on his hips waiting for the man to get closer.

He called out, "Where the hell is Anniston?"

There was no answer. "Hey, Garret, is that you?"

By the time the man got close enough for Dack to make out his face, he knew he was in trouble. Dack reached under his suit jacket for the weapon strapped at his hip.

But it was too late.

The man raised a SIG pistol and fired. The bullet whizzed out of the gun and straight into Dack's heart. His knees hit the ground first before his body fell forward. Dack Hawkins ended up face down in a puddle of mud at the edge of the asphalt.

Garret and Anniston had done a lot of running around that afternoon. Because of it they were doing their best to be no more than five minutes late for their meeting with Dack. Especially since Anniston had picked him up and exceeded the speed limit all the way up US 1.

"I can't believe you let those guys touch your car. What if they did something to it, like mess with the brakes? Or put a tracking device on it?"

She slanted a look at him from behind the wheel. "I watched them through the glass. All they did was change the oil."

"How can you be so sure?"

She let out a sigh. "Are we getting that paranoid?"

"You mean me?"

"No, I guess I mean everyone involved. I noticed Dack leaned a little toward that this morning. I've never seen him so amped up."

"Dack did look stressed out, like this case is getting to him. I refuse to believe it isn't solvable. And today you found that Dandridge has access to a laser jet printer and so does Baskin."

"Not to mention the entire town. I discovered the library's technology room uses that same HP model so anyone in town could've had access to that printer. Anyone could've walked up to one of the workstations there, slid in their flash drive, and printed out that note. It's like a salesman came through town and offered a fire sale on HP printers."

"I guess I see where Dack's coming from. Just when you think you have another piece of the puzzle figured out, it goes south and loses strength. The question is why would Dandridge or Baskin bother writing the note in the first place unless it was to brag about the murders. Jackson immediately believed the letter was genuine. Which man possesses the ego and type of personality to share details about the murders with the victims' families?"

"Let's not get tunnel vision," Anniston cautioned. "Let's say Baskin tried to get into the Vitamin Hut at 9:09

p.m. the night of the murders. He almost gets caught in the act and decides to go to the Buchanan home instead. He's looking for something and confronts Walker and Livvy at the house. He comes up with a good enough story to not only gain entry inside, but he somehow manages to get the entire household into the minivan, including the kids."

Garret picked up the narrative. "Then Baskin takes them to an unknown location where Dandridge is waiting. Both men begin beating and torturing Walker and Livvy, ostensibly with the purpose of getting information out of them. They threaten the kids to get what they want. Then one, or both men, take it up a notch and kill the captives, beginning with the kids. I mean, what else are they gonna do with four people who can so easily recognize them?"

"So they put the bodies in the fifty-five-gallon drums and take them out to the Gulf. They didn't use Walker's boat, the *Misty Dawn*, because the tracklog doesn't show it ever moved out of the marina. So, who owns a boat that Dandridge and Baskin would have access to?"

Goose bumps formed along Garret's arms. "That's easy. Dave Oakerson owns a string of them. The boats take tourists out on fishing expeditions and sunset cruises every day. Take your pick as to which one Dandridge or Baskin might've used to dump the bodies. And afterward, Dandridge has to get rid of the van to make it look like the family took off on their own. So he gets caught speeding toward the Tampa Bay airport, sticks it in a satellite lot where it takes a week to locate it."

"Paired with what you found in Walker's man cave— the bundle of cash and all those maps—what was the motive? The cash or the treasure?"

"Gotta be the hope and lure of Nazi gold. Hugo's name—old German sailor with supposed firsthand knowledge—was all over Walker's notes."

"Which means we have a lot to share with Dack."

"Like a bargaining chip? What do we get out of it? I'm not sure I want to share anything with Dack if there's a hint of truth that his own office is holding back. What if they're in on it? Or getting paid off?"

"Now you are sounding paranoid."

Garret twisted in his seat. "There's a reason for that."

"So what do you suggest we do? Hold back, too? I'm not sure that will get us anywhere. We have to trust Dack to do his job, Garret. We have to."

"Okay. You're the pro here. I'm trusting you to know what you're doing."

Anniston noted they were getting close to the rest stop and put on her blinker to exit. She headed into the parking lot, spotted Dack's car. "He's already here." She glanced at the digital clock. It read 7:03. "We're only a couple of minutes late." But just when she made the turn into one of the slots, her headlights shined a beam on someone lying in the dirt. "What is that?"

She saw his head, the blond hair, and the blood. "Oh my God. Is that Dack? He's down. Call 911!"

She started to bolt out of the vehicle but Garret grabbed her arm. "Wait a damn minute! Make sure there's no one else around first." He tried to scan the length of the lot but the fog made it impossible to see farther than twenty feet.

Anniston's hands were shaking when she snatched up her weapon and threw open the door. She stepped out into the mist and haze, hunched down next to the Crown Victoria using it for cover.

Garret skirted the front of the SUV, dropping down beside her next to the wheel well. He kept low trying to pick up any movement at the end of the parking lot. "I think they're gone."

He hoped like hell he was right as he inched through the mud toward Dack's body. Once he reached him, he used his fingers to try and find a pulse, checking Dack's wrist and his throat. When he detected nothing, he took out his cell, punching in the numbers for help.

By this time, Anniston had also crouched next to Dack's body.

"He's gone, Anniston," Garret said quietly as he tried to pull her back.

"How did they know he'd be here?" she said, sobbing. "I didn't tell anyone about the meeting. Did you?"

"Not a soul." Heartsick, Garret told her, "They probably followed him out here, maybe hoped all three of us would show up at the same time. They must've been disappointed when we were late."

For the next few minutes, Garret dealt with the emergency dispatcher, explaining the situation.

After that, the rest stop erupted in a chaotic scene. The EMTs showed up first, followed by a succession of Florida state troopers, followed by scads of crime scene people.

Garret and Anniston were pushed back to the entrance. They watched from that distance for another three hours while the crime scene crew collected evidence and took photographs of the entire area around Dack's body.

Garret couldn't help it. As he stood there studying law enforcement's reaction to the death of one of their own, he noted the difference. Four members of his family had died. But their murders had failed to garner this type of attention from the cops. He could only hope if anything at all came from Dack's death, it would be that it shook things up.

He decided the promise he'd made to keep quiet had come to an end, because now he intended to tell his brothers about what he knew. There was no longer a reason to keep it quiet.

When Garret spotted Sinclair making his way to where they were standing, he decided he could afford to play it with attitude. "Isn't this is a little out of your jurisdiction, Chief? We're at least fifteen miles out of the city limits. What are you doing here? Shouldn't you be in bed by now or maybe protecting the mayor from his constituents?"

"I came out here to ask what you two are doing way out here with a dead investigator."

Garret shook his head. "Sorry. No can do. I promised that trooper over there I'd wait around and give my official statement to the state police. Looks like you're out of luck,

Chief. But I'm sure there's still time for you to harass the common folk, maybe make sure Oakerson is tucked up for the night and doesn't have to answer bothersome questions from the voters."

Garret took some satisfaction from the glower Sinclair sent him. He tightened his hold on Anniston as they made their way toward the car.

Later, after the adrenaline faded, and Garret had crawled behind the wheel of the Explorer to take them back to town, Anniston found her heart actually aching.

"The sight of Dack lying in the mud, face down is something I'll carry with me for the rest of my life."

He squeezed her hand. "I know it hurts. I wish I could take the pain away."

"Back there as we waited, I made a promise to him. I'll solve this case or die trying. I refuse to let his death be in vain. Dack must've been getting close to something, Garret. It's the only reason they'd risk taking him out like they did."

"I know that. It could've been us face down in the dirt, as well."

"I'll have to go see his girlfriend Shonna. Will you go with me?"

"Sure. When?"

"I think it should be soon, maybe tomorrow."

"Are you sure you're okay enough to do that?"

"I have to be." She sniffled and laid her head back on the headrest. "I think I'm coming down with a cold."

He stroked her hair, curled in ringlets around her face from the damp weather. "You know what's good for that?"

"What?"

"All-night sex."

It made her smile.

"Seriously though, the best thing for a cold is noodle soup from Lee Fong's Palace."

"That does sound good."

"How about I take you back to the hotel and stop at Fong's along the way. They're open until eleven."

"You'll stay with me tonight, won't you?"

He leaned over the console, placed a kiss on her brow. "Absolutely."

Back in Anniston's hotel room, Garret recognized the shock hadn't yet worn off. He got the shower running and helped her peel out of her clothes. He made sure she was settled, gave her enough time under the hot spray to let her emotions play out before stripping off his clothes and joining her.

As the water sluiced over their bodies, he held her while her shoulders shook and the tears came again.

"I'm sorry. I don't seem to be able to stop."

"Shhh, it's okay. If only I could take the pain away, I would."

"You're doing great. You're here with me and that's what counts. This is how you've been feeling these past weeks, isn't it? I'm so sorry. I'm sorry if I've been anything but supportive to you and your family."

He framed her face in his hands. "Where's this coming from? You've been great. I think your grieving process is kicking in and doesn't know exactly which way to take you."

"I know. I'm having a hard time trying to balance the sadness with the anger I feel. If these assholes think they can kill a cop, a man that was my friend, I'm going to show them different."

"I'm counting on it." He nibbled gently at the corners of her trembling mouth, drew her into a slow, simmering kiss. "All I can do is try to make you feel better, take your mind off what you saw tonight."

He slathered fragrant soap along her tense shoulders, worked the foam down to her breasts. His hands massaged her knotted muscles.

She let out a moan as she began to relax and let her mind drift to other things. She took her turn, running her hands along his chest and down across his firm ass, enjoying the feel of each toned muscle.

Lathering each other became secondary.

His blood scorched with need. His teeth scraped over her breasts. On a sigh and a hurried clip of breath their bodies joined. With the scent of vanilla and jasmine hanging in the air, against a slippery shower wall, he pumped everything he had into the moment. And could only thank God when they dragged each other through the blinding light.

Chapter Sixteen

Garret had a rough night sleeping. He wouldn't admit it to Anniston, but he kept picturing Dack's vacant eyes and the way they'd stared back at him. It was the first dead body he'd ever seen up close. He hoped it would be his last. In death, Dack's face reminded him of what his sister and her children must've endured, how they must've looked inside that barrel. It was a disturbing thought that left him unable to think straight.

Anniston's eyes popped open to the unmistakable warmth of a male body nestling against hers. Last night he'd been there for her. When she'd needed to forget, he'd seen to it. He'd done things with his mouth that had made her unable to think. It was exactly what she'd needed.

When she realized he was already awake, she ran her hands along his chest, toyed with a few hairs. "Thank you."

Garret nuzzled her throat. "Now that's one way to start a morning. Grateful. What did I do?"

"You stayed with me and helped me get through the night."

"Let's see, I got sex out of the deal, multiple times. I showered with a beautiful woman, slept beside her. I'd say I'm the one who should be thankful." He fixed his mouth to hers and worked out a nice little hum of appreciation. "So how do you like your eggs? I'm starving."

"The kitchen downstairs makes a delicious eggs benedict. I'll take that."

As she made a mad dash to the bathroom, he picked up the phone on the nightstand, placed the order. "And could you send up some aspirin with that? Thanks."

He hung up, crawled out of bed and yanked on his pants. A drumming headache forced him to take a seat on the bed. He had to tell his family about the speeding minivan and the burglar alarm. It didn't seem to him that the madness would ever end.

When she came back into the bedroom, she dropped down beside him and took his hand in hers. "I just realized something. Death makes you face the fact that life is far too short. Dack didn't wake up this morning with Shonna, didn't get to make love last night like we did, didn't get to eat his supper or have a night to himself to relax."

Garret nodded, still feeling a bit dazed. "I keep thinking that of all the siblings, Livvy had it made. She seemed to be living the most normal life. Do you have any idea how difficult it is for me to learn the secrets she carried around? I always thought of her as the typical, busy soccer mom with two kids. Now it seems I discover her life was anything but normal or typical."

"It's hard to accept that these were regular people— Livvy, two little kids, Ryan, Dack—and now they aren't here anymore."

He put his arm around her. "I think we have to stop putting them up on a pedestal. Livvy, Walker, Dack, they were just people going about their everyday lives doing the best they could to get through it."

"Until they crossed paths with their killer. Yesterday I sent off the tissues that I took out of Dandridge's wastebasket to the lab. They should know something the first of next week. Hopefully, we'll get a hit in CODIS as to Dandridge's true identity."

"That's another thing about coming back here where I grew up. I used to think this place was the classic small town, a place where the likes of Jimmy Stewart would fit right in. Now, I have to accept that the town's obviously been hiding felons for years."

"Is anything really what it seems?" Anniston asked, as her cell phone chimed with a text message. "My brother's ETA is about fifteen minutes away."

Garret got to his feet. "Then I'll head on out and give you some time to get him up to speed. Why don't you bring him by the house later and we'll brainstorm about the next step."

"It sounds like you're leaving."

"I think it's best. Offer him my breakfast. I need to head home anyway and play catch up with my brothers. They'll need to know the blow-by-blow details from last night. And I have a lot of errands to take care of before the memorial service."

Sebastian Marcelli rolled into town in a pissed off mood. It wasn't every day he lost a friend like Dack. The two had gone to high school together, played sports together, had lost their virginity within weeks of each other.

A good cop had been executed, plain and simple.

Sebastian wanted to get his hands on the person responsible. He drove to the Mainsail Lodge in a Ford

Explorer similar to the one his sister owned. According to her, it'd be a waste of time to stop and have a chat with the chief of police. Anniston had emailed him the dossier on Sinclair. It was an ugly history she'd uncovered showing Sinclair's time spent with the highway patrol had been anything but heroic.

When he walked through the double doors to check in, he was surprised to see Anniston waiting for him in the lobby.

She took one look at the guy with the dark hair that matched hers—he still wore it cropped in a longer version of a police cut, but today he'd stuck a Marlins baseball cap on his head, and little tufts of wispy strands poked out. He'd turned the cap around, probably to look cool, she noted, as she threw her arms around her big brother's neck. "You're early. I'm guessing it's because of what happened to Dack."

He picked her up off the ground and whirled her around. "Good to see a welcoming committee. After you talked about this place I wasn't so sure what kind of reception I'd get."

"Most everyone's nice." She pointed to the cute redhead behind the front desk. "That's Molly Flax, she's a sweetheart. You'll find most of the locals friendly. But a few are downright..."

"Killers? I get that. After your phone call last night, I tried to sleep. I couldn't. So I got up at three this morning, threw my stuff in a suitcase and drove the six hours straight through from Daytona." He cocked his head to study his sister. "You look less stressed than I thought you would."

Anniston decided it was too soon to tell him about Garret. Instead, she led him to where Molly could check him in and waited around while he went through the process of handing over his credit card. "You did ask for a room near mine, right?"

Sebastian gave the attractive clerk the once over. "You'll have to ask this beautiful lady."

Anniston watched young Molly's face blush crimson. "You watch out for this Italian charmer, Molly. Promise me you won't go giving the likes of him your heart."

Molly's eyes twinkled with delight, enjoying the flirtatious attention. "I put you on the same floor down at the end of the hall. It's quieter."

"Appreciate it," Sebastian said. "Is everyone around here as pretty as you are?"

Molly blushed and handed over his cardkey. "If you need anything you let me know. I'm on until three."

Anniston shook her head and led him to the elevator. "What are you gonna do if Molly shows up outside your door wearing nothing but her raincoat?"

"Ah. That case in Pensacola really heated up after that."

She punched him in the arm. "No distractions. Breakfast is on its way up. I thought we could sit down over food and I'll tell you what I know."

"I talked to Dack's supervisor, Paul Briggs. He's as broken up about the murder as we are."

"That's odd because Dack mentioned his captain wasn't exactly supporting his efforts down here."

Sebastian sent her a strange look just as the elevator came to a stop on the third floor. "Paul left that part out."

When they reached her door, she slid her room key into the reader. "I bet he did. Your room is that way, end of the hall. But come on in, breakfast should be up any minute." After getting settled, she went into a catalog of the crime scene, trying to think of the smallest detail to share.

Because it was too early for the maid to come around and she hadn't taken the time to straighten up the bed, it was as messy as when she and Garret had crawled out of it. Sebastian seemed to take notice.

"You weren't alone last night." It wasn't a question. He cocked a brow, stared at his sister. "Not at the rest stop either. You took the client with you to meet with Dack? Why?"

"One of them. And he wanted to go."

His forehead creased into frown lines. "Are you having trouble with the case because you're already sidetracked with this particular client?"

"Sidetracked? I'm not."

"Are you certain? Because it's difficult to maintain focus when you're involved. You're sleeping with this guy, aren't you?"

"That's unfair. And don't start with me," Anniston tossed back. "You've been here five minutes and formed an opinion already. It's none of your business."

"It might be if you've been distracted. Maintaining a relationship takes all kinds of added energy and always takes away from the case. And this case might be one for the record books. Even Dad says so. Any time my partner doesn't keep her eye on the ball, it's cause for concern."

"Oh stuff it. If you're hinting I won't have your back because of Garret, that's ludicrous. You're completely off base. And I resent the implication. Try to start that crap with me and you can just head on back to Miami without bothering to unpack."

His lips curved up. "That's more like it. That's the fiery emotional heat I expect to see out of a Marcelli. Anything less and I start to worry. Do I need to have a brotherly talk with this treasure hunter?"

"What?" She laughed at that about the same time there was a knock on the door, indicating breakfast had finally shown up.

"You think I'm involved with Mitch Indigo?" She shook her head and threw the notepad off the nightstand at his head and watched it bounce off his chest. "Wrong brother. It's the hot surfer I'm interested in."

The waiter set up the food near the sliding glass door with a view of the white caps churning in the Atlantic surf.

Sebastian stared out at the scenic picture it made. "This seems like such a cute little town. It's hard to imagine all the things you've been telling me about it are true."

Starving, she sat down and started to dig into her eggs. "Wow, do I need to catch you up to speed!"

Chapter Seventeen

Garret spent the rest of the morning with his brothers filling his parents' house with music. Mitch sat at the piano, Jackson took up his guitar, and Garret tapped his snare as they rehearsed what they recalled were Livvy's favorite songs.

The first note, the first chorus, were definitely forced and rough. But as they stayed with it, the harmony began to flow from the heart.

In order for them to play at the memorial service, they pretty much had to put the grief they felt on display for everyone to see. Sharing their sorrow and sadness wasn't easy for any of them to do.

But to create the versions they liked best, the ones that came from deep down in the soul, took a certain amount of mettle out of each brother. Working to achieve the right melody, the right tone, gave them an opportunity to keep their minds occupied and off the subject of murder.

But it also created friction.

As band mates tend to do during the creative process, they squabbled about notes and refrains and which one kept coming in late on the beat.

Frustrated, Garret tossed his drumsticks in the air and headed into the kitchen to get a bottle of water. That's when the wall phone rang. That's how he ended up being the one to take the call instead of his mother.

Daniel Shugart had been the owner and operator of Shugart's Funeral Home for as long as Garret could remember. Daniel had taken over the job from his father who had been the town's only mortician for more than fifty years.

Daniel's voice was somber and professional. "I thought you might like to know that I just got all four bodies down here from the county coroner's office. They released them to me this morning."

"Okay. So, what happens next? What do we need to do?"

"I'll take care of getting them ready for burial. But you should tell your parents they need to start thinking about picking out caskets by tomorrow."

Garret felt a lump form in his throat. "Got it. I'll pass the info along."

The call had been brief but devastating. He turned to see his dad hanging on every word. The man looked as though he'd aged ten years in the last ten minutes.

"I guess that's it then," Tanner told Lenore.

"It's hard to believe I'll never see my daughter again or have Friday night sleepovers with Blake and Ally." Lenore's eyes went moist as her fingers worked her knitting needles. "I want to finish this sweater top for Ally. She picked out the mint green color herself. I thought maybe we could bury her in it along with that little plaid skirt she loved so much."

"One of us should probably call Royce," Jackson suggested. He cut his eyes to his dad. "Not you. Okay. Me. I'll make sure he knows about the service on Monday."

"Why bother with Royce?" Mitch snarled. "Do you see him anywhere around here concerned about any of us?"

"It's a courtesy," Jackson began. "We didn't get along with him when Livvy was alive. She knew that. The least we can do is try to maintain some kind of civility while we bury her and the kids."

The atmosphere was tense as they continued to practice for a little while longer. But they were never able to achieve the same pace or harmony as before the phone call.

When they agreed to end the session, Garret caught Jackson's attention, then Mitch's. He bobbed his head toward the backdoor indicating he wanted them to follow him to the backyard. Each man grabbed a beer out of the fridge and wandered outside.

Once they'd gone far enough away from the house for privacy, Garret told them about the burglar alarm going off at the Vitamin Hut, about the car that looked like Baskin's spotted nearby, and the Alton Rennie incident near Port Charlotte.

"The picture Dack showed me of the man driving the minivan could've been Boone's twin. I think someone stole Rennie's driver's license at the track because he looked similar to Boone, enough that the cop didn't question it. I'm convinced the driver outside Port Charlotte was Boone heading to the airport to ditch the van."

"It's looking more and more like Baskin and Dandridge are the killers."

"Yeah, well, Dack said it wasn't enough evidence to prove either man had anything to do with the murders. So we need to find the proof ourselves. They're also probably the ones who shot Dack."

Mitch rubbed the stubble on his chin. "There's just one problem with your theory. Last night I was watching Dandridge. I know he left church at five-thirty and went straight to his house. He never left unless he managed to slip out the back. We haven't been covering the back. I must've missed seeing him sneak out. Which means I have terrible surveillance skills. As soon as I learned about Dack's murder, I checked with Walsh. He says Baskin never left the auto repair shop until around nine-thirty."

Jackson took a slug of his beer. "That's really late to stay and work at a garage. Most people expect to have their cars in there for repair overnight or even several days. The problem is how do we prove either man slipped out the back without you or Walsh knowing about it?"

Mitch finally folded himself into one of the lawn chairs, stretched out his legs. "As far as I'm concerned that's exactly what they did. The failure in surveillance comes if you don't cover all your bases. That's on me. I thought I could handle it by myself. Maybe Dandridge spotted me days ago and ditched me to go out with Baskin. We need to do a better job."

"Anniston will be bringing her brother over later. She says he'll help us out. Maybe one more person means we can split up into pairs. There's something else, though. Last night's scene at the rest stop makes me realize it's time we arm ourselves. I was out there in pitch dark with Anniston, unable to defend her or myself—not that she isn't fully capable of protecting anyone, anytime. But she had a gun and I didn't. It was an ideal situation where I could've used my own weapon. It was an eerie feeling. And that was before I saw Dack lying on the ground dead."

"I'm all for arming ourselves," Jackson chimed in before taking another swig of his beer. "In fact, it's overdue."

"Good, because I already called Michael Tang this morning and made arrangements for us to go by his store and check out his inventory. You know he has a gun range next door."

"I don't need weapons," Mitch told them. "I have an arsenal on the boat."

"Those are for you and your crew," Garret pointed out. "Jackson and I need to pick out our own anyway. Something else to consider in all this, if we don't turn this thing around and fast, I'm not sure who we should trust now in law enforcement. Dack was our in because Anniston had a history with him. Now he's gone. Without him, I don't see anyone on the horizon we can talk to."

"I was thinking the same thing. Sinclair isn't even worth bothering with," Mitch said in agreement.

Garret had one more thing on his mind. "I think we should try to talk Dad into taking Mom out of town after the funeral. Make sure they don't come back here until this thing is over."

"Do you think he'd do that?" Jackson asked.

"If we handle it right. Maybe."

"It won't hurt to put it on the table, especially if we let them know how things are heating up."

Michael Tang had excelled in the same class as Mitch in school. Where Mitch had languished near the bottom, Michael had graduated valedictorian. He'd become a savvy entrepreneur who owned several businesses in town. One of those enterprises sold hunting and fishing gear along with guns.

Garret studied the pistols under the glass case. He didn't see what he was after. "What about a SIG-made P210? You sold any of those lately?"

"Too pricey for most folks around here. I can order it for you, but it'll take at least a week plus the three-day waiting period."

"Do you carry any SIGs at all?"

Michael reached behind him and unlocked a cabinet. "Oh sure. I carry any number of SIG Sauers, mostly P230s and 238s."

"I'll take one of those."

Michael pushed paperwork toward the men. "Three days. Plus, you guys need to take some time at the gun range, go through a safety course."

"I'll teach them everything they need to know," Mitch offered.

Garret bumped Mitch's shoulder. "I never thought I'd throw down a thousand dollars on a gun. It feels like I'm living in a parallel universe."

"For that kind of money I damn sure want to know how to use it," Jackson tossed back. "You ever shot anybody?" he asked Mitch.

"Nope. Never had to. Certainly never thought it would rear its ugly head in the place where I grew up. Maybe on some of my expeditions around Somalia, it got close. But it never reached that point."

"Look at us, carrying guns in our own home port," Garret noted. "Things have really changed."

For their first meeting with Sebastian, Lenore spent the morning over a hot stove, frying up plenty of chicken. Garret commandeered one of the burners to boil his pasta for the macaroni and cheese casserole he planned to make. He counted on Mitch creating the gooey, cheesy sauce from scratch that held it all together.

Mitch had to share space at the kitchen counter with Jackson and Tessa, who tackled the job of peeling a bag of potatoes for potato salad. Tanner agreed to make the beer run.

By mid-afternoon they served up the feast in the backyard picnic-style. When Anniston walked in with her brother, she made sure he remembered faces and names.

"It's a lot to remember," Tessa said, patting Sebastian on the arm. "My first time here I was flat-out overwhelmed."

"The Indigos are like that," Raine added. "But they're good, decent, hardworking people."

Sebastian's first impression of the Indigos was that of a typical American family, down to earth and welcoming. But it wasn't in his nature to be shy, too many years spent as a nosy cop. Even though Anniston had given him a clear heads up, he still had a lot of questions.

Sebastian couldn't shake one important fact. Dack's presence here among these very people had contributed to putting him in danger. This case had cost Dack his life.

Garret shoved a beer toward Anniston's brother. "Thanks for coming. We could use all the help we can get."

"I wish I'd been able to break away sooner and be here to help Anniston more."

"She's done a great job. It's just that this is a lot for one person. I think Dack would've agreed. That last morning he met with us, you could tell he was stressing out. He seemed to have a lot on his plate." Garret drank generously from his own bottle of brew. "Dack had planned to give us Walker's emails."

"Dack was at that rest stop to share evidence with me. Someone must've known that. Dack must've been close to something important—something that implicated Baskin and Dandridge. I should've searched the car for a flash drive before the EMTs got there. I didn't, but the killers probably did and beat us to it," Anniston said, resting her head in her hands. "I'd planned to use that info to see if Walker contacted Dietrich. Twenty-four hours later do we even know who's picking up the investigation?"

"Already asked Briggs that very question. This morning he hadn't even assigned anyone the case," Sebastian complained. "So there's no one yet to bug."

Garret decided it was time to level with his parents. He told them about Baskin's car seen near the Vitamin Hut that Wednesday night and that a Dandridge lookalike might've dumped the minivan in Tampa. "And Dack uncovered the fact that Dandridge couldn't be Roland Wainwright from Oregon. The height doesn't match up. We don't know who Dandridge really is, only that he came to Indigo Key twenty-some odd years ago. Before that, Anniston can't find anything on him."

Tanner pushed his plate of chicken away, uneaten. "Goes to show how you never really know anyone. Trust. That's a big word. Your mother and I trusted Dandridge, not just as a man, but also as a pastor. And so did Livvy and Walker." He wiped away a tear. "That's what hurts the most."

Lenore circled her arms around his shoulders. "The day he stood in the living room and said all those things about Livvy taking off, that was it for me. I knew something was wrong. Dandridge—or whatever his name is—has to be involved. The question is why would he harm an entire family, members of his own congregation?"

Seeing the emotion firsthand, Sebastian's heart went out to the family. "We'll find out. Anniston wants me to go over every surveillance camera in town. That's a tall order but it's something I'm willing to tackle. I'll beg the business owners if I have to. We also agree that finding this Hugo Reiner guy is essential. If the treasure hunting scheme was what started all this, then Hugo has to be the key link straight to Dietrich."

Anniston let out a deep sigh. "So you see, there's still a great deal to do."

"My brothers and I want to help you find Hugo. We suspect he's hiding somewhere along the coast. It's where he's known to hang out. We've even talked about starting in Key West, but right now keeping an eye on Dandridge and Baskin has to be the priority," Garret explained.

"What if we could do that using a remote security camera for surveillance?" Sebastian offered.

Mitch chewed his lip. "I don't think that would work. What if they go after someone else like they did Dack? What if they decide to go after Jackson and Tessa in Nana's cottage? Or what if they go after Mom and Dad in the middle of the day when we're busy doing something else? We'd find out about it too late to save them just like Dack."

"So we all agree that those two had something to do with Dack's death?" Anniston asked, looking at Garret.

"As far as we're concerned, they're responsible for obliterating an entire family, shooting Ryan, and killing a cop. We have to be willing to put them under watch twenty-four-seven."

"Your mother and I are up to watching Boone," Tanner added.

"That means we all have to take a shift," Raine decided. "I'll take 6 to 2 a.m."

"You can't do that. You have the restaurant to run," Mitch reminded her. "It isn't practical for you to work all day and then spend eight hours on a stakeout."

Tessa got up to get herself more lemonade. "Not only that, it's dangerous if we don't work in pairs. If we think these men are coldblooded killers, it means any one of us could end up in a precarious situation we're unable to handle alone."

"That's why you need to take a turn at the gun range," Jackson stated.

"I'm not opposed to that, especially when you consider that either of these men could've been the one to fire the rifle at us out at the preserve in broad daylight. They could've gone out in the early evening hours to kill Dack. These aren't bogeymen who wait until the midnight hour to strike. We have to be prepared for anything at any hour of the day or night."

"Good point. Are we in over our heads yet?" Raine asked in jest. "The only weapon I have is the one Danny used in the army, an M9. I've never even fired the thing before, not sure I want to."

Mitch bobbed his head toward his brothers. "When we make the trip to the gun range, bring Danny's handgun and I'll show you how to use it."

"Thanks for that," Raine returned. "But there's an issue no one's talking about. What do we do when we find out Dandridge and Baskin *are* the ones responsible? We can't exactly call up Sinclair to help make an arrest."

"That's why it's vital to keep the door open with the state police," Sebastian said. "If not, we're pretty much screwed."

Garret looked up from his plate about the same time a tall, gorgeous, model-thin woman came through the back gate. His jaw dropped when he realized it was Dominka Karetnikov. The woman had graced the covers of *Sports Illustrated* in little more than a bikini and the pages of Victoria's Secret wearing skimpy lingerie. She wasn't wearing much more than that now—a mini skirt that showed off her ass and a short-cropped top that barely covered her boobs.

Dominka waved to Garret and spoke in a heavy Russian accent. "I rang doorbell. No one answered. I heard voices back here so I come back here. Hi! I find you! Finally."

Garret stood up and went over to the beautiful blonde. "Dominka, what are you doing here? I thought you were in Belize on a photo shoot."

"No. You get it wrong…again. Barbados. I was in Barbados. I hear others talking about your sadness, your sister, your niece and nephew, your brother-in-law, all gone. I had to come see you for comfort."

"That's really sweet." And who knew she was so unselfish, Garret decided. When he found all eyes staring at him, he cleared his throat. "Uh, everyone, I'd like you to meet a friend of mine. She's originally from a tiny town in Russia. Dominka, this is my mom and dad."

He proceeded around the table until he got to Anniston. Her dark eyes narrowed down to steel traps. They kind of scared him.

"I'm from Vorkuta," Dominka corrected.

"How do you know Garret?" Anniston asked through clenched teeth.

"We go to Tahiti where he gets medal for surfing."

Anniston's eyes tapered into furious slits aimed at Garret. The expression on her face was cold and distant. "I thought you flew here from Queensland."

"I did. This…" He waved his hand between himself and the model. "Me. Dominka. Was a long time ago. Tell her, Dominka. We haven't been together in…months."

"Ah. Yes, long time ago. Last summer. I come here to comfort."

Tanner rolled his eyes and elbowed Mitch in the ribs. He leaned over, whispered, "Let's see how he gets out of this one."

Mitch in turn snickered and said, "Five bucks says he grovels."

"You're on."

Jackson cut his eyes toward the two of them, held up a hand indicating he was in for five, as well. He angled toward his mom and discovered Lenore was doing her best to stifle a laugh.

Instead of laughter, his mother went with manners. "Well, why don't you sit down and eat something? You must be tired after such a long trip from Barbados."

Dominka stared at the food on the table, her eyes growing wide at all the carbs. Horrified at the idea of putting anything like that in her body, she shook her head at the Southern-style spread. In broken English, the model explained, "No chicken. I eat green salad. Only."

"The only salad we have here is potato salad," Jackson revealed. "Made it myself."

Dominka puffed air in her cheeks. "Potatoes make me too fat."

Ignoring her declaration, Tanner dished up the pasta casserole onto a plate, handed it toward the too-thin woman. "We call this comfort food. Take a bite. Mitch and Garret put a lot of hard work into it. I supervised."

Once again, Dominka stared down at the macaroni and shook her head. "No…cheese makes me fat."

During Tanner's pitch, Anniston got up to leave. "If you'll excuse me, Sebastian and I need to get back to work."

Garret blocked her path. "No, you don't. Let me explain. This is a completely innocent thing. I had no idea Dominka would come to Florida. Ever."

"I think it's a good thing she showed up. It tells me a lot about you as a person."

That boosted his temper into overdrive. "What does it tell you exactly? That I have a friend who cares enough to come all this way to see if I'm okay after a death in the family? That I've had girlfriends before? That's a given. I'm twenty-eight years old. I haven't lived a life of celibacy since I was fifteen."

Out of desperation, Garret turned back toward Mitch. "Tell her this is completely harmless."

Mitch smiled and repeated the mantra, "It's completely harmless."

Garret rolled his eyes and went with desperation. He grabbed Sebastian by the arm and dragged him toward Dominka. "Meet the lovely Dominka Karetnikov who graced last February's cover of the swimsuit edition. Dominka, this is Sebastian. He's a real fan of yours. He went on and on about you not two days ago."

Dominka looked confused. "I come at bad time. I took taxi. I go back to hotel now."

"Which hotel?" Sebastian asked quickly.

"Uh. Lodging in blue and yellow building near water."

Sebastian's lips curved up into a grin. "That's my hotel. I'm happy to take you back there."

Dominka sent him her most charming smile and put an arm through his. "That would be good. We order salad, yes?"

Mitch slapped his brother on the back. "Way to think on your feet. For a minute there I thought you'd drowned in the middle of losing the war."

Garret grinned and turned back to Anniston, spread his palms out face up. "See. Problem solved. Dominka doesn't care anything about me other than as a friend. She was simply trying to do a nice thing and show up for emotional support."

Anniston made a face and put her hands on her hips. "You call solving the problem foisting your girlfriend off on my brother?"

"*Former* girlfriend. You were about to leave." He lifted a shoulder. "I choked."

"More like groveled," Mitch pointed out. To his dad and brother, he added, "Pony up the ten bucks, guys."

But Anniston wasn't so easy to placate. She punched him in the arm.

"Ow! What'd you do that for?"

"Principle."

Lenore had held her amusement in check long enough. When she started hooting with laughter, everyone else followed suit.

Raine put down her fork. "You know who would've found this scene hilarious? Livvy."

"Oh, she definitely would have," Lenore agreed. "Then she'd have taken Garret into the house and read him the riot act."

Garret felt he had to defend himself. "What did I do wrong exactly? I'm sitting here eating lunch, minding my own business. I didn't ask Dominka to jump on a plane and come to Florida."

"What kind of person doesn't eat potato salad?" Tessa wanted to know as she scooped up a second helping.

"That's what I was thinking," Raine noted as she dug into the pasta. "And who wouldn't want to try Mitch's casserole?"

Mitch gave her a wide smile. "I do make good macaroni and cheese. It's the real cream and cheddar that sets it apart from everyone else's."

"If you ever give up salvaging, there's a job for you in the kitchen at the restaurant," Raine added. "I'll put the Indigo specialty on the menu."

Mitch leaned back in his chair, took a swig of beer. "Go ahead. You have my permission to use my recipe. I should post it on my blog."

Garret took exception to that. "Now wait just a minute. Your recipe? I'm the one who came up with how long it needed to bake and at what temperature in order to come out of the oven with the perfect crispy crust."

Despite her previous anger and jealousy, no one enjoyed the banter more than Anniston. She realized then that she fit in with these people, maybe even this man. Like Tessa and Raine had done, she went back for seconds of everything and sat down with her plate, more content than before. "Everyone should eat up. We have stakeouts to plan."

Chapter Eighteen

Like most everything else, the surveillances over the next three nights turned out to be a team effort. Lenore and Tanner stuck to Boone during the day. Tanner stationed himself out front in a discreet spot, while Lenore covered the back alleyway. Jackson and Tessa took over at night when they did the same at the pastor's personal residence down the street from the church.

Mitch and Walsh covered Baskin during daylight hours, watching him at his repair shop, and at the back near the body shop.

That meant Garret and Sebastian kept track of the man's whereabouts at night. They would always end up at the same place, the sprawling Buchanan estate where Sebastian watched the front gate, while Garret kept his eyes glued to the guest cottage and its back entrance.

Anniston and Raine were left to do most of the legwork on their own.

It made for long grueling hours and short tempers all around. When things got too tense, they switched up the pairing.

Added to all their other activities, Raine and Tessa spent the weekend putting the finishing touches on the memorial service. They'd put their heads together to come up with a simple, low-key service Tanner and Lenore could be proud of.

The brothers rehearsed over and over again in between their shifts until they were happy with the songs.

So when Monday morning arrived they were all grateful the day started out warm and muggy with blue skies overhead.

With help from Jackson, Mitch, and Garret, the women arranged the stage, put up portraits of the family, and lined up friends and family to speak.

Having just gone through this with her brother, listening to the grief of friends was almost too much of a reminder for Tessa. But she stood spine straight next to Jackson and handed out the little keepsake booklets they'd printed up. Each had a bio of what Livvy and Walker and Ally and Blake had cared about in life. Raine had added some of the artwork from the kids, pictures Blake had drawn of the sea, of dolphins, of fish. Ally's love of horses was evident in her drawings. It also seemed she adored mermaids and turtles.

By nine-thirty, the park started overflowing with people who'd known the family the longest. The media showed up with their cameras from as far away as Pensacola. Noticeably absent were people like Boone Dandridge and anyone from the mayor's office. But no one seemed to miss them or care if they were no-shows.

Anniston had put on a black skirt and jacket with a white shirt for security detail. Her brother had worn similar attire—what she called his "Secret Service" suit. In the glaring sun, brother and sister had slipped on polarized wraparound sunglasses. With weapons strapped to their bodies, they were prepared for anything. They maneuvered through the crowd looking for anyone who might have an agenda.

The processional began when the nineteen-year-old twins Quentin and Joss Kade took the stage. Despite the dozens of magazine articles written about them starting at the age of six, the kids with Seminole roots were as down to earth as they come. Most locals referred to the siblings as prodigies. When it came to instruments, the pair played a variety—violin, cello, and the flute. Plus, they could tickle out the tender strains of Chopin on the keys of a Steinway.

Quentin showed his skill by picking up his maple violin and matching the soulful strings of his sister's cello. With their long black hair trailing down their backs and dressed in their Sunday best, Quentin and Joss switched to flutes, teasing out the Native American tunes they'd learned as children. The lilting melody flowed from the woodwinds, an original song Joss had written just for Blake and Ally. The tribute hung in the air in a timeless serenity, a reminder that life is precious.

Later, it would be Mitch at the piano, Jackson on guitar, and Garret on drums as they played a string of Livvy's favorite songs.

Halfway through a refrain, Jackson made the mistake of looking down from the stage at his parents. There was such sadness in their eyes, he didn't think it would ever dissipate. From that point on, he had trouble getting through the lyrics without tears rolling down his face.

When it was time for Tanner to speak he took the stage with slumped shoulders, heart breaking, and tears already forming.

"No father ever wants to stand where I stand today. No father should ever have to bury a child. I come here today with the daunting task of having to say goodbye to my only grandchildren. Many times, they'd beg me to bring them to this very park. I always relented. I'm glad I did. I used to do the same with their mother. Livvy grew up down the street. She roamed this park as if it were her own personal playground. I remember pushing her on those swings right after the city first installed them. Her mother and I were sure she'd be safe here where she grew up. We thought that same safety and security extended to Blake and Ally. It didn't. And here we are. I could tell you Livvy was a great mother, but you'd just think I was biased. The truth is Livvy was a wonderful human being. She was kind and loved helping people."

As Tanner went on, Tessa stood to the side, moved by the man's homage to his daughter and grandchildren. She turned to Raine and whispered, "I've never been to anything like this before, where the loss included kids."

Raine said nothing as the melodic flutes brought out memories of another time and place. It wasn't Danny's funeral that came to mind, not today. Emotion bubbled up inside her and she swallowed it back.

As if Tessa understood that she was thinking about her brother, she squeezed Raine's hand. "I tried to push out thoughts of Ryan to get through this. I know these past few days have been hard. You've had to do the same with Danny. It hurts to revisit all that pain."

Raine decided Tessa deserved a hug for that. She put her arms around her. "You know, you're the first person I've met in a really long time who totally understands that about me. For years, my mother was a basket case after losing her son. To some degree she still is. I get through the hurt by working practically night and day at the restaurant."

"I've seen you do that. Don't ever feel like you have to hide your feelings from me. You aren't mad at me for moving out, are you?"

Raine sent her an understanding little grin. "It was certainly the shortest roommate agreement on record. But I would've done the same thing. How do you like living in Nana's cottage?"

"It's such a homey place. I'm going to do my best to keep up her garden."

"That's the one regret I have about living on the houseboat. No dirt around to plant a seed. I make do with containers."

"That's what I did back in Nags Head." Tessa suddenly put her hand over her mouth as she realized Jackson was having a tough time singing the words. "Look at him up there, I feel so bad for what he's going through. He was so upset last night he couldn't sleep a wink. And look at him now, he can't even get through the song."

"You two are so cute together."

Tessa beamed back at that. "We are. Imagine finding him during the worst time of my life. Jackson's made this so much more bearable for me. Do you think you'll ever give Mitch a second chance?"

Raine let out a huge sigh. She glanced up on stage at the man in question sitting at the piano—and found him staring back at her. "I'll tell you something about my friendship with Livvy that most people don't know. And it says a lot about what kind of person she was. She knew the reason I was so angry with her brother. And yet, all this time she kept my secret. She never once tried to interfere or play peacemaker or matchmaker. Livvy just let the history between Mitch and me…be…without judgment or prejudice or trying to mend fences."

"Is that a polite way of telling me to butt out?"

Raine smiled. "Haven't you heard? No one can rewrite history. What I'm saying is that there's no point in trying to get us together. What's done is done." Uncomfortable with the topic, she changed the subject to something much lighter. "What do you think of Anniston's brother?"

"What's not to like? I'm on record as wanting more hunky Italians coming to town."

Raine stifled a laugh. "That isn't fair. You don't get to have more than one hunk."

"Says who?" She bumped Raine's shoulder. "Truth is I'm good with the one I have. I couldn't believe Garret got out of that thing with Dominka. I could see him sinking into quicksand right before my very eyes. It was painful to watch. I wanted to throw him a rope but…"

"That boy always was clever. Even when he was twelve, he could think on his feet."

Lenore made her way over to where the women stood and took the time to admire the sea of faces in the crowd. "Look at this turnout. You have no idea how wonderful this is, so much better than holding it inside Life Stone. I can't thank you enough for all your hard work."

Tessa gave her a hug. "How are you two holding up?"

"Tanner and I are doing okay. The tough part will be the final goodbye tomorrow at the cemetery." She turned to Raine, who had agreed to hold the wake at The Blue Taco immediately after the service today. "Are you all set at the restaurant? Is there anything I can do?"

"Nope. All set. As we speak, my assistant manager Charlotte is putting the finishing touches on the food. Don't worry. It'll go off without a hitch."

"Oh, honey, I'm not one bit worried. You and Tessa have been lifesavers through all this. I'm not sure what Tanner and I would've done without both of you pitching in every day with ideas and suggestions, things I never would've thought of, like the little handouts. I'm forever grateful."

"That's what we like to hear," Raine said. "In fact, I think I'll run over there now and check on everything."

Raine needn't have worried. When she walked in, her assistant manager had the eatery all ready to go, the food all set out. The place looked like it could handle the crowd.

Charlotte Townsend had been like the sister Raine had never had. During the four years since she'd taken over running the restaurant, the perky brunette had been crucial to its success.

"They'll be coming this way within ten minutes or so," Raine noted, looking around at Charlotte. "You did a marvelous job. Thank you."

"I didn't mind even though it was a lot of extra work. In fact, maybe we should add catering in the near future. Who knows? It might take off."

"I don't know how we'd work that in. We'd have to hire more hands for sure."

"We could do it."

Raine smiled. "You're always encouraging me to think big. Trouble is," she threw her arms out wide. "This is about all I can handle. I'd need ten of you to keep up."

Charlotte hugged the woman she thought of as a sister. "Oh look, they're starting to drift this way. How was the memorial service?"

"Big crowd," Raine said, drifting toward the front window. She wasn't surprised when Mitch was the first one through the door.

He bent to kiss her cheek. "My mother is grateful you're providing such a unique venue like this where people can relive stories about the family."

She patted his arm. "Don't be silly. I'm happy to do it." Raine turned her attention to the others who streamed through the door behind him. Greeting each one personally, she took her role as hostess seriously, pointing them toward the buffet-style food set up on two tables.

As soon as Garret walked in, he repeated what Mitch had done and pressed his lips to her cheek. "Thank you for this. You're an angel."

She patted his face. "You're welcome. And I'm glad I could help. Anniston came in a few minutes ago. She didn't look happy."

That prompted Garret to go looking for her. He found Anniston sitting on the patio among the honeysuckle and orange blossoms. Her eyes were distant. She seemed preoccupied. It wasn't like her to look so glum. "What's wrong?"

"I just got an email from the man who does the voice analysis. He hasn't completed his evaluations yet, but I asked for a preliminary report. In his professional opinion, all four men were lying the day you guys went face to face.”

“He said that?”

“Pretty much.”

“You can’t be that shocked.”

“Shocked? No. But I am disappointed. I thought maybe he could zero in on *one* man. One, Garret. I certainly didn’t expect him to tell me that he recognized stress in all four, enough that the point system he uses was pretty much off the chart. He looks for changes in their voice pattern and it was enough to indicate their word, their statements, are all useless.”

“Not necessarily. Men with nothing to hide, tell the truth. Obviously, these men didn’t. We know the mob enforcer probably hasn’t changed his ways, even though here in town he’s looked up to as a successful businessman. The lying politician still lies, in debt up to his ass, taking political contributions right and left that he deposits directly into his personal bank account. And a preacher—my parents trusted implicitly—has a history that only started twenty years ago. Your guy verified they’re all deceitful liars.”

“That’s one way to make me feel better.”

“The interviews weren’t a waste of time if that’s what you’re worried about.”

“I was.” She tilted her head up to his. “How is it you’re always able to boost my confidence?”

“Because I’m taken with how hot you look in that suit.”

She put her hand up to her mouth to stifle a laugh. She gave him a little shove with the other. “Go mingle. Your family needs you in there today.”

Over Garret’s shoulder she spotted Royce, sitting by himself. “Besides, in my mood I’m ready to piss someone off. I see a good prospect.” She nodded her head toward the old man.

“Ah. Be good now,” Garret said, kissing her hand before working his way back inside.

Anniston decided it was as good a time as any to rattle Royce's cage. She detoured through a side door into the kitchen where she picked up a pitcher of lemonade off the table and a bottle of whiskey from the counter.

She headed back toward Royce with one purpose in mind. It didn't hurt to approach the wealthiest man in the county with a little honey instead of a vat of vinegar. "How are you holding up?"

"Many more days like today and I'll be joining Carla, Winnie, and Walker in the family crypt. They've left me alone, an old man with his memories of better times."

"I'm truly sorry." She held up both the pitcher and the bottle. "I noticed from across the room you looked thirsty. Refill? Your choice."

"On a day like this, I'll take the whiskey, even though Doc Whitten will probably have my head for it."

"He won't find out from me."

Royce chuckled. "That's one reason I like you."

"Glad to hear it." The man was also perceptive, she decided as she watched his eyes glow with a twinkle.

"What do you want to know?"

"Ah, I like a man who's insightful. How'd you know I came over here with questions on my mind?"

"Why else? A pretty thing like you wouldn't waste ten minutes on an old coot like me if you didn't want a bit of information."

"Okay, I'll get right to it then. Have you ever heard of a woman by the name of Darla Pendleton? To jumpstart your memory, she was the sister of Braden Pendleton. She disappeared in 1992 from right here on the island."

"I wouldn't say I knew her. But I am the one who brought her to town. She was supposed to interview for the job as my assistant."

It sounded so innocent, thought Anniston. But she wasn't in the mood to buy a bunch of lies today. "What happened?"

"I interviewed her in my conference room, spent about an hour with her and she went on her way."

"That's it? She wasn't your mistress?"

He choked on his whiskey. "No. I barely knew the woman. If you're interested in getting to the truth of what happened to her after she left my office, you might want to ask Jessup Sinclair. I always thought he had something to do with the woman's disappearance."

"Well that certainly came out of the blue. Why would you think that?"

"From my office window I saw him leaning on her car, a blue sedan waiting for her in the parking lot. And it was Sinclair's first year here. It's the same year he was elected police chief. He had a dark history when he was with the highway patrol. You don't believe me, check it out for yourself."

"I'll do that." She already knew about it, of course, but decided it would be much better to keep Royce talking. She took a seat next to him. "Why do I like you so much?"

"Because I'm not the monster Tanner Indigo has made me out to be."

She wanted him to prove it. She chewed her lip and realized she'd have to find a way. In the meantime, Anniston listened to Royce as he went on about Walker. To her, he sounded like a typical father who greatly missed his only son.

"You aren't upset the Indigos are burying Livvy and her babies in their family plot, are you?" Anniston asked.

"As long as they let me have my boy to put alongside his mother and sister, I don't care what they do."

Chapter Nineteen

It was around two o'clock when The Blue Taco cleared out and Raine ushered the last of the guests out the door. She flipped the lock to keep the public at bay for a little while. That left behind the small group of Indigos to meet with Anniston and Sebastian. Even Dominka stayed.

When Sebastian cornered Garret near the restrooms, he leaned over to whisper, "You aren't upset that I brought Dominka, are you?"

Garret gave him a half smile. "Not really. Unless you think she's becoming a nuisance. Because I already told you when we were on stakeout, I'll talk to her about leaving if you want her gone."

"She's more of a distraction for me than anything else."

"I don't like the sound of that. Your focus should be on the case."

"I didn't mean that. Did you know she started out in a coal-mining town near the Arctic Circle? She has a great sense of humor, although she barely eats. I'm from an Italian family that loathes the idea of turning down pasta or pizza. She turns her nose up at both."

Garret slapped him on the back. "I doubt that'll change. But I know she eats eggs and avocado. Get her to eat one of Raine's avocado sandwiches over there on the table. I bet you five dollars she stuffs her face with the veggie lover's dream."

"You're on," Sebastian said, elbowing him in the ribs. "Anniston's ready to start the meeting. We have an announcement to make."

Sebastian strolled over to the dining room and picked up an empty glass, clinked it to get everyone's attention. "My sister and I talked this over and came to a decision last night. From this day moving forward, we won't take another dime of your money."

"Please tell me you aren't resigning," Garret said, cutting a look at Anniston.

She slid her arm through his. "Not at all. We're working toward a common goal. Sebastian and I grew up with Dack. Our families are very close, always have been. We now have a personal stake in catching the people responsible for all these murders. So, we've decided to work this case for free. Sebastian's already uncovered an important aspect of what happened the night Dack was killed. It involves Baskin."

Sebastian had been waiting for this all day. He took out his laptop and flipped it open. "Anniston mentioned that you guys weren't quite sure if Roger Baskin could've slipped past the man you had watching him. The answer to that is yes. Baskin's auto garage shares a building with the body shop he owns around the corner. I found a surveillance camera on another commercial building across the alleyway. The owner of that business is Royce Buchanan. He gave me permission to go through the video."

He hit a few keystrokes and brought up a grainy image. "This is Thursday night at 6:10 p.m. See the time stamp. It clearly shows Baskin leaving out the backdoor of the repair shop and going the thirty feet or so through the backdoor of the body shop. He gets into a gray Chevy Malibu that was probably in for body work and drives off."

"So Baskin knew he was being watched. He had access to another vehicle and didn't hesitate to take advantage of it," Mitch said, not surprised. "Walsh had Baskin covered during the day. I was on Dandridge. But neither one of us considered the possibility the men would evade by sneaking out the back. That's on me again, my mistake."

Sebastian zoomed in on the frame. "Dandridge lives about a block from the church. His house sits looking south toward the marina. We know he didn't leave out the front. So the nearest camera to the back is affixed to the roof of the florist shop, right about here. I found video from that angle that shows Boone walking down the alleyway eight minutes later, at six eighteen. A gray Chevy pulls up at the end of the block and Boone hops into the car."

"But all that really proves is they didn't stay put," Garret growled.

Sebastian nodded. "Unfortunately that's true. If we could get video near the rest stop that would be the nail in their coffins."

Garret dug his hands into the pants pockets of his suit and roamed between the tables. "I don't want to step on any toes here, or make anyone mad, but I'm beginning to think our time would be better spent looking for the old sailor."

"Why?" Tanner roared. "Why not stay on Baskin and Dandridge?"

Garret didn't back down. "Because we're already convinced they're responsible. It'd be nice to build a case against them. Hugo might be able to help us by filling in some blanks. We have to try."

Mitch folded his arms across his chest. "At the risk of making a wrong step here, I didn't want to say anything, either. But I think the stakeouts are a waste of time. I think both men know we've been watching them. For the past three nights, they'd go to work, go back home and act like choirboys in between. We're getting nowhere."

"I'm not too keen on spending the next week sitting in a car all night. I agree we need to watch Boone and Baskin. But how do you catch them doing anything if they know we're sitting down the street? Maybe it's time we shift our focus. There has to be a better way to keep track of those bastards," Jackson suggested.

"There is," Sebastian offered. "As I suggested before, we install our own set of cameras. Strategically placed, they'd do our work for us. I'd do the monitoring."

Mitch lifted a shoulder. "Let's do it."

Garret angled to look at his dad. "There's something else we need to talk about. And we don't want you to blow a gasket at the suggestion. We think you should take Mom and get out of here for a little while. Just until we can bring this thing to a resolution."

"No way. You want me to run?"

"No. I want you to take my mother out of harm's way and keep her safe. Hear us out for a change, will you? There's no way we can be everywhere. Whether it's staking out those jerkwads or going after Hugo, for the next week or so, we'll likely be stretched to the limit. If you and Mom were to go somewhere safe, it'd be one less thing to worry about." Garret glanced at his brothers for a little backup.

Mitch stepped up to use his wild card. "Protecting Mom would almost be like protecting Livvy and the kids."

Jackson cut his eyes toward his mother. "It's okay to leave town. Neither one of you are abandoning us. After the service at the cemetery, feel free to fly to New York and use my loft there."

"Better still, fly to Oahu, stay in my house," Garret suggested. "It's right on the beach and the weather's perfect this time of year."

"See, there are any number of options you could take to get away for a little while," Mitch proposed. "The stress you've been under has to be taking its toll. You've lost a child. No one knows what that's like."

"Let me think about it," Tanner finally said.

Bone-tired from all the talk about murder and conspiracies and plans for the future, Raine left the dining area visibly upset and ducked into the kitchen where she could be alone for a few minutes.

She wasn't happy to look up and see that Mitch had followed her.

"Are you okay?"

Raine started wiping down counters. "No. The truth is I may never be okay again. I just need a minute."

"You did a good thing today," he said as he stepped closer.

"I did it for Livvy and the kids."

"You did it for my family. I appreciate it. Do you realize it's been four whole days since we last yelled at each other?"

She cracked a smile. "That has to be a new record. We should circle it on the calendar."

"Definitely." He stalled, picked up one of the dishtowels and twisted it like he was nervous. "There's something I need to say to you. It's long overdue. I'm sorry I didn't come back for Danny's funeral. I didn't even know he'd been killed until the following Christmas. By that time, it had been months. And I didn't know what to say, so I said nothing and avoided you while I was in town. I even stopped coming into the restaurant for a couple of years after that. I want you to know, I'm truly sorry. I loved Danny like you loved Livvy."

"And they're both gone. You're good at avoiding things. People," she corrected. "How do you do that? How do you manage to throw people away like an unwanted piece of trash any time you feel like it? If they aren't convenient to you, they're gone." She snapped her fingers. "Just like that. You know narcissists do that. It's one of their traits."

His back went up. "So now I'm a narcissist? Things change between two people when they're apart. Long-distance relationships don't work."

"You would know that infinitely better than most. As I recall, you didn't even give long distance much of a chance."

"There was a time you knew me better than anyone else ever did. The only one I could talk to at a time in my life when I was too young to know what I wanted. You used to be the one I came to when I needed advice about my life, my future."

"Why was that? Because you knew I wasn't part of the long-term plan?"

"See, I can't come within five feet of you before you start spouting nasty things at me."

She held up a hand. "Never mind. I'm not doing this again. I'm wasting my breath with you. What's important now is that we understand this town's very different from the one we grew up in. Sometimes I wake up at night and realize how hard it is to accept all this evil happened right here, where we used to trust and love and care about each other. The town we knew is gone. I'm not sure we'll ever get it back." She turned and busied herself at the counter, grinding beans for a fresh pot of coffee.

He came up behind her, stilled her hands. Over the sound of the grinder, he whispered, "Raine, honey, we used to love each other. Talk to me. You don't have to make coffee right this minute. Why don't you sit down? You look exhausted. All this work on the memorial service is catching up with you. What you need is a good night's sleep."

"We could all use eight hours of uninterrupted shuteye." Her stomach jittered at his touch. He was too close. She couldn't breathe without her chest tightening. If he didn't step back, she thought she might be sick.

"Something's wrong. You look like you're about to drop."

"I'm fine. I have to stay busy. For me, that means being in the kitchen, cooking, making something. I should probably put on some taco meat. Your parents will be getting hungry soon." She tried to make it to the commercial fridge, but he snatched her hand.

"Raine, look at me." He turned her around and was surprised when she leaned into him, all but melting in his arms.

"This isn't about me or you. Today is about comforting you and your family," she said in protest. "Not the other way around." She rubbed her forehead where a headache began to throb. "I'm making a mess of this again."

"Come on, Raine. Life is too short. I think it's time we comfort each other. Livvy would've liked the idea, don't you think?" Without waiting for an answer, Mitch ran his fingers into Raine's blond hair, tugged her head back where he could tilt her mouth up to his. At the first touch of lips he recognized old familiar territory—old magic versus a skill or two he'd picked up in the last dozen years or so.

Her lips parted as his tongue teased out that seductive pull in the belly. Her pulse skidded as the space closed between them. She yearned to have him run his fingers along her breast. As if reading her mind, he brushed his hand over a nipple through the satiny fabric of her blouse.

She didn't protest because today she needed it there, wanted him to put his hands everywhere. When he dropped them to cup her butt, she felt her feet leave the floor.

They went at each other like hungry wolves. The urge to mate nipped at the fringes.

As abruptly as the volcanic kiss started, Mitch set her back down on the floor. He said nothing as he left her like that in an aroused state, still wanting, yearning for what might've been.

She'd barely opened her eyes before she caught a glimpse of his back disappearing out the door.

Annoyed with the way he made her feel, she was embarrassed he could still make her shudder like a schoolgirl.

Raine had to give her heart time to settle before she could move her feet. Shaken to the core, she forced her brain to work, made it engage again. She had a business to run. She checked the food on hand in the cooler, knowing full well that after the wake she'd have to reorder almost everything.

Damn him, she thought. All these years she'd been able to hold her feelings in check until that smoldering kiss changed everything. It was probably his plan. How exactly was she supposed to get over the man she'd once loved with every fiber in her body? And now, he'd awakened all those dormant emotions she thought she'd locked away forever.

Raine took a seat on one of the kitchen stools. She took out her purse from under the counter. With her hands still trembling, she dug out the picture she'd hidden behind her credit cards, the one she kept there and carried with her wherever she went.

After so many years the paper had seen better days. Worn and frayed around the edges, it even suffered from a stain or two.

But it mattered little to Raine. She stared at the image and felt the tears stream down her face. "Oh, Livvy, what have I done? So much animosity built up and for what? If you were here I know exactly what you'd tell me to do, something I should've done years ago."

Raine stood up and dried her face. "If it isn't too late I have to set things right."

Before she could pull herself completely together, Anniston and Tessa walked in. The women exchanged looks. "Are you okay? We looked up and noticed you were gone."

"There's fresh coffee," Raine said, still in a daze.

Tessa turned the lock on the kitchen door so no one else could enter the room. "Screw the coffee. Tell us what's wrong?"

"Did Mitch do something?" Anniston wanted to know.

How could she answer that? "Give me some time to make things right with Mitch and I'll tell you everything. But right now I have to go see my mom."

Two streets over, Raine came to a stop in front of a Cape Cod with dormer windows on the roof. She walked up the flagstone pathway to the long front porch, past eclectic-painted rocking chairs, and looked into the entryway via the beveled glass on the door.

She found it strangely quiet and turned the handle without knocking.

Marla Manning was still dressed in her black dress, the one she'd worn to the memorial service. She'd kicked off her heels and left her feet bare and propped up on the coffee table. She leaned back into the cushions of her sofa, sipping on her glass of vodka on the rocks.

The small terrier in her lap, named Buffy, let out one yippy bark as soon as the pooch spotted someone entering the living room. Raine watched Buffy settle down the minute he saw the familiar face. The teacup-sized dog curled up beside Marla again without making a fuss.

"You've got some guard dog there, Mom," Raine said as she plopped down on the other end of the couch.

"That was a lovely service you put together," Marla said, her words slurring slightly from the alcohol. "Reminded me of Danny's."

Raine should've known her mom couldn't let five seconds go by without mentioning her son's name. "I know."

"What are you doing here? Is something wrong at the restaurant?"

"If I said yes, would you go there now and help me out?" Knowing the answer before she asked the question, Raine patted the cushion and waited for Buffy to come say hi. The little dog gingerly waddled over.

"You know I can't do that. Your grandmother's taking a nap. I couldn't leave her alone."

Some things never changed, Raine thought as she brushed her fingers through the dog's coat. "Then I guess there's nothing wrong. As always, everything's peachy. Lenore appreciated you and Grandma showing up to the service."

"Lenore told me. I talked to her for a few minutes until everyone started crowding around. Told her if she needed anything to call."

And what would you do if she did? Raine thought. She let out a deep breath. Maybe she did have too many issues with the past that she needed to get over. "At least you took food over to the Indigo house with me. I wish you'd get out more, Mom. You need to be around people."

"I'm around your grandmother every day. You know I'm not that social any more. Why are you here? To make me feel bad? Don't be mean to me today. I have a terrible headache."

Raine stared at the cocktail glass wondering where her mother had hidden the bottle. She hadn't left it out, but then she never did. "I just need to look for something in the attic."

"What?"

"Just some old photos."

"Well, there's plenty up there. Don't make a mess, though."

"Sure, Mom." She handed Buffy back to her mother and got to her feet. "Don't worry. I'll straighten everything up before I go."

Chapter Twenty

Somehow they managed to get through the graveside service the following day. Burials on the Keys tended to be done above ground in mausoleums. They'd been doing it that way for two centuries or longer.

For the entombment, the crowd was small—only a few outside the family had been invited. They gathered at the Indigo family crypt on a warm October day to say goodbye.

It wasn't Boone who led them in prayer but Daniel Shugart. The funeral director was a bear of a man, but soft-spoken. God had given him a deep tenor, a singing voice that rivaled Elvis Presley's. Daniel could perform a hymn without music or accompaniment—his song list was extensive and varied. Maybe that's why his vocals didn't let anyone down today.

Tanner had picked an old gospel song called *Lighthouse* that he'd heard Daniel sing many times before. Lenore went with *There Will Be a Day*. For Ally and Blake, Garret pressed him for *My Heart Will Go On*, knowing it was from Livvy's favorite movie of all time, *Titanic*.

In a final tribute, as family members filed past each casket, they placed a yellow trout lily on top—the flowers courtesy of Cozelle Dunfrey and her container garden.

The service was brief and over within an hour's time. But Garret's somber mood remained well after the last hymn. Added to the sadness was a rage building inside him that kept biting at the edge. It snapped and frayed and dangled there on a razor-thin tether.

A few hours after the final goodbyes, a group decision was made to end the stakeouts. The surveillance had only lasted four nights, but come Tuesday evening, no one could work up the energy or the right frame of mind to go near Baskin or Dandridge. They didn't trust themselves to remain in the car. And since Garret had picked up their new weapons that afternoon from Michael Tang, it didn't seem wise to tempt fate.

Anniston couldn't stand to see Garret like this so she offered a solution. She talked him into burning off a mad fury at the gun range. In turn, he brought the gang along where Anniston and Sebastian could go over gun safety. They made sure everyone in the group knew how to load and unload their respective weapons. Even Lenore and Dominka took a turn at target practice.

Raine seemed uneasy handling Danny's M9 so Mitch tried to help her feel more at ease. "It's a powerful weapon that holds fifteen rounds with very little recoil."

"I'm not much of a gun person," Raine admitted, hoping Mitch would move on to someone else. She should've known better when he took even more of an interest.

"Where sand might jam other guns, this one is built to fire in desert conditions," he went on. "It had its problems early with reliability but the army modified it to accept different sights, even a laser."

"None of that helped Danny make it back home," Raine said, her voice tinged with bitterness.

"No, I guess not," Mitch said quietly. He showed her the safety lock, directed her to remove the slide and then showed her how to load and reload. He let her go through the same routine three times before announcing, "Let's get you a pair of ear muffs." He readied the gear, stuck it on her head, and brought the target within fifteen feet.

She looked around at everyone else's firing station and frowned. "That's really close. Garret's target is way back there near the wall."

"It's at twenty-five yards because he's used a firearm before."

Raine wasn't sure she bought that explanation. Even Dominka's target was farther back. But she kept her mouth shut for once without popping off because she was nervous enough already. The last thing she needed was to provoke Mitch into an argument. Somewhere during all this, she had to suggest they find a place to talk.

Mitch noted how tense she looked. "Relax." He showed her a comfortable firing stance and how best to grip the weapon to reduce needless tension. After letting her practice her hold, he turned her around toward the target and rubbed her shoulders. "Take a deep breath. Now pull the trigger."

She let loose with a string of shots. "It's pretty awesome firing the same pistol Danny used. How'd I do?"

Mitch scratched his chin. "You did very well. Are you sure this is the first time you've fired that particular weapon?"

"Absolutely. It's the first time I've ever been to a gun range."

"I'll move the target back. Try it again."

Even at twenty-five yards she was surprisingly accurate.

"You have a knack."

"Hmm, maybe I've found me a niche, other than slinging hash all day at the restaurant."

Anniston sidled up to review Raine's target. "Not bad. I'm impressed. Never underestimate the female eye when it comes to aiming and firing a weapon with such accuracy."

Raine let out a laugh. "How'd Tessa do?"

Tessa heard her name mentioned and walked over. "Jackson says I need work."

"You did fine with a target ten yards away," Anniston assured her. "It's not necessary to be that consistent at long range."

"That's what I like to hear," Tessa exclaimed. "But with every shot I kept thinking of what cold-blooded tactics it must've taken for the killer to aim at Ryan's head."

"Same here," Jackson added. "I wake up nights in a cold sweat knowing there's someone out there, close by, who beat and tortured four people. Maybe the timing wasn't the greatest to do this so soon after saying goodbye. But I have to tell you, with each shot I fired, I thought of getting justice."

Garret began packing up his stuff, putting away the firearms in a duffel bag. "For me, the timing was perfect. I needed to vent and Anniston recognized it." But out of the corner of his eye, he caught a blur of female wrath, or so he thought. Raine had left their little circle to go over to where Mitch stood. He braced himself for the fireworks that usually followed.

There was something Raine needed to get out of the way before she left for home. She tapped Mitch on the shoulder as he unloaded a steel Smith & Wesson 9-millimeter.

"I thought you were on your way out the door."

"Thanks for helping me…earlier…with Danny's gun. I appreciate it."

"Any time you want to shoot, let me know, and I'm happy to meet you here."

Raine fiddled nervously with the strap on her handbag. "Look, you know what happened yesterday after the memorial service was a reaction to grief. That's all it was."

Mitch sent her a confident grin. "Got it. You keep telling yourself that."

She sighed, knowing full well he didn't buy it. "We did have a long history together. That kiss in the kitchen was completely normal, something between two old friends."

"Friends? We were more than that. Three years all through high school, fifteen to eighteen, were our formative years. You even taught me how to kiss."

She found that funny. "Me? And here I thought you schooled me in that fine art."

"Come to think of it, we probably learned together."

She pivoted to look up into his dark eyes. Here, too, was power. No wonder she'd had trouble resisting him when she was so young. "We should talk."

"Okay. But if this afternoon is still freaking you out…"

"It's not."

Mitch saw the serious face, read the body language. "How about I come by your place after I leave here?"

"All right. I'll see you then. Text me when you're on your way."

"Sure thing. And Raine?"

She turned back. "What?"

"Be careful." Mitch watched her leave and wondered if he'd hit some kind of nerve.

"What was that all about?" Garret asked.

"No idea. Women are mysterious creatures. But that one seems more so than anyone I know. Maybe it's just me but it's almost like she has something heavy hanging on her mind."

"They don't think like we do. That's for sure. I thought she was coming over here to ream your ass," Garret said flatly. "I watched you with her tonight. You're still in love with her."

He supposed there was no point in a fat denial. "I'd better get over it because she's as prickly as a pear cactus around me. I'm not sure her attitude will ever change."

"My advice is to use some of that Indigo charm you're so famous for." That was as far as Garret got with the advice when his cell phone rang. He stopped to take the call and watched the rest of the group head out to the parking lot.

By the time Garret caught up with them outside, Mitch had folded himself into the Nissan Titan and was about to pull away.

Garret waved him down. "That call was from Willie Desoto. He finally ran across someone who remembered the name of Hugo's boat. Clay Don Bigelow swears the name is *Schneewind*. I even had him spell it out. I wrote it down."

"Weird name. Although Clay Don would know, he owns the fueling station at the marina."

"But it's important because Clay Don backs up Willie's claim. Clay Don says he filled up Hugo's boat the day word got out they'd found Livvy and Ally. He's sure of the date. That means Hugo clearly took off *after* the bodies were discovered. We need to jump on this, Mitch."

Anniston had wandered over to ask Garret what was taking him so long. Her eyes widened at the news. "If we have the name of the boat that gives us something concrete to go on. Let's see what I can find out on my phone. I just need a few minutes to search the name, maybe get into the boat database the state keeps."

By then, Raine had pulled out of her space and spotted the others assembling around Mitch's pickup. She slowed to a stop. "What's up?"

Garret told her about the update on Hugo's boat. "We're headed back to the house now. Anniston's trying do some research. Why don't you follow us there?"

Raine shook her head. "Not tonight, Garret. I'm really beat. It's been a rough two days for me. You guys go ahead."

"Are you sure?"

"Positive. I'm heading home to get some sleep. Tell Mitch I'll talk to him another time."

They were still huddled around Mitch's truck when Anniston held up her phone in triumph. "Found something. Searching the word Schneewind gets me several thousand hits. *But* the most interesting one of all is the name Fritz Schneewind. He was the captain of a German submarine, U-183."

Garret peered over her shoulder, read what was on the screen. "183 went down in the Java Sea in April, 1945. Schneewind was eventually awarded the German Cross in Gold. That's the highest award recognized by Hitler. He gave out gold for recurring acts of bravery or success in battle. I'd say Hugo naming his boat after this guy sounds to me like a case of definite hero worship left over from Nazi Germany, which fits with what we know so far about Reiner."

Garret chewed the inside of his jaw and exchanged looks with his brothers. "I think we should take *The Black Rum* out tonight and start looking for this guy. Now. No more wasting time."

Raine made it back home to her houseboat within a few minutes and jumped in the shower. She made herself an egg salad sandwich and settled down in front of the TV to watch late-night reruns of *Frasier*. She usually adored the show, but tonight she couldn't focus on a single line. It wasn't because she already knew most of them by heart.

Her eyes kept coming back to the leather-bound keepsake book on the coffee table that she'd retrieved from her mother's attic. A low-level hum of regret ran through her as she picked it up. Almost reluctantly, she flipped inside to the first page.

What a naïve girl she'd once been, she thought, as she studied each photo. She'd kept every memento from high school in a scrapbook carefully preserved in between plastic sheets. It wasn't her fault that most of the stuff consisted of pictures of her and Mitch. She chose one at random. The teenage couple smiled and mugged for the camera and by all accounts adored each other. It had been taken on a June trip to Disney World® when they'd been sixteen. She flicked to other pages that held silly birthday cards, banners, even little love notes sent between the two. She read a poem he'd written over that same summer, a little rhyme declaring his love.

But something about it caught her attention. She took out other poems, read other verses, and realized in each one he always mentioned his love for the sea, the ocean, the outdoors, how one day he'd go looking for treasure. Had she somehow mistaken his words of affection for how he felt about her?

Tired of thinking about the past *and* Mitch Indigo, she snapped the book shut and shoved it off her lap to the other side of the sofa.

She picked up the remote, switched channels to the news. The weather service had already issued an alert about a tropical depression building in the Atlantic. Winds were expected to exceed fifty miles an hour.

She'd plugged in her phone to charge and left it on the counter. But when she heard the signal that she had a text message, she dragged herself off the couch and went over to check it out, hoping it wasn't from Mitch. But of course it was.

Going out tonight on the Rum to find Hugo. Will talk when I get back.

She shook her head and typed in a response. *Watching the weather now. You're going out when there's a storm moving in?*

He sent a reply within seconds. *I'm a good sailor with an excellent crew. It'll be fine. Don't worry.*

That's the trouble, she decided. She'd spent way too many years worrying about someone who would never change. What kind of life would she have had sitting home in her little world on Indigo Key running a taco stand while the man she loved spent his time at sea facing all kinds of harrowing weather conditions?

She came to one conclusion. The couple in those old photos no longer existed. And it was way past time she came to grips with that fact.

Chapter Twenty-One

Back at the Indigo house, Anniston spent an hour trying to talk Garret into waiting until morning to go look for the old sailor. But his mind was made up.

"You're the most hard-headed, stubborn man I've ever tried to reason with. What possible harm could it do to wait until the storm passes?" Anniston shouted as she watched him throw clothes into the same bag where he'd stored all the weapons.

"Mitch knows what he's doing and so does his crew. They've dealt with storms before. Besides, it's the perfect time to go out and look for that old geezer. With the storm blowing in, he'll have to anchor somewhere until it passes. This is the best time to catch him in port."

He shot a look over at Sebastian. "You're staying here, right? Because someone has to stay behind with the women and make sure they're safe."

That set her off on another outburst. Anniston put her hands on her hips in a defensive pose. "What did you just say? If you'll recheck my resume, I think you'll find I'm the only female in this room who routinely carries a weapon *and* I'm trained to use it. I hardly need my *big brother* around to ensure my safety."

That brought out responses from all the other females standing nearby. Lenore folded her arms across her chest and glared at Tanner. "Don't you stay behind because you're worried about me. You should know better. I have your army-issued .22 rifle here and I'm not afraid to use it."

Tessa speared a finger at Jackson. "After the firing range, I might not be accurate at long distances, but as Anniston reminded me, I don't have to be. I can hit the target at ten yards. Plus, I have access to a very sharp butcher knife. I'll sleep with it under my pillow if necessary while you're gone. Although I do wish you'd wait until the weather clears up."

Dominka piped up, "I travel many places. Always bring with me full can of pepper spray wherever I go. I protect myself."

"That's the spirit." Anniston glanced around the room. "See, I think you'll find the women here are fully capable of looking after themselves while the men go off to sea. Now that I think about it, you should dash off into the dark of night if that's what you want to do. Don't let me stop you."

Garret let out a tired sigh at her attitude. "Fine." He reached down to the ankle holster he'd strapped to his leg and drew out the SIG P230 he'd bought from Michael Tang. "It's not the fancy 210 you lusted after, but it's a well-made firearm. I bought it as a backup. Keep it here with you while I'm gone."

Anniston's fiery temper melted. Disarmed by the offer, her shoulders slumped. She eyed the blue-steel slide and her heart thawed the rest of the way into slush. She crossed the ten feet separating them and curled her fingers over the gun. "No, it's okay. You keep it for now…as backup. I'm sorry I've been upset with you since you decided to pull this crazy stunt."

"Upset? You passed upset…never mind. I accept your apology. It's not a crazy stunt, though. We need to find this German guy. You want to find the link to Walker, I think Reiner might be it."

She tugged his hand and led him into the kitchen where they could say their goodbyes without an audience. She framed his face and leaned into him. "I don't know what it is about you."

He slid his arms around her waist, covered her mouth. "I'm glad you're worried about me, but there's no need. I'm not exactly a newbie on board a boat, although I'm not fond of the small space where you have to bunk and shower."

She linked her arms around his neck. "I just wish you'd listen to reason."

"I got that."

"Yeah. Well. I've been slightly miffed at you ever since Dominka arrived on the scene."

"And I tried to explain you have nothing to worry about. Besides, she's Sebastian's problem now." He kissed her mouth again and teased out a slow moan.

She patted his chest. "I got over Dominka. She's actually not a bad person. I just want you to be safe out there. Come back to me in one piece. Not like that movie, *Perfect Storm*, where everyone gets caught in a gale."

He laughed and nipped her bottom lip. "You write me a love note while I'm gone and send it to me. I promise I'll put it to memory."

"Hmm, Bobby did that with Christina's, didn't he? Most romantic thing about the whole movie. I'll have to make mine an email, gets there quicker, and no one will read it but you."

In the living room, Mitch dealt with the hysterics over the storm. "I've been doing this for a dozen years now. I'm a good sailor. I've picked the best available men for my crew. Count on me taking care of my brothers while we're out there. Going out with a depression building is nothing to laugh at, but I assure you, we'll be fine."

Jackson threw an arm around his dad's shoulders. "It's okay to stay behind to keep an eye on Mom."

"You know, I think with the weather so nasty, I'll hang around the house. Despite your mother's assurance that she'll be okay, I don't think I want to risk leaving her alone."

"Good call. While you're at it, could you keep a watch on Tessa for me? Maybe you could ask her to stay over here until I get back."

"Consider it done."

By midnight Garret watched the crew of *The Black Rum* get underway with skill and precision. Mitch punched in the coordinates that would potentially hug the coastline and motored the boat out of the marina.

In the command center, Walsh had used the latest software to check with the National Weather Service out of Miami and learned it had downgraded the tropical depression.

"The weather service says Hanna is losing strength. She won't even make it to a Category 1, but she'll still pack a punch. Expect winds as high as forty miles an hour. The good news is we're not in her direct path. She's staying on the east coast of Florida and moving north. Since we intend to keep to the west side of the Keys we should be okay. But don't kid yourself, it's gonna get plenty rough even if she stays eastward and doesn't veer off course."

"We've hit rougher seas before," Mitch tossed back. "Are you worried?"

Walsh studied the choppy waters in Sugar Bay and knew the swells would get a lot worse once they hit the open sea. "I'm cautious. I've been around long enough to respect Mother Nature."

"It'll be bumpy until we turn south and head toward Key West."

"You really think this Reiner guy is important enough to head into a gale like this?"

"I wouldn't take the risk if I didn't."

"I just hope this odyssey pans out," Walsh mumbled. "Nobody asked me anything, but do you think it was wise to give up the surveillance on Dandridge and Baskin like we did? That didn't sit well with me."

Jackson came up to the helm and slapped Walsh on the back. "They obviously knew we were tailing them. We made a judgment call. We're counting on Anniston and Sebastian to keep track of them via video surveillance. I'm not sure where they'll install the cameras but they assured us it was a better solution than sitting in the car all night. Let's hope they're right."

"How's baby brother doing?"

"Garret's fine. The bumpy ride isn't the problem. He'll sit back like he's on a roller coaster and enjoy every minute. It's the closed up quarters that get him every time." Jackson went over to the chart table. "So, how do we do this?"

Mitch lifted a shoulder. "For starters I stationed two men on lookout—one on the bow, the other on the stern—using infrared, high-powered binoculars. They'll keep watch for two hours, then we'll rotate the shift."

"Fresh eyes every couple hours, good idea."

Walsh brought over a pot of steaming coffee, poured the black liquid into three mugs. He dumped two fingers of whiskey into his own cup. "Night like tonight, who needs cream in his coffee?"

Jackson chuckled. "You've got the right idea. Hit me."

Walsh obliged, more than generous with the bourbon. He got comfortable near all the digital readouts, sipped. "Do you ever wonder how those guys—Baskin and Dandridge—are communicating with each other including whoever they're working for? It's gotta be a covert operation."

"What are you thinking?" Mitch asked, taking a slug of his java minus the booze.

"That they have to be using an encoded message system in order to chat back and forth."

Garret came through the door heading for the coffee pot. "You mean like spy stuff?"

"CIA does it all the time."

Garret grinned. "I don't even want to know how you came by that info. Something tells me I'm glad you're on our side, though." He dumped sugar in his coffee, added enough cream to turn it into a white blend resembling café au lait. "I'll relieve Jenkins when we make the turn south around 3 a.m."

"Same here," Jackson muttered. "I'll take over the three to five shift from Blaine and then try to catch a few winks afterward. Remember, I spent several months on a research vessel. I'm fully capable of taking over at the helm if you need me."

Mitch sent him a wry smile. "Good to know. But for the next few hours, I'll be wired. Walsh and I will take turns handling the wheel until daylight. Mainly because we could navigate these waters blindfolded. But we will need some relief at some point."

"If we do find this old guy, how do we get him to come back with us, short of kidnapping him?" Garret contemplated.

Walsh didn't have to think about it too long. "Friendly persuasion."

Hours later, the rain continued to fall as Garret took his turn on the bow of the ship. Dressed in a rain slicker, he peered through the infrared goggles as the wind battered his face. At the opposite end, Jackson stood at the stern doing the same thing. The brothers communicated using walkie-talkies.

"See anything yet?"

Even though it was the middle of the night, Jackson found that funny. "All I see is a bunch of rain. How about you? Let me know when it stops on your end."

Garret chuckled. "To think it's heading toward four in the morning, you're a funny guy."

"I'm trying to stay awake. I tried listening to music through my headphones but the damn things are soaking wet now."

They kept up the chatter until five on the dot, when a young crew member by the name of Prentiss appeared next to Garret.

"I'm here to relieve you, sir."

Garret stretched his back. "Thank God. I feel like I'm about to drop. I remember when I used to party till dawn and still have the energy to cut through a wave."

"You're the surfer. What's it like to make a living on a surfboard?"

Garret studied the man's eager face. "Do you surf?"

"I used to. I'm from San Diego. I don't get much chance anymore."

"We should go sometime. I'll show you some moves you can use back home to impress the women."

"That'd be great. I been kinda bored staying in port all this time," Prentiss admitted.

"I imagine so, especially when you're used to hunting for treasure."

"It's not what I thought it'd be, you know? I miss my family back in California. I might go back soon. I haven't told Mitch yet though. I'm trying to stick it out here and not leave him shorthanded."

"He'd appreciate that. In fact, my entire family would. I'm glad you stayed." Garret slapped him on the back and looked up at the sky. He caught the little peep of sun beginning to break through the horizon. "I haven't seen any sign of the *Schneewind* yet. But it's almost daybreak and the rain's letting up so that's good news." He shoved the field glasses toward the fresh-faced seaman. "Hopefully, you'll have better luck than I did."

By mid-morning all the men were bleary-eyed and dragging but still fervent about locating Hugo's sailboat. Running on adrenaline and caffeine, they scanned the busier ports, as well as dots on the map where coves offered little or no fuel supplies. They even checked the string of private docks along the way.

While the lookouts were stationed above deck, the rest of the men gathered in the galley. The hub of the ship was a roomy place to eat and assemble where Mitch could hold meetings, or the crew could kick back and relax. They could often be found passing the time drinking coffee, or playing video games.

"You have a homesick sailor on board," Garret revealed when Mitch sat down to enjoy a plate of scrambled eggs. "Maybe when we get back to port we should invite your crewmembers over to the house. It might ease the monotony for them."

"Who was bitching?"

"He wasn't complaining. The man's homesick. Besides, what difference does it make who it was?"

Mitch stopped eating long enough to look at his brother. "Let me guess. Prentiss. He's my newbie. I worried about giving him the job, too immature, too green."

"Maybe it's his first time away from home."

"It is. That's what I meant by immature. But he needs to find a way to suck it up."

Under the table, Garret shifted his leg and kicked his brother. "You're such a hardass. Not everyone handles being away from family with the same cool, indifferent approach you do. Your crew could use a break. Think about it. Sitting around, spending the day playing cards like they've been doing stuck in Sugar Bay isn't as exciting as looking for sunken treasure in the Bahamas."

Mitch sipped his coffee. "Yeah, well, Prentiss signed a contract. He needs to keep to it."

"Do you hear yourself? When did you get to be so cold dealing with people?"

"I run a business, not a daycare. Like you would know what it's like to make payroll. I pay these guys top dollar and medical benefits, in addition to them getting a piece of the action when we locate and bring up the goodies. What more do you want me to do?"

Garret stood up. "Grow a heart."

With that, he walked out to go find Jackson.

When it was his turn to take watch again, Garret found the sun overhead warm and soothing, a slight breeze wafted out of the south and hit his face. He took in the blue skies, grateful the storm had moved on. He much preferred the outdoors to spending time in the bunk area, closed off like a jail cell.

The boat had just passed Sugarloaf Key, near the campground, when Garret spotted a good prospect through his field glasses. The antique listed in the water at a slight angle. The length of the hull was right, probably forty feet, and it looked like the clipper class sailboat he remembered, with the same markings—white on top and a faded blue at the water line. He radioed Jackson to check out the old tub on the starboard side of the ship. "What do you think?"

Through the binoculars, Jackson found the schooner and searched for a name, but it was angled the wrong position to make out the lettering. "That's gotta be fifty years old. We should definitely check it out."

Garret used his walkie-talkie again to alert Walsh, at the helm, to slow their speed so he could get a better look.

Mitch came out on deck to make his own assessment. "That's it. I'm sure that's Hugo's cutter. All engines stop!"

Garret rushed to the railing. "We can fit three in the dinghy. It shouldn't take more than that."

"You hope," Jackson stated, beginning to change into his wetsuit. "We should take two just in case."

Garret scratched the side of his jaw where he hadn't bothered with a razor. "If we have to wrangle this guy into the skiff we're already in trouble." He reeled toward Mitch. "You coming?"

"You bet. I want to meet up with this guy."

They hurriedly changed into wetsuits in case they encountered the swarms of jellyfish that hung out around the jagged reef.

Rough chops filled the surf with whitecaps as they lowered the dinghies over the side. Mitch took one raft while Jackson and Garret took the other. They motored over to the U-shaped island, fighting eight-foot swells all the way.

When they got close enough to shore, they jumped out, left the lifeboats, and waded onto the beach. The spot seemed devoid of tourists, a nice place to hide out in a fairly deserted stretch of Key.

They approached the ancient sailboat planked in well-worn teak. Garret pointed to the bow and the name, *Schneewind*. "Jackpot," he whispered.

As they climbed on board, they noticed the smell. The tub reeked of stale beer, puke, and fish, and maybe even a backed-up toilet. The hull looked as though it hadn't seen a paintbrush in twenty years. The deck definitely hadn't been cleaned in this decade.

"Who goes below?" Jackson murmured.

"I'll rock-paper-scissors you for it," Garret offered.

"Step aside. I'll do it," Mitch said. "Can't you hear the snores coming from below deck? The guy's obviously sound asleep."

Mitch disappeared down the boat's stairs to the cabin below. He found the old sailor on his back sleeping one off in a grimy bunk.

Hugo had a crop of white hair. His wrinkled face, aged by sun and weather, hadn't seen a razor in at least a week. His eyes showed the ravages of booze and a poor diet. From the looks of the boat's galley, he didn't have much food on hand, which probably was the reason he didn't weigh more than a hundred and fifty pounds soaking wet. His clothing consisted of a tattered shirt and filthy pants that hadn't seen a washing machine in five years.

Mitch waved a hand in front of the old guy's face. "Whew, smell the rotgut whiskey."

"He has to be pushing seventy-five if he's a day," Garret noted from the doorway.

"This place is in really bad shape," Jackson noted, checking out the living quarters. "Maybe we're doing the man a favor by taking him out of here."

"Whether we approve of it or not, this is the guy's home," Garret reminded them. "It's hard to believe this is the same man who was able to talk Walker into looking for gold."

"I was thinking the same thing," Mitch said. "If I met this guy in a bar, I likely wouldn't believe a word that came out of his mouth."

The back and forth banter never even caused Hugo to stir.

"So how do we get him out of here? I'm not carrying him," Mitch declared. "In fact, I'm not sure I want to touch him."

"Then we have to sober him up."

"He's gonna love that," Garret surmised. He walked over and tried to shake Hugo awake. "Hey! Mr. Reiner, wake up!"

Hugo uttered something in German.

"Come on now, wake up! What's German for wake up?"

Jackson rubbed his chin, thought for minute. "Uh, wach auf."

"Louder."

"Wach auf! Wach auf!"

Speaking German did the trick. Hugo sat up quickly, rubbing his aching head. But when he saw three strangers standing in his cabin, he began a rapid-fire dialogue in his native tongue. "What do you want? Why are you on my boat?"

"Are you Hugo Reiner?"

"Who wants to know?" he replied, still in German.

Mitch didn't understand the comeback so he stated, "Look, we know you speak English, so cut the German. We aren't here to harm you."

"Get off my boat! Now!" Hugo demanded in English, laden with a German accent.

Mitch put his hands on his hips. "Let's try this again. Walker Buchanan was my brother-in-law. He ended up beaten to death and stuffed in a barrel along with his little boy, our nephew. Same thing happened to our sister, Livvy Buchanan, and her six-year-old daughter, our niece. We're here to ask *you* what you know about it. And don't bother denying you knew Walker. That's not gonna fly. We have witnesses that place you in Mattito's Bar talking to him on numerous occasions. So we can do this here, on your boat, or we can yank you off this tub and take you back to talk to the cops in Indigo Key. Your choice. But we aren't leaving here without some information out of you."

Hugo's eyes went big as saucers. He swung his legs out of his bunk and staggered to his feet. "I tried to tell your stupid brother-in-law to stay away from Werner Dietrich. But he refused to listen to me. It's not my fault he ended up like he did. Before I say more, I need a drink."

Mitch grabbed the old man's arm. "After. You talk and I'll get you a case of whatever it is you drink but right now I want you sober while you're telling the story. You got that?"

Hugo nodded. "Three against one. Not so fair." He raised his shoulders. "No choice."

"Let's go up on deck. Maybe take the launch over to *The Black Rum*. What do you say to that? We'll get some food in you. When's the last time you ate?"

"Yesterday." Hugo tapped his chest. "I catch my own supper. Always."

Mitch wasn't sure how he did that, as wobbly on his feet as the man appeared. But he had to take the man's word for it, since Hugo was obviously still kicking.

Garret led the way up on deck while Hugo followed. Jackson and Mitch lagged behind to make sure the old sailor made it up the stairs.

It took another thirty minutes to persuade Hugo to get in the raft and another hour before he agreed to a hot shower on board *The Black Rum*. After providing him with a decent pair of pants and a clean shirt, he finally felt like talking. And that was after a pot of coffee and a feast of scrambled eggs, hash browns, and five sausages, two of which he wrapped up and put in his pocket for later.

"Good sausages," the old sailor declared.

Impatient, Garret had been biting his tongue. Now that Hugo's belly was full, the questions poured out of him. "How did you meet Walker?"

"Mattito's Bar, like you say. I always go in there when I have a little money left at the end of the month."

"Why Nazi gold? Of all the made-up stories, why would you try to push that one off on a married man with two kids?"

"Push? I did not push him into anything. He made up his own mind."

"How did you convince him of such a harebrained scheme?"

"You think Nazi gold is rubbish? It's there, just waiting to be found, waiting for someone to pluck it off the sea floor. But just as I warned Walker—and I'll tell you the same thing—it's guarded by the ghosts of brave U-boat heroes. You won't steal it without cost. Walker looked at all my maps and decided for himself it was worth going after it. He even stole one of my maps from me. Stole what belonged to me. The thief, he steals my diary, he steals my papers. Schmutzig schwein!"

Hugo translated the insult without being asked. "But the filthy pig didn't get everything." He tapped the side of his head. "The rest is up here. Your Walker thinks he will get me drunk and I will tell him everything. Hugo is much smarter than that!"

The old man took a wheezy deep breath. "That idiot of yours went to Dietrich and that's what got him killed. No one blackmails Dietrich and lives to tell about it later. And Dietrich, he will kill me for what I know if he ever finds me."

"How do you know this guy so well?" Mitch asked.

"I know all Werner's secrets. If you have the heart to kill this man, I will help you. If not, you are like everyone else, too scared of him. And we will go our separate ways."

The old man's eyes darted around the galley. "This is a fine boat. You should use it and I will lead you to the gold. All I ask is that you return the bullion to Germany. They will give you a large finder's fee. It is true. And if we find my father's bones inside the sub, we will bring all who rest there back to their native country for burial. I want my father resting next to my mother's grave in their little village."

"Touching story. You ask a lot for an old man," Walsh said from across the room. "Walker listened to you, and now his entire family is gone."

"No. Walker tried to blackmail Dietrich using my papers, papers he stole. Stupid, stupid man."

Hugo's rapt audience traded looks.

Garret remembered what they'd found in the safe. "By any chance is this diary bound in faded black leather?"

Hugo's rheumy blue eyes glistened with interest. "Ja. Have you seen it?"

Sensing this was the way to get Hugo back to the Key, Garret replied, "Not only did we see it, we have it in our possession. We thought it was an old family Bible."

"No Bible. It is my father's account of where to find the gold. If you have it, then there is nothing stopping us from getting to it first. And then we will finish Dietrich off, once and for all, ja?"

"What took you so long to go after this fortune?"

"No one believed me."

"Okay, if we buy into this story, you need to start from the beginning."

Hugo stopped to sip from his cup. He eyed the bottle of bourbon on the counter. "Maybe something to flavor my kaffee before I go on?"

Walsh picked up the whiskey, tipped it into the man's mug. "There. Now keep the stories coming."

Hugo licked his lips and began, "My father was a twenty-five-year-old lieutenant assigned to U-boat 492 in the final days of the war. This was between December 1944 and April 1945. When I was a much younger man I went looking for information about him. Of course, I already knew his sub had gone down along the US coastline in April just before the war ended. After that time, my father was presumed missing at sea. But I didn't know much more than that. I searched the war archives and discovered among other things my father was involved in ferrying high-ranking Nazis out of Germany on their way to South America to start a brand-new life. On one of his trips, there was a high-ranking SS Colonel traveling with his five-year-old son. My father made notes about how revered this man was for committing major crimes during the war. That man's name was Dietrich, and Werner was the boy."

Garret took out his phone and used the Internet to look up information about U-492. "But this site claims 492 was scrubbed in 1943."

Hugo shook his head. "Nein. Fake documentation. There were five subs left intact so that the Allies would never know they still existed. 492 was one of those." He held out his cup for more of the bourbon.

Again, Walsh obliged. "Go on."

"It was much, much later when my mother went to see a friend of hers in the little town of Bariloche. She hadn't seen this woman in twenty years."

Once more, Garret used the search engine to look up the town to verify Hugo's claim. "This website says Bariloche is located at the foothills of the Andes in

Argentina. It's reputed to have been a haven for fugitive Nazi officers and their families."

"See, I tell the truth," Hugo declared. "My mother's friend had the cancer in the breast and was near death by the time she reached the town. She gave my mother a packet filled with photographs of my father standing next to those he ferried to South America. Many, many photos. I have pictures of Werner as a boy and his father standing proud in his SS uniform."

Hugo leaned across the table and lowered his voice. "And old Nazi ID cards with more pictures that belonged to Dietrich's family. I also keep the passports and logbooks with the coded messages about gold bullion carried in the belly of my father's U-boat. Not only locations but also the routes they took to get to Argentina. Walker stole these from me. Until I met him, I had been waiting for someone to believe me. But people dismiss my story as just coming from a drunk looking for someone to buy him many drinks."

Mitch was unconvinced. It was unimaginable to him that kind of valuable documentation would be kept on the stinking tub he'd just left. "So Walker stole all of it?"

Hugo shook his head. "Nein, not everything. I have a few documents left."

Mitch exchanged looks with his brothers. "Make me believe it," he said in challenge. "Show me what you have."

Back on the *Schneewind*, Hugo left the brothers on deck while he scurried below to retrieve his incriminating stash.

Garret heard noises coming from the cabin. Thirty minutes went by before Hugo reappeared carrying a waterproof, German-issued trunk, circa 1939, about the size of a large metal briefcase.

"Let's see this trove of documentation," Mitch demanded.

But Mitch found Hugo Reiner had a feisty side to him.

"I'm not going with you. I won't leave my boat."

"I'm not leaving you here. And we can't tow this tub back to Sugar Bay. We can't," Mitch emphasized. "It'd be like sending up a giant red flag. Too many people know we've been looking for you. The *Schneewind* shows up in port and Dietrich will be all over it."

"Nein, I won't leave my boat," Hugo insisted again. "Someone will steal everything I own. I won't part with my trunk."

"Hugo, be reasonable," Jackson pleaded. "Mitch is right. You want to avoid Dietrich's detection, this is the only way."

Mitch stabbed a finger at the old guy. "I didn't want to say this earlier, didn't want to scare you. But do you realize all those nights you sat in Mattito's Bar, bragging about gold bullion, you were talking to Dietrich's men directly?"

"What do you mean? I was talking to Walker."

Mitch cut a lethal glare Hugo's way. "I'm telling you everyone in that place heard you. Roger Baskin works for Dietrich, and so does probably half the town, too many to count. You ran your mouth and now we can't just drag this tub back to Indigo and let it sit in the harbor on display."

Garret knew how stubborn his brothers could be. Since it seemed they were at an impasse, he intervened. "Look, we could tow it to Shock Island. I have a friend there. I'll call ahead and see if Gary has a place to dock it where it's completely out of sight."

"Whatever," Mitch finally said. "Let's just make it happen and get moving." He turned to Jackson but pointed his finger at Hugo again. "I'm putting you in charge of *that*. Don't let him out of your sight for five minutes."

Chapter Twenty-Two

While Garret was busy with the mysterious Hugo, Anniston had plenty of work to keep her busy. There were calls to make, research to finish. She'd set up a command center in her hotel room where she and Sebastian could monitor the surveillance on Baskin and Dandridge. If nothing else, it might be the only way they'd gather the evidence they needed to take it to the state police.

They'd already gone through hours and hours of video at two workstations. One near the window, the other at the little desk Anniston had set up on the smidgen of counter space. In addition to that, she'd enlisted Tessa and Raine to help her go through the rest of the security videos from various business owners around town. More eyes meant better to find what they were looking for.

Tessa sat down ready to get to work. "When's Raine due?"

"Any time now."

Tessa went on, "With the storm moving through, the streets are flooding in some places. I hope she isn't having trouble with that old roadster she drives."

"I'll give her a call, ask her if she needs us to swing by and…" The knock at the door got Anniston to her feet. "Let's hope that's her."

Raine came into the room carrying her umbrella, drenched from the downpour. She nodded toward Anniston. "Sorry I'm late. But I had to persuade Charlotte into covering my afternoon shift."

"We were worried you had car trouble," Tessa said.

"That too. I walked over from the restaurant."

"You should've called me or Sebastian for a ride. There's hot coffee on the counter. But first, you need to get out of those wet clothes." She went to the dresser, found a pair of sweatpants and a top. "Here. Bathroom's in there."

Raine hung up her raincoat and umbrella over the tub, changed into the dry clothes, and came out fluffing her damp hair with a towel. "I found something online I think you should see. But I need to borrow your laptop."

Anniston rubbed her hands together. "I love it when a protégé hits her stride." She relinquished her MacBook and said, "Help yourself."

Raine went over and sat down at the computer and switched windows. She typed the name into the search engine to bring up another site. "First of all I need to give you the backstory on the keywords I used. Do you remember when Garret found that Day-Timer belonging to Livvy? A couple of days ago I asked Mitch if I could look through it, mostly out of curiosity. I noticed that Livvy used this catchphrase over and over again that she wrote in the margins, at least ten times."

"What was the phrase?" Tessa asked.

"'Faith is belief that turns into bravery.' I found it odd, yet strangely familiar. Sure enough, I went online, typed in the phrase and basically got two hits. One was Boone's sermon he'd posted on the church website in the archives section. I remember the day Boone delivered it. I was there. And so was Livvy. The other was posted on a religious blog written by a man by the name of Willis Hartman over twenty years ago. It seems this Hartman wrote a post about what he called foundational life concepts. Turns out, it matches almost word for word the archived sermon Boone delivered five years ago to his congregation. Which means, either Boone plagiarized this Hartman guy off the Internet, or the two men are one and the same and Boone simply dragged out an old homily from the past."

Sebastian, who'd been focused on his computer screen, spared a glance toward Raine. "Let me see that." He went over to the laptop, read the blog post and then the archived document from Life Stone Church. "This is brilliant work, Raine."

Anniston looked on proudly at Raine before turning to her brother. "I told you these people were motivated and talented. You didn't believe me when I told you Tessa had the foresight to snap pictures of all those license plates."

"I'm a believer now," Sebastian said as he reread the blog post. He angled toward Raine, kissed her on the forehead. "Do you realize you may have just popped this case over the fence? Anniston and I have been agonizing over how to uncover Dandridge's true identity."

Anniston clarified. "The lab texted me this morning and said they ran the DNA profile through CODIS and got zip. Not a single hit from that wad of tissues I sent them. Sebastian and I know the man reinvented himself just before he arrived on the Key. But if Dandridge hasn't been picked up for anything, we're dead in the water."

"And now this." Sebastian sat back down at his laptop and began a series of rapid keystrokes. "I'll hunt down Willis Hartman while you guys keep at the surveillance."

"There has to be something in those videos that we've overlooked," Anniston stated.

Raine switched gears and tapped into the videos Tessa hadn't yet viewed. "After getting my neighbor to give up her camera feed from the houseboat next to me, I'm beginning to agree with you. With the angle from where Deidra located her camera, I see a straight shot to Walker's yacht. If only we could get lucky and catch a glimpse of Ryan getting on that boat."

"Maybe we'd learn who Ryan was with besides Walker," Tessa finished. "Persistence has to pay off sometime," she said as she moved through more videotape from the string of shops downtown.

When Anniston's cell phone dinged she turned to check the readout. "It's Dack's boss back in Tallahassee."

She put her fingers to her lips for quiet. "Hello, Captain Briggs. Thanks for returning my call. I won't keep you long. I just need to know a couple of things about Dack's murder. The night he died, what did the police find in his car at the rest stop?"

"Nothing of evidentiary value if that's what you're asking. Why? What was supposed to be there? What was Hawkins doing meeting you at that rest stop anyhow? Where were you when it happened? I've read your statement and the one your client gave. I'm pissed off about that."

Anniston recounted the plan to meet up and the reason for it. "I was about four minutes late. If I'd been on time Dack might still be alive."

"Why was Hawkins giving you information? He knew that was against policy."

Anniston balked at revealing anything more. "Look, Sebastian and I go way back with him. We're determined to find out who killed him. So did they find anything in the car? That's the question."

"I can tell you one thing. Whoever killed him took his cell phone. Bastards. What the hell's going on in this little town, anyway?"

"Six people dead and counting," Anniston fired back. "Did Dack ask for help while he was here?"

"All my detectives in the field ask for help, Marcelli. It's a daily request. I'm shorthanded as it is, due to budget cuts. I only have so many detectives to send out."

Same old song and dance, thought Anniston. "Do you know what caliber gun was used?"

Briggs didn't hesitate. "The state troopers agree it's some type of large caliber 9mm."

"Could it have been a SIG-made P210?"

"I guess. I'd need to talk to ballistics. Why?"

"Because that's the same caliber that killed Ryan Connelly."

There was a long pause. "Jesus Christ. I'll pull my two best detectives off what they're working on and get them up to speed. But don't expect them to buddy up with you and share anything about the investigation."

"So you refuse to keep me in the loop?"

"It's an active investigation," Briggs began. "We're trying to keep a lid on things. Hawkins should never have given you any information."

But Anniston cut him off. "Just remember, the same person who killed Dack also murdered a couple of kids. We're trying to find out who that is before he kills again."

After ending the call, she eyed the others. "Okay, so I shared with Briggs and he's decided to shut us out. What should I have said?"

"You did the right thing," Sebastian agreed. "If we have no one in law enforcement left to turn to, then we'll do this on our own."

She plopped down on the bed, held her head in her hands. "Like you said, there has to be something we're missing. Something that's right in front of us."

Raine had a thought on that. "Something occurred to me the other night after I went home from the gun range.

Where is this wealthy Dietrich guy staying? No one's really seen him except for Tessa that night at Royce's house. There's no scuttlebutt making the rounds. Why is that? Am I the only one who finds that odd?"

"Excellent question. I don't know the answer, but let's find out."

"How?"

"There is a direct approach. I ask his business partner, Royce Buchanan. Royce kind of likes me. He has to know where the guy is living, right? The thing is I want y'all to come with me."

"Us?" Raine said. "I don't think so."

"What about you, Tessa?"

"You know, I saw him at the memorial service and he looked like a man deep in sorrow. At least, that's how he seemed to me, like a grief-stricken father. I'll do it. I'll go with you. I'm done letting this guy make me wonder if he's the same kind of monster as the right-hand man."

Tessa bumped Raine's shoulder. "Come on, come with us."

"Okay. But one of you should do all the talking. That man's always made me really uncomfortable."

Anniston made the appointment to see Royce inside the plush offices at Buchanan Industries. His secretary gave her directions. On the drive across town she turned to the other women. "Don't you think Royce deserves to know he's harboring his son's killer in his own guesthouse?"

"Whoa, I'm not willing to trust Royce just yet," Tessa said from the backseat. "I mean, do you feel that kind of confidence he isn't mixed up in these murders in some way?"

"I'm with Tessa on this," Raine said. "The jury's still out to what degree we should trust that old man."

"Tell you what. You're both coming with me into his office. I'll let you two judge whether or not he's leveling with us. How's that? You make the call on his honesty."

"He'll have to convince me," Tessa warned.

In a small environment like Indigo Key, the Buchanan Industries building was about as high-rise as anything in town. At four stories, it sat on the east side looking out on the waters of the Gulf of Mexico.

The irony of that wasn't lost on Anniston. She swung into the parking lot, cut the engine to the SUV, and pivoted in her seat. "Why didn't anyone tell me that Royce's workplace overlooks the area where the bodies were dumped?"

"I thought the Indigos would've mentioned it," Raine said. "It wasn't that far offshore."

"You're telling me," Anniston grumbled as she got out, her umbrella in hand. She took in the view of the coastline and then looked up at the building. "If Royce's office turns out to be on this side, I'm beginning to get an eerie feeling."

Raine skirted the hood, holding her own umbrella so she could share with Tessa. She waved her hand toward the top floor. "His office is in the corner, to the left."

"That's an almost direct line to where the shrimper netted the barrel. Let's get out of this wet." Anniston led the way inside, leaving the rain gear in the lobby.

Once they reached the fourth floor, Royce's secretary—a tidy woman in her forties with her hair pulled back in a bun—ushered the three women into a lavishly decorated corner office. Royce was sitting behind his mahogany desk, and got to his feet when the women came in.

"Esther, would you bring us some fresh coffee, please."

"Certainly, sir."

"Have a seat. What on earth brings you out on a nasty day like today?"

Tessa and Raine got comfortable in the pair of leather club chairs in front of his desk, but Anniston remained standing. She went over to the window and stared out at the torrent of rain still coming down.

Anniston had always preferrred the direct approach. "Royce, have you been honest with me? I mean, I'm asking because it's vital that you tell me the truth now."

"Of course. What's this about?"

"You have a business partner in the resort project named Werner Dietrich. He's been staying here in town but not at the hotel. Where exactly is he living?"

Royce narrowed his eyes. "South of town there's a gated community. I own a house there. Why?"

Anniston crossed her arms over her chest. "How do I put this? How well do you know this guy?"

"Well enough to take his money and hope there's a healthy return on investment one day."

"Or else Dietrich would be very pissed off. Am I right? Did Walker know that Dietrich was such a dangerous guy to do business with?"

"I was the one who found Werner and brought him in on the golf course deal. I did business with him, not Walker. I've already gone into this before. You were right there when I did."

"Royce, what if I told you that big deal Walker bragged about last summer involved Dietrich." Anniston watched his eyes bug out, watched his face go white as a sheet before the man clutched his chest.

Anniston went over to him, bent down in front of his chair. "Are you okay?"

"Pills…in…top…drawer."

Anniston found the digitalis and shoved one under his tongue. "You have heart problems? Arrhythmia?"

Royce nodded. He leaned back in his chair, closed his eyes.

"Do I need to call the paramedics?"

Royce moved his head slowly from side to side.

Anniston picked up his hand, squeezed his fingers until the meds kicked in.

About that time Esther came back in with the coffee. She set down a tray holding a silver pot and four pale-green bone china cups. When she turned to do the serving, she saw Royce's face. "What's wrong? Is he having trouble breathing? There are pills…"

"I think we have it covered. Does this happen often?" Anniston said, turning to Esther.

Esther hesitated but then admitted the truth. "Lately, yes. A lot of people don't understand what this man's been through. It hasn't even been a year since he went through this same thing with Winnie."

"I agree. He's had a rough time of it."

After the pain had subsided, Royce took out a handkerchief from his breast pocket and wiped his brow and upper lip, which had broken out in beads of sweat. Embarrassed to show such weakness, he waved the linen like a flag of surrender. Each breath labored, he finally got out the words. "You…were saying? Walker did…business with…Dietrich?"

Anniston cut her eyes toward Esther.

"Esther, I'm fine now. I'm okay. You…please, go back to your…work," Royce ordered softly.

Anniston waited for the secretary to leave the room. "I'm reconsidering. I don't think you're strong enough to hear this."

"I am. Go on. Please."

"Okay." She told him about the Nazi gold. She could see in Royce's eyes a horror at the notion Walker would go after something so huge. She also could see he believed her.

"You're saying Dietrich killed my son?"

"You know as well as I do that he has henchmen to do that. Let me ask you something else. Did you bring Roger Baskin here to the island?"

"Baskin was recommended to me by Braden Pendleton long before he became a state senator."

"I see. What about Dandridge?"

Royce's words came out slowly. "Life Stone needed a pastor. Boone sent in his resume. I liked his philosophy so I recommended him to the church deacons. They got together at a meeting and agreed he was the best man for the position. I didn't hire him, all I did was put his name into the hat."

With great energy, Royce threw out his bony finger at Anniston. "Now, you tell me who killed my boy."

Anniston looked at Tessa and Raine, waited for them to give the go-ahead or not. Once they both nodded, she went on, "Roger Baskin used to work for the Dixie mafia as an enforcer. He's well-versed in murder. We think he's working for Dietrich."

"That son of a bitch."

"You have a killer living in your guesthouse," Anniston said flatly.

"You have proof?"

"I won't go into what I have or don't have. Mainly because those women over there are my clients. I owe it to them to hold something back to take to the cops…eventually." But she pointed beyond the window to the view of the Gulf waters. "You want proof right now, here, today? Look out the window and beyond to the water." When he turned his eyes to the rain coming down, she went on, "Five hundred yards from this office is where your son's body was dumped. I guarantee you that wasn't a coincidence."

Royce's jaw locked. His hands clenched into fists. "I'll kill him myself."

"No you won't. I'm serious, Royce. Don't even think like that. You may have known Baskin for two decades but when a fortune is at stake, loyalty flies out the window. We all know that. Right-hand man or not, he's younger than you are, stronger, cunning. And if you shoot him dead, we won't get all the answers."

"But I may not live long enough to see him pay."

"You will. Take your meds and do what the doctor says, you will."

"What about Boone?"

She shook her head. "Honestly, we don't know who Boone is. But he didn't exist before he arrived in town."

Royce swallowed hard, then used the handkerchief again to pat the sweat from the corners of his mouth.

"Does it sound like we're on the right track?"

The old man bobbed his head. "I believe you are. The question is what do you want me to do?"

"Ever played poker?"

"Yes."

"How good are you at bluffing?"

Royce's lips curved up. "I haven't forgotten how, if that's what you mean."

"Good. Because you need to act as though you still trust Baskin, totally. Will you let us run a wire into your guesthouse?"

"Absolutely. I'm surprised you asked."

It was Anniston's turn to grin. She spread her arms out wide. "I'm a law-abiding private detective just doing my best to earn a living. You need to let us know when there's a clear path to the cabana."

"You're welcome to put a bug in my study, too. Baskin is often in there to talk business."

"No. I'm not asking you to play informant or wear a wire. You need to understand that in Walker's venture there are *millions* at stake. It pales in comparison to the return on investment from the casino deal. You can't go questioning a killer about what he's up to even in your own study. Are we clear on that?"

"Sure. And Anniston?"

"What?"

"Thank you."

"No problem. I keep my word. I'm trusting you to do the same."

Back in the Ford Explorer, Tessa was the first one to toss cold water on the deal. "I hate to bring this up, but there's not an Indigo anywhere around who'll be pleased with this turn of events. When Jackson finds out you trusted Royce like this, he'll be furious."

"Same with Mitch. He won't understand at all why we even came here today."

Anniston sighed. "Neither will Garret. I knew when I was standing in Royce's office I'd have to describe the man's emotional state in order to make my case with Garret."

"I never would've believed it unless I'd seen it with my own eyes," Raine said. "I think he was mad as a hornet when you mentioned Baskin's betrayal."

Tessa added, "You have instincts there, Anniston. You knew all along Royce wasn't involved."

"No, I didn't. But after talking to him face to face the first time I decided he was a greedy landgrabber, a ruthless businessman, but not a murderer. And he adored his son. He would've given up his own life to protect Walker."

She backed out of the visitor space and exited the parking lot, heading south. "I know it's pouring rain, but I need to check out this house Dietrich's living in."

"Go for it," Raine said. "For the first time in weeks, I feel like we're finally getting somewhere."

"You don't think Royce would go after Baskin by himself, do you?" Tessa asked.

"That's the wild card. I hope not. I need to get Sebastian in there as soon as possible to bug the place before Royce changes his mind."

Chapter Twenty-Three

Walsh hadn't been far off the mark.

Roger Baskin communicated with his associates through a coded message chat room. That's how the group got wind of Dietrich's latest madness. He'd taken things to the next level and acted on his own—bad idea even for the moneyman.

What would they do now if the irrational twit had brought down the entire house of cards? It had taken them so long to reach this point, it would be a damn shame if everything was for naught.

In his auto repair shop, Roger paced the full length of the garage. At times, it never ceased to astound him how stupid rich people could behave.

In one afternoon, Dietrich had singlehandedly sent everything into a tailspin. Everything they'd worked for, everything they'd planned was at risk. If it imploded now, they'd never get to the gold.

For years, he'd sacrificed his own life, his owns dreams, slaving away for someone else, doing their dirty work, doing their bidding.

Roger was done being Royce's lackey—at his beck and call no more. Throwing in with Dietrich and getting to the gold had been his only chance at the life he deserved, the life he should have had years ago while still in his twenties and young enough to enjoy it. Why did he keep hooking up with losers?

It was one thing to kill a naïve pest like Ryan Connelly, who stumbled on the truth. It was quite another to eliminate a cop and get him out of their hair. But killing an entire family because one old man got rattled and worried was something else entirely. The very man who'd ordered Walker and his family dead, had now, in fact, committed a tactical blunder, one that might not be able to be corrected or fixed, one that could easily send them all to Florida's death row.

As his computer dinged with another message, this one from Sinclair, Roger felt cheated.

Stupid old bastard, he decided, as he sent a reply back to Sinclair, Oakerson, Dandridge, and Frawley.

Chapter Twenty-Four

The Black Rum motored into port at five-fifteen in the morning under a heavy greenish fog. The pea soup had made it a major pain in the butt trying to get back to Sugar Bay. But it did provide one huge benefit. They had the shroud of mist and the cover of darkness to hide Hugo's presence from anyone who might be watching.

Not that Mitch planned to let him leave the ship. He left Walsh under strict orders. "Stay glued to his side. No one guards him but you. We both know Hugo could easily talk his way past Prentiss, Blaine, or Jenkins."

"Gee thanks. How do I go to the bathroom? I'm not taking him with me."

"Lock him in his cabin if necessary. He's to communicate with no one but you. Surely you can keep a seventy-five-year-old man from getting off this boat."

"Don't be so sure. How do you think that old geezer's lived this long? That's one cagey dude. Imagine what he'd be like if he didn't booze it up."

"No thanks. I'm well aware we can't fully trust him. He'll likely explode when he finds out I've taken the chest, which I'm putting under lock and key in a safe place."

"So you want me to explain it to him."

Mitch frowned. "I'm not in the habit of asking my brothers to do my dirty work for me. All I'm asking is to keep him from going crazy so he doesn't spoil this whole thing. I want you to call me as soon as he wakes up. I'll let Hugo in on the plan then."

The first thing Garret did was text Anniston that he was back. If he got a reply, fine. It meant she was awake and he'd head to the hotel. If he didn't, he'd go home and grab a quick shower and sleep on the couch for a couple hours of much-needed shuteye.

She surprised him with a text message. *How soon can you get here?*

He grinned as he hefted his bag over his shoulder and started trekking down the path toward the hotel. As he walked past the front desk, he sent a wave to the pretty redhead behind the counter and headed through the lobby to the elevator. It occurred to him he needed a cover story for anyone curious enough to ask where he'd been. He decided fishing was as good as any and he had the makings of a beard to prove it.

He waited what seemed like five minutes for the elevator but when the light seemed stuck on two, he took the stairs up to the third floor and knocked on her door.

As soon as she opened it, he dropped his gear on the floor and hauled her up against his chest. As if he'd been away for months, he kissed her with a fervor he hadn't felt before now. She tasted like warm vanilla with a hint of cinnamon. "I know I need a shower but..."

She ran her fingers through the stubble that was just beginning to soften up. "I missed you."

He framed her face, looked into her chocolate eyes. "That's what I like to hear."

"So what happened? I'm dying to know."

He showed her an image he'd captured on his cell phone. He'd learned through the years that a visual always made the story so much better. "We found him near Sugarloaf Key, passed out on his bunk with a hangover, stinking to high heaven of booze and BO." He went through Hugo's story, trying not to leave anything out.

"Bless his heart," Anniston said, eyeing the photo Garret had taken of a down and out man. "He looks like a homeless person. You're saying this is the guy who holds the key to this entire thing."

"That remains to be seen. We had to sober him up to get him to talk, get some food in him, and now we have to keep him somewhere Dietrich doesn't know about. Who knows how long Hugo will be happy staying on *The Rum*? My guess is not for long."

He dug in his bag and pulled out a cup in a plastic baggie that he'd taken from the boat. "I want you to check this for fingerprints."

"Sure, I can send this through the system. But if his father was involved in Nazi activities, I doubt Reiner is his birth name anyway. The same holds true for Dietrich. If Reiner's father got these guys to Argentina the way Hugo says, they started life over with completely new identities. It's historically amazing to me that Reiner's father made all those trips back and forth to South America carrying SS officers but his sub ends up going down right off the Florida Keys."

"I've been thinking about that. Why was this sub so close to the US coastline? There's a story there somewhere."

"No doubt a fascinating one. You know you can't let anyone in town know Hugo's here."

"That's what I've been saying. But this is a small island. Things have a way of getting out whether you want them to or not."

"I know the perfect place."

"Really? Where?" He eyed her with open curiosity. "How would you know a place where Hugo could bunk? You aren't even from here."

"But I think outside the box, which means I'm creative. Raine tells me her family owns a little house on Ramrod Key. Hugo could stay there."

"Not by himself. This guy needs a keeper. Otherwise he'll just try to take off, get back to his boat. This guy's a piece of work, he's uncooperative one minute and plays people the next. He's fine for now on *The Rum*. But at some point, we'll have to think of something more permanent."

Done talking about it, he wrangled off his shoes, yanked his T-shirt up over his head and moved toward the bathroom while shedding his jeans. "I need a shower in a regular size tub."

She laughed and started to turn the other way, but he snatched her hand. "You look like you're ready to get wet."

She lifted a brow. "There are benefits to having been away from each other for three days."

"I'll say. Which is why we should lock ourselves in this room and not come out until tomorrow morning."

"We do need a break from everything. It'd be nice to spend *one* day together without any disruptions or distractions."

"And no talking about murder. Murder's off limits." He reached over and turned on the water, let it get hot before crossing to her and sliding off the lavender-colored robe she wore. He kissed a bare shoulder, brought his lips to each corner of her mouth. He toyed with her tongue as he splayed his fingers along the small of her back, where he knew she liked to be touched. He deepened the kiss, then lifted her up and over the rim of the tub and into the rising steam.

Anniston wrapped around him like a vine as he lapped the water off the curve of her breast. She let him trail his tongue up to her neck. That primal need was already in charge. She soaped his chest and belly and ran her hands along his butt. He washed her like she did him, exploring slick skin and enjoying wet flesh.

Their appetite for each other had to be sated.

Soft curves met hard abs. As the water sprayed over them, he leaned her back against the tile and took. The joining was just the beginning. A ravenous hunger ripped through them. There was no time to savor. They rushed to feast, to fill the craving, matching each other greed for greed. The climax came with a burst of magic and awe.

He rested his brow on hers. "I think you did miss me."

She ran her hands through his wet hair, then jerked his head back and kissed his mouth. "I thought you'd never get back. I'm not usually so impatient."

"Lucky for me that you were."

"You want breakfast?"

"Maybe later," he said as he dried off with one towel, handed her the other. He walked out of the bathroom naked, crossed to the bed, and dropped onto the sheets. "I have to have some sleep. We took turns all night keeping an eye on Hugo."

She crawled in beside him, jerked the covers around them and snuggled into his side. But he was already asleep before she could throw her arms around him.

When he woke three hours later, he ordered breakfast from room service.

They lounged in bed over blueberry pancakes. When they got hungry again, they called Lee Fong's Palace and had the order delivered.

Garret finally got dressed at seven-thirty that evening to open the door for the delivery guy.

Over twice-cooked pork, Anniston was the first one to bring up murder. "Dack's funeral was yesterday, back in

Miami. I saw Shonna there. You remember Dack's girlfriend, right?"

"I'm sorry you had to go there alone."

She smiled. "I didn't. I talked Raine and Tessa into coming with me. And then there was Sebastian. He even brought Dominka. What's with her anyway? She doesn't seem inclined to leave."

Garret chuckled. "Dominka is a woman who sets her sights on something and usually gets it. That little girl from a coal-mining town grew up to be a force."

"Is that what she did with you?"

Sensing an irreversible relationship error that might shatter the mood, he decided to beat a tactical retreat and changed the subject. "How'd it go at the funeral?"

"Like you'd expect. Dack's mother, Kate, is grief-stricken. Chuck is devastated. And Shonna is inconsolable. I think they appreciated all of us coming. When we got ready to leave, his family offered to do anything to help us catch the people responsible."

During the meal, Garret had noticed she seemed preoccupied. "What else is wrong?"

"There's something I should probably tell you."

He picked up his glass of wine and leaned back in his chair. "Okay."

"Royce agreed to let Sebastian wire the guest cottage." She held up a hand. "There's more. He told me where Dietrich's been staying."

"Why did he do that? Don't tell me it's out of the goodness of his heart."

"Look, Garret, I made a judgment call. My belief is that Royce has nothing to do with this cockamamie gold scheme. I told him about Baskin."

"You did what?" He couldn't believe what he was hearing. He ran both hands through his hair. "Oh, my God. You didn't? You can't trust Royce Buchanan. Don't you know that by now?"

"I think your judgment about him might be severely clouded."

His temper flared like a rocket. "Oh really? So, because you've known him for a few weeks, you're dismissing my opinion of a man I've known for most of my life? I've watched that money-hungry developer do some downright despicable things to get what he wants. And you want me to discount what I've seen with my own eyes because you formed this immediate bond with him? I don't think so."

"Did you ever consider your father might have overblown this bad-guy image?"

"Are you nuts? This has nothing to do with my dad's point of view. I know all I need to know about Royce."

"For your information, I took Tessa and Raine with me, and they both agreed Royce's grief is genuine."

"I see. So Tessa's known Royce for what, three weeks now? And Raine is scared to death of the guy. Always has been. So yeah, that really proves he's free and clear in all this. That's bullshit."

"Then why is he willing to help us get Baskin?"

"Maybe he gave you the *illusion* of helping *us*? Did you consider that? I think since you and Sebastian decided to give us up as clients, you've basically been acting on your own behalf."

"That's not fair. I didn't tell Royce about Willis Hartman."

"Who the hell is Willis Hartman?"

She went into how Raine had made the discovery and perhaps found a link to the pastor. "Dandridge and Hartman might be one and the same guy. So as you can see, I held certain things back from Royce, too. I didn't disclose everything."

"And that makes it somehow okay? I don't think so. You're going to Royce spilling what I wanted to keep secret pretty much tells me you plan to do what you want in this, regardless of what I think. You seem to forget that my dad butted heads with that man for decades. Why? Because Royce Buchanan is a shark. I go out of town and boom, you decide on your own to trust him. Think about it, Anniston. You're trusting a guy who didn't even show emotion for his own grandchildren. If that's what you consider a decent human being, then we have nothing left to discuss."

With that, Garret grabbed his gear and walked out, slamming the door behind him so hard it rattled the windows.

Outside, Garret wasn't sure where to head first, the boat or to his parents' house. He decided to veer off down Waterfront Street and found himself standing in front of what used to be his Nana's house. The beachfront bungalow now belonged to Jackson, who didn't seem the slightest bit inclined to resume his life in the big city.

He was glad to see the two had kept the flowerbeds popping with wildflowers. When he thought of his Nana, Garret always remembered an acre of blossoms. He studied the seashell-white cottage with its red trim and the red-tiled roof, and fondly recalled spending his time here. He recalled the many times his Nana wore her big, huge hat that protected her face from the sun while she worked for hours in her garden.

Garret sent Jackson a text message before knocking on the door. He didn't want to intrude on an intimate moment if the couple were thus occupied.

Standing out front. You busy?

Nope. Come on in. Mitch is here.

Five seconds later, the front door opened.

Mitch noted the bag on his shoulder. That didn't bode well for a happy homecoming after three days at sea. "What happened?"

Garret dropped his bag at the door and glanced toward Tessa. "I'll tell you what happened. While we were gone Anniston told Royce everything. She decided to take him into her confidence without so much as asking me first. She unloaded our entire theory on him and believes that he's totally trustworthy."

Tessa licked her lips and cut her eyes toward Jackson. "I'd planned to tell you about that."

"You knew?" Jackson stared at her.

Tessa went on, "We went to Royce's office. He has some kind of heart condition. He almost passed out right in front of us. Anniston made a judgment call. Raine and I support it. We don't think Royce knew anything about Walker's gold scheme. She even got Royce to agree to let Sebastian bug the guesthouse. He offered to do more." When the trio of men didn't look convinced, she added, "I guess you just had to be there and see it play out."

Garret sent her a disheartened look. "That's not the point. I don't care about you visiting Royce at his office or getting information out of him. What bothers me is Anniston took this tack knowing we didn't fully trust Royce. Do I know for certain that he's involved? No, I don't. But I can look back at all the dirty deals Royce has put together over the years and voice my concerns based on his lousy track record."

"I agree," Jackson said. He stuck his hands in his pockets and turned to look at Tessa. "There was a time you didn't trust Royce either."

"That's true. But it was mostly based on things you said about him."

"What about your taking pictures of all those cars in his driveway? You didn't trust him that night. Hell, you didn't even trust me," Jackson accused.

"Again, true. But the thing is I went out there to his office very skeptical. Just ask Anniston and Raine. But by the time I left I was convinced Anniston had made the right call. It's as simple as that."

"It's not," Mitch said quietly. "Take this thing with Hugo. There's something off about him. I can't put my finger on it exactly, but that feeling is called a gut instinct. And I don't take it lightly. I won't fully put all my eggs in Hugo's basket until I vet the situation more. The same thing can be said for Royce. Both these guys haven't put all their cards on the table. And until they do...I won't put everything we've worked so hard on at risk. If you lined up five people in town and forced me to pick the man I least trust, I'd pick Royce Buchanan every time. It's just the way it is."

"There you go," Garret said. "I don't know what role, if any, Royce played. But I've yet to feel that I have complete faith in him. It's the same thing I felt with Walker. He wasn't a man who gave off a good vibe when it came to trust. Not for any of us."

Tessa bit her lip. It was time to remind the men that she had a lot at stake, too. "I understand. If I find out Royce had anything to do with Ryan's death, I'll be the first one to react." She stepped to Jackson, rubbed his back. "I'm sorry you're upset. But it's a different gut reaction for me."

Jackson took her hand, looked at his brothers. "How do I change someone's mind who doesn't have thirty years of knowing the bad guy in town?"

"I don't know. But Anniston said my judgment was clouded because of Dad. My mistrust isn't based on Dad. Not this time." Garret took a step toward the door. "Look, I didn't mean to cause problems here. I should probably go."

Mitch stopped him. "We were just about to open up this chest I took from Hugo. You should stay for that."

But popping open the little trunk only added to the list of questions.

"I don't see any ID cards, passports or photographs in here. This looks like nothing more than mementos from his mother." Which prompted Garret to ask, "Where's the leather-bound diary we thought was a Bible?"

"Before we reached port, it was in Mom's dining room hutch. Now it's locked up in a very secure place." Mitch went on, "The diary is written entirely in German, so we'll need to hire a translator to crack what's written in it."

But Jackson began to see another disturbing pattern. "If Hugo doesn't actually have the documents in his possession, then where are they? We didn't find them in the house or in Walker's safe." He began to mutter out loud. "If Walker had the diary, then chances are he had the ID cards that Dietrich doesn't want anyone to find out about, enough to kill whoever's got them squirreled away."

"Motive," Garret muttered. "We finally have a motive. They were murdered to protect the world from finding out Dietrich's father was a fucking Nazi." He got up to roam the room. "So where are these precious documents? Would Walker have given them to Royce for safekeeping? Did Walker and Livvy have a safe deposit box at the bank?" He turned to Jackson. "Your banker friend disappears, could he have drilled into their safe deposit box?"

Jackson threw his hands up. "How would we know that for certain? How could we prove what was in there unless we find the bastard."

Mitch tossed out another worrisome piece of the puzzle. "There's another angle to this, guys. Hugo must've known the documents weren't in the trunk. He snookered us."

"Which makes me wonder what else he's bullshitting about," Jackson said, looking straight at Tessa. "We don't trust Hugo until we know with certainty he's on the level. It sounds like he's more of a con artist than we thought. Agreed?"

"Absolutely. I think it's time we hit the Vitamin Hut. If the documents aren't there, then we're looking for another needle in a haystack."

For three hours they searched the supplement shop, going through inventory, ripping through shelves, rifling in drawers, looking under the counter for a secret safe, and generally tearing the place upside down. Near midnight, they gave up.

"I gotta get some sleep, guys," Mitch admitted. "Walsh has been placating Hugo all day. But come tomorrow morning, we'll have to confront him about what we didn't find in the trunk. For that scene, I'll need to be at the top of my game because this old guy is crafty, more so than he looks."

Chapter Twenty-Five

The next day, Garret joined his brothers on the boat. He'd dragged himself out of bed to sit in front of the lying sack of shit that called himself Hugo Reiner. In the galley, they all gathered around watching the old sailor drink coffee and eat his breakfast.

"Did you sleep well, Mr. Reiner?" Mitch began. "Yesterday, we thought we'd give you some time to recharge. We hope it worked."

"Ja, it worked fine."

"Good. So maybe now you'll cut the bullshit and tell us why there was nothing in the trunk like you described, no passports, no damaging Nazi ID cards, certainly nothing of any real value pointing to gold bullion."

"Schmutzig schwein! That pig Walker stole my stuff!"

"Now, see," Garret started. "The filthy pig thing won't work. You knew two days ago that there were no papers in your cache, which means you lied to us."

Hugo's affable mood changed. "You can't keep me here against my will."

"So, you're in Dietrich's backyard but you're no longer afraid of him? Interesting. How about I let you wander around on the dock and see if you'll last an hour? What about that?"

"I'm an old man, more valuable to Dietrich alive than dead until he gets his hands on those papers. Then sadly, I have outlived my usefulness to anyone, even you."

Mitch narrowed his eyes at the old man. "So let me get this straight. Walker stole the documents from you. Then he tried to blackmail Dietrich with them because the papers are that damaging. He doesn't want the world knowing that he started his company with money taken from the Nazis. You say Walker looked past the danger dealing with Dietrich all because Walker needed a backer?"

"Ja, that is correct."

"Walker told you all this, confided in you, right there in the bar?"

"He has very big mouth when he drinks."

"Okay, so Dietrich gets pissed off at being blackmailed. He desperately wants to find the documents Walker has in his possession. He wants these papers so badly that he commands a lackey to kidnap an entire family. This flunky he sends tortures them to learn the whereabouts of all this Nazi crap that would expose his sorry ass to the world. But the plan doesn't work. Dietrich comes up empty because his little gutless minion kills Walker and Livvy without learning the location of this cache. Have I got it straight so far?"

"Ja. I want my diary back."

"We'll get to that in a minute. So Dietrich is still looking for these papers?"

Hugo's accent thickened. "Ja, ja. Dietrich keeps looking. He needs the diary, which you claim to have, to find the gold and the documents to keep from losing all he's built over the years. His wealth, his dynasty, his assets depend on keeping his secret. If it were to get out, become public knowledge where his money came from…everything Dietrich has would crumble into nothing. Dietrich would be branded an outcast by all those he values."

Mitch met Hugo's eyes, clearer and bluer today than they were yesterday. "Then following the logic of that, there are three possibilities as to where these papers could be. One, Walker put them somewhere and the stash of documents are still hidden because Dietrich murdered them all before anyone gave up the location."

Mitch laid a hand over his heart. "Now me, my personal opinion, killing and torturing little kids, and then not getting what you want out of it, is incredibly stupid. Dumbest move I ever heard of, a flat-out blunder on Dietrich's part. And they say this man is a genius at business?" He turned to Jackson. "You ever heard of anyone so stupid?"

"I'd go with sadistic and cruel with a major case of stupid."

"Exactly. Now where was I? Oh, yeah. The second possibility is that someone else stole the stuff from Walker before he was murdered. Of course, there is a third option. Mr. Reiner here is lying through his pearly whites, and this is a cleverly constructed pile of shit."

"Again, you think I lie?"

"As a matter of fact I do. Here's what we're gonna do for now. Your ass is gonna sit on my boat under heavy guard until you make a believer out of all of us. So far, that hasn't happened. And until it does, your ass isn't going anywhere. Are we clear?"

"Kidnapping is what this is," Hugo muttered as Walsh led him back to his cabin. "I want my diary back!"

After Hugo was safely out of earshot, Jackson pointed out, "Here's something to consider. Hugo was in rags when we found him. But I noticed today when he was talking, his teeth are in pristine condition. His nails look like he's had a manicure recently. And there are no calluses on his hands. Shouldn't a man living off the grid have teeth that need work, uneven nails, and rough hands? Does anyone else find that odd?"

Garret went over to the coffee pot and filled a mug almost to the rim. "I find this whole damn thing odd. What if all we really have is Hugo's boat and not Hugo?"

Mitch pondered that as he drank deeply from his own cup. "Call your friend on Shock Island and get him to go over that tub with a microscope."

"I'll do that. I hate to bring this up but we know Livvy was having an affair with Nathan. Could that bastard have found the papers or taken them out of the safe deposit box and now he and these documents are God knows where?"

"I don't know. But as long as we can't put our hands on them it means we have to keep searching, maybe tear the house upside down again. Because if we fail to turn anything up, we can't hold Hugo indefinitely."

"It's a waste of time to search the house," Garret stated. "There's one thing we know with certainty. If Livvy and Walker had known where those documents were, they'd have handed them over in a heartbeat to save their lives. They wouldn't have let Blake and Ally die."

"Which means Walker might've had the papers at one time and someone stole them," Jackson said. "Are we all picturing Nathan in that role?"

"I believe we are."

Afterward, Garret jacked up his music and locked himself away from the rest of the world in the solace of his dad's workshop to think. If his mother needed shelving in the utility room, he damn well intended to give her shelving while he could.

In the humidity he was sweating like a pig in his T-shirt and shorts. Not to mention the pair of safety glasses he had on made his head hurt. He should've hit the surf instead of closing himself off inside four walls.

He stood in front of a table saw with a cast-iron top in the middle and steel wings on the side. It was his father's pride and joy. He might not have been the carpenter his father was, but Garret slid a long piece of red oak through the blade, listened as the saw ripped through the wood.

Tanner came in holding two bottles of water, handed one off. "You're making me look bad, Garret Davis."

Garret reached to flip the switch on the saw to off and raised his goggles. He twisted off the cap and gulped down half the bottle.

"I noticed you slept here last night."

"If you know all that, then you know why. Anniston went to Royce, had a nice little talk. She revealed everything we'd discussed because she's come to the conclusion the man should be trusted."

"Your mother and I have disagreements all the time."

"Yeah, but they're usually about whether or not it's time to put on a new roof. Or shelving. Or how much to put away in savings. This is a fundamental problem between us."

"You think so? When all this happened, your mother was convinced Royce couldn't have been involved. As I recall, it pissed me off."

"There you go. The difference is Mom didn't go to Royce behind your back and tell him stuff he'd never have known otherwise. Anniston did. I feel like she betrayed the case we've worked so hard on. And me."

Tanner scratched his ear. "Maybe she was right to meet with him, to reveal Baskin for what he is. Maybe Royce didn't have anything to do with the murders. Maybe Walker did keep him in the dark about this treasure hunt for gold."

"Maybe. But as I see it that's not the point. She didn't value my opinion enough to take it under consideration. She put her trust in a man I warned her about. In fact, we all warned her."

"That's because we've known him longer."

"That's right. And our opinion should've mattered, should've carried more weight."

Anniston had been leaning up against the doorframe, listening. "You're right. I should have considered how you felt." She looked around the workshop at all the lumber and tools and machinery. "You're a man of many talents." She sent a smile toward Tanner. "You both are."

"You're just now figuring that out?" Tanner said.

He slapped his son on the back with pride. "This one is a true wonder. All my kids were talented, but this guy was always willing to help out his old man, get his hands dirty doing some type of carpentry job. Whether it was cabinets or knocking out a wall. Every time he comes back home, he never fails to find his way into the workshop and take the time to build something for his mother."

Garret sent him a crooked grin. "It's okay, Dad. You don't have to tout my good points. Anniston's already seen my temper."

She placed her arms across her chest in a gesture of surrender. "I'm here to apologize."

Tanner started for the door. "I'll leave you to it unless you need a referee."

"We'll be fine," Anniston assured him.

"Why are you apologizing exactly?" Garret wanted to know.

She let out a sigh. "Because I got caught up. Whether or not I'm taking your money now, today, doesn't matter. You're still my client. I should've respected your wishes and not gone anywhere near Mr. Buchanan other than to interview him about the specifics of the case. It was unprofessional on my part. Even though I do disagree with you, I shouldn't have disclosed anything to him, certainly not aspects of the case. I'm very sorry. I meant well. You're welcome to replace me with Sebastian."

"Oh, for God's sake. I was pissed and thought you were way out of line, but you don't have to quit over it." He went over, linked his fingers with hers, drew her in for a kiss.

"Just so you know, Reiner's fingerprints didn't show up in any databases. They checked Interpol, nothing."

"I was afraid of that." His cell phone went off. "I gotta take this. It's about Reiner's boat."

Listening to the caller, Garret nodded through most of the conversation until it was time to hang up. "Thanks, Gary. I appreciate you looking. I'm sorry I pulled you into all this. I know you were just doing me a favor. Okay. Talk to you soon."

Ending the call, he turned to Anniston. "I asked Gary to recheck Reiner's skiff. Gary didn't find anything suspicious except a blood splatter near the galley. It could be fish blood."

"We could test it."

"We could spend time doing that, but if you'd seen this old tub…it reeked with all kinds of stinky smells. So it's not surprising Reiner gutted his fish in the galley."

"Shouldn't that be done on deck?"

"Normally. But this guy calling himself Reiner is different, beyond odd. He's just not adding up."

"That gut instinct thing?"

"Yeah. If you don't listen to your gut, what else do you have?"

"There's another reason I came by. It may not be related, but it's weird. This morning a fisherman found two bodies floating near Sugarloaf Key, very near the spot where you found Reiner."

"Coincidence?"

"I wonder."

"Maybe we should tell the others and let them decide for themselves."

Within the hour everyone, except Raine, had assembled in Lenore's dining room. She'd put out a tray of snacks—pretzels and veggies with smoky jalapeño-ranch dressing for dipping. Tanner had made the iced tea and lemonade. But no one seemed to be interested in food.

"So other than the small amount of blood Gary found in the galley, there was nothing out of the ordinary on the *Schneewind*," Garret explained. "But the two bodies washing up are problematic. What if the remains have something to do with this guy we have locked up? What if he's as murderous as Baskin and Dandridge?"

"My line of thought exactly," Mitch decided. "Reiner was in the vicinity. And we don't know for sure who he is exactly."

"Since the fingerprints were a bust, I'll keep checking with county to get the autopsy results on both of the unidentified remains. I don't even know if they were male or female, if they drowned or suffered trauma. This is all very preliminary information picked up from a news report," Anniston prompted. "Maybe it's time to remind you that you're in a gray area by keeping that man a prisoner on your boat."

"What do you suggest we do, call the authorities and hand Reiner over to them? Which authorities would that be exactly? Or have you changed your mind about Sinclair, too?" Mitch asked.

Lots of attitude, Anniston decided. "I've apologized to Garret about my visit to Buchanan. I'll apologize to everyone here again. It was wrong of me. There? Satisfied? I'm not suggesting calling Sinclair, nor would I, but we have to turn over the man you have on board to someone…eventually."

"If it comes to that, I prefer taking him back to his sailboat and letting him resume his wandering lifestyle. I prefer that to handing him over to someone I don't trust…like Sinclair." Mitch crossed his arms over his chest. "Satisfied?"

"I believe I am," Anniston said.

"What about that Willis Hartman guy Raine found online?" Garret asked. "Anything on him?"

"Other than his date of death? No. I found an obituary that showed a Willis Hartman dying in 1992 here in southern Florida around the time Dandridge showed up in Indigo Key. Other than that, nothing. His daughter still runs the website Raine found. But it'll take a trip up to Port Saint Lucie to talk to her."

"I could do that," Sebastian began. "But there could be another more important factor right now. I had a long talk with Walsh. I took the information he gave me and ran with it. I think he's onto something. Baskin is likely using a private chat room with encrypted code to communicate with his buddies. I could hack my way in, but first I'd have to get access to one of his computers, or that of his cohorts. Since Royce let me into the guesthouse once, we could ask him again, and obtain the IP address of the chat room that way. By posing as the administrator I could monitor their posts."

"Are we okay with asking Royce for another favor?" Anniston asked.

Garret met Mitch's eyes to see if they were on the same page. "As long as we get something out of it, I suppose so."

There was another matter she needed to bring up. "You already know that Dack suspected the type of caliber that was used to kill Ryan came from a SIG-made P210. Turns out, the same caliber gun was also used to take down Dack. I ran Baskin's name through a state database. And what do you know? He owns a registered P210."

"We're getting closer," Garret noted.

Anniston went over her notes. "I'm just full of information today. I mentioned before that Royce told me where Dietrich is staying while he's here on the Key. I think we should…"

Garret sat up straighter. "That's right. I forgot about that. Where is he?"

"You won't believe it. The property is less than a quarter of a mile from where Jackson and Tessa were shot at, very near the preserve."

"That big estate that sits behind iron gates?" Jackson asked. "What does he do, watch the preserve from his window waiting for the bulldozers to show up?"

"Probably. The place has boat access," Sebastian added. "So potentially it could be checked out from the water."

"That sounds fine by me," Mitch said. "I want my turn at questioning Dietrich. Garret got to get in Oakerson's face, Jackson went head to head with Baskin, Raine got Frawley to talk, and even Mom and Dad had the satisfaction of watching Dandridge squirm. I want my chance at Dietrich."

The wheels started turning in Garret's brain. "And you'll get it, but not right now. The timing's wrong for a face to face. But I have a better idea. Instead of that, what if I went on a little scavenger hunt inside the premises?"

Garret turned to Sebastian. "Could you get me the floor plan of that place? Any kind of pictures would help. Maybe it's been for sale or for rent at other times. If so, there should be photos online of the house."

"I'll see what I can do. But why?"

Anniston thought she already knew the answer. "You're going in there to steal from Dietrich?"

"Not unless I find something worthy of taking the risk. Stealing isn't the goal. I think it's important to know what he keeps in that house. Maybe see if he already has the documents. I'll go room by room and see what I can find, get the lay of the land."

Anniston didn't like the sound of that. "It's too dangerous, Garret."

"I know what I'm doing. You guys take care of getting back into the guesthouse or wherever Baskin has a laptop. You might consider his string of businesses, even the used car lot. It's vital we break that communication code. I'll take care of finding out anything I can about Dietrich."

Mitch took out his phone as if expecting a call. "Does anyone know where Raine is? I know it's her day off but she should be here by now."

"I haven't talked to her all day. Usually she calls the restaurant to make sure everything's running smoothly, but not today," Tessa offered.

"I haven't talked to her since we got back from Dack's funeral," Anniston admitted.

Mitch sent Raine a string of text messages that went unanswered. He grew impatient first and then broke out into worry. He began to call around looking for Raine but no one had heard from her. "Okay, this is nuts. I'm going over to the houseboat."

"What's that all about?" Jackson asked after Mitch left. "If he thinks he can prod Raine into being a part of this, he's mistaken."

"She's been pulling away since that night at the gun range," Tessa suggested. "She's not too keen on being around Indigos at the moment. No offense."

Lenore grabbed a carrot stick and swiped it through the dip. "None taken. But I think it's just one Indigo she butts heads with more than anyone else. It must be difficult for her to have such strong feelings for Mitch and only see him once a year."

Anniston turned to study Garret's mother. "Raine is fine with seeing him once a year. The problem comes from having to be around him so much during this ordeal. Repressed emotions and all."

Garret didn't get it. "Am I hearing you right? The only feeling Raine has for Mitch begins and ends with loathing."

"Men. Raine still carries that love she had for him as an adolescent. She can't help how she feels," Anniston told him.

Garret frowned. "If you say so, but personally, I think she just hates his guts, has for years."

Chapter Twenty-Six

Mitch stood on Raine's deck and knocked on the door of her houseboat, painted aqua-blue with a bright cerulean trim. An improvement, he decided, over Danny's color scheme—ugly white. Leave it to Raine to go bold. She'd always had a bohemian spirit, an avant-garde approach to life. It's one reason he'd been drawn to her in high school.

No one told Raine Manning what to do or how to do it. That's why he'd been so surprised when he'd learned that she'd let herself get roped into taking on the duties of running The Blue Taco. She'd always said she'd never get stuck behind the counter taking orders for life. And yet, she seemed happy doing just that. Which just goes to show you how much people could change, Mitch thought.

He knocked on the door again and waited, tapping his foot impatiently on the wood floor. Standing there, he looked around at the work she'd done on the place since he'd been in town last. There were rows of houseplants sitting along the sundeck in containers, mostly stuffed with red, white, and blue asters, their big and bold blossoms making a colorful statement. She'd put out a carved jack-o'-lantern with a crazy Igor-like face. It was so like her to remain grounded in the middle of madness.

The door popped open and she stood there, her hands on her hips, a rebellious attitude at the ready. "Yes, I got your texts, but I've had a rough week and I really, really, want to be left alone tonight. Is that so hard to understand?"

Mitch looked her up and down and noted she'd been crying. Just as ready for a battle as she seemed to be, he fired back, "It takes five seconds to reply to a text. If you didn't want anyone, *me*, to come check on you, then you should've texted back."

"Yeah. Well. Silly me. I'm not up on my text etiquette."

"So the snotty attitude is back again?"

Instead of closing the door in his face as he'd expected, she opened it wider. "Okay. Fine. Let's do this and get it over with, once and for all. Come on in. Would you like something to drink?"

A little stunned at the change of heart, Mitch stepped inside her living room. "A beer would be great."

Raine went into the kitchen, brought back two bottles of nut-brown ale, handed one off to him.

She took a seat on one end of the couch as far away from him as possible and tucked her feet under her to get comfortable. "Go ahead, have a seat." She deliberately took a deep drink from the bottle.

"Such a sweet invitation, but I don't think so. Something tells me I won't be around here all that long."

"Suit yourself. So you were worried about me? Wow. Why?"

"Because I haven't seen you since that night at the gun range. You said you wanted to talk. Now it seems you've changed your mind and decided to go into avoidance-mode."

She took another drink of beer, hoping to find courage in the alcohol. "You're right. I do need to tell you something, something I should've told you a long time ago."

"Unless it explains why you hate me so much, what's the point?"

"It does. Well, partly." Raine took another deep drink. "I'm just gonna say it. You left out of here right after graduation. I mean we went through the whole commencement thing, walked across the stage at noon to get our degree, and by six o'clock that night you'd packed your bags and were gone. Is that a fair statement?"

"What was the big deal, Raine? You knew what my plans were all along. I told you about them for six months before it happened. I told you what I'd decided to do with my life. Not only that, two nights before graduation I reminded you about everything. After all this time, I still can't figure out why you're so upset about it. We said our goodbyes the night before we graduated."

"That's just it. I didn't realize you were serious about leaving town and heading off on the first salvage boat that hit Sugar Bay. I didn't realize you planned to take off and be gone for a year before I'd see you again."

She took a deep breath to calm down. "Which I suppose is my fault. You did tell me your plans in detail and I, like an idiot, thought you were just blowing off steam. It never occurred to me you really intended to go through with it and be gone for good. But when you left on that salvage ship, what was the name?"

"*The Outlander.*"

"When you left on *The Outlander,* when you sailed out of port, I was pregnant with your baby. There, I said it. What a relief! It's finally out. The day you left town without a backward glance, I was two months pregnant."

Mitch was so stunned he had to grab the nearest chair for support and then folded himself into the cushion. "And you never bothered to mention this after a dozen years? So where's our child?"

"Ah. That. Because luck always seems to be on your side, I had a miscarriage at eighteen weeks."

Rage built so fast he was unable to sit. He got to his feet again, closed the distance between them. "Luck? What a horrible thing to say to me! And so unfair. You can talk to me like that when I didn't even know. How was I supposed to know, Raine? How? Telepathy? I'm not a mind reader."

"Well, listen to you. *You're* outraged and taking on the role of the wronged party because you're the one who left town and didn't hang around to know. Am I right? I didn't even have a way of contacting you. And as I recall, you didn't even bother with a postcard until six months after you'd been at sea. I opened the mailbox one day right before Thanksgiving and there it was. Some card with a picture of Madagascar and on the back was your brief but cheery update about how great you were doing."

"You could've told me instead of carrying around all this resentment toward me…for years. So don't deny that part of it. I've been back in town for holidays off and on since I owned my own boat. You could've picked a dozen times, maybe more, to lay into me about this. But you chose to keep it to yourself and to keep building up the hate toward me. That's what's unfair!"

"I did, at one time, intend to 'lay into you' about it. But after the fact, what would've been the point?"

"I'll tell you the point. Honesty. How many times did I ask you what was wrong? Why you were so frigging angry. I might not have been here for the miscarriage, but I damn sure gave you the opportunity to be upfront with me. Not only that, you could've told me before I left. Two months? You had to have known or at least suspected. What were you waiting for back then?" he shouted.

Her temper could match his. "And thank God I did keep it to myself. If you'd have known, you might've stayed around a place you obviously hate to marry me. If I'd told you back then, you'd have surely resented me. You'd have ended up resenting the child. Every day you spent confined on this island, you would've hated your life here. So don't even try denying that."

He couldn't because that much was probably true. "Did your mother know?"

"Hard not to. She and my grandmother were completely supportive. Dr. Whitten knew because he treated me. After it happened I spent a few days with my cousin in Key Largo and then came right back to town, picked up my life at the taco shop as if nothing had happened. And later, I told Livvy after the fact. I needed someone to talk to and she was it."

Mitch felt like he'd taken a punch to the face. "Livvy knew?"

"Yes. I think it's the one thing that put us on the path toward a real friendship."

He rubbed the pain in his forehead. "But your world had obviously turned on its end when you lost the baby." He narrowed his eyes as if he'd just thought of something. "That's why you left the room the other day at the restaurant."

"What are you talking about?"

"Because I mentioned that my mom and dad were the only ones there who knew what it was like to lose a child. My God, Raine, I'm truly sorry."

He paced a couple of steps away as if he meant to leave it at that, but then he turned back. "Look, is there any way we can get past this and stop yelling at each other every single time we get within five feet? I loved you once."

"See, that's what I don't understand. You say you loved me. But you left me as though you couldn't stand looking at anyone in this town for one more day. That included me, Mitch. I've tried to come to terms with how someone does that, to reconcile that kind of declaration of love, and then walking out as if three years together didn't matter. But I just can't do it."

She went over and picked up her wallet, dug out the image she'd spent too many hours studying. "Here, I've carried this around for way too long. I think now it's your turn. This is an ultrasound of the baby at sixteen weeks. That's about four months. It was a little boy. After I got home from Dr. Whitten's office that afternoon, I decided to name him Taylor…after his father."

"My middle name." Mitch stared at the black and white image on the sonogram and his heart cracked. He'd been a father and hadn't even known about it. There'd been loss but he'd been shut out.

"Yes." She bit her lip to keep from crying, but the tears ran down her face anyway. "About two weeks after that, I started having stomach cramps in the middle of the night. My mom called Dr. Whitten and he met us at the hospital. But it was too late. After he told me what had happened, I persuaded my mom and Dr. Whitten to call Daniel Shugart at the funeral home. I begged them to let me have some kind of service for Taylor. Daniel pointed out that they don't usually do that for a miscarriage, certainly not one that happens at four and a half months. But I threw such a fit about it, that my mother and grandmother piled on and helped me convince Daniel to do it. I know it may seem like a silly teenage girl kind of thing…"

"No, it doesn't. I wish I'd been there for you."

She smiled. "I can see that now. I remember the service that day. The rain poured down in buckets as if even heaven was in tears. At least that's the way I looked at it. I stood there under my umbrella thinking it was all a nightmare. But it wasn't. We buried Taylor in the family mausoleum where my grandfather had been laid to rest. Later, we put Danny there when we received his body back from Afghanistan. And now a few rows over, Livvy and Ally and Blake rest nearby. At least now, maybe Taylor won't be quite so alone."

He reached to wipe her tears away. "Raine."

She held onto his hand and kissed the palm. "I don't blame you anymore. I can't. I can't go on carrying around all this anger inside me. It's too heavy and too much work and takes way too much energy. And I'm sick of looking at myself in the mirror for doing it."

Mitch plopped down on the sofa and took her into his arms. "Stop beating yourself up."

"There's something else. I spent hours rereading some of your cards and notes from high school. I think I might've misunderstood your words. You were telling me how much you loved the sea, how much it meant to you and I thought you were declaring your love for me. I'm sorry."

"Oh, God, Raine, don't think like that. I did love you. Do. I loved you in every way a teenage boy loves. We were so very young. I didn't leave because I wanted to get away from you. I left because I wanted what all young men want. Adventure. To see the world. To experience more than Indigo Key had to offer. It wasn't about you, Raine. It was an emptiness inside me if stayed here."

"I know that now."

"I wish you'd told me. I wish…things could be different between us. Not back the way they were, but—"

She put her fingers up to his lips. "Stop. We can't change history, Mitch. What happened, happened, and there's nothing either one of us can do to change it."

When Mitch made the trip to the cemetery he didn't go empty-handed. He pulled up to the same gates where his family had said goodbye to Livvy and her family less than a week earlier.

He shoved out of the pickup, grabbing the flowers he'd bought at the florist from the passenger seat. He headed toward the aboveground vault belonging to the Indigo line. He stood for a few minutes before placing part of the bouquet of lilies at the feet of the sculpted angel, the one raised on a pedestal with her arms outstretched in welcome. He knew she'd faithfully watched over those he'd lost over the years.

Too many, he thought now. But someone was missing.

Downhearted, he lumbered among the headstones toward the other side of the graveyard where the vaults were newer. As he approached the Manning family crypt, he tried to blank his mind and tamp down his emotions.

It had been there since the sixties, ever since Diane and Douglas Manning settled on island in 1962. The couple had bought a larger plot after Douglas Manning, Raine's grandfather, had dropped dead of a massive coronary inside his taco stand.

Next to Douglas, Danny's name had been etched into the marble headstone. But it was the other simple words Mitch studied. His eyes drifted to the name carved next to Danny's that had been there for a dozen years without him even knowing it existed.

He'd had a son. Baby Boy Taylor.

Mitch didn't plan it, but he dropped to one knee on the grass. He ran his fingers over the lettering as his eyes began to water. His vision blurred. It was impossible not to feel loss, a loss he'd known about for exactly one hour. There on bended knee, he struggled with his emotions, all the while trying to figure out how he'd tell his folks about another grandchild, dead in the ground before they even knew anything about him.

On board *The Black Rum* Mitch was in such a foul mood, the crew deliberately avoided him. Around seven that night, Walsh had had enough. He pounded on the door of Mitch's private quarters just to see if he could get a response. The fact that he couldn't pissed him off. If Mitch intended to ignore him, he decided there was only one thing left to do.

Stationed in front of Reiner's cabin door, Walsh pulled out his cell phone and thumbed through his contacts. Since he considered Mitch like a brother, Walsh figured that if one family member couldn't get the job done, maybe three would have better luck.

Fifteen minutes ticked by before Walsh looked up and spotted Garret and Jackson making their way down the narrow passage to Mitch's cabin.

Walsh greeted them with a curved grin and a wink.

"What's wrong with him?" Jackson asked. "Did he take a swing at Hugo?"

"Not yet." Walsh thumbed a fist toward Mitch's room. "I've never seen him like this. It's like he's possessed. What happened on shore?"

Jackson leaned back on the wall, lowered his voice. "Damned if I know. He went to find Raine and never came back to the meeting."

"Ah." Garret rocked back on his heels. "He must have found her all right. And it didn't go well. If we want him to talk, we should get him drunk. That usually works."

"Gotta get him to come out of his cabin first," Walsh said. "Although he does have his own liquor cabinet in there."

"I could pick the lock," Garret pointed out. "But it is his personal space. He should be entitled to his solitude when he needs it. How long's he been in there?"

"He came back in a bad mood over four hours ago," Walsh answered.

"Then he's had plenty enough time to pout," Garret reasoned. "I know how to get a rise out of him. Watch the master." He rapped on Mitch's door while Jackson and Walsh stood back to take in the scene. "Hey, you in there, Raine told us what a total piece of shit you are."

The insult worked its magic. The door flew open and Garret rushed past his brother. The two struggled in arm locks until Garret tossed Mitch back against the wall. He smelled whiskey and cut his eyes toward his audience. "Looks like the boss man has already been hitting the sauce." He picked up an almost empty bottle of scotch, and held it up so the others could see.

"Kiss my ass," Mitch slurred. "Now get out!"

"What the hell's the matter with you? Now's not the time to fall to pieces like this."

Mitch staggered over to the bed, put his head in his hands. Quietly, barely above a whisper, he muttered, "Please, get out. I don't want to talk about it."

Walsh and Jackson stepped further into the stateroom, but it was Jackson who sat down next to his brother and threw an arm around his shoulders, if for no other reason than to hold the man up. "Did Raine do a number on you?"

Mitch let his head fall back against the headboard. "What did she tell you?"

Garret traded furtive glances with Walsh and took a seat in one of the chairs. "Let me guess, she finally told you why she carries all that hate inside her."

Mitch finally looked up. "But you said…didn't you talk to her?"

"Oh, that. It got you to open the door, didn't it?" Garret reached back, took out a bottle of water from the compact fridge and handed it off to Mitch. "Drink this. You said if she ever gave up her secret, we'd be the first you'd tell. So start at the beginning. Don't leave anything out."

Hearing his words thrown back at him, Mitch drank half of the water to quench a dry throat. "Close the door," he mumbled. He pointed a finger at Walsh. "Is Hugo secure?"

"That old man ain't going anywhere. He's locked in his cabin, good and tight," Walsh promised. After closing the door, he went over to Mitch's miniature galley and started a pot of strong coffee. "So what happened?"

Once Mitch opened his mouth the story came tumbling out in a mix of anger and guilt. He left nothing out as he recounted each painful detail. By the time he was done, tears dribbled down his cheeks.

Shock brought on silence that collapsed around the men like the ceiling had fallen in. The sway of the boat didn't help. Each one felt a little sick at his stomach.

When Mitch tried to get to his feet, Jackson held him in place. "Let me get this straight. You were just beginning to start things back up with Raine again when she brought out the big guns from the past. Now you're hurt and pissed off about it. Royally."

Garret let out a laugh. "Do we need to remind you that you love this woman? You said so yourself not three nights ago."

"What's your point?" Mitch asked. "She could've contacted me, let me know what was going on."

"Really?" Garret took a beer from the fridge, twisted off the cap, sat back. "I'm just curious. How was she supposed to do that exactly? You left end of May, right? I didn't even know where you were until you called Mom around the Fourth of July. Remember? That summer everyone in town must've asked me five times a day where you were, including Raine. I didn't know what to tell her. I didn't know what to tell anybody."

Jackson nodded. "I remember that. I came home from school for a week in between summer classes. Mom was worried sick. We knew you hadn't been shanghaied because you'd packed up most of your belongings, clothes, and other stuff. You just up and left without a goodbye to anyone. In other words, if your own family couldn't find you, then how the hell was Raine supposed to know how to reach you?"

"Because I told her!" Mitch erupted. "I told her my plans not two nights before I took off. Don't you guys understand that? I started telling her my plans months before I took off. I might not have known the name of the ship then, but I kept updating her every time I got a response from a ship's captain. I must've sent out two dozen inquiries. Then *The Outlander* sailed into port. The timing couldn't have been better for me. The freighter was headed to the Indian Ocean right where I wanted to go. It was the opportunity of a lifetime. I had to go. They were leaving here Saturday night at six on the dot. I had to be on that ship."

"And you were. But did Raine know the name of the freighter? Because we didn't, not until weeks later."

"Face it," Walsh added. "You blew it, man. You left her in the dust."

"But I didn't know about the baby," Mitch insisted, desperate for some support, for someone to see his side of the situation. "I wouldn't have left her like that. I would've married her."

"And where would you be now? Raine obviously wasn't your first choice unless the pregnancy was the deciding factor," Garret said softly.

He tapped his brother on the knee. "The sea won, Mitch. You think Raine doesn't know that? Believe me, she does. She's had twelve years to consider all the possibilities. She knows you might not have this boat or the kind of life you have now. It's exactly what you wanted. No doubt, you guys had an unfortunate turn of events. But the question is what do you plan to do about it now. Sit here and feel sorry for yourself? Or figure out a way to be with the woman you love?"

Walsh drained the remaining scotch from the bottle. "We love you, bro. But at times you come off as unbelievably coldhearted. Not to mention, a bit of an ass. Don't let this resentment continue. You'll have to make things right with the woman eventually."

Garret veered from that point of view. "Clear the air, yes, but not until you've figured out what you want from Raine this time around. Either you'll work things out, or you won't. But one way or the other, you need to get a clear path in your head as to what comes next. Either leave the woman be or go for it all."

Jackson put in his two cents. "You have to stop this tendency you have of playing with her affections. Garret's right. You have to ask yourself what you want. Do you want to settle down with Raine here on island? She was head over heels in love with you once and you left. Every time you get near each other, there's no doubt about the chemistry. But frankly, I don't see you settling for a life behind the counter at the taco shop. What else would you do here, Mitch? Take tourists out to look for gold on the weekends? That doesn't sound like my brother, the adventurer."

Mitch didn't see himself doing either one of those things. It saddened him to the core.

"And is chemistry enough?" Garret went on, "Everyone in this room knows when you're ready to leave the Key again, you will. You'll take off without a backward glance because it's what you do."

"In other words, you'll do what suits you and won't think twice about hurting Raine again," Jackson noted. "So be sure what you want this time."

Garret took the long way to get to the heart of his advice. "So until you decide that staying put with Raine is what you want, I'd suggest you think long and hard about approaching her."

Walsh bobbed his head toward Garret. "That's a good point. Yeah, stay away until you've got your head on straight."

"So my own brothers are condemning me for wanting to get Raine back?" Mitch implored. "Unbelievable. You don't think I'm ready to settle down? You think I'll hurt her again? What's wrong with wanting to have my life at sea *and* Raine Manning waiting back here at home? Why can't I have both? Other men do it."

Garret exchanged a look with Jackson. "You don't get it, Mitch. Raine may want something other than a life with a sailor. That's something the two of you will have to work out. If it's meant to be, if Raine will accept your life in the salvage business, or you decide to stay here in Indigo, it's up to you two. It's possible it could work out, depends on the two of you."

"You don't sound all that hopeful," Mitch said.

"That's because you both have to get past all the anger first. Looking at you right now, let's face it, that's a big hurdle. We all come with baggage. What happens in the past makes us who we are. There's no getting around that. Bottom line is if you want Raine, you'll figure out a way to make it work. If not, you'll have to let her go."

"I already did that."

Garret slapped him on the shoulder. "Come on, pull yourself together. I have a house to break into and I need you to have my back."

Fuzzy-brained still, Mitch asked, "You're still doing that? I thought Anniston would've talked you out of that by now."

"I'm still doing it," Garret stated. He tossed a glance at Jackson. "Looks like you'll have to back me up. I don't think Mitch is up to it."

Mitch staggered to his feet. "No, I'm okay." But his head was spinning like a scene out of *The Exorcist*. He had to sit down again. "On second thought, take Walsh. Take one of the lifeboats. I'll stay here and guard the infamous Hugo."

For the next couple of hours, Garret got his gear ready. He loaded up a bag with the stuff he'd need, including the weapons he would bring. If only he didn't have to have an argument with Anniston about going. "This is the next step. I'll be fine."

"I wish you wouldn't do this."

"Stop worrying. I'm not going in alone. With Jackson and Walsh, I've got this covered."

"I should go with you."

"There's no room in the dinghy for a fourth," he pointed out, watching the worried frown lines spring up on her face. Some part of him inside brightened with the joy that she'd fret over him while he was gone.

"Sebastian's done most of the surveillance. He's done the legwork and I've done my homework. There's no need to get all tied up in knots."

"Just be careful," she said, linking her arms around his neck.

"I always am," he told her as he patted her rear end.

Anniston checked her phone for an update from her brother. "The good news is Sebastian's latest report says that Dietrich doesn't have guard dogs, at least not the canine variety. Although he did see Baskin and Dandridge hanging around earlier. But at last report the men left around 10 p.m. No other visible supporters anywhere around the property that he can see."

"Awesome, because I'll need enough time to locate the moneyman's bedroom in the house, and enough time to take a tour, then crack the safe without interference from any of his bodyguards. Sebastian knows if he spots anyone around the perimeter, he'll have to create a distraction to get them away from the rental, otherwise they'll screw this whole thing up."

"We don't want that. Text me as soon as you're out of there and on your way back home, okay?"

He took her chin and planted his lips on her mouth. "I'm beginning to think you're a worrywart."

"I guess I am when it comes to you."

"I like the sound of that."

"Be careful."

"I'm the epitome of careful." He let go of her hand to join his band of brothers and pushed off in the dinghy.

Like men on a mission, the three guys began to row. Above them, low in the night sky, a waxing moon glistened on the water in a show of silver and light. The waves slapped the little skiff, bouncing them up and down in the surf.

Garret didn't start the motor until they were halfway across Sugar Bay, well away from the busy marina. They hugged the coast to the south, using the lights on shore as their navigational point, the shadows to hide their presence.

The moonlight helped them once they reached the beach. Dressed in all black with ski masks hiding their faces, the trio left the dinghy bobbing at the water's edge, a good seventy yards away from the estate.

Grabbing the backpack he'd brought, Garret led the way through a canopy of tropical palms.

Walsh shoved a device in Garret's hands and whispered, "Use this as soon as you get within ten feet of the house. It's guaranteed to jam the sensors and take care of the security cameras and the alarm system in one fell swoop, forcing them all into shutdown mode no matter the location."

"How does it do that?"

"It intercepts the data, deciphers the commands and changes the encryption so that it can't authenticate any signals."

"I'll take your word for it," Garret said as his face broke out into a grin. "I'd give you a big kiss on the mouth if I didn't think you might take it the wrong way."

"I hate to break it to you, sweetheart, but you aren't my type. Now get out of here, kid. And don't get yourself caught."

"I don't plan on it. One question, though. How do I reengage the systems after I get out? I don't want Dietrich finding out I've been in there."

Walsh pointed to a button on the side. "Once you're out, hit this. It'll reset everything."

Jackson stood a few feet away next to a flowering ponytail palm. "If you need help, you know the signal. Walsh and I have your back."

Garret sent him an eye roll. "If I get caught there won't be any time to send up a flare. You guys take the raft and get out of here. Period. Don't wait for me."

"You're joking, right? If you get caught I doubt Dietrich will bother calling the cops. We'll likely hear gunshots long before he bothers asking any questions."

"Thanks for that image," Garret grumbled as he took off toward the house, veering through the property's flora for cover. Hiding behind banana and banyan, he trekked through wild tamarind until he reached the outer courtyard.

Modern in design, the oceanfront villa was a tri-level gem at just under twelve thousand square feet. Garret intended to take his time with the premium tour.

There were no lights coming from anywhere inside, which made the house look deserted. But then he wouldn't expect revelry at two-thirty in the morning.

When he found himself standing in the middle of a garden surrounded by shrubs and flowers, he brought out the device Walsh had given him and adjusted the dial that would send out radio waves to block the frequency and jam the data.

He made his way around the side of the house into the gleaming backyard pool setup. He took a few extra seconds to admire the oasis—surrounding sandstone deck and gurgling waterfall—that glowed like a beacon in the night. It was so bright back here he almost felt exposed. Even if he kept to the shadows, he doubted he'd need his penlight to see to pick the lock—it was that bright.

From his bag, he took out a pair of black gloves, tugged them on. He removed a grappling hook with a forty-foot rope. The metal flukes had been taped so they wouldn't clink when the hook hit concrete or metal and make needless noise.

He tossed the hook up and over the balcony, then tested it to see if it had caught and the rope would hold his weight.

Behind him, Jackson and Walsh waited in a thicket of blooming poinciana. After signaling to them that he was ready to make the climb up to the second story, he shimmied up the rope like a ninja. He grabbed hold of the railing and hauled his body over the ledge in one fluid motion.

Standing on the veranda, he saluted the men below letting them know that he was in position. Out of habit, he ran his fingers along the frame of the French doors, checking for those sensors Walsh had mentioned. Finding no contact wires at all, he took out his handy dandy burglary kit from his backpack to pick the lock.

Concentration and skill had him standing inside a hallway the size of a grand ballroom.

Thanks to the floor plans Sebastian had procured, Garret had the layout committed to memory. His first stop was the master bedroom where Dietrich was hopefully fast asleep. When he opened the door a crack to peer in, he was stunned to find the bed neatly made and empty. He checked the bathroom, just in case, and the walk-in closet that was the size of a playroom. He found two-thousand-dollar suits still on hangers, freshly laundered shirts in the drawers. But Dietrich was nowhere in sight.

Disappointment began to scuttle through him. What was the point of breaching Dietrich's personal castle if the wealthy guy wasn't around to try to thwart the invasion?

Puzzled by the uninhabited quarters, alarm bells went off in his head. Thinking it might be some sort of a trap, he looked around for any cameras that Walsh's device had failed to jam. But he found nothing that would indicate a live feed or that he was being recorded.

His good mood returned. He took off to explore the rest of the second floor and found no one occupying any of the bedrooms. Not a maid or a servant anywhere in sight. Odd that the house would be so void of people this time of night, he thought, especially when Sebastian had reported Baskin and Dandridge on the premises four hours earlier.

Caution sailed through Garret as he began to consider the possibility that he was in the wrong house. To verify the address, he made his way to the study downstairs.

But once he reached the first floor, the first thing he went after was the alarm system. Garret had to make sure himself that no part of it could send out a signal. And when he found it DOA he smiled, and had to admire Walsh Kingston's creativity.

The library had the look of money—rich mahogany woods, leather furniture, and gold accents that gleamed in the dark. Garret took his time perusing the bookshelves, noting many titles were in German. The books looked to be first editions and collector's items. A good sign he was in the right place after all.

Turning to the desk, he spotted what looked like a cheesy hourglass front and center. He flipped it upside down and watched the grains of sand filter through to the bottom. The piece seemed out of place among the Cartier fountain pens and mocha leather. For a man with such expensive tastes it was an odd trinket to have on hand, thought Garret.

Skirting around to the other side, he jiggled the drawer to the desk, not surprised to find it locked. He took out his torque, slipped it inside the keyhole and twisted until he felt the mechanism pop. He found mail inside addressed to Werner Dietrich—finally proof that he was in the right spot.

Feeling better, he went in search of the safe. A lower panel at the end of the bookcase revealed a cheaply designed box. He grinned as soon as he saw the brand name—another safe that required nothing more than an electronic code.

He dug in his bag again, took out a yellow zippered case that held an earth magnet the size of a hockey puck. The disk was already tucked inside a cotton jewelry pouch. Placing the magnet in the upper left corner of the safe where the solenoid device was angled, he waited ten seconds for the magnetic energy to scramble the safe's chip and wipe the memory clean before he tried the handle. When the door clicked open, he rummaged through the contents inside.

He found two Glock pistols, an assortment of loose diamonds and rubies, a stack of cash, along with a dozen or so business contracts, many with Royce Buchanan's name on them. There were other signatures from the usual suspects—the mayor, Baskin, Dandridge, Frawley, and Sinclair. But nothing to indicate Dietrich held the antique papers that proved his Nazi origins were for real.

With his camera phone, Garret took pictures of the paperwork and tried to leave everything just as he'd found it. But as he turned to go, it ran through his mind that he ought to be able to have a little fun and mess with the German's head. Since the magnet had wiped the chip clean, he entered a different code into the keypad. Try to get into your safe now, Garret thought.

He was grinning from ear to ear when he strolled out through the first-story double doors and back out into the courtyard.

Two hours later, he'd made it back to Anniston's hotel room and was stretched out on the bed, exhausted. But while he tried to close his eyes, she was in the mood to rehash…everything.

She'd already gone through the photos of the documents and found them damning. "My God, Dietrich has been Royce's business partner for more than five years. The man kept a detailed list of people he's paid off and how much he gave them."

"The Nazis were known to keep immaculate records. So it stands to reason that with Dietrich's upbringing it'd be ingrained in him to do likewise."

"Well, right after Royce brought him into the golf course project, the guy didn't waste any time meeting with as many congressmen as would meet with him and getting them on his payroll. If we ever do nab this guy, we could bring down all his crooked politicians."

Since she insisted on talking about it, Garret rolled on his side and propped himself up on one elbow. He watched as Anniston slathered fragrant cream on her toned arms and up and down her long legs. The picture was sexy as hell.

"Why wasn't Dietrich at home?" she persisted, not letting the subject go. "It's weird."

"No idea. It didn't look like anyone had been there for several days." He patted the sheets next to him. "Come to bed."

But since he'd gotten back, she couldn't get her mind to let go of that one fact. When she crawled between the sheets, she was still thinking like a detective. "Then why were Baskin and Dandridge there earlier?"

He ran a hand up one silky thigh. "Checking up on the place for an absent Dietrich, I guess. I don't know. You're full of questions I can't answer."

"Okay, then did you at least find out what happened between Mitch and Raine?"

"That's a long story," he said as his mouth closed over hers.

She poked him in the ribs, nuzzled his neck. "Come on, before you go to sleep, tell me what happened between Mitch and Raine."

He sighed, gave up the idea of foreplay and settled back into his pillow, gathering her close. He kissed her brow and began the sad tale of two star-crossed lovers destined to take different paths in life.

Chapter Twenty-Seven

For weeks, Werner Dietrich had been on Franco Duarte's ass. The captain of the *Patagonia Pike* had worked for the wealthy owner for eight insufferable years. But Duarte was determined to make this particular salvage operation pay off like no other. Nearing retirement, he wanted to settle down with his wife and spend some quality time with his grandkids, far away from Dietrich's relentless domination.

But with every resolute day, Duarte found Dietrich more intolerable. He had to admit he'd never seen the boss this involved with a hunt before, certainly not to the level he saw now.

The owner insisted on hourly updates, which Duarte resented. The constant inquiries on the crew's progress were annoying and bothersome. It seemed to him,

Dietrich's intervening—he had to know what was happening on the ship at all times—was the main cause for delays.

Duarte had kept quiet when Dietrich insisted on handpicking the new divers himself. Even though the men had come highly recommended, Duarte hadn't been given the opportunity for input. It didn't matter to him that the men were good at making deep-water dives, even if each dive appeared to be getting longer in duration and more dangerous than the last.

It was the owner's constant interference that was getting to him. Werner expected and demanded perfection. Add to that, the time crunch they were under was insane. Duarte felt a heightened sense of urgency in the air that had a hold on the ship and wouldn't let go.

Most days, the crew rushed from one task to the next. So far, they'd tried several different locations, but each one had been nothing more than a wild goose chase. They didn't stay in one dive spot for long. After all, Dietrich wasn't known for his patience. Because of that, during the last few weeks, the boss had questioned Duarte's judgment at every turn. In his communiqués to him, the owner had insisted the crew be more productive, charging his employees with wasting precious time.

Dietrich had a thing about wasting time. He didn't like to do it. While the grains of sand dropped through the hourglass the German kept on his desk—a sand timer he claimed came from the tomb of an Egyptian pharaoh— Duarte had noticed Dietrich's agitation increase.

As the days passed and they hadn't located what they were looking for, Duarte knew they were quickly losing their advantage. You couldn't keep a major hunt like this secret for long. Someone, somewhere would figure out what they were doing diving off the Keys. Spies were everywhere, in every port. If their goal was to steal the prize out from under an opponent, they had to expect the same kind of attitude from other competitive salvage operations.

Fear of that was always an issue, especially on a mission this strategic, this important. Not only that, but Duarte was beginning to think he had a saboteur on board. Since the start of the operation, things seemed to go wrong for no reason. He'd even mentioned it to Dietrich. But the boss had accused him of making excuses.

Duarte had narrowed down the prospects to the three newest crewmembers he felt were responsible. It wasn't his imagination that as soon as they'd come aboard things had started to unravel. He'd never had to deal with sabotage before now. But since Dietrich had practically forced him into hiring three strangers, he knew how to take care of it.

Duarte was no fool. Even though the boss didn't believe him about the sabotage, he refused to trust the man he'd already tagged as the culprit.

Mistrust took over again as the captain fingered the 9mm Beretta he wore at his hip. He hadn't caught him in the act yet, but he would. And when he did there would be no whining to the boss about it. The body would simply vanish into the ocean. He already had a believable explanation at the ready. A man going overboard happened all the time at sea. Duarte was done letting the newcomers create more havoc on his ship. He'd made up his mind. He didn't intend to take the blame for failure any longer.

The grueling days coupled with the pressure he was under made Duarte short-tempered and a little paranoid. Losing patience with everyone, he stood on deck shouting one brusque order after another.

Duarte pivoted on his heels and headed to the bridge, where he pulled out several charts with the locations marked in red. He opened an underwater survey chart and compared the red markers to the next site. He decided that one had more potential than where they were anchored now.

The captain stepped outside the operations room and yelled toward the deck below, "Call the dive team back up and get them on board. We're moving to another site."

Back at the helm, he turned to his watch officer. "Sandoval, as soon as the dive team's out of the water, weigh anchor. Chart a course for dive site F-88."

"Aye, sir."

Duarte turned on his heels, heading for his quarters. He needed alone time. For the next several hours, he took a nap and caught up on his emails. He did some work on his computer-generated maps, trying to commit the unfamiliar Florida coastline to memory.

He fixed himself a warm bath, finished reading Stephen King's novel, *Finders Keepers*, and talked to his wife back in Buenos Aires via satellite telephone.

Several hours later, a knock on the door indicated they'd reached their destination. Seventy-five miles from the shore of Indigo Key, the ship dropped anchor again. It was getting dark. They'd already had their evening meal when Duarte ordered two divers into the water.

Braxton Evans had worked on a Dietrich operation before this one. But he had to admit this salvage operation seemed different than the others. The owner seemed determined to take what he deemed to be unnecessary risks at every turn.

The times Dietrich had shown up on board, he seemed paranoid, almost to the point of having psychotic episodes. Either that, or this hunt was indeed plagued by a series of ill-fated occurrences that were dooming them to failure.

Braxton wasn't happy about diving in total darkness. There were always additional hazards diving at night. Anything could happen when you were a hundred and twenty feet below the surface. Torchlights could fail and cause the loss of visual positions. The ability to read instruments and gauges was vital to controlling depth and awareness of your surroundings. Any experienced diver could list a number of hazards associated with going down at night. Separation from a diving partner, equipment failure, and the inability to locate the boat were all excellent reasons to wait for daylight. But Braxton had already butted heads with Dietrich about it once before, to no avail. The owner had simply reminded him he was under contract to do a job. Pleading his case to Duarte had been just as ineffective.

Braxton thought of all these things as he dropped over the side with his partner of three weeks, a man he didn't know all that well named Todd.

The pair reached the sandy bottom fairly quickly. All seemed routine when they signaled to each other the target was within sight and to their right. Both divers made their way over to what looked to the untrained eye like a large sand dune. But as they swam closer to the mound, they could make out twisted pieces of metal under the silt.

It was then Braxton noticed his partner began to grab at his mask, fighting for air. Todd started to panic when he checked the gauge on his air tank and realized his air supply was already way too low. He signaled to Braxton for help.

Braxton responded by swimming over, thumped the instrumentation and read the gauge himself. Shocked to see it was almost empty, he tried to get Todd to calm down. But when you were fighting for your next breath true panic brought on fear. Todd began to kick his legs wildly, as he fought to take a breath. Braxton saw him take off and head for the surface. Knowing Todd had to decompress or he'd get bubbles in his blood, Braxton tried to grab his feet, doing his best to slow Todd's ascent.

By this time Todd was in full panic mode and hyperventilating. He was obviously scared and determined to get to the top. The fear of taking his last breath had him shooting straight upward without stopping to decompress. Braxton tried in vain to catch him. When he realized he couldn't, he alerted the crew above to the situation through his headset. "Diver Todd surfacing. Air tank failed. Get oxygen ready to revive!"

Standing on deck at the railing, Sandoval saw Andre Todd break the surface of the water fighting to get his dive helmet off. He watched as Todd ripped the regulator out of his mouth. The watch commander shouted orders for the crew to get him on board.

Once they hauled Todd out of the water and up on deck, Sandoval removed the diver's helmet and heard the guy begging for help, struggling for air. "Can't…breathe…can't…breathe!"

Sandoval noted the diver's condition—pale skin, blue lips, blue fingernails. "We have an emergency, Captain."

Duarte shouted, "What the hell's wrong with him? Didn't he do the decompression stops before he surfaced?"

"No. Braxton's says Todd's tank ran out of air. Someone must've messed with it because Braxton's tank is working fine."

By this time, Braxton was about a quarter of the way up. He used the dive com on his wrist to measure his decompression stops, unwilling to take the chance of getting the bends.

But on deck, anger moved through Duarte. "Get Todd into the decompression chamber. Now!" He clicked on the dive com again, speaking to Braxton directly. "Take your time coming up. I don't need another accident. Don't get in a rush."

"Checking my dive computer now, should be up in thirty, working my stops now," Braxton responded.

Five minutes later, the crew was dealing with yet another problem.

"Captain, the decompression chamber malfunctioned."

"What are you talking about? I checked it myself this morning. It has to be working."

"No, sir. It won't even come on. And Todd's shoulder's hurt bad. He's coughing up blood, too. There's liquid in his lungs."

"Take him to sick bay. Put him on one hundred percent oxygen and keep him on it until I tell you otherwise. Check his vitals every fifteen minutes." Duarte turned to his watch commander. "As soon as Braxton gets on deck, weigh anchor."

"Aye, sir."

"Radio the Coast Guard and tell them we should be back in Sugar Bay in two hours. Tell them we have a diver with DCS who needs medical assistance and the use of a decompression chamber."

The captain tossed Sandoval his keys. "You, take the crew chief and unlock the gun cabinet in my quarters. Make sure you lock up our three newest crewmembers in the storage compartment. We're going to get to the bottom of these mishaps before we reach port."

Chapter Twenty-Eight

Garret had offered to take a shift at watching the cagey Reiner. When his time ended and Walsh relieved him, he headed to the bridge where Jackson and Mitch sat around the chart table listening to the Coast Guard scanner. Jackson's software program had generated a detailed map of the Keys. He studied it, doing his best to pinpoint the exact location of the *Patagonia Pike*.

Jackson circled a longitude and latitude point. "Their last known position was here. If we assume a twelve-knot cruising speed per hour in calm seas, then it could be anywhere inside this circle."

"That's a lot of water," Mitch groaned. "Fortunately I'm game for a winner-take-all chase."

Garret went to the coffee pot, dumped the old grounds in the trash and put on a fresh pot of coffee. "Hugo is starting to piss me off. He complained about the food again. For a man used to fishing for his own supper, you'd think he'd be more grateful when he gets a ham and Swiss cheese on rye."

"For a guy living off the grid I noticed he's a fussy eater," Jackson pointed out.

"Downright picky," Garret added. "By the way, Anniston found a translator for that diary, a retired German history professor from Florida State. He comes highly recommended."

"As long as he's someone we can trust and knows German like it's a second language, he sounds fine," Mitch chipped in.

All of a sudden, the International Distress channel squawked to life. It was Dietrich's ship calling the Coast Guard about a near-fatal diving accident and the victim they had on board.

Garret ran his hands through his hair. "I don't believe what I'm hearing. This is perfect. We don't even have to go out and look for her. She's coming into port. They're bringing in the injured man for treatment, which means she'll likely be here only long enough to refuel and then be gone by morning."

"We could use a plan."

Garret chewed his jaw, trying to think. "Do you still have those radio tracking devices on board?"

"We should. We use them all the time to track great whites whenever we dive in shark-infested waters."

"Okay, here's what we do. When the *Pike* rolls into port, I'm in my wetsuit ready to go into the water the minute that ship docks. They'll be so busy getting the injured man seen to, I should be able to slip under the belly and attach one of those tracking units, no, two would be better, onto the hull of the ship. After that, all we have to do is ease back and follow them from afar. They'll never know we're tracking them."

"That's not a bad idea," Jackson said.

Garret went on, "We'll need a camera with a telephoto lens to get pictures of all the crewmembers while they're in port. Sebastian has one he used on surveillance for his last case in Daytona. We'll borrow that. Once we get photos, we'll know each and every man who we're dealing with on board. We'll email the pictures back to Anniston so she can run them through facial recognition to ID each one."

Mitch gave his brother a man hug. "That's brilliant. You *are* more than a pretty face."

"I'm glad you like it. Once I leave the boat to fasten the tracking devices to the hull, Jackson gets out the Nikon and he locates a spot out of sight where he starts acting like the paparazzi." Garret cautioned, "Try not to miss a man, because it's essential we know every face on board that ship."

"Why do you get to swim over?" Mitch asked as if he'd just realized Garret was having all the fun.

"Why do you think? I'm a better swimmer than either one of you."

"That's not true," Jackson challenged.

"Wanna bet?" Garret dared. "We could hold a meet right here and now, but there's no time. I'm offering to take the risk."

After much discussion back and forth, Garret won out.

Over the next few hours, the brothers devised and refined the plan that would ensure they knew where Dietrich's vessel was at all times. During the span of time it took the ship to make it into port, they assembled what they needed.

Mitch pulled out a pair of binoculars to watch from the small dock where *The Rum* had spent the last two days out of sight from the main docking area. He spotted the Coast Guard and EMTs waiting at the busy pier for the *Patagonia Pike* to bring in the injured man.

The minutes crawled by until he noticed Dietrich's ship on the horizon. "Garret, get in the water and get ready. They should be docked within ten minutes."

Once the *Pike* neared the wharf, the crew's attention focused entirely on the injured diver and getting him to the paramedics. The captain was also stuck for at least an hour completing the report and going over the incident with the Coast Guard.

In his wetsuit, Garret adjusted his mask and slipped underwater to make the long swim over to Dietrich's ship. He stayed close to the bottom on a straight line. As he enjoyed the glide through the water, he noted all the garbage dumped near the beach from the slips. It always infuriated him how people could be so careless as to trash their own harbor. He ought to do something about it. Maybe he'd become more vocal like his dad and hold a cleanup campaign when all this settled down. Deep in his outrage, the ship's hull suddenly came into view.

Jackson had stationed himself near the pilings where Jimmy Don Bates rented out Jet Skis to the tourists. From a hundred yards away, Jackson turned his baseball cap around and played photographer. He clicked away each time a different crewman aboard the ship showed his face within camera range.

Through the lens he spotted a familiar face. He blinked several times when the man appeared on deck. Jackson took another look through the viewfinder, snapped several more frames for proof. Just when he'd decided it was a mistake, the man was jerked back into a cabin out of sight. He hoped his eyes were mistaken. Maybe he was seeing things. But when developed, the film wouldn't lie.

While Jackson went on a photo-taking frenzy, Garret inspected the hull for the best place to attach the tracking units. He'd brought heavy-duty zip ties hoping to fasten one to a rudder hinge and the other to the propeller guard. He had to be quick, though, because if they started the engines for any reason, he'd be fish bait in about ten seconds.

He got the first unit in place on the rudder hinge in record time. Now for the tricky part, he looped the zip tie around the prop guard metal tubing, made sure it was secure, and swam the hell out of there.

It was a difficult thing for Jackson to accept, but the images didn't lie. He slapped a series of photos down on the table in the galley, pointed to the man in the pictures. "Even with the beard, I *know* that man is Nathan Hollister."

"Looks like your friend got over his fear of the water," Garret said. "In a hurry."

"In spades," Mitch added.

"Look closer. That crewmember standing behind him is holding a semiautomatic weapon to Nathan's head."

"I can't say I feel one bit sorry for the bastard," Garret intoned. "But the sad fact is we need to pull that lying son of a bitch off that ship. There's no other way. If we intend to find out the truth, he's part of it."

"We said we needed to figure out the weakest link." Jackson tapped the photo. "I think we're looking at it. In case you missed it, that's fear on his face, in his eyes. He's scared shitless. Nathan's obviously not a popular man on board."

"So now we're talking about kidnapping Nathan?" Mitch drawled. "I like it. But we're running out of cabins on board. I guess I could change the focus of my business to running a prison ship," he added in jest.

Garret found that funny. "Is there money in that?" Without waiting for an answer, he added in seriousness, "Kidnapping Nathan is something Walsh and I will handle."

"In your dreams," Mitch growled. "This time I'm not staying put."

"Yeah you will." Garret let those words fly with a stubborn bent. "You have to stay here in case something comes up with Reiner that the other crew members won't be able to handle."

Mitch put his hands on his hips. "It's annoying the way you're right most of the time."

Patient up to a point, Anniston wasn't having it this time. "Come on, Garret, this is crazy talk. You can plainly see right there in the photo that crewmember is armed and dangerous. He isn't one bit happy with that asshole Nathan. Don't do this."

He gripped her shoulders, rested his brow on hers. "I know what I'm doing. Trust me. It'll be okay."

"You always say that!"

"And everything always works out, doesn't it?"

She looked at Mitch, then at Jackson to back her up. "Do something. You aren't just going to let him try to board the *Pike* by himself, are you? It's insane. This is your brother. Think about it, long and hard."

"Not so insane," Jackson admitted. "But we'll need a diversion."

Garret picked up the logic and went on, "What's the weather report for tonight. We could use a fog bank. That'd work enough as a diversion. And we'll need to be able to shadow the *Patagonia Pike* and mirror her route, wait until she's moored at a specific spot. We already know the crew is one diver short. And for some inexplicable reason, they like to dive at night. So we wait until two more divers go into the water and that's when I board the ship."

"It's all about timing," Anniston concluded. "Two less men to worry about."

"You bet. I'll need to know the precise location of the cabin where they're holding Nathan. No guessing. So getting that will take some reconnaissance. I'll go in there fast and silent and move out quickly before they know what hit them."

She put her hands on her hips, beginning to get caught up in the plan. "At the risk of losing my license, if you insist on doing this, then I'm going with you this time."

Garret's lips curved up. He nipped her around the waist. "As much as I'd like to have you, you're not putting your livelihood in jeopardy for me. But I appreciate the offer."

Unmoved, she dug in. "You aren't going without me and that's final. Think about it. I'm a tactical asset. More than."

"She is," Mitch pointed out. "If I can't go, then you should take her. She moves fast and she's deadly with a weapon."

"There, see?"

Walsh stepped into the galley. "We have a situation. Reiner is screaming his head off about having a belly ache."

Mitch reached for a bottle of Pepto-Bismol and tossed it to Walsh. "Here's a bottle of pink stuff. The man bitches about everything. The way he makes demands, you'd think he was lord and master of the universe. Unless he's suffering from appendicitis, I don't want to hear about it. He's not getting off this boat."

From the bridge, Garret heard shouting. He recognized Anniston's raised voice as she yelled back at her brother. Sebastian's tone was just as mulish.

"They're talking about kidnapping a guy off a boat, Anniston. Think long and hard about the consequences of that. Do you want to lose your license? Piss everything away that you've worked so hard for these past few years? It's a crazy idea. Not to mention dangerous."

"Sheesh, you sound just like Garret. I'm more than qualified to do this."

"I didn't say you weren't. But it's risky. What if you get caught? The *Patagonia* crew works for a ruthless man who couldn't care less about legalities. Dietrich is a force to be reckoned with. If you get caught who knows what he'll demand in return, a million dollars in ransom? He's insane enough to do it."

"We won't get caught."

"You don't know that," Sebastian charged, throwing his arms up in the air. "You're so wrapped up in this guy, you don't see how harebrained this is. This isn't like you at all. You're normally so levelheaded."

That brought out the fire in Anniston. "I'm wrapped up in Garret? Please. What about you? You don't make a move without bringing Dominka along with you. So it's okay for you to drag her everywhere you go? I don't think so. You even brought her with you when you did the stakeout at Dietrich's hideout. Don't deny it. That was a stupid thing to do. You're usually so...it's not levelheaded. What's the word I'm looking for? Wait for it...pigheaded is what you are!"

Garret stepped up to the railing. "You guys need a referee?"

"No, I'm done arguing," Sebastian said as he walked off toward the stern in a huff.

"Sorry to interrupt your sibling war of words, but there's something about me you should probably know."

She crossed her arms over her chest. "If you've finally decided to come clean and tell me you've worked for the CIA in the past..."

Garret laughed. "Nope, not my style."

"You *are* a cat burglar," Anniston guessed with wide eyes. "I knew it."

"Jeez, will you just let me tell you."

"I did a background check on you. No priors, never even been picked up for stealing. You have a healthy bank account, but that's not surprising seeing as how you're a world-class surfer with hefty sponsors and endorsements. What gives?"

"That right there tells you not to believe everything that shows up in a background check. Before I made it on the circuit, I had a job as a locksmith. You already know as a kid I used to break into stuff around town all the time. It drove my parents nuts. But as long as I didn't steal anything, they figured it was just a weird, quirky phase that would eventually run its course."

She stepped closer. "And?"

"For a time, I turned that eccentric little hobby into a useful way to pay the bills, especially when I was starting out and had nothing."

"Are you telling me your sideline started to pay off in other ways? You *did* steal."

"Just listen. About eight years ago I got picked up by an undercover cop in Paris."

"You got arrested?"

"That's another word for it. I like to call it making new friends. It was my first time in the city and I was mesmerized by the vibe of the place. As a tourist I wanted to see everything so I decided to go sightseeing on my own. I came across this little art gallery in the Le Marais district. But it was closed for the night. I was there and didn't see the point of having to come back in the morning when I would likely run into a natty salesperson who would ruin the ambiance of the place by hitting me up with a tried and true sales pitch. So I picked the lock."

"Garret Davis Indigo, you didn't?"

"Now you're sorta sounding like my mother. Anyway, this guy appears from out of nowhere. He certainly wasn't wearing a uniform. He was dressed like me, in jeans and a T-shirt, but he came with an attitude toward Americans, exceptionally snotty. He started blathering away in French. I only caught about every other word. The gist of it seemed to be, that he had taken exception to the unconventional way I got into the building. Turns out, he was an off-duty cop trying to make a few extra bucks working as a security guard for the owner of the gallery. He took me downtown and put me in a holding cell until he ran me through Interpol. Once he realized that I hadn't stolen anything and I wasn't a terrorist, or a thief with priors, he let me go…with one condition."

"That you never set foot in Paris again?"

"You'd think that would be where this story would end up. But no, he wanted me to retrieve something from his ex-brother-in-law's house."

"Don't tell me he wanted you to steal back a valuable piece of jewelry."

"That's what I thought, too, but nothing quite so glamorous as that. It turns out all he wanted me to take was a family photo album that the ex-brother-in-law kept telling his sister he no longer had."

"That's it?"

"That's it. But Henri and I became lifelong friends. So you see, I'm more than capable of getting Nathan out of a locked cabin without you putting your job in jeopardy or making things bad between you and your brother."

She threw her arms around his neck and kissed him long and hard. "You might be the most fascinating guy I've ever met."

"Then you've lived a sheltered life."

She put her arm through his as they walked around the deck, enjoying the sunshine and the southern afternoon breeze.

"Is it true what your brother said? Are you wrapped up in *this guy*?" Garret asked as he looked deep into her soulful eyes.

She smiled. "You know, I think I am."

Chapter Twenty-Nine

There was planning to be done. For that, they lounged in the galley and ate Blaine's slow-roasted, barbecue brisket sandwiches.

To everyone's surprise, it was Sebastian who got things rolling. "We have a minor setback. About the encrypted chat room Baskin uses. These guys have set up their own server farm with a private portal. I haven't yet found anyone who's been able to hack it, certainly not me. Walsh and I have discussed this and as long as they change their passwords on a regular basis, it'll be almost impossible to monitor."

"Sometimes that's the way it ends up in the game," Walsh declared. "It just means we'll have to find another way."

"We're still keeping track of Baskin and Dandridge, correct?" Garret wanted to know.

"Yep. The good thing about surveillance is you can set it up from anywhere," Sebastian assured them. "Now for reconnaissance on the *Pike*, why don't we use a drone with a camera? I could disable the safety chip to get it to fly higher so the crew wouldn't even hear it circling above."

"I thought you were vehemently opposed to this little mission," Anniston snarled.

"I decided if my sister is so morally flexible that she'd get involved in something this stupid, it ought to be planned in precise detail—less risk, less chance of it going south."

Anniston glanced around the room. "Morally flexible? Nice. I'm pretty sure he just insulted all of us. It's not like we're running with drug dealers."

"That's about the only thing we haven't encountered here," he lobbed back. "Safety should be paramount in any operation."

Garret picked up his iced tea. "I agree. But let me remind you that we're taking Nathan off that boat for one big reason. He's being held against his will. We don't know why or how he got there. But we do know the guy holds some secrets that are probably the key to unlocking this whole thing. That's the reason we're going in. So how about we cut the hostility? Anniston made up her own mind to do this. I respect that. You don't agree. Fine. But that should be off the table for discussion. So there'll be no more arguing about it. We're on a timetable here. Agreed?"

Sebastian bobbed his head with some reluctance. "Sure."

"So you have access to a drone?" Mitch asked him.

"I know where I can get one."

"Then you'd better see if your supplier is able to get it quick, like tonight, ASAP because this is coming together fast."

Sebastian stood up. "I'll go make the call."

Jackson steepled his hands. "With any luck, when the crew discovers this guy's gone, they'll simply think he broke out of his cabin, slipped over the side, and tried to swim for shore."

"We ought to be able to tell where they're holding Nathan by where the guard is stationed."

"If Sebastian comes through with the drone, I'd prefer relying on that for confirmation, otherwise, we'll go with it."

"We need to check the weather forecast, keep on top of any marine layer moving in. We could use a nice cloud cover tonight."

Mitch ended the meeting with a terse directive. "So if we're done here, y'all need to go home and get your gear. You know what you need to bring. Meet back here on the boat in two hours." He looked at his watch. "In maritime speak, that's thirteen hundred hours. You need to come back prepared to haul ass—because I plan to catch up to the *Patagonia Pike*."

Mitch got under way an hour behind Dietrich's ship.

Jackson sat in the command center at a laptop, tapping away at the keys. He logged into the GPS software, pulled up the data coming from the tracking device. He opened a chart and mapped the path of the other ship as it took a southern route out into the open sea. But he had to be patient while the ship decided where she wanted to drop anchor for the night. Another hour ticked by before her engines came to a complete stop.

Garret and Anniston stood behind Jackson watching the data come up on the screen.

"What we need is a place to hang out near them and be able to sneak up on the ship without being detected by their radar," Jackson explained.

Garret studied the images of the coastline and pointed to a reef consisting of several sandbars. "There, we can come up from this direction and anchor there offshore, without being detected. Then we wait for nightfall and hope for that nice fog to roll in. It's the season for it."

"Looks as good a place as any," Jackson agreed, relaying the coordinates to Mitch.

At top speed, *The Black Rum* had the other ship on visual within an hour of leaving port.

It didn't appear that the *Pike* had spotted them. When she remained where she was without moving, Mitch maneuvered into position between the sandbar and a narrow coastal ridge, just under a quarter mile from the other boat.

"Tell Sebastian he needs to get the drone airborne," Mitch ordered Prentiss.

On deck, Sebastian was ready. He got his Phantom 2 prepared for a flyover. The device was small but sturdy, with a range of two thousand feet. It had a speed of thirty miles per hour and a flight time of fifteen minutes. But Sebastian had jacked everything he could into this little baby. He figured he might have to invest three or four flybys to obtain enough information.

He took a couple of practice laps to make sure everything was working correctly before he sent it soaring into the sky, watching it glide toward the other ship in the distance.

Garret and Anniston joined him on deck in time to witness its takeoff.

"There she goes. Notice it's white so it easily blends into the clouds. It'll take the photos as it flies and store everything it sees on a SIM card. Now we wait for it to come back."

Everyone was on deck and applauded when the drone returned.

"Let's see what she was able to get." Sebastian removed the SIM card and handed it off to Jackson who shoved it into his laptop.

"We have pictures from bow to stern." He flipped through the disk. The last three frames contained images of the main deck. He zeroed in on the single crewman who stood guard in front of a cabin door.

"This is where they're holding Nathan. If you pull alongside here and climb on board, you're out of view of the guard. Plus, it's the shortest distance to his cabin. The plan is to overpower the guard, pick the lock, secure Nathan, and get him back in the lifeboat. Be sure to paddle out five hundred feet or so from the ship before starting the motor. It should only take about thirty minutes to get back here."

Garret looked at Anniston. "I think we can do better than that. What do you say?"

"Absolutely."

They changed into their wetsuits and waited for nightfall. Mitch ordered the power cut to the boat. There could be no lights on board *The Rum* to give away their position.

For them, darkness came early.

But across the water, it was a different story. When the marine layer moved in and the mist brought shadows, they could tell the moment the *Pike* came to life. The boat was lit up like New Year's Eve. The crew got busy on the port side, as divers dropped into the water.

By Garret's count that left eight men still there. He turned to Anniston. "Are you ready?"

"You bet. I'm stoked."

Sebastian hugged his sister, and said, "Don't forget your night vision goggles and the two-way in case you get into trouble. You let me know, and I'll come in hot and fast to get you."

She kissed him on the cheek. "I'll be fine. Let's hope we don't need a rescue."

She followed Garret over the side and into the raft. The navigational point wasn't hard to determine. Even in the mist, they could still make out the lights and headed straight toward Dietrich's pride and joy. Halfway there, Garret cut the motor. They picked up oars and paddled the rest of the way.

On the moonless night, neither one said a word on approach.

Through her binoculars, Anniston scouted the deck to see if anyone was moving around. She zeroed in on the one man stationed as lookout. They bobbed up and down, letting the motion of the current carry the raft closer to the *Pike's* side.

"All clear on my point," Anniston whispered.

"Clear on mine," Garret replied. When he was close enough that he could touch the side, he quickly secured the lifeboat to the ship.

Garret was the first up and over the railing. Once he stood on the deck, he turned to help her as she climbed aboard. They hugged the ship's wall, so they wouldn't stand out, and moved swiftly to the first corner, where they stopped.

He held out a small mirror to peer around the edge. To his surprise, the guard wasn't there. He moved quietly into the hallway and Anniston followed, taking a position across from him to keep watch.

He put his ear to the door to listen for any sounds. Maybe the guard was actually inside the cabin with Nathan. But he heard nothing coming from that side. He went to work on the simple lock while Anniston had his back. In less than a minute he had the door open. Anniston scooted in behind him as they both ducked into the cabin and shut the door.

In the dim light, Garret could make out a man sleeping on a bunk. He crept toward the still figure. Once he was standing over the man, he signaled that it was indeed Nathan.

He removed a hood from his pack and yanked it down over the banker's head. In one quick motion, he rolled him over on his back and planted a knee in his chest, subduing him. He pulled out a length of tape and wrapped it around the hood to secure his mouth shut. When Nathan began to struggle, Garret punched him in the face through the cloth.

"Try that again, and it'll be the last thing you do," Garret murmured. "Now get on your feet. You're coming with us."

Anniston jerked Nathan's hands behind his back and slapped a pair of handcuffs on him.

Garret opened the door to make sure the coast was clear. He motioned for her to follow with Nathan as he disappeared back around the corner.

But a second after that, he put his fingers up to his lips for quiet. They had to wait for a crewman to finish dumping garbage from the galley over the railing and into the sea below.

After the shipmate disappeared down the corridor, they hugged the wall again until they spotted another member of the crew out on deck, taking a smoke break. Ten long minutes went by before they could head to where they'd left the lifeboat tied up.

This time, Anniston went over the side first. Once she was safely in the skiff, Garret turned to Nathan and tied a rope around his waist. "You try to wriggle out of this or make one sound and you're a dead man."

It took every muscle in him to lower Nathan into the raft before he scurried over the side and climbed down. The minute his feet hit the bottom, he untied the rope and shoved off. Anniston took out her paddle and started rowing away.

From somewhere above, a shot rang out. Garret heard shouting overhead.

They paddled harder for a few minutes until Garret said, "To hell with this. I'm starting the engine." He gunned the throttle, and the lifeboat picked up speed, disappearing into the foggy night.

When Nathan squirmed and tried to talk through the tape and hood, Anniston poked him in the back with the end of her paddle to make him think it was the barrel of a gun. "Stop that. Don't do it again."

Nathan took the hint.

No one said another word until they came alongside *The Black Rum*. Garret killed the motor, secured the raft, then looked at Anniston. "Go on up."

She scuttled up the ladder and waited on deck for Garret. She saw Mitch and Jackson rush over to lower the winch that would haul up their captive.

Still in the lifeboat, Garret attached the hoist to Nathan's back and waist, then let the crane lift Nathan out of the raft.

Garret sat there a minute contemplating the close call they'd had. He held out his hand and waited for it to stop shaking before he reached around the back and unzipped his wetsuit. When he thought his wobbly legs could make it, he climbed the ladder up to the deck and looked around for Anniston.

The minute Garret hopped over the railing, she pushed everyone else aside to get to him and locked her arms around his neck. "That was awesome. We did it! We kicked ass. You sure know how to show a girl a good time."

That's when she saw the blood. "Oh my God, you've been shot!"

"What?" He glanced over at the stream of red trickling down his bare arm. "I'm okay. I didn't feel a thing. Adrenaline. It's just a scratch, a little shoulder wound. I'll be fine."

She framed his face in her hands and spread kisses everywhere. "I've never been shot at before and you took the bullet."

He laughed, picked her up, and whirled her around in a circle. "I took a scratch for you. I hope it leaves a scar just for you. How do you feel about living in Oahu?"

"How do you feel about moving to Miami?"

Turn the page for a sneak preview

of the third book in the trilogy

Indigo Justice

Indigo Justice

Jackson almost didn't recognize his best friend from high school. The man certainly didn't look like the bank president who'd been so helpful at the bank the day they'd started the search for Livvy and the kids.

Nathan Hollister had dyed his hair an awful shade of platinum blond and let it grow out, but his dark roots were beginning to show. He'd also grown facial hair, a little goatee that made him look very much like the cartoon character, Mr. Van Driessen from *Beavis and Butt-Head*. It wasn't a flattering look.

When the hood was yanked off his head, Nathan's eyes darted around the galley. When he tried to move, he found one hand cuffed to the table. He was surrounded by

Indigos. Maybe that's why he should've been more prepared for the fist to the face.

Jackson connected to Nathan's nose and flexed his right hand. "I haven't hit anyone since Mitch ran my car into a ditch and broke the axle the night before high school prom. But I swear to God, I'll beat you senseless if you don't tell me what the hell's going on. What are you doing helping Dietrich look for treasure? What the hell did you get Livvy involved in that got her killed? You're nothing but a low-life snake!"

"You broke my nose!" Nathan screamed, the words coming out very nasal.

Mitch ignored the blood and stepped in front of Nathan's face. "I'm gonna break more than your nose if you don't start talking. Jackson is the levelheaded PhD, the scholarly one. You know it's true. Me? I'm volatile and unpredictable. And you were never my best friend. So start talking, Hollister."

"Okay. You caught me. I need a doctor first."

"No, first we ask questions and then you answer," Jackson fired back. "What happened to your fear of the water, Nathan?"

"Uh, well, I live on an island. I finally got tired of watching everyone else enjoy what the place has to offer. I did something about it. I took lessons from Dave Oakerson's outfit."

"I bet you took lessons from the esteemed mayor. So now you're good at diving, are you?"

"I'm okay. I know enough to not get the bends on deep dives."

Jackson wanted to smash his lying face again. "Enough to get Dietrich to hire you on the *Pike*? That sounds like you're more than okay. You want to tell me how you and your new pals killed Livvy?"

"What? No. I loved Livvy."

"Then why did you disappear and go to work on Dietrich's boat using a disguise? You colored your hair. You changed your appearance from the dull and stoic banker to make yourself look more like a member of a motorcycle gang wannabe. What are you hiding? What do you know about Livvy's murder? Come on, you snake, spill it."

"Livvy and I've been so secretive over the years, it became second nature to keep quiet."

"We know you're lying through your teeth," Garret said, getting to his feet. He circled the man, then reared back like he intended to throw another punch at Nathan's face.

The banker flinched and put his free hand up in defense. "Okay. Okay. I'll tell you what I know. Livvy and I were planning to take the kids and get out of our lousy marriages. Livvy mentioned Walker's plan to find the gold. He'd been obsessed by it for months. Walker seemed convinced he could find it with Werner Dietrich's help. That's when things started going south. Royce had brought Dietrich in on the resort development—the project that was going to make everyone involved a bundle. That is, if they could squeeze your old man into giving up on the preserve and get him to stop fighting them at every turn."

Mitch exchanged a look with his brothers. "So now you're saying that Dad's environmental stance got an entire family killed? That's not what happened, Nathan. Try a different fairy tale."

"Sure. Okay. The truth then. One night Walker met up with Hugo Reiner in Mattito's Bar. You remember Hugo, that old sailor who tells all those outlandish stories about knowing how to find Nazi gold. He claims some U-boat went down around here off the coast in '45 carrying gold bullion."

"It seems everyone in town suddenly got interested in it at the same time," Jackson stated.

"Well, Walker certainly did. He swallowed it like a catfish on a grub worm. The two started plotting. But Walker knew they couldn't go looking for gold using his yacht or Hugo's tub of a sailboat. Neither man had the means or the equipment to pull off that kind of operation.

And Dietrich? Walker had already met him a couple of times before through his dad. Walker knew Dietrich had a successful salvage operation. According to Livvy, Walker contacted him for help, got turned down a couple of times in the process."

Mitch interrupted him. "How do you know these kinds of details?"

"Livvy. Walker went home at night and told Livvy about all of it. She in turn, told me. During all those nights drinking at the bar, Walker had been listening to Hugo's tall tales about Dietrich's ties to the Nazis. Hugo claimed he had papers to prove it. Livvy told me Walker stole the papers and tried to use them to coerce Dietrich into cutting him in on the gold. But you don't blackmail a man like Dietrich and get away with it."

"So we've heard."

"By that time Dietrich had his own salvage operation heading to the Keys. He must've had his own leads about Hugo. I know for certain the *Patagonia Pike* won't stop until it locates that sub. Dietrich certainly didn't need Walker or Hugo to get that done. But he must've wanted those other documents back, enough to kill them all. Livvy and I thought we could use her share to start a new life together. But then things unraveled. It all went to hell."

"And you knew all this that day I walked into the bank and asked you for help," Jackson charged. "What a nasty piece of work you are."

Jackson reared back and smacked Nathan across the face again. "You lying sack of shit. You got Livvy killed because you stole the papers from Walker. You betrayed Livvy."

"Me? Not me. I wouldn't do that. It had to be Dietrich's henchmen who killed them."

"Oh, we know that, Nathan. But the murders are on you. You got them all killed because you took the papers and when Baskin tried to beat the information out of them, Walker gave up the location to save his family and himself. But when his accomplice, Boone Dandridge, went to retrieve them, the papers were gone. They weren't where Walker said they were. So Baskin turned his wrath on Livvy. Unfortunately, Walker had already given up the information. Livvy had nothing new to offer, nothing to divulge. She trusted you. And she and the kids lost their lives because you'd already stolen the documents out from under her. So their deaths are on you, buddy. It's your fault they all died!" Jackson said, his fists still clenched at his sides.

"No. I loved your sister. For years, I had to watch her live with that lying, cheating Walker. It made me sick. I…I wanted to take her away."

Mitch picked up the narration. "You were so concerned about Livvy that after she went missing, you weren't all that interested to find out what happened to her. Why is that, Nathan? Because you already knew."

"I was afraid I already knew. Yeah. Dietrich had gotten to them all. I was scared, afraid for myself."

"You were afraid for yourself? Poor guy. So what were you planning to do, Nathan? Take off with all that gold without Livvy? You don't look like you've been in mourning all this time. You don't look grief-stricken either." Mitch glanced around the room. "Is it just me, or does he look like he's taking his lover's death really well?"

Garret cocked his head, studied Nathan's face. "To me, it looks like he's gotten over Livvy just fine and moved on to count the gold he hopes to get. Plus, he felt like he was entitled to a bigger share than everyone else. So he took a job on board the *Patagonia Pike* and began to sabotage things for the crew. One by one, his goal was to eliminate anyone who was entitled to their fair share of the loot."

He turned his attention to Nathan. "Duarte apparently caught on to your little scheme, that's why you were locked up. You've been a busy boy since you lied to your wife about going to Denver."

Jackson circled Nathan. "Ah, I'm beginning to get the picture. You never lied to Wendy. That's why Anniston had such a difficult time talking your wife into filing a missing persons report. Wendy dragged her feet because she already knew where you were all along. And my guess is you planned on dropping Livvy at the first opportunity if she'd lived. After Walker had done all the legwork to get the gold, you and Wendy were off to Fiji. How long had you been using Livvy for information, Nathan? Maybe you knew Dietrich planned to kill them all along since you wanted to keep the gold for yourself. And then there's your wife. She wants the gold as badly as you do. And so does her lover, Dave Oakerson."

"No, that's not it," Nathan protested.

Jackson grabbed hold of his shirt. "Bullshit. You're such a lying weasel. The murders didn't have a thing to do with Dad trying to protect the damn preserve. When did you become such a scum sucker? Where are the documents Dietrich killed for? When exactly did you steal them? You already admitted Livvy told you where they were."

Nathan's eyes got bigger. "How do you know the rest of that stuff?"

Jackson leveled a deadly gaze at his former friend and decided it was time to bluff. "What did you take out of the safe deposit box, Nathan? There's surveillance video of you going in there, coming out fifteen minutes later. You might as well tell us."

The banker started twitching in his seat. "You couldn't possibly know that."

"We know more than you think we do. We've been talking to Duarte since Garret took you off that boat. Matter of fact, Duarte wants you back, bad. He wants to cut your throat himself because of all the misery you caused on board his ship. So it sounds to me like you've worn out your welcome there. No gold for you, Nathan."

"Hey, that's not fair."

"Neither is murdering a family of four, add two more to that count—Ryan Connelly and Dack Hawkins didn't deserve bullets to the head. I got news for you. You aren't even welcome on *The Black Rum*. I could send you back to Duarte and let him take care of you." Mitch turned in his chair. "Bring in Hugo Reiner."

A few minutes later Walsh brought the old sailor into the galley.

Nathan went icy-white. He started to hyperventilate and sputtered out, "What the hell is *he* doing on your boat?"

"Hugo? We agreed to keep him away from Werner Dietrich."

Nathan stared at the old man, his eyes blinking at a rapid rate. The wheels were turning in his head. Beads of sweat popped out on his brow. Tears began to stream down his face until he broke into genuine sobs. His chest rattled out a high keening sound as he continued to weep and moan and twist in his chair trying to get his cuffed hand loose. He tried to catch his breath enough to speak. When he finally took a gulp of air, the sudden crying stopped. He started wheezing again.

As quickly as he'd turned on the waterworks, his mood changed. The wheezing became a hysterical howl that turned into laughter. He laughed so hard that he doubled over. Blood dripped down his face from his busted nose. But the banker ignored it. He looked like a half-crazed man losing the slim tether he'd had on his sanity.

When Nathan did manage to open his mouth, his voice was a high-pitched, unnerving squeal. He screamed, "You fools! Don't you realize, we've all been played!"

Dear Reader:

If you enjoyed *Indigo Heat* please take the time to leave a review.
A review shows others how you feel about my work.
By recommending it to your friends and family it helps spread the word.

For a complete list of my other books visit my website.
www.vickiemckeehan.com

Want to connect with me to leave a comment?
Go to Facebook
www.facebook.com/VickieMcKeehan
I'd love to hear from you!

Don't miss these other exciting titles by bestselling author

Vickie McKeehan

The Pelican Pointe Series
PROMISE COVE
HIDDEN MOON BAY
DANCING TIDES
LIGHTHOUSE REEF
STARLIGHT DUNES
LAST CHANCE HARBOR
SEA GLASS COTTAGE
LAVENDER BEACH
BENEATH WINTER SAND

The Evil Secrets Trilogy
JUST EVIL Book One
DEEPER EVIL Book Two
ENDING EVIL Book Three

The Skye Cree Novels
THE BONES OF OTHERS
THE BONES WILL TELL
THE BOX OF BONES
HIS GARDEN OF BONES
TRUTH IN THE BONES

The Indigo Brothers Trilogy
INDIGO FIRE
INDIGO HEAT
INDIGO JUSTICE

ABOUT THE AUTHOR

Indigo Heat is Vickie McKeehan's seventeenth novel.
She writes romantic suspense and makes her
home in Southern California.

You can find Vickie online at
https://www.facebook.com/VickieMcKeehan
http://www.vickiemckeehan.com/
https://vickiemckeehan.wordpress.com

Printed in Great Britain
by Amazon